D1393791

This edition, issued in 1961, is for members of The Companion Book Club, 8 Long Acre, London, W.C.99, from which address particulars of membership may be obtained. The book is issued by arrangement with the original publishers, Michael Joseph Ltd.

Also by

HENRY CECIL

★

FULL CIRCLE
THE PAINSWICK LINE
NO BAIL FOR THE JUDGE
WAYS AND MEANS
NATURAL CAUSES
ACCORDING TO THE EVIDENCE
BROTHERS IN LAW
FRIENDS AT COURT
MUCH IN EVIDENCE
SOBER AS A JUDGE
BRIEF TO COUNSEL
NOT SUCH AN ASS

SETTLED OUT OF COURT

and

ALIBI FOR A JUDGE

"A blessed companion is a book"—JERROLD

SETTLED OUT OF COURT

and

ALIBI FOR A JUDGE

*

HENRY CECIL

THE COMPANION BOOK CLUB
LONDON

Made and printed in Great Britain
for The Companion Book Club (Odhams Press Ltd.)
by Odhams (Watford) Limited
Watford, Herts
S.761.W.A.

CONTENTS

★

SETTLED OUT OF COURT

ALIBI FOR A JUDGE

SETTLED OUT OF COURT

CHAPTER ONE

NOTHING LIKE THE TRUTH

"TAKE it easy," said the warder, who led Lonsdale Walsh down the stairs from the dock in Court 1 of the Old Bailey, "you can always appeal."

The warder was a kindly man and realized that the prisoner was upset. He was not altogether surprised. A lot of prisoners became upset, even when they were convicted of lesser crimes than murder. Some of them shouted, some of them cried, some of them collapsed. Lonsdale Walsh did none of these things. He simply went very red in the face, very, very red. The warder rightly assumed from this that Lonsdale Walsh disagreed with the verdict of the jury, and he was preparing to add a few further words of advice about appealing. Not because he thought that an appeal would be likely to succeed, but simply out of kindness, to give the man some hope.

The warder had not been surprised that Lonsdale Walsh took the verdict badly, but he was most surprised and pained by the answer to his kindly advice. The convicted man was a very wealthy financier and, apart from the unfortunate matter of the murder, had never been in the hands of the police. Some prisoners have two warders to accompany them down the stairs, some even three. One should surely be enough for an otherwise respectable financier; but he was not. Lonsdale Walsh's answer was to turn round and knock out the warder with a well-aimed blow to the chin. Having thus relieved his feelings to a small extent, he then waited quietly for the inevitable to happen. But there was not much they could do to him. You can't add anything useful to imprisonment for life.

Later, Lonsdale Walsh arranged for £200 to be sent to the warder, with the result that that kindly man remarked to his wife that he wouldn't mind being knocked out again at the same price, preferably just before they took their holiday.

It will be realized from this payment that Lonsdale Walsh had no grievance against the warder. He had simply been compelled to lash out at someone, and the warder was nearest to hand.

It must be very unpleasant to be convicted of murder and even more unpleasant to be so convicted on perjured evidence. Any reasonable man would resent this. But there was a special reason why it was worse for Lonsdale Walsh than for anyone else. He was allergic to lies. Just as some people break out into a rash if they come near a cat or a strawberry, so a deliberate untruth had from his childhood revolted him. It was not a question of morality or religion at all. His devotion to the truth was like a purely physical complaint. No doubt he himself would have told a lie to save his own life or the life of someone for whom he had a sufficient regard or to save his country, but he had never been put in the position of having to do any of these things. He had told no lies at his trial, not even to his own solicitors and counsel. And the evidence against him was almost entirely perjured from beginning to end. With the possible exception of their names and addresses nearly everything stated by the chief witnesses against him had been untrue.

If this would be difficult for an ordinary person to bear, it was impossible for Lonsdale Walsh. And so the warder got his £200. Take it easy indeed!

Lonsdale Walsh was the child of well-to-do middle-class parents. They were very ordinary, decent people and, except to the extent that no one is absolutely normal, they were without "isms" or allergies of any kind. Nor, curiously enough, did they notice anything wrong with Lonsdale until it was pointed out to them. But one day they were a little surprised to be asked by Lonsdale's headmaster to come to see him. They wondered whether the discussion was to be about the boy's career or whether he had got into trouble of some kind. They were not unduly alarmed. Lonsdale was a big boy for his age and good with his fists. But they could not think that he would be guilty of anything worse than a schoolboy prank. So perhaps it was his career after all. But, then, why ask them in the middle of term? Perhaps he had been bullying smaller (or even larger) boys. They knew that he was very determined to get his own way but, as he never told lies to his parents and never tried to knock them down, they could not imagine that he had done anything terrible. On the way to the school they discussed every possibility they could think of, but they were still somewhat mystified by the time they were shown into the headmaster's study.

"Nice of you to come," he said. "So sorry to have to trouble you, but we're a little worried about Lonsdale."

The parents were relieved. This couldn't be anything very bad. You can't be "a little worried" about a boy whom you're going to expel.

"Oh?" said Lonsdale's father.

"I thought you might be able to help us," went on the headmaster.

"What's the trouble?"

"Well," said the headmaster, "you must know all about it, but it is becoming a bit embarrassing."

"Embarrassing? I'm afraid I really don't know what you're talking about."

"I'm sorry," said the headmaster. "It's this truth business, you know. It's really getting us down a bit."

"Truth business?" said Lonsdale's father. "I haven't the faintest idea what you're talking about. Has he been telling lies or something? It's not like him."

"Lies?" said the headmaster, "indeed no. I'm afraid I wish he would sometimes."

"Look, headmaster," said Mr Walsh, "my wife and I are simple people, but I hope I may say of average intelligence. Would you kindly explain in plain intelligible language what your complaint is about our boy?"

"It's not exactly a complaint," said the headmaster uncomfortably, "but, to put it bluntly, we think he ought to see a psychiatrist."

"Who's we?"

"His form master, his housemaster and I."

"Why on earth should he see a psychiatrist? He's a normal enough boy. He works well, doesn't he? He's good at games.

Bit of a bully, perhaps, but that you can easily cope with at a school like this."

"What you say is quite right, Mr Walsh," said the headmaster. "It's quite true that he is inclined to fight his way through, if he wants anything badly enough but, as you say, we're quite used to dealing with that sort of thing here. No, it's something much more unusual. Indeed, it's unique in my experience. But I can't imagine that you don't know all about it."

"Well, I'm afraid we don't," said Lonsdale's father. "Will you be good enough to enlighten us?"

"Well, anyway," said the headmaster, "you must have noticed that he always tells the truth."

"Really!" said Mr Walsh. "I'm a very busy man and it's quite a long journey here. You haven't asked us to come and see you just because we've tried to bring our boy up decently."

"Please don't be annoyed," said the headmaster, "I assure you that I have only the boy's interests at heart—and yours too, of course."

"I'm sorry," said Mr Walsh, "please forgive me. But my wife and I would really like to know what you are driving at."

"Well, as you don't seem to know," said the headmaster, "I'd better start from the beginning. Now naturally we like boys to tell the truth. But, of course, the normal boy doesn't always do so. Usually it's to avoid unpleasant consequences for himself or someone else. But occasionally it's simply out of kindness. Just as we don't hurt people's feelings by saying what we really think of them."

"You find that Lonsdale speaks his mind too freely, is that it?"

"He certainly does, but that isn't it by a long way. Not only does he invariably say exactly what he thinks, not only does he invariably tell the truth, however unpleasant the consequences for himself or anyone else, but, if he knows that anyone else is telling a lie, he . . . he . . . well I know it may sound ridiculous to you, as you don't seem to have noticed it at home—so let me say something else first. As I've said, we like boys to tell the truth, but equally, or perhaps even more important, we don't encourage sneaks."

"You're not suggesting——" began Mr Walsh indignantly, but the headmaster held up his hand.

"Please let me finish," he said. "I am quite satisfied that your boy is not a deliberate sneak—that is to say, he never deliberately tells tales about other boys. I'm sure it's not deliberate."

"What isn't deliberate?"

"Well, every time Lonsdale knows that someone is telling a lie he—he goes red in the face, red like a turkey cock. In other words, if the truth is in question and Lonsdale knows it, the master has only to look at him to find the answer. I repeat, I'm quite sure the boy can't help it. He's got an allergy. Lies make him nearly burst. It isn't healthy, Mr Walsh. It doesn't so much matter here, but I'm thinking of his later career. Of course, truth is very important. We all realize that. And I must congratulate you on Lonsdale's truthfulness. But—but—now I'm not a psychiatrist, but, in my view, if he goes on like this without any assistance, if he goes into the world with this allergy, a world which unfortunately abounds with lies, he may very well find himself in a mental home. If you had seen the look on that boy's face sometimes when he knew the truth was not being told, you would understand why I am warning you. Now, of course, he may adapt himself to the behaviour of the world, I may have sent for you unnecessarily, but, in my view, I should be failing in my duty as his headmaster if I did not say that, in my opinion, your boy ought to be seen by a psychiatrist as soon as possible."

Mr and Mrs Walsh said nothing for a moment. They simply looked at each other. Then Mr Walsh said:

"I must confess we've never noticed anything very peculiar. Now I come to think of it, the boy is very outspoken. But I've always liked that, and rather encouraged it. Are you sure it's more than that?"

"If you will treat the conversation as entirely confidential, then I'll send for the boy and ask him a question."

"Certainly," said Lonsdale's parents.

Lonsdale soon arrived and greeted his parents in the normal way. "Tell me, Walsh," said the headmaster to Lonsdale, "what do you honestly think of Mr Thompson?"

"Bloody awful, sir," said Lonsdale.
"There's no need to swear," said his father.
"The headmaster asked me what I honestly thought," said the boy. "That was the only way I could express it honestly."
"This Mr Thompson," said Mr Walsh to the headmaster, "what is your opinion of him? In confidence, of course."
The headmaster coughed.
"He's a very good man," he said eventually.
Lonsdale blushed furiously.
"May I go now please, sir?" he asked.
A month later Lonsdale was interviewed by an eminent psychiatrist, Dr Harvey McLong.
"Well, how's school?" began Dr McLong.
"All right," said Lonsdale.
"I see," said Dr McLong. "Nothing more than that? Just all right?"
"Yes," said Lonsdale, "it's all right."
"And what's it like at home?"
"All right," said Lonsdale.
"No better than at school?" asked Dr McLong.
"It's different," said Lonsdale.
"I see," said Dr McLong, and there was a pause. "I gather," he went on, "that you're happy both at home and at school?"
"Yes," said Lonsdale.
"Nothing the matter?"
"Not that I can think of."
"Why d'you think you've come to see me?"
"Because I'm growing up, I suppose, and you're going to tell me things."
"I see," said Dr McLong, and there was another pause. Then he decided he must get nearer the subject.
"Do you always tell the truth, Lonsdale?"
"As far as I know, I do."
"Why?"
"Because I do."
"Is there no other reason? Isn't it because you want to be trusted?"
"I've never thought."
"D'you know the story of Cassandra, the Trojan prophe-

tess, who had a curse laid on her that she should always prophesy the truth and never be believed?"

"That's a horrible story," said Lonsdale, and went very red in the face.

"A thing like that upsets you?"

"Yes, it does."

"Why?"

"How should I know? I don't like it, that's all."

"You like the truth, don't you?"

"How d'you mean, like it?"

"Well, you always tell the truth yourself and you like other people to do so too."

"I suppose so."

"Why?"

"I don't know. I just do. Same as I like stewed apricots and not stewed prunes."

"Good," said Dr McLong. "You've never thought of joining our profession, have you?"

"No," said Lonsdale.

"Why not?"

"Because I think it's a lot of . . ." and Lonsdale then said a word which was seldom used in Dr McLong's consulting-room, except by men friends who happened to be calling on him for a chat, and a few women patients who wanted to show off.

"People used to make that sort of remark about a lot of things which have since proved to be very useful. We're a fairly new profession. You must be indulgent with us."

Lonsdale said nothing.

"When I mentioned the story of Cassandra to you, you went very red in the face. Did you feel anything?"

"I felt hot."

"Why?"

"Because I didn't like the story."

"But you don't feel hot when you see stewed prunes, do you?"

"No."

"Or when you see someone you don't like?"

"I suppose not."

"Then why at the story of Cassandra?"

"Because I do."

"And you feel the same if you hear anyone tell lies, don't you?"

"Yes."

"Why?"

"Because I do."

"It isn't really an answer to say that. We don't eat because we eat. We eat because we're hungry. That's right, isn't it?"

"I suppose so."

"Then why d'you feel hot when somebody tells lies?"

"Because I don't like it, I suppose."

"But you don't feel hot at everything you don't like?"

"No."

"Then why at lies?"

"I don't know. I just do."

"But you must realize that in a civilized society lies have to be told. Sometimes you have to lie to be kind to a person. If a girl asks you whether you like her dress, it wouldn't be kind to say you didn't, would it?"

"No."

"Don't you want to be kind to people?"

"Sometimes."

"Which would you prefer, to tell the truth and hurt someone's feelings or to tell a lie to avoid hurting them?"

"To tell the truth."

"But that wouldn't be kind."

"I didn't say it would."

"What is your object in life?"

"To be a millionaire."

"Why?"

"Because, if you're a millionaire, you can do lots of things."

"What sort of things?"

"Oh—I don't know, have swimming pools and yachts and things."

"And girls all round the place?"

Lonsdale said nothing.

"Well, what are you thinking about?" asked Dr McLong.

"I thought you'd have got there before."

"To girls, you mean? You thought you'd come here to talk about girls?"

"Yes."

"Are you disappointed that we haven't talked about them?"

"No."

"Why not?"

"Plenty of time for them later, when I grow up."

"What d'you like talking about?"

"Depends who I'm talking to."

"What would you like to talk to me about?"

"Nothing."

"I see," said Dr McLong. "You're not exactly co-operative."

"What's that?"

"You're not trying to help me."

"Help you do what?"

"Help you."

"I don't want any help."

"I think you do. D'you want to go through life getting red in the face every time someone tells a lie?"

"I don't mind."

"You will."

But it was many years before Dr McLong was proved right. Until his conviction for murder, Lonsdale was not personally affected by his complaint. Indeed, to a considerable extent, it stood him in good stead. During his career it became known by everyone with whom he had dealings that, though he would use every effort to get his own way, the lie was the one weapon he would not use. "Walsh's word" became a synonym for the truth.

It was the other people who suffered, not he. He would not tolerate lies in any circumstances. Once, an office boy in a company of his started to take money out of the petty cash to put on horses. Eventually he had a lucky win and paid it all back. By a miscalculation, however, he paid back rather too much and his offences were discovered. His immediate superior, however, was so impressed at the boy's honesty in repaying the money that he tried to hush it up and told a lie about it. When this was discovered, Lonsdale immediately ordered the dismissal of the man who had covered the crimes of the office boy. The latter was allowed to remain.

Lonsdale's allergy only related to the spoken or written lie. Mere dishonesty was a totally different matter. He had no particular objection to the burglar, even if he used violence. But the woman who lied to the customs authorities in order to smuggle in some trifles provoked him to fury. He could have sympathy with a man who murdered his wife, but none with a man who tricked a woman into bigamy by pretending he was single. He never considered whether he over-valued truth at the expense of other qualities, any more than the average sufferer from one disease seriously considers whether he would prefer to have another.

CHAPTER TWO

DISCOVERY AND CONVICTION

LONSDALE WALSH started his career as an accountant and he soon became deeply interested in finance. His parents left him a little capital and by careful, speculative investment he quickly increased it. By the time he was forty he was of importance in the City. By the time he was fifty he was a very wealthy man, and by the time he was convicted of murder, at the age of fifty-five, he was pretty well a millionaire.

His conviction arose as a direct result of the battles which often take place between financiers. Sometimes the contestants are on the same board, and it was so in this case. A great struggle was taking place for the control of the Anglo-Saxon Development Corporation Limited. This company had been nurtured by Lonsdale Walsh almost from its birth, and it had become one of the biggest and wealthiest companies in the country. Lonsdale was determined to retain control of it, but he had an equally determined opponent in Adolphus Barnwell or, more accurately, in Adolphus Barnwell's wife.

Jo Barnwell had been a singularly attractive girl and at forty-five she was as attractive a woman as Lonsdale knew. But there was no doubt at all that it was she who kept Adolphus at it. Probably he would have preferred to retire into the country and farm. But that sort of life was not for Jo. She liked to be at the centre of things. She enjoyed a fight. But though she did not lead her regiment from behind and would have been the first to admit her influence over her husband, she preferred to win her battles through him. So she never personally went on the board of any of Adolphus' companies. She contented herself with telling him what to do when he was on them. He gladly accepted her advice for two reasons. It was good advice and it made things easier at home. Once or twice in their early days he had made a mild protest at some of Jo's more outrageous suggestions, but she quickly put him in his place, and it must be said that, until he was murdered, he was very happy there.

Jo and Lonsdale often met and they each enjoyed those occasions. It was the attraction of opposites. Jo would tell a lie as soon as look at you, if it would serve her purpose, but she was highly intelligent and realized that, if you want to make the best use of the lie as a weapon, it should not be used too often. And it must be a good one. She was the one person whose lies had a fascination for Lonsdale. He loathed them instinctively but in her case they had the attraction which repulsive-looking objects have for some people. He would even try to provoke one on occasion, much as a person sometimes squeezes a painful sore to make it hurt more. No one is quite sure whether that is done because of the relief when the pressure stops, or whether there is something masochistic about it. Whatever the reason, Lonsdale enjoyed meeting Jo, and they danced many times together, while Adolphus sat quite happily in the background.

Lonsdale's wife had died young, and he had never remarried. But his relationship with Jo was completely blameless on the surface. Most of the time they fought and in their words and actions towards each other there was never the slightest hint of the affection which may well have existed under the surface. Apart altogether from their verbal battles which were little, if anything, more than play, they fought in earnest behind the scenes. Had the opportunity arisen, each would cheerfully have made the other bankrupt. They asked each other for no quarter, and never gave it. The only difference between them was that Jo knew that she could always take Lonsdale's word, while he knew that he could never accept anything she said with any degree of assurance, unless it was on a matter of no importance to her.

The battle for the control of the Anglo-Saxon Corporation had only been in progress for a short time when the events, which were to place Lonsdale in the dock, started to take shape. In the course of gathering his forces together for the main attack, Lonsdale had exchanged a number of important and highly confidential letters with some of his associates. Knowledge of their contents would have been of the greatest possible value to the Barnwell forces. Jo indeed considered the idea of a burglary, but rejected it as too dangerous and too doubtful of success. She was quite right to reject the idea. Lonsdale had taken sufficient precautions to deal with that possibility. He kept all such correspondence at his bank. So Jo had to think again.

One day Lonsdale received a letter from the Barnwell solicitors informing him that their client, Adolphus Barnwell, was proposing to bring an action for slander against him, and asking for the names of solicitors who would accept service on his behalf of such proceedings. The nature and occasion of the slander were mentioned, and Lonsdale knew that it was a pure invention. He was not unduly worried, although he had a vague feeling that there was more behind the threat than he could see. He went straight to his solicitors, Messrs Slograve, Plumb & Co., and interviewed Mr Slograve.

"What's this all about?" he asked.

"Did you say what the letter alleges?"

"Certainly not. I didn't even discuss the matter. What's behind it?"

"Let me think," said Mr Slograve. After a moment or two, he said: "I'm afraid I think I know what they're after. You're not going to be pleased."

"What is it?"

"The Annual General of the Anglo-Saxon is in about nine months, isn't it?"

"Yes. But what's that got to do with it?" Lonsdale was becoming a little apprehensive.

"This slander action will be so framed that the correspondence we all know about and which Barnwell would dearly love to see before the Annual General, will be material to the action."

"And?"

"Accordingly you will have to disclose it to them."

"I'll do nothing of the kind."

"I'm afraid you'll have to. You'll have to swear an affidavit saying what documents are in your or your agent's possession."

"We'll destroy them."

"Then you'll not only have to admit that fact but they can ask you what was in them."

"My God!" said Lonsdale. "It's that bloody woman. What can I do about it?"

"I really don't know," said Mr Slograve. "We could try to drag things out, but we'd never succeed in avoiding discovery before the meeting."

"But the whole action's a fraud. It's just brought to get a sight of the correspondence."

"I know. The more I think of it, the plainer it becomes."

"But surely you can prevent a thing like that? It's an abuse of the process of the Court. Isn't that what you'd call it?"

"Certainly it is. But how can we prove it? All they have to do is to call their witness to say you said what's alleged."

"But it'll be rank perjury."

"But how can you show it to be? There's only your word against his."

"It's an outrage," said Lonsdale. "Surely the law is strong enough to deal with a situation like this."

"I'm afraid not," said Mr Slograve. "Of course, we'll go to counsel about it, to see if we can avoid disclosing the letters, but, as the whole project of the action is to look at them, I can't conceive that they won't frame their allegations so as to make any case for refusing to disclose them untenable."

"So that anyone, who's unscrupulous enough, can just invent an allegation in order to look at someone else's private documents?"

"I'm afraid that is so, provided it's skilfully done and provided at least one person is prepared to commit perjury.

Of course, we can fight them all the way, but in my view we shall lose and, however much we appeal, we'll never keep the fight going beyond the meeting. We can only hope that Mr Barnwell has a coronary thrombosis before discovery."

"What good would that do? That woman would carry on after him."

"Well, she couldn't, as a matter of fact. A slander action dies when the plaintiff dies."

"I thought the executors could carry on with an action started by a man who dies?"

"That rule doesn't apply to libel or slander actions. I don't pretend to be a great lawyer, but that's one of the things you can take from me."

It was not long after this conversation that Adolphus Barnwell died, not from coronary thrombosis—but suddenly and violently. That was the end of the slander action, but not of Jo Barnwell. And, three months after her husband died, she saw to it that Lonsdale stood in the dock charged with the murder. And the jury said "Guilty," and the judge said "Imprisonment for life."

CHAPTER THREE

SPIKEY LEE'S CHANCE

FOR the first few days after his conviction Lonsdale was hardly sane, but he pulled himself together sufficiently to sign his Notice of Appeal to the Court of Criminal Appeal. He was present when his appeal was dismissed. Once again he had to be forcibly restrained. He was led away shouting unintelligibly.

After a few days in the prison hospital he recovered sufficiently to take stock of his position. His counsel advised him that it was impossible to apply to the Attorney-General for leave to appeal to the House of Lords, as there were no grounds for making such an application. So Lonsdale petitioned the Home Secretary and wrote to his M.P. for help. All his attempts to have his case reviewed failed, and the governor of the prison eventually told him that it was useless for him to batter his head against a brick wall and that he would be well advised to accept his sentence with resignation.

"But there wasn't a word of truth in the evidence for the prosecution, sir."

"I'm afraid a lot of convicted people say that. Now, you're an intelligent man. Your sentence will be reviewed in ten years and any time after that . . ."

"Ten years!" said Lonsdale. "That makes it a bit early to be measured for my coming out suit."

After a few months in prison, Lonsdale asked his only daughter, Angela, to visit him, and he was eventually allowed to see her.

"I want you to do something for me," he said.

"Of course. What is it?"

"I want you to go round the Courts and find a barrister whom you consider to have intelligence of the highest class and to have a resilient mind. A chap who isn't hidebound. A man who's prepared to consider new ideas or new situations, not just dismissing them because he's never come across them before. I don't mind if he's old or young, well-known or not, but he must have the qualities I've mentioned. He won't be easy to find, so go everywhere. Take your time. High Court, County Court, Sessions, Old Bailey, Magistrate's Court—but find me the right man."

"Of course I will, father, but what . . ."

"Never mind the reason. Find him. Now there's something else I want you to do. To some extent you can do it at the same time. I want you to find a High Court judge with the same qualities, someone of the highest intelligence but who's still prepared to learn. Will you do it?"

"Well, of course, father, if it'll make you happier."

"It will," said Lonsdale, "and, when you've made your selection, let me know their names and addresses."

While Angela was making her tour of the Courts, her father was concentrating on the plan he had made. A person of his character must have something to live for, something in the not too distant future. By the time of his conversation with Angela, Lonsdale had completely recovered from the appalling shock of his conviction and the sense of utter frustration. At once his agile and determined mind began to consider ways and means of attaining his object before it was too late to be worth while. Neither the decision of the Court of Criminal Appeal nor the rejection of his plea by the Home Secretary, nor the governor's advice had in the least altered his resolve, which was to have the jury's verdict in his case set aside and, incidentally, to show Jo Barnwell that it was not as easy as she must have thought to put Lonsdale Walsh in prison for life. He gave her full credit for what she had achieved. It required ingenuity and boldness, and, if it had not also entailed the use of the lie from start to finish, Lonsdale might even have admired her handiwork.

Day after day and night after night he pictured the scene of his triumph and of Jo's anger when, in spite of the apparently insuperable difficulties, he finally triumphed over her. But, though he allowed himself these dreams as a necessary entertainment during his drab prison life, he spent much time in working out, from the practical point of view, how he was going to attain his object.

His first step was to find a co-prisoner, due for release in a few months, whom he considered a suitable ally. He must be a man with many previous convictions, someone for whom crime was simply a means to an end and who had gone on too long in the business to become respectable, who indeed would consider himself a recidivist if he took an honest job. He must be a man who, as Becky Sharp might have been, would be honest on ten thousand a year. In other words, he must not be a man who enjoyed crime for its own sake and who needed the excitement involved. Such men are often exhibitionists and would be very dangerous to employ. Lonsdale needed a man for whom money and not notoriety was the spur. Eventually he chose Spikey Lee as someone who came nearest to his requirements. Spikey was a versatile criminal and was as prepared to go in for a long-firm fraud as to climb up a drainpipe and tie up the lady of the house with her husband's pyjama-cord, preparatory to ransacking the bedroom. On one occasion his calculations went wrong and the husband was there too, with the pyjama cord safely round him. He had also tried, not very successfully, a little forgery, and once (and he was heartily ashamed of this) a little blackmail.

"Honest, guv," he said to Lonsdale (who was known in prison as "The Guv"), "honest, I wish I 'adn't. And that ain't 'cos I got five years out of it. It's the only time I meant it when I said I was sorry. The old basket didn't believe me any more than 'e did the other times. But I told 'im straight —'I'm sorry, my Lord,' I said. 'Straight I am. It's a dirty game, and I swear I'll never do it again. But the money seemed so easy,' I said. 'You see, my Lord,' I said, 'I take a lot of risks when I go climbing up a drainpipe. I may fall and break my blooming neck for one thing. And I may get caught for another. And there may not be anything worth taking in the end. And when I saw this easy money—with no drainpipes, no householders with rolling pins, nothing at all except to say "more please" and out it comes all nice and easy, well I fell for it, my Lord. And I'd like to say to Mr X and Mrs Y and Miss Z that I'm really and truly sorry for what I done to 'em, and if I still 'ad the money I'd give it back.' I can't say I really meant that bit, guv, but it just come out and it didn't make no difference as I'd spent it all long before. 'I believe you're sorry,' said the old basket—'you're sorry because you were caught.' 'Well, that's true, my Lord,' I said, 'but I'm sorry for what I done too. I don't say I'll go straight when I come out, but I'll never do that again.' 'You won't get the chance for some time,' he said. 'Five years.' It was quite fair, guv. It's a real dirty game and I don't 'old with it. Easy, though."

And Lonsdale observed a look of regret on Spikey's face, as he savoured in retrospect the ease of the living which he had renounced.

It was not the renunciation which made Lonsdale think that Spikey was his man, but his obvious desire for ease. Here was the man who would work for money and who would certainly not exchange it for his picture in the Sunday newspapers and a pat on the back from the police. In other words here was a man who could be completely trusted so long as he was paid. And Lonsdale intended that he should be paid.

The whole prison population knew who Lonsdale was

and accordingly Spikey could believe his ears when Lonsdale mentioned what he was prepared to pay for Spikey's co-operation. To Spikey it was the fulfilment of his life's dream. Always to know where the next pint was coming from and without having to work for it. It was like winning a football pool. For Lonsdale had promised Spikey a substantial lump sum and an annuity. And, once again, Lonsdale had the reward of his passion for the truth. Spikey really believed that he meant it. Anticipation is often sweeter than realization, and Spikey's last few weeks in prison were some of the most enjoyable he had ever spent in his life.

CHAPTER FOUR

A TOUR OF THE COURTS

ANGELA WALSH was a double First but she had the great advantage of looking and talking like a charming Third. She was as intelligent as her father, not quite so determined and with an unexaggerated regard for the truth. She was devoted to her father but she had told him the normal lies which normal children tell normal parents, with this qualification, that from a very early age she never told him an untruth without being quite certain that she would not be found out.

She was deeply distressed at her father's predicament and anxious to do all she could to help him. She had but the vaguest idea of what was behind his request, and she did not attempt to find out. She knew that she would learn in the end and she simply concentrated on the task which her father had given her. Had the circumstances not been so tragic, it would have been a most interesting assignment and, even as it was, she was able to get considerable interest and even amusement from her tour of the Courts. At the end of it she could have written a most entertaining little book containing sketches of judges, barristers, solicitors, witnesses and the other people who are involved in civil and criminal trials. It was a highly concentrated tour and, in the course of it, she reflected that it might be no bad thing if such a tour could be introduced into the curriculum of children about to leave school, or at any rate of university students. Although there would obviously be periods of boredom in such a course, it would for the most part, she thought from her own experiences, combine instruction with entertainment to such a high degree that even the dullest student must learn a good deal.

Although, in view of her father's wealth and previous position, she could easily have obtained introductions to solicitors or barristers to show her round, she thought it better, to begin with at any rate, to go entirely by herself. She did not want her own judgment to be affected by the views of lawyers of experience. She must make this choice by herself. Once a well-known lawyer had advised her on the subject, she would have difficulty in relying on her own inexperienced judgment. How could she tell whether the judgment of the lawyer was right? Only the barrister she was looking for could have given her the right advice.

So round the courts she went by herself. She heard impassioned pleas at the Old Bailey, dry legal arguments in the Chancery Division and incredible evidence by bankrupts, explaining how they had managed to dispose of certain untraceable assets, explanations which no one pretended to believe and which the bankrupts themselves sometimes put forward rather apologetically, as the best they could do at short notice. She heard husbands' and wives' stories of marital unhappiness, and motorists' protests at the diligence of the police in prosecuting them for obstruction while armed robbers remained loose, and so on. A little book! She could have written several volumes. Sometimes she could not resist waiting, although she knew that no one in the case was the man for her father. Very sensibly she felt that she must have some relaxation and she used such occasions for that purpose. And she would have been very sorry indeed to miss such incidents as the cross-examination of a witness by Mr Tewkesbury, the astonishing solicitor, who could give a tight-rope walker points in the way in which he managed to remain on the roll of solicitors.

Mr Tewkesbury's client was a lady of easy virtue. She chose to be defended instead of pleading guilty because she had come before a magistrate who was well known for his habit of exercising his powers under a very ancient Act of Parliament. These powers in effect enabled him to send prostitutes to prison, although the maximum fine for the offence with which they were charged was forty shillings. The method was to call upon them to find sureties for their good behaviour. In default of such sureties being found, the ancient Act entitled the Court to send them to prison. So Mr Tewkesbury was from time to time, when he was sober enough, pressed into service by these ladies. And excellent service he gave. Magistrates in the districts where such ladies abound have very full lists, and, if every one of them insisted on pleading not guilty, no magistrate would be able to get through his list. Moreover, the offences with which they were charged were not always easy to prove, as it required proof that at least one member of the public had been annoyed. As, normally, no member of the public is prepared to come and give evidence that he was annoyed, the witnesses in such cases almost invariably consist of policemen. Mr Tewkesbury knew that, by spinning out the case to the greatest possible length, he might eventually prevail on the magistrate to dismiss the charge, not simply to put an end to the ordeal but because, in the course of asking so many questions, it might well happen that some kind of doubt might emerge. The lady in question was entitled to the benefit of the doubt, and, after three-quarters of an hour of Mr Tewkesbury, a magistrate could not be blamed for being in doubt. Indeed, the endeavours to follow conscientiously all Mr Tewkesbury's questions and submissions sometimes made more than one magistrate doubt if he was fit for anything else that afternoon.

It is not always appreciated by members of the legal profession and the public that the conscientious judge is always listening, listening intently, even when his eyes are half-closed, and it is an extremely wearying ordeal to have to listen intently to arguments which vary in infinite variety between the intelligent and the unintelligible. Interruptions in an effort to make a point clear usually only succeed in making it even more obscure, and the business of sorting out the various arguments and trying to make some reasonable sense of them occasionally almost reduces the listener to tears. He does not actually cry, but his exhaustion is sometimes indicated by a sudden exasperated remark from a judge who is noted for his placidity.

Mr Tewkesbury's cross-examination during Angela's visit was directed to the policeman's evidence that a man had been annoyed by his client's solicitations.

MR TEWKESBURY: Now, officer, I want you to follow this next question very closely.

CONSTABLE: I try to follow all your questions closely.

TEWKESBURY: And with what measure of success?

MAGISTRATE: You needn't answer that question.

TEWKESBURY: But, sir, with the greatest possible respect, am I not entitled to an answer?

MAGISTRATE: No.

TEWKESBURY: But, sir, unless I know the measure of success which the officer has in following my questions, it becomes more difficult for me to frame the next question.

MAGISTRATE: So far you seem to have overcome your difficulties most manfully. I have observed no lack of questions.

TEWKESBURY: Your Worship's courtesy overwhelms me.

MAGISTRATE (*to himself*): I wish it would.

TEWKESBURY: Is it now convenient, sir, that I should resume my cross-examination where I left off?

MAGISTRATE: Very well.

TEWKESBURY: Well then, officer, would you be kind enough to tell me the measure of success with which you have understood my previous questions?

MAGISTRATE: I've just said he needn't answer that question.

TEWKESBURY: But, sir, did I not understand you to change your mind and say I may ask it? If I may say so, the greatest judges change their minds. *Judex mutabilis, judex amabilis,* if I may say so.

MAGISTRATE: Mr Tewkesbury, would you kindly continue your cross-examination of this witness. I've fifty summonses to hear after this.

TEWKESBURY: I don't know how your Worship does it and retains your good humour.

MAGISTRATE (*quietly, to his clerk*): I've about had enough of this. Is he sober?

TEWKESBURY: Perfectly, sir. And my hearing is perfect too.

MAGISTRATE (*to himself*): Oh—God!

TEWKESBURY: Now, officer, I want you to follow this next question very closely.

CONSTABLE: I follow all . . .

MAGISTRATE: Be quiet, officer. That was not a question.

CONSTABLE: Sorry, sir.

MAGISTRATE: If you will confine yourself to answering questions, and Mr Tewkesbury will confine himself to asking material ones, we may get on.

TEWKESBURY: That would be an ideal cross-examination, if I may say so, sir. But (*shaking his head sadly*) *Non cuivis homini* something something *Olympum*.

MAGISTRATE: *Corinthum,* Mr Tewkesbury. *Contingit adire Corinthum.*

TEWKESBURY: Bless my soul, sir. I beg your pardon. I must be slipping. *Quantum mutatus ab illo Tewkesbury.*

MAGISTRATE: This isn't a Latin class. Please get on.

TEWKESBURY: If you please, sir. To resume, officer, when did you last see a person annoyed?

For a fraction of a second the constable looked at the magistrate and then hastily withdrew his eyes.

CONSTABLE: I'm not sure.

TEWKESBURY: Well, be sure, officer.

MAGISTRATE: How can he be?

TEWKESBURY: He can tell me the last occasion he *remembers* seeing anyone annoyed.

MAGISTRATE: That's a different question.

TEWKESBURY: Then I ask it. And remember, officer, you're on oath.

CONSTABLE (*after a slight cough*): I saw a pedestrian this morning annoyed by a motorist.

TEWKESBURY: How did he show his annoyance?

CONSTABLE: He shook his fist.

TEWKESBURY: Excellent, constable. He shook his fist.

MAGISTRATE: Don't repeat the answers, please, Mr Tewkesbury.

Tewkesbury: I was savouring it, sir.

Magistrate: Well don't.

Tewkesbury: And when was the last occasion before that when you saw someone annoyed?

Constable: I cut myself shaving this morning.

Tewkesbury: And what did you say, officer? You may say it in Latin if you prefer.

Magistrate: You may not.

Constable: I said "damn," your Worship.

Tewkesbury: Excellent. Damn. I'm so sorry, sir. I was savouring again. And the time before that?

Constable: I can't be sure I get the order right.

Tewkesbury: Of course not, officer. You couldn't possibly be expected to remember such things in correct order. *Lex non cogit ad impossibilia.* Well, constable, let us have another example of someone being annoyed.

Constable: I once saw someone slip and fall down in the street. He said "bloody hell", as far as I remember.

Tewkesbury: And the next? Your wife perhaps has burned herself in the kitchen, or dropped something?

Constable: I broke a plate the other day.

Tewkesbury: And what did she say? You may write it down if you like.

Constable: She called me a clumsy lout.

Tewkesbury: Admirable. And the next, please. Did your mother or father never hit you if you annoyed them?

Constable: I was smacked occasionally.

Tewkesbury: You were a good child, no doubt, officer?

Constable: Normal, sir.

Tewkesbury: And at school perhaps you have seen a master get annoyed?

Constable: Sometimes, sir.

Tewkesbury: Can you think of any particular incident?

Constable: I saw one throw a book at a boy once. It missed.

Tewkesbury: Thank you, officer. Well, that will do for the moment. You have given me six examples of people being annoyed. And now, officer, will you be good enough to tell me what the man did in this case? Did he shake his fist? Did he say "damn" or "bloody hell" or "you clumsy lout"? Did he smack my client or throw a book at her? Did he do any of these things?

CONSTABLE: No, sir.

TEWKESBURY: But you say he appeared annoyed?

CONSTABLE: Yes, sir.

TEWKESBURY: Then I'm afraid I must trouble you for some more examples, officer.

MAGISTRATE: How long is this going on for?

TEWKESBURY: Well, sir, that depends on what the officer says. I am proposing to take him through every example of a person being annoyed that he remembers. And I then propose to ask whether the man in this case did any of those things.

MAGISTRATE: Why d'you say the man appeared annoyed, constable?

CONSTABLE: He just did, sir. The look on his face.

TEWKESBURY: But you had never seen the man before, officer, had you?

CONSTABLE: No, sir.

TEWKESBURY: Then he may have had a twitch? Or an itch? Or he may have just thought of something disagreeable. How can you be sure that he was annoyed? He said nothing, he did nothing, and you'd never seen his face before. You can't be sure he was annoyed with my client, can you?

CONSTABLE: I thought he was.

TEWKESBURY: But you're not absolutely sure?

CONSTABLE: Not absolutely.

TEWKESBURY: Then you're not sure?

CONSTABLE: I'm sure but not absolutely.

TEWKESBURY: I'm afraid that's impossible, officer. If you're sure, you're sure, aren't you?

CONSTABLE: I suppose so.

TEWKESBURY: You're sure, aren't you?

CONSTABLE: I suppose so.

TEWKESBURY: Well, if you're sure, you're absolutely sure, aren't you?

CONSTABLE: Not necessarily.

TEWKESBURY: Well, if you're not absolutely sure, you mean you're not quite sure?

CONSTABLE: I suppose so.

TEWKESBURY: Then the truth is that you think the man was annoyed but you're not quite sure. (*To the Magistrate*) I can go on for some time, sir, but I respectfully submit that I have now disposed of this little matter. If the constable isn't quite sure, your Worship certainly can't be.

MAGISTRATE: I think there's a doubt. Case dismissed.

TEWKESBURY: I'm much obliged to your Worship. (*In a whisper*) Don't be too annoyed, constable.

Angela tore herself away from Mr Tewkesbury with difficulty. The next call she paid was at London Sessions, where once more, she had to admit to herself, she stayed less on her father's mission than for relaxation. There she found Mr Sumpter Hedges in the full flow of his eloquence. She soon discovered that, although Mr Hedges had no difficulty in finding his voice, the barrister in John Mortimer's little classic, *The Dock Brief*, was much too near a reality for the liking of those who want criminals to be adequately defended. Mr Hedges was addressing the jury in a case where his client was accused—most properly—of receiving goods knowing them to have been stolen.

"Members of the jury," Angela heard him saying, as she came in, "you are men and women of the world. Suppose this had happened to you. Put yourself in my client's position. Not his present position in the dock. I would not suggest to you, members of the jury, that any of you would ever find yourselves there. But his position at 10, Elephant Road, when he came into the house and found these cartons of cigarettes in his room. Sixty thousand of them. What would you have done, members of the jury? My learned friend for the prosecution sneers at my client's explanation of what he did. But that is what the prosecution is for.

CHAIRMAN: It is nothing of the sort.

HEDGES: Please don't interrupt.

CHAIRMAN: I shall always interrupt when you make improper remarks.

HEDGES: Then I shall leave the court.

CHAIRMAN: Continue with your address, Mr Hedges, and behave yourself.

HEDGES: I shall try again, members of the jury, but only

for my unfortunate client's benefit. I was saying, when the Chairman thought fit to intervene, that my learned friend sneered at my client's explanation of what he did. Well, what would you have done? Why must the worst motives always be attributed to everyone? That is what the world suffers from today. Too little charity, too much suspicion. Why must every unusual action, every unusual event be presumed to be in bad faith? My client, who was once in the tobacco trade, finds these cigarettes in his room. Now, if you had once been in the tobacco trade, what would you have thought? It would have been different if they had been oranges and apples, or silk stockings. But they were not. They were cigarettes. And, members of the jury, I shall not be straining your knowledge of the world if I ask you to reflect that cigarettes form the bulk of the tobacconist's trade. Indeed that is admitted. Mr Jones, whom I cross-examined on the subject, agreed that, so far from cigarettes being a strange thing to a tobacconist, they are in effect his life-blood. Well, members of the jury, my client comes home and finds his life-blood on the floor. What more natural than that he should put it in the cupboard? My learned friend suggests that my client ought to have gone to the police. Why on earth, members of the jury? Why should he assume that there was something sinister about these cigarettes? What does a tobacconist expect to find on his premises? Iron bars, members of the jury? Flowers? Chimney pots? No, members of the jury, tobacco, and, above all, cigarettes. And now, if you please, members of the jury, the prosecution suggests that, because a tobacconist finds that a normal delivery of cigarettes has been made, he ought to assume that they have been stolen. At this rate no retailer could accept any deliveries without going to the police.

Chairman: I'm sorry to interrupt you again, Mr Hedges, but I cannot allow you in your enthusiasm to try to mislead the jury. The accused is not a tobacconist and never has been one. Twenty years ago he spent three months as a boy in a tobacconist's shop. He is not a shopkeeper at all. He is a window cleaner. He found the cigarettes, so he says, in the sitting-room of the house where he lodges. It is a private residence, not a shop.

HEDGES: Very well, my Lord, I shall retire from the case.

And, throwing his brief down on to the desk with a bang, Mr Hedges stalked out of court.

Angela waited to hear how the situation was resolved. The Chairman asked the prisoner what he would like to do—to carry on with the case himself, or to have an adjournment and a retrial with another barrister to defend him.

"I think I'll plead guilty and be done with it," said the prisoner. "I wanted to from the start."

From London Sessions Angela went to the High Court, where she was relieved to find that the standard of advocacy was higher. First she sampled Mr Justice Storer's Court. The judge was speaking as she went in.

"I suppose you're relying on these cases, Mr Brownlow," she heard him say, and then go on to mention the names of six cases dating from the eighteenth century down to 1950 and to give all their references correctly. Angela could not, of course, be sure whether the cases were relevant or the references correct, but, as counsel stood saying nothing, she assumed that they were. The judge then went on to refer to eight other cases and to quote from three of them. Counsel remained silent. The judge continued. Angela even began to wonder if she were seeing things and if the judge were really counsel and counsel were the judge. Certainly Mr Brownlow appeared to have one of the qualities which Angela had understood from friends was useful in a judge, the ability to keep quite quiet. Mr Justice Storer, on the other hand, appeared to be a remarkably good advocate. For, having put Mr Brownlow's case fully, as far as the law was concerned, he then proceeded to deal with the facts, and, there again, all Mr Brownlow ever said was, "Yes, my Lord," or "If your Lordship pleases." He once tried to say: "Your Lordship is putting it so much better than I could have done," but Angela could not tell that he was going to say that, as all the words after "Your Lordship" were drowned in the further remarks of the judge.

Angela began to be extremely sorry for the other side, who, she gathered, was a lady called Mrs Perkins, represented by a young barrister called Space. But she soon found that her fears were quite groundless. For, as soon as Mr Brownlow had completed his almost entirely silent submission, and Mr Space had got up to reply, the judge proceeded to tell Mr Space what his argument was and to quote, Angela again assumed correctly, just as many cases as he had quoted in favour of Mr Brownlow. On Mr Brownlow's behalf the judge had certainly convinced Angela and had appeared to convince himself that the whole of English law and all the best English judges were ranged entirely against Mrs Perkins. But, once Mr Space was standing up, all the cases quoted by the learned judge appeared to show that the law was firmly established, by all the judges who mattered, in her favour. And, when it came to the facts, the same thing happened.

"And you would say, Mr Space, I suppose," said the judge, "that, unless your client is telling the truth, the evidence of the plaintiff himself doesn't make sense?"

"Indeed, yes, my Lord," Mr Space managed to slip in.

"A very good way of putting it. Thank you, Mr Space," said the judge.

Eventually, when Mr Space considered that the judge had nothing more to say, he sat down.

Thereupon Mr Justice Storer gave judgment.

"I am most indebted," he began, "to counsel on both sides for their succinct and admirable arguments. But, if I may say so, each of them appears to have omitted several important considerations both of law and fact."

The judge then began to refer to a dozen other cases which he had not so far mentioned, and to point out that it was really in those cases that the law applicable to this particular dispute reposed. He then proceeded to arouse that part of the law out of its sleep and, in a few well-phrased sentences (which, though of inordinate length, never got out of hand), he showed that neither Mrs Perkins nor her opponent really knew what was legally good for them.

"It is unfortunate," he added, "that the plaintiff did not plead this case in trespass. Had he done so, very different considerations might have applied. He could then have relied upon an entirely different line of authority."

Having quoted eight cases in support of this proposition the judge, rather sadly, it seemed to Angela, sent them about their business with an almost curt:

"But, as I have said, that aspect of the matter does not arise."

But, if the plaintiff had blotted his copybook by not pleading his case in trespass, the unfortunate Mrs Perkins had done no better. For she had failed to put forward the defence of "leave and licence". Had she done so, that would have temporarily resuscitated another eight cases. The judge referred to these, not, as he said, because they were really relevant to the matter he had to determine but so that, if the case should happen to go to the Court of Appeal, that Court would appreciate that he had those cases well in mind.

By the time Mr Justice Storer had finished, Angela had come to the erroneous conclusion that she had heard the names of all the cases that had ever taken place in the English Courts. She was wholly unaware that Mr Justice Storer had only quoted a tiny percentage of the cases which his mind obstinately refused to forget.

Angela also formed a great admiration for the unbiased way in which the judge appeared to be determined, at one and the same time, that the plaintiff should win the case and that the defendant should not lose it. But, although she thought that this was a signal example of British fairness and of the complete impartiality of the English Bench, she felt somehow that Mr Justice Storer was not quite the man for her father. Judges, she remembered, were supposed to hear and determine cases. Admirably as Mr Justice Storer no doubt determined his cases, she did wonder when he actually heard them.

In the next court she tried, she arrived during counsel's closing address. He sounded an able man and seemed to have an extremely good case. He ended his speech with:

"And so, my Lord, with some confidence I ask you to find for the defendants."

Whereupon the judge, without troubling counsel for the plaintiff to argue, gave judgment against the defendants for the full amount claimed by the plaintiff.

"Mr Barnstaple has, with his usual eloquence, endeavoured

to persuade me to take a different view of the transaction. In my opinion there is nothing in his argument at all. Indeed, it is plain beyond a peradventure that the plaintiff's claim is made out. The only matter which has occasioned me any surprise is that the action was defended at all. The defence was doomed to failure from the start."

Angela decided that Mr Barnstaple was not the barrister her father wanted. She realized that she was not able to judge of the merits of the case, but the point she took against Mr Barnstaple was his use of the words "with some confidence". If he did not know that he was going to lose the action, then, in view of the terms of the judgment, it showed that he must have a lower standard of intelligence than she at first thought. Alternatively, if he realized that he was fighting a hopeless battle, it was silly of him to use the cliché "with some confidence", when he had in fact none.

Next she went into one of the Courts of Appeal which, at that particular time, was more like the Centre Court at Wimbledon, except that there was no applause. A singles match between two Lords Justices was in progress. Each was using Counsel rather like a ball boy, while the presiding Lord Justice acted as umpire.

"I suppose you say to that," said Lord Justice Keen to Counsel for the appellant, "that that point was never taken in the Court below and is not open to the respondent now?"

"I do, my Lord," said counsel, dutifully supplying Lord Justice Spenlow with the ball.

"What about paragraph 6?" asked Lord Justice Spenlow, making the chalk rise on the sideline.

"That quite plainly is only dealing with equitable estoppel," replied Lord Justice Keen.

Before counsel could pick up the ball, Lord Justice Spenlow picked it up himself and returned it at speed with:

"Isn't that what we're talking about?"

"No," said Lord Justice Keen.

By now the ball boys were standing almost idle, though ready to pick one up, whenever required.

"This is 1958 not 1872," said Lord Justice Spenlow.

"Might I respectfully suggest," said the presiding Lord Justice, "that if we continue much more on this topic it will be 1972 before we reach the main point of the case."

Lord Justice Keen immediately queried the umpire's decision, which can be done with more decorum in Appeal Court One than at Wimbledon.

"The rules of pleading must be observed," he said.

"And the rules of common sense, fairness and justice," replied Lord Justice Spenlow.

Counsels' heads were now moving much like the spectators' at the side of the Court at Wimbledon.

"And those rules require that a party should put his case fairly into writing, so that the other side knows what he has to meet."

"Personally," said the presiding Lord Justice, "it seems to me that that has been sufficiently done in this case."

Angela translated this immediately into "Fault called."

She never learned what the case was about. She realized that it involved intricate matters of law, which laymen cannot be expected to understand. Nor could she judge of the ability or resilience of mind of the judges, as she could not follow the subject-matter with which they were dealing.

She went out into the corridor. She was standing there, looking a little disconsolate, when a young barrister in robes approached her.

"You look lost," he said. "Can I help you at all?"

"How kind," said Angela. "I wonder if you could."

"What Court are you looking for?"

"As a matter of fact, I'm looking for a judge, not a court."

"What's his name?"

"I've no idea."

"That does make it difficult. Can you describe him?"

"Not physically. But he's the best you keep. Quiet on the Bench, quick, but not too quick, at understanding what's said to him."

"By 'not too quick' I suppose you mean that he doesn't interrupt counsel before he's finished a sentence, by saying: 'I suppose you mean so-and-so,' when, if he'd let him finish, he'd have found out that counsel meant nothing of the sort?"

"That's right," said Angela. "And he doesn't object to new ideas and doesn't ask questions if he knows the answers. In fact, as I said, he's the best judge you've got, full of learning but not parading it, courteous, kind, firm, with a mind of his own but ready to listen to other people's views before he comes to a conclusion. In which Court shall I find him?"

"Well," said the young man, "I'm not a judge yet, but meantime I think Halliday's the man you want. He's in Q.B.3 today. I've just done a case in front of him."

"Would you mind telling me your name?" asked Angela. "I might want a barrister one of these days."

"I'm sorry to hear that."

"I've nothing special in mind, but one never knows. And you've been very kind."

"I'm afraid that doesn't necessarily mean that I'm any good at the Bar."

"Aren't you?"

"It's difficult to tell. I don't think I'm bad, but then I shouldn't be much use if I did. I can't be good yet, as I haven't been going long enough."

"Well, if you can tell a good judge when you see one, that must be a recommendation."

"Oh, everyone knows Halliday. What he says today the House of Lords says tomorrow. He's for stardom. The only question is where and when."

"That sounds like my judge," said Angela. "Could you tell me which way to go?"

"I'll take you there, if I may."

"It is good of you."

"Not at all. I should like to."

On the way to Court 3, Angela asked her guide when she could have the chance of hearing him in action.

"I don't often come here," he said. "I'm mostly in the County Court at present. Don't suppose you'd be interested, but I'm at Hampstead tomorrow."

"Could I come?"

"Well, of course, but I can't conceive why you should want to. Now here we are."

Angela found that the qualities of Mr Justice Halliday had not been exaggerated to her. There was no doubt at all about it. This was the judge her father wanted. He might have been made to measure. She had succeeded in one part of her task. Now for the other. She wondered about her companion.

"You haven't yet told me your name," she said.

"It's Southdown as a matter of fact, Charles Southdown. May I be introduced?"

"I'm Angela Walsh. How d'you do? You've been a tremendous help to me. I am grateful. May I come to Hampstead tomorrow?"

"I'll call for you and drive you there if you like."

"No, I won't let you do that," said Angela, "though it's extremely kind."

She was not particularly anxious to disclose that she was the daughter of Lonsdale Walsh, and, as she still lived in his house, disclosure would in all probability be necessary if the young man called for her. It was not that she was ashamed of her father. He had told her that his conviction was based on perjury and she believed him implicitly. But it was sometimes embarrassing and she hated people being sorry for her.

They walked along the corridor. Charles pointed to a Court.

"Old Boniface is in there," he said. "He tried Lonsdale Walsh, you know. Oh, of course, your name's Walsh. No relation, I suppose?" he added with a laugh.

CHAPTER FIVE

CAUGHT UP IN THE MACHINE

When Lonsdale heard from Angela that she had found his judge and that she had considerable hopes that she had found a barrister too, he went into conference with Spikey and began to formulate his plans in greater detail.

Spikey listened with the happiest anticipation. When Lonsdale had finished Spikey said:

"Now, the bloke you want is the Boss."

"Can he be trusted?"

"Now, look, guv. Do you trust me?"

"Would I be telling you all this if I didn't?"

"Right, you wouldn't. Then why do you trust me, guv?"

"Because I think you want the money and, provided there's enough money and not too much risk, there's no reason not to."

"Right. Well, the Boss is the same. If he likes the job and the pay's right, 'e's safe as me aunt's grandmother and she died ten years back."

"Good. Where is he now?"

"Well, unless 'e's 'ad a bit of bad luck, 'e's out at the moment; going straight they call it."

"All right, Spikey. You go and see him as soon as you get out and tell him what we want. My daughter will give you all the money you need. I've already told her that you'll be calling on her when you get out and that she's to give you all the help you ask for. She'll understand that but, just to be on the safe side, try to smuggle this out with you."

Lonsdale gave him a minute piece of paper on which he had written: "And I mean all."

"Angela will look after you and the Boss all right. Now, the only thing is, how are you to let me know?"

Spikey winked.

"You'll know all right," he said, "if your daughter understands this note. There ain't a prison wall which fifty nicker won't go through—and less," he said.

"Right," said Lonsdale. "Well, I hope it won't be long now."

Some little time before, Angela had gone to the County Court to hear Charles perform. She had formed an immediate liking for the young man and realized that she must guard against prejudice in his favour. She did not precisely know why her father needed his services, but she was quite determined not to recommend anyone just because she had a liking for him. Her father had said, however, that experience was less important than intelligence and mental resilience. So he was certainly a possible. But she was taking no chances and proposed to listen to him in action, even more critically than she had listened to the others.

She arrived at the County Court and sat in the public benches as near the front as possible. Judge Smoothe was presiding, an elderly man of a kindly disposition; not a profound lawyer, but with a keen sense of justice and a desire to do the right thing between the parties. Moreover, he was not simply anxious that the result of every dispute should be fair but that it should, as far as possible, also be satisfactory to both parties. In consequence he was known at the Bar as "Old Settlement," for, in a very large number of cases, he persuaded the parties to agree to a compromise judgment. He did not always realize that, though such behaviour on the Bench may be of great value, it is a two-edged weapon. In a good number of the cases where, as a result of the judge's desire to satisfy everyone, the case was settled, the consequence in fact was that no one was satisfied. Judges and lawyers are good at trying to heal wounds and bring warring parties together and they are often successful, but it is important to ensure that this method of approach is not used or pursued to the end in inappropriate cases.

Sometimes Judge Smoothe would smile happily to himself, as he disrobed, about a settlement he had procured, and even make a remark on the subject to the usher who was assisting him.

"Very satisfactory, don't you think, Walters?"

"Very satisfactory indeed, your Honour."

Naturally Mr Walters always agreed with his judge, but there was no sycophancy about it at all. He had been the judge's usher for many years and it was not strange that they began to think alike. Indeed, the usher could have given most valuable advice to the parties in many of the cases.

"Much better than fighting it out," the judge went on. "No one would have gained. A lot of mud slung, probably another day's costs incurred and no one any the better off."

"Very lucky they had you to try it, your Honour. I'm not sure that the parties always appreciate what you do for them."

This was unconscious humour on Mr Walters's part, because at that very moment both counsel in the case were having the greatest difficulty in parrying the verbal blows of their respective clients.

"I came here to get my rights," said the plaintiff. "And what have I got? A bloody sausage."

"Well, you did agree to the settlement," said his counsel timidly.

"Of course I agreed. What else could I do with the old basket looking at me over his spectacles and telling me I'd bloody well got to?"

Judge Smoothe had not put it so indecorously, but unquestionably the plaintiff had got the point correctly. What the judge had in fact said was:

"Of course, if the plaintiff wishes me to try the case, I will do so. That is what I am here for. But I think he would be wise to bear in mind that no case is won until judgment is given, and, even then, it may be reversed on appeal. Moreover, even if the plaintiff should win, would it give him real satisfaction to live in the same house as a person over whom he has triumped? Injunctions between neighbours do not make for good relationship. A friendly smile is worth far more than damages. I repeat that, if the plaintiff is prepared to take the risk of losing, or of winning and finding it a barren victory, I will, of course, proceed with the hearing. But don't you think it would be wise, Mr Gathermore, if the plaintiff consulted you before taking the final decision?"

"Bloody well settle," is certainly shorter but it is not the way judges talk.

On the day when Angela went to Judge Smoothe's court, Charles was appearing for the defendant in a case where a lady had somehow or other got her hair tangled in a washing machine. She complained that the machine was unsafe or alternatively that there ought to be a warning on it that people with long hair should tie it up before using the machine. Fortunately her hair was not torn off and her main complaint was the shock which she had suffered. Her husband had come into the kitchen just in time and cut off the current. The plaintiff now said that she was too nervous to use the washing machine, and that in consequence she had either to do the washing in a tub, which took much longer, or send it out, which was more expensive. In addition she and her husband said that instead of being a happy, gay young woman, she had become moody and irritable.

"I hope," said Charles, when he rose to cross-examine her, "that I shan't irritate you too much. I shall try not to do so. Tell me, Mrs Small, do you feel irritated at the moment?"

"I feel nervous."

"A lot of people feel like that in the witness box," said the judge, "and I'm not surprised. I'm only surprised at how calm most of them appear on the surface. Would you like to sit down while you give your evidence?"

"No thank you, your Honour."

"What form does your irritability take?" went on Charles.

"I just feel irritable."

"And how do you act when you feel irritable? Do you bite your husband's head off?"

"I wouldn't say that."

"Well, that's something. Do you jump if you hear a bang?"

"Yes, I do."

"And didn't you before the accident?"

"I don't know. I suppose I did."

"Do you burst into tears suddenly for no reason?"

"I wouldn't say that."

"Then what form does your irritability take? I've made a few suggestions. Can you help me at all about this?"

"I just feel irritable."

"Could anyone tell that you feel irritable?"

"I don't know. I suppose so."

"Why do you suppose so? Unless you do something to show that you're irritable, how should anyone know that you are?"

"I don't really know—now you put it like that."

"Perhaps 'irritable' is the wrong word. Perhaps you just have bouts of being moody and depressed? Is that right?"

"Yes, perhaps it is."

"I suppose that happened to you occasionally before the accident, as it happens to most people?"

"I suppose so."

"If you get a large award of damages in this case, do you think you will feel less depressed?"

Before the witness could answer, Judge Smoothe intervened.

"I don't think that's quite a fair way of putting it, Mr Southdown," he said. "The witness hasn't said she's depressed at the moment, only that she's nervous."

"I'm sorry, your Honour," said Charles. "Do you feel depressed at the moment, Mrs Small?"

"It's all so strange here, I don't really know."

"Did you feel depressed yesterday then?"

"Not all yesterday."

"Then did you feel depressed at some time yesterday?"

"I think I did."

"When?"

"I can't be sure."

"Why did you feel depressed?"

"I don't know really."

"Were you thinking about the case?"

"I may have been."

"That depressed you?"

After a further short cross-examination about her shock and extra expense, Charles turned his attention to the question of liability. Within a very few minutes he had tied up Mrs Small in much the same way as the washing machine had tied up her hair. And half an hour later Judge Smoothe, in giving judgment for the suppliers and manufacturers of the washing machine, said this:

"There seems to be an impression today that, if someone is injured, someone else has got to pay. I cannot conceive any other reason for this action being brought. It was doomed to failure from the start. The accident was obviously due entirely to the plaintiff's carelessness. There was nothing whatsoever wrong with the machine. As for the suggestion that there ought to be a warning notice on the machine, you might as well suggest that the manufacturers of the machine should supply a nursemaid with every machine. If you bang your head against a wall it will hurt. If you hang your hair over moving machinery, of course it may get caught up in it. The case is too plain for argument. I can only hope that the depression which may descend on Mrs Small as a result of this judgment may be of short duration. My advice to her is to forget all about it and to start using the washing machine again. But she should keep her hair up when she does so, charming as it must look when it is loose."

At the close of her day in Court, Angela was satisfied

that, in spite of his inexperience, Charles would do as well as anyone for her father. She wrote and told him so. Within a short time of his receiving the letter, Spikey was released and things began to happen.

CHAPTER SIX

INVITOR AND INVITEE

SPIKEY called on Angela the day after his release, and produced the note from her father.

"How much d'you want?" she asked Spikey.

Spikey told her.

"What d'you want all that for?"

Spikey told her.

"I see," she said, "and when is all this going to happen?"

"That depends on the Boss, Miss. 'Aven't seen 'im yet. 'E may 'ave some other engagements. But I don't suppose 'e'll be long. 'E's got to get everyone organized, though. You can't rush these things."

But, though things were not rushed, they happened, and, as a direct consequence, Douglas Broadwater received a telephone call which, though it pleased his wife, was a very great surprise to them both. Douglas had been Treasury Counsel at the Old Bailey for some years and he had in fact been one of those engaged for the prosecution against Lonsdale. Mary Broadwater was very anxious for Douglas to become a judge in due course, and she complained to him from time to time that he did not attend legal gatherings enough. She believed—quite wrongly—that, by associating regularly with the right people, Douglas would increase his chance of promotion to the Bench.

Douglas was not a particularly sociable person, and did not care for garden parties, cocktail parties, or the like. Indeed, he did not much care for going out to dinner. He was an able man at his job and had few other interests, except reading. He and Mary were very happily married and their disagreement on the subject of going out and about did not disturb their happy relationship. But

Mary never stopped urging Douglas to do what she wanted.

They were both equally surprised at the telephone call, but Mary was delighted.

"You'll accept, of course," she said, and on this occasion Douglas did not feel that he could refuse, though he was completely astounded at the invitation. He had answered the telephone and been told that Mr Justice Halliday wished to speak to him. He had appeared before Halliday on a number of occasions but he did not know him personally and he could not conceive why the judge should suddenly telephone on a Thursday evening. That was odd enough, but the conversation was even more odd. For Halliday had invited Douglas and Mary to come and spend the week-end with him. If he had not clearly recognized the judge's distinctive voice, he would have imagined that a practical joker was responsible. But there was no doubt about it. It was Halliday speaking. It was true that the judge apologized for the shortness of the notice and added that he had been wanting to invite them for some time but had never got round to it, but it was none the less one of the most extraordinary things that had ever happened.

"I just can't understand it," he said to Mary. "He doesn't know me. We don't belong to the same club. I don't think we've ever met out of Court. Why on earth should he invite us? It doesn't make sense."

"Well, I don't know why it is," said Mary, "but it's a jolly good thing. He's just being sociable, I expect. Probably thinks that the Bar and the Bench should get together a bit more. You remember this when you're a judge. I'm glad I was in the room when he phoned, or I believe you'd have refused."

"I must say he made it very difficult for me to say 'no'. It was almost like a Royal Command. What time shall we start?"

Mr Justice Halliday was a bachelor who lived in a house in the country called Howard House. It was not far from London. He had made a very large income at the Bar in the days when a man could retain a reasonable proportion of his earnings after paying income tax and surtax, and his attractive house stood in the middle of about ten acres of land. As Douglas and Mary drove up the long drive they were still discussing the possible reason for their visit.

"I wonder what a policeman's doing outside the front door?" said Mary as they were driving up to it.

"I expect he's had a threatening letter or something," Douglas suggested.

The judge opened the door to them himself and welcomed them.

"I'm afraid you must have thought it a bit odd being invited at the last moment, but I'm delighted you could come."

He was about to show them to their room, when Douglas suddenly remembered an important telephone call that he needed to make.

"I'm so sorry, judge," he said, "but might I use the telephone?"

"Whom d'you want to phone?"

"A chap in London."

"I'm afraid not," said the judge.

Halliday had no reputation for meanness, but Douglas could only assume that he grudged the amount of the toll call.

"I'm terribly sorry to be a nuisance," he said in a somewhat embarrassed voice, "but the call is rather important and—and—of course, I'd want you to let me pay for it."

"That's beside the point," said the judge. "I'm afraid you can't use the telephone, and that's all there is to it."

"Well," said Douglas, "I'd better go down to the village and make it. It is rather important. I want my clerk to alter a conference for Tuesday."

"Tuesday will keep," said the judge.

"But I'd really like to let him know now, judge, and if you'll forgive me. . . ."

"I'll forgive you certainly," said the judge, "but you can't go down to the village, and there we are. Shall I take you to your room?"

CHAPTER SEVEN

THE HOUSE PARTY

MILES HAMPTON, who was one of the witnesses for the prosecution at Lonsdale's trial, had had a varied life. He had never been very successful. Possibly his greatest success was in the witness box at the Old Bailey, where he withstood all the efforts of defending counsel to make him deviate from his original story. He came out of the box in the same good state and condition in which he went in. No sweat pouring down the face; no glass of water for him; he required no assistance from the judge. As calmly as his jerky method of speaking allowed, he told his story, and one juryman actually said quietly to his neighbour:

"Well, he's obviously telling the truth."

And so it appeared. Yes, it had been a good day for Miles Hampton.

He did not have so many good days. He was the kind of man for whom no one is sorry, because he never appeared to need sympathy. One day he would be found in the Thames, or under an omnibus, and his friends and acquaintances would wonder why on earth he did it. Such a happy type. Not a care in the world. Up to a point they would be right. Apart from a desire to know where the next meal and the rent were coming from, Miles had few cares. But he took almost a childish delight in keeping up appearances. He certainly had no success at making money or love or any of the things which most people think important, but it was his ability to keep up appearances which made people think he had nothing to worry about. He wore well-cut expensive clothes, for which he sometimes paid. Usually by instalments ordered by the local county court judge.

"But really Mr . . . Mr Hampton," Judge Knight had said to him, "if you can afford to go to an expensive tailor, you can afford to pay him."

"I'm afraid that doesn't follow, your Honour," Miles had replied blandly. "I find it much cheaper to buy one really good suit than several shoddy ones."

"I've no doubt you do, if you don't pay for it."

"But I shall, your Honour, given time. Unfortunately I have been out of employment for the last three years."

"What is your occupation?"

"I've told your Honour, none—at the moment."

"But, when you do get a job, what sort of job do you do?"

"Anything honest within my capabilities, your Honour. I have no particular qualifications. I would take up brick-laying but I gather it's a skilled occupation. I would do ordinary labourer's work, but unfortunately I have a weak heart. I would sell newspapers but I can't get a pitch."

"What are your qualifications?"

Miles looked down at his feet inside the witness box and then up again to the judge, as though making a swift appraisal of himself.

"I have had some administrative experience, your Honour. I was a major during the war. For a short time I was a permanent president of Courts Martial. I learned a little law then, but not really enough to become a qualified lawyer."

"What are you living on?"

"I sometimes wonder myself, your Honour. I have had National Assistance, though I prefer to do without it when I can."

"This is hopeless," said Judge Knight to the creditor's solicitor. "Your client had better forget it. Unless you'd like to make Mr Hampton bankrupt. The debt is £60, I see."

"I don't think that would do much good," the solicitor had said.

"If only I could get a job I'd pay the debt at once," Miles had said, and he meant it.

At about the time Mr Justice Halliday was showing the Broadwaters to their room, Miles was sitting in his room, wondering how to spend the day, when his landlady sent a man up to him.

"Come in," said Miles.

The stranger came in.

"You Miles Hampton?" he said.

"That's right."

"Ever done any crowd work?"

"Films, you mean?"

"Yep."

"Twice," said Miles.

"Want a job?"

Miles repressed a choking feeling in his throat. He was a sentimental person and sentimentalized about himself. This incredible answer to his needs made him want to cry. After a moment he said:

"Yes, I could do with it. How many days?"

"Three or four. Can't be sure."

"When does it start?"

"Now."

"How did you hear of me?"

"You're on the list."

"Good Lord, I didn't know they were so efficient. Right. Where is it?"

"Just out of London."

"How do I get there?"

"I'll take you."

"That's very kind."

"Better bring a few things. It's on location. May have to stay there."

"O.K." said Miles.

Ten minutes later he was being driven towards Mr Justice Halliday's house. When they arrived, he pointed to the man outside the door.

"Real policeman?" he asked.

"You bet," said the man, and they went in.

The same afternoon Angela telephoned Charles's chambers, and spoke to him. He was delighted to hear from her again.

"I'm afraid you'll think this very odd after our very short acquaintanceship," she said, "but I wondered if by any chance you'd be free this week-end. I've been asked to take someone to a week-end party. I shall quite understand if you'd rather not, but could you come?"

"I should love it," said Charles. "I shan't even look to see if I've any other engagements, because, if I have, I shall cancel them."

"How nice you are," said Angela. "I deserved a snub."

"Nothing of the kind," said Charles. "How do we go? Shall I drive you?"

"That would be lovely."

They made the necessary arrangements and that evening Angela and Charles drove to the house of Mr Justice Halliday.

"Why the policeman?" he asked on arrival.

"Your guess is as good as mine," said Angela, a remark which would have made her father blush.

The party at Mr Justice Halliday's house was now beginning to take shape, but there were more guests to come.

One of the witnesses against Lonsdale was dead, and his widow was at home when a cheerful stranger called on her.

"Mrs Elsie Meadowes?" he asked.

"That's me."

"Widow of the late Kenneth Meadowes?"

"Well, I was, but I'm courting again."

"Glad to hear it, Mrs Meadowes. I've come just at the right time."

"Why? Who are you?"

"You go in for the pools, don't you, Mrs Meadowes?"

"I do sometimes, but never 'ave no luck."

"That's all changed, Mrs Meadowes. You've had some luck."

"Me? I 'aven't won, 'ave I?"

"Not in the way you expected, but you've won just the same."

"'Ow much?"

"Well, I'm not sure, but I'll explain. Although we get a lot of winners on our pools, we want to encourage the people who don't win. So we've decided that a certain amount of the money will be set aside and a prize given out of it each week to certain losers selected at random. And you're one of the lucky losers, Mrs Meadowes. Congratulations."

He held out his hand.

"Well I never. About 'ow much will it be?"

"Well, not less than a hundred pounds—perhaps more."

"Well, if that ain't the best thing I've 'eard since Jimmy got the compensation. When do I get it?"

"Now—if you come with me. The first award is going to be made in person."

Half an hour later they were on their way to Mr Justice Halliday.

"'Ere, where is this?" said Mrs Meadowes. "And what's a copper doing 'ere?"

"To see that no one pinches the stuff. Come along in, Mrs Meadowes."

The late Mr Meadowes had had a good deal to do with judges, who had imposed varying sentences upon him, but he would never have imagined that his widow was actually going to be entertained in a judge's house.

The house party was now nearly complete. One of the prospective guests, Herbert Adams, was difficult to find, but he was traced in the end. He was on a bench in the park. Two men approached him.

"Herbert Adams?" said one of them.

"Well?" said Adams suspiciously.

"We're police officers," said one of the men, "and we want you to come along with us to answer some questions."

"I ain't done nothing," said Mr Adams.

"Then that's all the better for you," said the man. "Come along."

And Mr Adams, without further protest, walked with the men to a car and was soon being driven to Mr Justice Halliday's house.

"Wot's this?" he said on arrival. "This ain't a police station."

"It's temporary," said one of the men. "While the other's being repaired."

Jo Barnwell lived in an attractive house in the Regent's Park area. She was just leaving it when a small boy dashed in front of a car, narrowly missed it and then fell flat on the pavement and remained still. She at once ran to him. The boy was motionless. A fat man was getting out of the car. He helped Jo to lift up the boy. He seemed unconscious and his face appeared to be covered with blood.

"We'd better take him to the hospital," said the man. "I wonder if you'd mind helping?"

"Of course not," said Jo.

Together they lifted the little boy into the car.

"I wonder if you'd mind sitting with him while I drive?"

"Certainly."

The man got into the driving seat and drove off. He

stopped at the corner and two other men got in. One got in beside the driver and the other in the back.

"Which is the nearest hospital d'you think?" the fat man asked Jo.

Jo told him, but her attention was mainly taken up with the boy. So she did not notice for a few minutes that the car was not going towards the hospital she had mentioned.

"You're going the wrong way," she then said.

"I know the house surgeon at the hospital we're going to," said the driver.

As Jo had not seen the small boy rehearsing his part that morning several times, and covering his face with red paint, she did not become suspicious until the car was nearly out of London.

"Where are you going to?" she asked eventually. "This boy ought to be seen to at once."

"He's O.K.," said the man next to her. "All right, Tommy, you can wake up now."

Tommy sat up and grinned.

"Now don't make a fuss, madam," said the fat man. "You'll be quite all right, if you behave. But it's three and a half to one, and chloroform's a nasty business. We might give you too much."

"Where are we going?" she asked.

"You'll see."

And in due course Jo found herself at Mr Justice Halliday's house. She was momentarily relieved to see the man at the door.

"Officer," she called.

"Yes, madam," he said, coming up to them.

"I've been kidnapped by these men," she said.

"Well, if you'll go through the front door and take the first door on the right, they'll take all particulars."

Jo had not fully taken in this extraordinary behaviour by the policeman when her companions took her into the house.

One hour later another car drove up to the house, and Lonsdale got out and walked swiftly inside. A companion followed more slowly, after saying to the man at the door:

"That's the lot, I think."

CHAPTER EIGHT

ADDRESS OF WELCOME

HALF an hour later the guests were all assembled in the drawing-room, when Lonsdale came in.

"I might have known it," said Jo.

"Evening, Jo, nice to see you," said Lonsdale. "Now, if you're all comfortable, I'll explain. First of all, let me apologize to you all—particularly to you, Sir George, for the somewhat unusual methods I have been compelled to adopt."

"I hope you realize," said Mr Justice Halliday, "that, although you are undergoing a sentence of imprisonment for life, you can not only be sentenced for your present crimes with a sentence to begin after your life imprisonment is over . . ."

"That is hardly a deterrent, Sir George," interrupted Lonsdale.

"You know quite well what I mean. A sentence of life imprisonment is reviewed after ten years and normally the convicted person is released after serving anything from ten years to fifteen years. What I was going to add was that conduct such as yours will presumably result in your serving the maximum sentence for your original crime, in addition to the further sentence which I mentioned."

"That is a risk I must face," said Lonsdale, "but let me say at once that, as far as most of you are concerned, I do very much regret the steps which I have had to take. But I venture to suggest that you must agree that there was no alternative open to me. Now, what are the facts? Eighteen months ago I was convicted of the murder of Adolphus Barnwell. I was convicted on perjured evidence. There is the woman who procured my conviction by that evidence."

"There stands the man who murdered my husband," said Jo.

"Don't interrupt please, Jo," said Lonsdale. "You'll have plenty of time to say your piece later. After my conviction, I appealed to the Court of Criminal Appeal. My appeal was dismissed. I petitioned the Home Secretary, to no avail. I asked my Member of Parliament and other friends to have my case reviewed. It was hopeless. Nothing could be done. Now, Sir George, would you mind assuming, just for one moment, just for the purpose of argument, that in fact my conviction was procured as I have said. What other course was open to me? For most people there would have been no alternative but to suffer the sentence. But I was able to do something else. Admittedly I have had to break the law in order to do so. I have had to escape from prison and to induce all of you by one method or another to assemble in this house. You, Sir George, I have very regretfully had to make a prisoner in your own house. None of you I hope will suffer any more discomfort than is absolutely necessary. You will, I am sure, understand that every precaution will have to be taken to prevent you from communicating with the outside world. No one is going to come here looking for an escaped convict. But all the necessary steps have been taken to deal with friends and tradesmen who may call or telephone. None of you will suffer in the slightest degree, provided you make no actual or apparent attempt to get help. The judge has pointed out that my offences are already such that I have really nothing to fear from any further crimes which may be committed by me or on my behalf. So I do beg you all to be sensible and to make no show of resistance.

"Now, why are you here? Most of you will have guessed. We have the transcript of my trial, photostat copies of the documents, all the chief witnesses, except one, who gave evidence, and the lady who paid them. Now don't interrupt, Jo. You know you did. I am proposing, with the assistance of the two members of the Bar present, to go through the whole of the evidence at my trial in such a way as to satisfy the judge that what I have said is true. If, after this new trial, as I may call it, the judge is satisfied that my conviction was properly procured, I shall give myself up to the police and take the consequences of my actions. But if, as I am quite confident I can do, I satisfy him that hardly a word of truth was spoken at my trial, then I hope that in those circumstances the judge will take such steps as he thinks proper to put the matter right. I shall certainly surrender to the police, but I venture to suggest that no one can then fairly complain at my unorthodox methods of showing that the jury in returning their verdict of guilty were grossly misled. How long this trial will take I naturally cannot say, but in the intervals between the sessions every endeavour will be made to make you as comfortable as possible. Now, are there any questions?"

"What do you want us to do?" asked Broadwater.

"I should like you to be kind enough to conduct the case on behalf of the prosecution, and your learned colleague, Mr Southdown, to conduct the case on my behalf. I apologize for the absence of any solicitors to instruct you but, in the circumstances, I'm sure you won't mind interviewing the witnesses yourselves. It may be of some help to you if I say that, while the witnesses whom Mr Broadwater will see will tell him all manner of lies, I shall tell Mr Southdown nothing but the truth."

"Mr Walsh," said the judge, "if this affair is going to serve any useful purpose, I should advise you to stop persisting in saying that your case is right and the prosecution's is wrong. It doesn't impress me in the least. Dozens of rightly convicted criminals say the same thing, when they are trying to get off on appeal. It has no value at all."

"Thank you for your guidance, Sir George," said Lonsdale. "I will try to benefit from it. But I hope you will understand that the reason I emphasise these matters is because I feel very strongly about them. I have been in prison for eighteen months as a result of lies, and she knows it."

"There you go again," said Mr Justice Halliday.

"I'm sorry," said Lonsdale. "Now, I suggest that we have dinner shortly and go to bed early. In the morning Counsel on each side can get his instructions and by, say, twelve o'clock, they should be ready to present the case to you, Sir George. Will that be convenient to you all? Good. I take silence for consent. Spikey, could you arrange about drinks?"

CHAPTER NINE

NO ESCAPE

LATER that evening the judge explained to Charles and Broadwater how the whole thing had started, as far as he was concerned. On the Thursday evening he had been dining by himself when his manservant informed him that a police inspector would like to see him. He was shown in at once.

"I'm so sorry to disturb you, my Lord," he said, "but the police have just received some urgent information. It may be a hoax but we don't think it is. I don't know if you remember sentencing a man called Thorowgood—an inappropriate name, if I may say so, my Lord—for robbery with violence? He got seven years."

"You must tell me more about the case if you want me to remember. Names mean very little to me," said the judge.

"Well, either at the trial or down below in the cells, he was heard to swear vengeance against you. He said it was an unfair trial and an unfair sentence and, to use his own words, he was going to get you."

"I can't say that I remember anything about it," said the judge, "but convicted people do sometimes shout threats. As far as I know, no attempt has ever been made to carry them out."

"That's right, my Lord," said the man, "until tonight."

"What has happened?"

"Thorowgood has escaped."

"I've seen nothing about it in the papers, and there's nothing on the wireless."

"I know, my Lord. In view of the information we had, it was decided not to assist the man in any way. You see, my Lord, when it's published that a man has escaped, something has to be put in the papers as to the steps being taken to recapture him. You know the sort of thing, my Lord—his house is being watched, or a search is being made in the woods near so-and-so, or it is believed that he escaped in a small blue car heading for the North; road blocks are being established round a wide area. That information may be true or false but, whichever it is, it gives the man something to think about. Now, if nothing is said at all, it makes him jittery to begin with. The silence must worry him. Where are they searching? What are they doing? Indeed, has his escape been discovered yet? And so on."

"Yes," said the judge, "but where do I come into all this?"

"My Lord," said the man, "there is another very special reason why we don't want to publish anything at the moment. We have pretty reliable information that not only is he heading in this direction with a view to carrying out his threat, but that he is going to be accompanied by several armed men to assist him. They're a very determined gang, and the police are very anxious to catch the lot. With your Lordship's assistance, I think we can. Would your Lordship tell me who lives in this house?"

"I live here with a cook and a manservant only," said the judge.

"Trusted servants?"

"I've had them for years."

"I don't want to alarm your Lordship, but we have information that two masked men were in Brocket Wood, five miles from here. What the police would like to do, if your Lordship will permit it, is to fill this house with plain clothes police officers, themselves masked, and wait until the attempt is made. We then hope to get the lot."

"What's the object of the masks?"

"Well, my Lord, we believe that there are about ten or more men in this, coming from different directions. If one of them sees a masked man he will at once assume that he's one of the gang."

"But mightn't it be dangerous for your own men, if one of them mistook one of his colleagues for one of the gang?"

"That's all been provided for, my Lord. They will wear a special type of mask and, of course, in addition there's a password."

"I see," said the judge. "Well, it's all very odd, but, if that's what you want to do, I suppose I'd better let you do it. But I hope you won't make too much mess."

"You leave that to us," said the man. "Thank you very much, my Lord. I'd be grateful if you and your staff would all go into one room above the ground floor, so that we can give you complete protection."

"All right," said the judge. "When d'you want to start?"

Ten minutes later nine masked men were admitted into the judge's house, while he and his cook and manservant chatted in one of the bedrooms.

Not very long afterwards, the "inspector" came into the bedroom.

"There's been a bit of a mistake," he said. "Thorowgood hasn't escaped after all."

"Good," said the judge. "Then we can go downstairs again," and he led the way to the drawing-room. In it were eight masked men.

"You might remove those things now," said the judge.

"I'm afraid this is going to be a bit of a shock to you," said the man who had fetched the judge, "but we are not policemen."

"Then who are you?"

"That doesn't matter," said the man, "but I'd better tell you what is going to happen. We are going to hold you and your staff prisoners and the house will be in a state of siege. But, provided you do what we tell you, no harm will come to any of you. On the other hand, if there is the slightest attempt to escape or call for help, I cannot be answerable for the consequences. Is that understood?"

"I hear what you say," said the judge.

"Good," said the man. "Now, first thing in the morning, you will telephone to the Law Courts and say that you're not feeling very well and won't be able to sit that day and possibly not for a few days longer. If, in the course of that conversation you attempt to give the alarm in any way, it will be the worse for all of you. And you might bear in mind that none of us can be identified. You may have been surprised to notice that the uniformed man you first saw had a beard. Unusual in a police officer. And glasses. No doubt you'll be able to tell the police the colour of his hair and his approximate height. Any other information you give will be quite valueless."

"What is the object of this outrage?" asked the judge.

"You'll learn in due course. The next thing you must do is to telephone to a Mr Broadwater, a barrister, and ask him and his wife to stay here for the week-end."

"And if I refuse?"

"Don't," said the man.

There was a slight pause, and the man turned to the cook and said in a somewhat menacing tone:

"You don't want him to refuse, do you?"

The cook thereupon fainted.

"You see," said the man. "She'd like you to telephone, and so should we. Shall I get you the number?"

"But I don't know him, or his wife."

"You must make some excuse for asking him. After all, you're a judge and he's a barrister. He'll want to come. I expect he's appeared in your court from time to time."

And so it came about that the judge telephoned and invited Broadwater and his wife for the week-end.

CHAPTER TEN

CONVERSATION PIECES

AFTER the judge had explained what had happened, he lowered his voice and added:

"There is one thing we can do. I've done it already, as a matter of fact."

"What's that, Judge?' asked Charles.

"Well, it's only a possibility, but it's worth trying. But it depends on the wind. I've written several notes calling for help, and, if there was a bit of a breeze, thrown them out of the window. One of them went quite a long way."

"Did you see what happened to it?"

"I did," said the judge. "It was eaten by a cow."

"We can all try it," said Charles.

"Don't do it unless a wind gets up. Otherwise they'll just drop down and may be found."

At that moment Lonsdale came into the room.

"I hope you're not finding things too inconvenient," he said. "If there are any urgent messages you want to send to anyone, I'm sure it can be arranged—provided you make no attempt to give an alarm."

"How long do you propose to keep us here?" asked the judge.

"No longer than is necessary," said Lonsdale. "How long d'you think it'll take? The first trial took two days. This shouldn't take much longer. Perhaps not as long."

"I can't think what good you imagine it will do you," said the judge.

"Well," said Lonsdale, "without wishing to appear impertinent, you should. Supposing I did satisfy you that the whole case against me was a fake. What would you do?"

"I don't feel called upon to answer that question," said the judge.

"Well, of course not," said Lonsdale. "There's no reason why you should answer. But I can't conceive that any judge, who was satisfied that there had been a verdict procured entirely by perjury, would do nothing about it, just because he only learned of the fact through completely unlawful means. You'd do something about it, wouldn't you," he said, turning to Broadwater, "if you were a judge? And you?" he added, to Charles.

Both of them took their lead from the judge and said nothing.

"Well, it doesn't matter," said Lonsdale. "I've enough faith in you all to make me think this is worth doing. You all loathe injustice, and I'm quite sure that, if any of you saw what you believed to be a gross piece of injustice, you would take all the steps you could to have the matter put right. Almost anyone in the country would. And, whatever people may say about lawyers, I'm quite sure that they'd be the first to try to remedy an injustice they'd heard of, if they knew there was no one else who could do anything about it. Well, I mustn't detain you any longer, gentlemen. You know where you are sleeping, I think. I hope you'll have as good a night as possible."

Lonsdale next paid a call on Jo. She was in bed reading.

"Forgive me for not knocking," he said.

"I forgive you for nothing," said Jo. "Why did God make you such a bloody man?"

"My dear Jo, that's a line of enquiry which it would suit few people to indulge in. Even you, for instance. He'll have quite a lot of questions to ask you, when you get up there."

"Thanks for saying 'up'."

"I don't believe there's a down. We all go to Heaven. The only difference is that some of us won't like it. You, for instance, you won't find anyone to fight."

"What about you? You fight hard enough."

"That's only to get my way, not because I like it. You enjoy a fight for its own sake."

"Perhaps I do. I'll put you back in gaol if it's the last thing I do."

"You won't have to, Jo. I shall go back on my own, as soon as this is over."

"I'll get you back before it's over if I can, and I'll see you stay longer when you do get back."

"They may not ask you, Jo. Granted you put me there, it's not your business any longer. It'll be up to the judge then. It's up to me at the moment. What does it feel like to be in my power? Do you love every moment of it? It must be a new experience."

"A very unpleasant one."

"But you don't really dislike me—not really—any more than I hate you."

"That's all you know."

"But I do, Jo. I do know. If I were standing on the edge of a precipice you'd push me off as soon as look at me. But all the same, if things had been different, you'd have pushed the other fellow off instead. We'd have made quite a pair, you know. And I've never pretended I didn't like you."

"Funny way of showing it."

"It's a funny world. But it's true. I like you very much, Jo. And you like me."

"I've a funny way of showing it."

"True enough. May I kiss you?"

"I'm in your power, aren't I? What's to prevent you?"

"I shouldn't dream of kissing you by force. I told you, I hate fighting. I only fight when there's something I want to get."

"That's hardly a compliment."

"I don't pay you compliments, Jo. Not that kind anyway. I *am* paying you the compliment of having an extra guard outside your window."

"Why the window?"

"Just in case you thought of sending any little notes into the air. We like to keep the grounds tidy."

"You don't seem to have made much headway with the judge."

"How could you expect me to, yet? But you wait."

"I am waiting," said Jo.

And they kissed.

At about the same time Angela was paying a visit to Charles. She was very apologetic.

"You do see my point of view, don't you?" she said. "I know my father is innocent. He never lies. Wouldn't you have done the same?"

"I can't conceive the situation arising. But, when you say you know he's innocent, how d'you know? Most wives who are fond of their husbands believe them innocent. So would most children their parents. The courts have found him guilty and the Home Office can find nothing even to merit an enquiry. Why should they all be wrong?"

"He would never have pleaded 'Not guilty' if he'd been guilty."

"There you are wrong. It isn't telling a lie to plead 'Not guilty'. It is simply calling on the prosecution to prove your guilt."

"Well, anyway he's told me he's innocent and he's never told a lie in his life. I do want you to believe that."

"How d'you know he's never told a lie?"

"Because I do. Because I've lived with him all my life and you can't live with someone without knowing these things. He just can't tell a lie. You're going to appear for him and I do want you to understand that."

"Why? What difference can it make?"

"All the difference. If you don't believe in his case you may not bother."

"Of course I will," began Charles, and then stopped and laughed.

"What's the joke?"

"I said 'of course I will' automatically, as though this were going to be a real trial."

"It's going to be a very real trial," said Angela.

"You don't understand. In an ordinary case in the Courts it doesn't matter to me if I believe my client innocent or guilty. I put up the story he tells me for better or worse, whether I believe it or not. And pretty well everyone does the same. If a criminal's counsel had to believe in his innocence before he could raise any enthusiasm for the defence, there'd be precious few enthusiastic defences put forward, and most of those would be put forward by pretty stupid advocates. If your father's were a real case, I'd do the best for him I possibly could, whether I believed him or not. But this case is different. So that really you're quite right about it this time. If I really believed your father to be innocent, I should try much harder tomorrow. In any event, of course, I'll try sufficiently hard to prevent one of your bodyguard knocking me on the head. But I suppose that's all I'm prepared to do. Now if I really thought he was in the right, I would have a go."

"Well, thank Heaven I came to see you," said Angela. "You must believe me. Why d'you think he'd take all this trouble, spend all this money and risk getting many years of extra imprisonment, if he weren't innocent?"

"I'm afraid that argument can always be raised. It's sometimes said that there are two kinds of judges. One kind think that a plaintiff wouldn't spend the money on bringing an action unless he thought he had a good claim, and the other kind think that the defendant wouldn't defend unless he had a good defence. And the commonest cry by an obviously guilty thief in the witness box is: 'What should I want to steal it for?' No, I'm afraid that sort of argument doesn't cut any ice with me. I'm much more impressed with your obvious complete trust in your father. I say 'obvious' but I should say 'apparent.' I don't know you well enough. How do I know that you're not putting on an act?"

"You're very frank."

"No point in being anything else."

"Well, I can only give you my word. Mark you, I'm not a truthful person like father. I don't mean that I'm an inveterate liar. I'm just normal. Like you, I expect. But father's not. He's quite abnormal. He just never tells a lie, never, never. Please try to believe me."

"You certainly sound as though you meant it, but, if I accept that, how can I tell that you're right?"

"Well, do I strike you as a fairly intelligent person?"

"Very."

"Thank you. Well, then, if I am above average intelligence, surely I'm either putting on an act as you suggest, or I'm probably right? Obviously I can't ask you to be certain about it. I can only beg of you to think that what I'm saying may be true. You were quite right. This is not a real trial. But it's vital to us, and, if you believe in our case, it must be some help."

"Well," said Charles, "I'll promise you this. I will go into it with an open mind and then, if I find in the course of the case that you appear to be right, I'll do my damndest. I can't say more than that."

"No," said Angela, "I don't think you can. Thank you for being so sweet. Have you told the judge, by the way, that it's really your fault that this is happening to him? I chose you myself, but, if you hadn't told me to go and see the judge at work, I might never have heard him."

"Well, I haven't yet," said Charles. "I think I'll wait till it's over."

"Tell me," said Angela, "if we are right, and if we satisfy the judge that father is innocent, he will do something about it, won't he? He won't just let father go back to gaol and say 'serve him right for making such a nuisance of himself'?"

"No, I don't think he'd do that. If you ask my honest opinion, I don't believe for a moment that you'll do any good at all, but if I'm wrong, and if you really showed that your father's innocent, then I'm quite sure that the judge would do something about it. We all would, if it came to that."

"Father was sure of it."

"It's the first hurdle you've got to get over. And I don't believe you ever will."

"But you will try?"

"I will, but you mustn't expect anything."

"But I do."
"Why are you so certain?"
"Because I think the truth's bound to come out the second time. You'd say that it usually comes out, wouldn't you?"
"I don't know about usually, but often, certainly."
"Well, I can't believe that it won't this time."
"Well, good luck, anyway. At any rate I should never have met you but for this."
"Are you pleased?"
Charles paused.
"Yes," he said eventually. "In spite of being kidnapped and locked up and threatened with I don't know what, I'm pleased."
In what might be called the guards' common-room, Spikey was holding forth on the beauties of a life of ease.
"No more cops," he said. "No more stir. I wouldn't 'ave believed it if 'e 'adn't told me 'isself. Didn't know there was so much money in the world."
"How d'you know that he'll keep his word?"
"'Ow do I know! 'E's done all right so far, 'asn't 'e? If we didn't get no more we shouldn't do so bad. But I know 'im. 'E'll do wot 'e's said."
The advantage of Lonsdale's infirmity of always telling the truth was that he normally carried conviction with people, even in the most unlikely places.
"Thou shalt find no ease neither shall the sole of thy foot have rest," put in one of the guards, known to his friends as Holy Hal. He had spent many years in prison and the Bible had had a great attraction for him there. Not from a religious point of view. He simply enjoyed the language. He did not quote it either hypocritically or in order to moralize. Possibly he enjoyed showing off his immense knowledge, but his real pleasure was to relate everyday words and actions to phrases in the Bible for his own benefit. No doubt saying it aloud and creating an impression among his friends and acquaintances gave him added pleasure, but that was not the real source of his enjoyment. It cannot be said that he ever deliberately went back to prison to devote more time to his study, but this was hardly necessary. Like most habitual criminals, he was not very successful and usually found his

way back there soon after his release. Some prison chaplains found his knowledge a severe test of their own. One of them, in the hope that it might lead to better things, actually played a sort of Bible chess with him. Everything they said had to come directly out of the Bible from the beginning to the end. Any failure to reply with a quotation lost two marks. Any mistake lost one more. The parson had to confess that he looked forward to his visits.

"Why not look on the bright side?" said another of the guards, to Holy Hal.

"We wait for brightness, but walk in darkness," said Holy Hal.

"O.K.," said Spikey, "but it's round the corner. Me and the missus'll go travelling, I think."

"Do they put your previous on a passport, like they do on a marriage certificate?" asked another guard.

They discussed the pleasures of life and the various ways in which they would seek them out. Lonsdale had indeed put a very large sum aside for the purpose of paying the men without whose help he could not succeed. He was prepared to spend half his fortune or even more on ensuring the success of his scheme. Angela had already opened an account for the Boss, in which she had placed £100,000 to be distributed among them all equally, with an extra bonus of £10,000 for the Boss himself. Her father had promised another £110,000 to be paid on the completion without interruption of his new trial. Lonsdale did not consider that £220,000 out of a million was a penny too much to pay for the chance of freedom.

Naturally suggestions of this kind were taken most seriously by the Boss and his associates. Spikey had been quite right that the Boss was the man Lonsdale wanted. The combination of a public school and University with a prison education produced an interesting result in the Boss. He could mix happily in all circles. Among criminals he was trusted because he never deliberately let them down. His part in a crime was the organization. He seldom appeared himself—except in the dock. One of the things his associates liked about him was that, if they were caught, he didn't try to wriggle out and leave them to take the rap. Naturally, if the police never came to him, he was not expected to go to them. But he did not do what so many receivers do when questioned by the police (and later in the witness box), throw the entire blame on his accomplices.

This tendency on the part of receivers is a great help to the prosecution in some cases. When there is a charge against a number of people of conspiring to steal, everyone knows that usually one of the accused is the receiver and the remainder are the thieves. The prosecution put the receiver first on the record, so that he has to go into the witness box first. He attempts to give a display of wide-eyed innocence and, without the slightest hesitation, he throws on the thieves any blame there happens to be going round. In their indignation the thieves trip into the witness box and sink themselves and the receiver. The result is that, even if there isn't much evidence against the receiver at the beginning of the case, there is at the end—all provided by the defence.

The Boss naturally tried to avoid conviction, if possible, but never at the expense of his friends. His public school had done something for him.

He was a kind of independent contractor in crime. Some hostesses, when giving a party, instead of employing direct labour and buying the food themselves, employ a caterer to do the lot. The Boss was the equivalent of the caterer. If you wanted, for example, to crack a safe, or carry out an important warehouse robbery, he would supply everything, the men, the materials and the method. Naturally, he only took on jobs of sufficient size. He didn't supply buns and cups of tea for the Mothers' Union Summer Party. He would do the equivalent of a small dinner party for six, if it was exclusive enough, but in round figures he would not touch anything if there was not at least £1,000 for himself, not subject to tax.

He was against unnecessary violence, but he recognized that neither banks nor ordinary citizens would part with their valuables without sufficient inducement. Accordingly, when an exploit could not be carried out entirely in secret, which he preferred, he authorized the use of enough violence to achieve the object. But he always emphasized the necessity for as much care being exercised as possible. For example, gagging can be a very dangerous operation, and he had two specialists (who had been male nurses) who knew how to complete this delicate and sometimes difficult operation with as little discomfort as possible and no danger to the patient.

When in funds, the Boss went to expensive restaurants, where his cheques were gladly accepted. He never dishonoured a cheque, though his bank manager did sometimes wonder where the cash came from. Particularly did he wonder about this on one occasion, a month or so after his own branch had been robbed of over £10,000. Did Mr. Bostock's payments-in come, as he said, from winnings at the races? How lucky for the Boss that he was not like Lonsdale. Otherwise, presumably he would have had to tell the manager that it would have avoided a lot of trouble if he had just transferred the amount to his account before the robbery. It would have saved an elaborate and quite expensive plan, and the temporary disablement of a bank messenger and two policemen. It is sometimes difficult for a bank manager to decide whether to open an account for a man whom he knows to have convictions against him, or to keep the account open after a conviction. Just because a man has been convicted, he should not be denied ordinary services when he comes out of prison. Obviously, if the account is considered unsatisfactory, or there is something suspicious about the cheques paid in, the account will be closed. But the Boss's account was always conducted most satisfactorily. He never overdrew. On the contrary he normally had a large credit. Any cheques paid in were from obviously satisfactory sources, and, though most of the payments-in were cash, that is the case with many course bookmakers. And he always ascribed these payments to winnings at the races. The Boss would never have been so indiscreet as to pay in the proceeds of a robbery the day after it had taken place. It would have given him some amusement to return to his bank, for the credit of his account, the money he had stolen from it, the day after the robbery, but he had been to gaol sufficiently often to curb his sense of humour on that occasion. When he did pay in a large sum a month after the robbery, the cashier did say to him:

"Had a good day, Mr Bostock?"

"One of the best," the Boss had replied.

"I can't think why people bet," said the cashier.

"People are very stupid," said the Boss, "fortunately for me."

"Well, I suppose we all are if it comes to that," said the cashier. "If we'd been more careful we should never have lost that £10,000 a month ago."

"I don't know what else you could have done," said the Boss. "Tell me, what other precautions could you take?"

"We're taking them, Mr Bostock," said the cashier. "But walls have ears, even in a bank, you know."

"Well," said the Boss, "I expect they're unnecessary anyway. No one would go for the same place again so soon."

"That's a comfort," said the cashier. "The messenger will be pleased to know that."

"I hope he's all right," said the Boss. "I was very sorry to read about it . . . but there it is, it's a wicked world and these things will happen."

"Well, it's nice to know they won't happen here again for a bit. I wonder what I'd do if a gunman suddenly walked in?"

"Now—what *would* you do?" asked the Boss. "You ought to have a foot button you can press so that the doors close automatically and an alarm bell rings."

"That's an idea," said the cashier. "Thanks very much. I'll pass it on. I wonder why we've never thought of that before?"

"Of course," said the Boss, "the chap might get cross and try to shoot his way out. I should just have the alarm bell if I were you and leave the doors open. But, you know," he added, "there's only one thing that will keep a really determined burglar out."

"If it's not a breach of confidence," asked the cashier, "what might that be?"

"Don't have anything worth stealing inside."

"Oh—that's an old one," said the cashier.

"I know," said the Boss, "but it's the only one that works. Good morning."

The Boss had made the arrangements for Lonsdale's escape and retrial, with great care and efficiency. He had even gone to the lengths of arranging diversionary escapes at two other prisons, in the hope of providing employment for as many police cars as possible at the time of Lonsdale's escape. It had been a simple affair. Everything in these matters depends on exact timing. Three minutes were allowed for the whole operation. At the appointed moment a small car drew up to a particular place outside the prison wall. The street on which the wall abutted was not used a great deal and the precise spot which had been chosen could only be seen for about fifty yards in either direction. Between seventy-five and a hundred yards in each direction away from the place where the escape was to take place, two large lorries waited with their engines running, ready to block the road for a sufficient time at the crucial moment. At the appointed time two men got out of the small car and threw a rope ladder over the wall. Lonsdale was there, with a confederate to hold it while he made the descent. He went up quickly and down on the other side within a minute. The precise timing of the whole operation had been rehearsed most carefully several times to make sure that, as far as could reasonably be ascertained, they would have the necessary three minutes. The operation had been rehearsed without the rope ladder, so as to see that both sides were in the right place. Lonsdale was not an expert in climbing rope ladders but he made the journey safely, jumped in the car and was driven off. The two lorries never had to be used and drove away slowly behind the small car. By the time the alarm was given, Lonsdale was well out of the district, making direct for the judge's house.

The announcement of his escape was in the normal form. "Lonsdale Walsh, who is serving a sentence of life imprisonment for murder, today escaped from Northwall prison. A special watch is being kept at all ports and airfields."

But not at judges' houses.

CHAPTER ELEVEN

OUT OF TOWN TONIGHT

ONE of the few witnesses who was quite pleased to have been kidnapped was Miles Hampton. It was true that he was not to be paid as a film extra, but he was fed and housed and it was a new experience. His life had become increasingly dim and with little or no excitement in it. Now here was certainly an adventure which he would be able to retell over pints of beer. It hardly needed any exaggeration either. Indeed, it was so extraordinary that he doubted if people would believe it. That troubled him for a moment—until he suddenly realized with a thrill that, once it was over, it would make headlines in the newspapers. That thought quickly led to another. Perhaps he would be asked to write an article. He had heard that quite a lot of money could be made that way. Then again, he might be interviewed on the wireless—or even on TV. They might even revive *In Town Tonight*. He visualized something of this kind:

The Interviewer: Tonight we have someone who will interest viewers tremendously, someone who actually took part in the incredible proceedings in Mr Justice Halliday's house, someone who was taken for a ride, literally, and forced to give his evidence over again before the judge, literally, at the pistol point. Has there ever been such an astonishing story as was unfolded after Lonsdale Walsh eventually surrendered to the police? It was, literally, breathtaking. But you have read all about the story for yourselves and you don't want to hear any more from me. You want to see the man who was made to take a part, and an important one too, in the astonishing events which fell, literally, like a thunderbolt on the legal world. So, without more ado, here is Mr Hampton. How d'you do, Miles, if I may call you that. Nice of you to come here tonight.

Miles: Not at all. I'm very pleased.

Interviewer: I expect it will be a long time before you forget your extraordinary experiences?

Miles: Yes, I expect it will be.

Interviewer: Nothing like that has ever occurred to you before, I take it?

Miles: No, that's right.

Interviewer: Not the sort of thing that happens every day?

Miles: No.

Interviewer: Tell me, what did you find the most interesting part?

Miles: The most interesting part?

Interviewer: Yes, the part that interested you most.

Miles: In what way?
Interviewer: In any way.
Miles: I don't really know.
Interviewer: But it must have been very interesting?
Miles: Oh, yes, it was, very.
Interviewer: And frightening too. I'm sure I should have been very frightened.
Miles: I wasn't exactly frightened.
Interviewer: A little nervous perhaps?
Miles: Yes, I suppose so, at first.
Interviewer: It must have been all very interesting.
Miles: Oh, yes, it was, very interesting.
Interviewer: Didn't you wonder whether you would ever be rescued?

At this stage in the interview Miles suddenly realized with a shock that, if something went wrong, if a revolver suddenly went off, or someone hit him on the head with a blunt instrument, he might never be in *In Town Tonight,* or even in the world at all. The thought stopped his imagination for a few moments, and he spoke to his companion, Herbert Adams.

"D'you think we'll ever get out of this alive?"

"'Ow should I know?"

"I thought you might have some sort of idea."

"Well, I ain't, see. I been in worse spots and I been in better."

"Well, you got out of them all right."

"That don't mean we shall get out of this one."

"It doesn't mean we shan't."

"It doesn't mean we shall."

"One doesn't want to be too pessimistic."

His companion spat out of the window.

Miles returned to his thoughts.

Meanwhile Lonsdale was preparing for the trial in the morning. He chose the dining-room as the most suitable room, and it was arranged in the most convenient manner so that, while the proceedings would not be formal as in a court, they would be conducted with reasonable dignity. Angela had brought from his house three copies of the transcript of the proceedings at his trial, one for the judge and one for each barrister. He also had photographs of the exhibits. All these documents he had obtained for the purposes of his appeal to the Court of Criminal Appeal, and were brought by Angela together with notebooks and paper for the use of the judge and counsel. He had wondered whether the witnesses should be examined on oath but, after consideration, he saw no point in it; they had already committed perjury, so it was obvious that the fact of swearing on the Bible had no effect on them. And, whatever they said, they could not be convicted of perjury, as it was not a legal trial.

Finally he checked all the security arrangements and, after being satisfied that all was well and everything ready for the trial next morning, he went to bed. He slept reasonably well. He was happy in the thought that at last he was going to be able to prove that he was convicted solely by reason of a plot. The possibility of failure never occurred to him, even though he had no clear idea of how the prosecution's case was to be broken down. He had failed in breaking it down once. Why should he succeed the second time? The witnesses were the same, except for the man who had died. They would presumably tell the same story. Unless they were shown quite plainly to be lying, the judge would obviously believe them, and all his trouble would have been to no avail. But he did not believe this could possibly happen. He had not thought it possible at his trial. He had a different defending counsel then but, though he was sure Angela had made a good choice, it was not the change of counsel that made him so certain. It was the consciousness of right. Had he appreciated how gullible the jury would be on his original trial, he might have acted differently then. But now he knew that everyone was against him, everyone except Angela. That, he felt, made his task easier. He knew what he was up against. Overwhelming prejudice. But that was at the same time his own strength. Everyone except himself and Angela would start the trial believing that it was little more than a farce. Once an inroad was made into the case for the prosecution, its fall would be all the greater, just because it had appeared originally to be impregnable. It would be a day of triumph. It must be.

CHAPTER TWELVE

RETRIAL

THE following morning Charles and Broadwater spent some time preparing for the case to begin. It was finally decided to have an early lunch and to start the trial immediately afterwards.

"You will, I hope, forgive a light lunch," said Lonsdale, "but I am anxious that none of us should feel sleepy."

The judge did not feel called upon to comment, and Charles and Broadwater followed his lead. The cold ham and tongue and salad were eaten in comparative silence for about ten minutes. Spikey eventually broke it with:

"This ain't a funeral, is it?"

No one answered.

"Well—not if everyone behaves 'isself, it ain't," he added.

Miles suddenly visualized himself being interviewed again. It was a most interesting lunch before the trial, he would say. Why? he would be asked. "We had ham and tongue and salad" did not seem a very good answer. "No one said anything" was not much better. Perhaps he could start something himself and make the lunch interesting.

"I have a feeling," he said, "that this has all happened to me before."

"In that case," said Jo, "perhaps you'll tell us how it ends."

"I don't actually remember if it did end. I can only seem to think of this part."

"Well, pass the sauce, please," said Spikey, adding: "D'you remember that bit?"

They drank water or lemonade, and it was all over within half an hour, and then the proceedings began. Lonsdale opened them:

"I know that it isn't usual for the prisoner to start the ball rolling, except by pleading Guilty or Not Guilty, but I want to make one thing plain before we start. You know the object of this inquiry and, in order to achieve it, it is quite unnecessary that the proceedings should be conducted as at an ordinary trial. For example, there are all sorts of rules of evidence which normally have to be observed. A witness mustn't say 'what the soldier said.' I dare say that makes for justice as a whole. I don't know. Nor do I care. There'll be no such rules here. There'll be no objections to evidence on the ground that it isn't admissible. Everyone will have a free hand—subject only to the judge's requirements. For example, I see no objection to one witness being asked a question while another witness is in the witness box. Mr A says something; the judge or counsel can turn to Mr B immediately and ask him what he says to that. The only requirement is that the proceedings should not get out of hand and, if we all agree to do what the judge asks us to do, that aspect of the matter should be sufficiently taken care of. Does everyone understand?"

No one spoke.

"I take it from your silence that you understand what I mean," Lonsdale went on. "It should be a new experience for you all. Indeed, it might result in legal reforms being introduced. I won't pretend that I'm interested in that aspect of the matter. All I'm concerned about is to see that my original trial is fully investigated by every means at your disposal. Now, shall we begin? Unless the judge knows of some better method, perhaps Mr Broadwater will start by calling his witnesses for the prosecution. You have, no doubt, all read the evidence and know what the case is about. Unless, therefore, the judge wants to hear, or Mr Broadwater wants to make, a preliminary speech, I personally see no point in his opening the case. But, of course, as I have already indicated, there will be no objection to his intervening with an explanation or correction in the middle of the evidence. Indeed, all the things which you can't or shouldn't do in court can be done here, if anyone thinks they will help."

Broadwater's first witness was a man who had been present at the murder. He gave his name as George Allwinter. He was an artist. He had been brought to the judge's house on the pretext that he was to be commissioned to paint a picture. He said in evidence that he was walking near Adolphus Barnwell's house, although he did not know at the time that it was his house. He had heard of Adolphus as a financier, but did not know anything more about him or where he lived. As later evidence showed, Adolphus was on the way from his house to the nearest pillar-box to catch the last post, at the time when Mr Allwinter was strolling along the pavement thinking about a picture—or a model, he wasn't quite certain which. He would probably not have noticed Adolphus at all in a perpendicular position, but a large blue motor car came out of a side turning, where it might have been waiting, and changed the perpendicular to the horizontal. Mr Allwinter did not actually see the impact. He had an idea of a car coming out of the side turning, of a loud acceleration, a muffled exclamation (presumably of protest) by Adolphus, and the next thing he knew was that the car had disappeared and Adolphus lay dead in the middle of the road. He was unable to take the car's number. He went across to see what he could do for Adolphus, but saw that it was hopeless. He went into the nearest house and telephoned for the police. They were soon on the scene. He gave his account to a constable, and that was really all he knew about it.

Charles then cross-examined him.

"You have known for a long time that my client is charged with murder?" was his first question.

The judge interrupted.

"Southdown," he said, "I see no reason why you should call this escaped convict your client. He is not your client in any sense. You are doing what you are under compulsion."

"I'm sorry, Judge," said Southdown. "It slipped out. I hope you'll forgive me if it happens again. What d'you suggest I call him?"

"It is a bit difficult," conceded the judge, "but I must say that in the circumstances I resent the expression 'client'. He is a thug and a kidnapper."

"I don't mind what I'm called," said Lonsdale, "provided you all do your best to arrive at the right conclusion. I shouldn't take offence if you repeated what the judge has said, and referred to me as 'the thug'."

"I'll try to call him 'Mr Walsh'," said Charles.

The judge considered whether to suggest leaving out the "Mr". He was not one of those judges who refer to the prisoner by his surname without any prefix. But this case was different. A prisoner is presumed innocent, until he is found guilty. In the witness box he ought, therefore, to be treated like any other witness. But this man had been found guilty. He was a convict with a number.

Lonsdale sensed what the judge was thinking.

"My number's 1074, if you'd prefer that," he said.

The judge decided to leave the matter.

"Well now, Mr Allwinter," went on Charles, "you know that Mr Walsh has been convicted of murder?"

"Of course."

"And have known it for a long time?"

"Quite."

"And before he was convicted, you knew he was charged with murder?"

"Naturally."

"How long after you saw the incident did you learn that the charge was not manslaughter, nor killing by reckless driving—but murder?"

"I don't know exactly. When it was published, I suppose. I saw it in the papers. About two or three weeks after he was killed. I can't be sure exactly."

"From what you saw yourself, it might just have been an accident?"

"Why didn't he stop then?"

"He could have been frightened. Have you never heard of that sort of thing happening?"

"Yes, I have, but there's all the other evidence."

"That's exactly what I meant," said Charles. "You've heard or read all the other evidence. If it weren't for that, this might in your view have been just an accident, mightn't it?"

Mr Allwinter hesitated.

"Well," he said, "there was no one else in the road and no other vehicle. There was no need to hit him, was there? The road was wide enough."

"He might not have seen him."

"Driving with his eyes shut?"

"Have you never done that?"

"Driven with my eyes shut? Of course not. If I've felt sleepy, I've stopped and had a rest. But anyway this wasn't long distance driving. This was in London."

"I didn't ask you if you'd slept at the wheel. I asked if you'd ever driven with your eyes shut?"

"When I was awake? Of course not."

"Haven't you?" said Charles. "I should think again. Do you always stop your car before you sneeze?"

"I can't say that I do."

"Well, when you sneeze, you shut both eyes. And it's for much longer than just a blink. Have you never thought of that?"

"I can't say that I have."

"Well, I should," said Charles. "There are circumstances when it's very dangerous for a driver to sneeze when driving. We can test it if you like. Could we have some pepper, Mr Walsh, d'you think?"

Pepper was brought and the witness was induced to sneeze.

"D'you see what I mean?" asked Charles.

Not only the witness but everyone else could see that Charles was right.

"Well, Mr Allwinter," he went on, "how can you know that the accident wasn't caused by a sneeze?"

"Well, it didn't look like that to me," said Mr Allwinter.

"But you didn't see anything until after it had happened, did you? You just had the impression of a car coming out of the side turning and the next you knew was that a man was lying on the ground and the car was gone?"

"But look at all the other evidence."

"Exactly," said Charles, "that's what you've been doing, looking at all the other evidence. If it hadn't been for that, you'd have had no idea how the accident happened."

At that stage Broadwater said that he felt he must intervene.

"All this talk of sneezing is very interesting, and may indeed be profitable for those of us who drive, but it was never suggested at the trial that this death was accidentally caused by a sneeze."

"A lot of things may not have been suggested at the trial," said Charles.

"I think we ought to know," said the judge, "if you are going to suggest that death was caused by an accident. Because, if you are, we might as well save our time. I have read the other evidence. The case for the prosecution was that this was a deliberately planned murder. Either it was or it was not. Sneezes do not come into it."

"The point is, Judge," said Charles, "that the only person who the prosecution suggest may have wanted to kill Mr Barnwell is my—is Mr Walsh. If he isn't guilty of murder, it may have been an accident. Suppose Mr Walsh is right, and all the other evidence you're going to hear is perjured, the fact remains that the man was killed and killed by a car."

"I see what you mean," said the judge, "but it doesn't matter to you how he was killed, so long as your—this man isn't responsible."

"All the same," said Charles, "it's a little help—not much, I agree, but something, to show that accident is, apart from the other evidence, a possible explanation. Of course, if this other evidence is true, accident, I agree, doesn't come into it. It was a cold, calculated murder."

"All right," said the judge. "I see what you're driving at. Shall we get on? Is there anything else you'd like to ask Mr Allwinter?"

"I'd just like to ask him about this once more. The dead man was found about the middle of the road, wasn't he?"

"About."

"It's a good wide road?"

"Yes; he could have missed him quite easily. He could have driven either side of him."

"If he saw him."

Fortunately for Charles, at that moment Mr Allwinter sneezed. The pepper was still doing its work.

"Quite," said Charles. "Or, if he wasn't paying sufficient attention as he drove, he might have seen him suddenly and hesitated which side of him to go, in case the man went that way. You know, like two people bumping into each other in the street."

"Then he would have stopped after the accident."

"Most people would. But some people panic. And suppose this driver had previous convictions for dangerous driving, or suppose he was disqualified at the time he was driving, those would be reasons for someone not stopping."

"I suppose so."

"Then suppose he'd just stolen the car? That would be another reason, wouldn't it? You see, Mr Allwinter, you are not able to identify the car—or the driver—are you?"

"That's true. It happened too quickly."

"So, for all you know, it might have been a thief, a disqualified driver or a man who sneezed and panicked. You have heard of hit-and-run drivers, haven't you? Why shouldn't this have been one of them?"

"But the other evidence," began Mr Allwinter.

"Exactly," said Charles.

"Suppose we get on to the other evidence," said the judge. "You've made your point quite clearly. If the other evidence comes to nothing, Mr Walsh should have been acquitted—but, if it's to be believed—as it was believed by the jury—he was plainly guilty, as you yourself have said, of a calculated murder."

"If you please, Judge," said Charles, "I only wanted to establish that, apart from this other evidence, this might have been another of those cases where a driver doesn't stop after an accident."

"Well, I think you've established that sufficiently," said the judge.

"I respectfully agree," said Broadwater.

"Good," said the judge. "As we're all agreed, we can get on. The sooner we finish, the sooner this outrage will come to an end. At least so the . . . the. . . ."

The judge could not think of the right word. Lonsdale was not "the accused". He had already been accused and convicted. He was not "the prisoner", as he was free. It was the judge and counsel who were the prisoners. He could not keep on calling him "the escaped convict". It was too heavy. To call him the "murderer", when he was at least going through the motions of investigating the crime, offended his judicial sense. He was at a loss for a word. Eventually he went on:

"At least so the man who has brought us here has promised."

"I keep my promises," said Lonsdale. "But I must make it plain that I should not feel called on to keep this one, if the investigation were conducted as a pure formality. I expect the case to be gone into thoroughly to the best of your ability. I apologize for being dictatorial in this matter. But it is the whole object of the exercise. Unless I get a fair hearing here I might as well have stayed in prison."

"Are you saying that you did not have a fair hearing in the Courts where you were tried and where your appeal was heard?" asked the judge.

"No," said Lonsdale, "I'm not. As far as I could see, both hearings were perfectly fair. But mistakes have been made at fair hearings before and all I say is that my case is another example of such a mistake."

"Very well," said the judge. "Your next witness, please, Broadwater."

Jo came forward and sat in the seat which was being used for the witnesses. First of all she described her husband's position, and his relationship to Lonsdale.

"They were the leaders of opposing factions," she said, "and matters came to a head in regard to the management of the Anglo-Saxon Development Corporation Ltd. My husband had a very good chance of ousting Mr Walsh from his control of that company. Indeed, but for his death, I have no doubt that he would have obtained the necessary support for a resolution he was about to propose for the purpose of removing Mr Walsh from his position of Chairman and Managing Director of that company. Now, a short time before that meeting, my husband brought an action for slander against this man. In the course of that action Mr Walsh had to produce certain documents, but, shortly before the day fixed for the production of those documents, the action came to an abrupt end. It came to an end automatically because my husband was killed. And here is the man who was responsible for his death."

"Let us avoid dramatics as far as possible, Mrs Barnwell," said the judge. "He has been convicted and sentenced, and there is no need for you to emphasize his guilt almost every time you speak. This is not the case of a man who is assumed innocent until he is proved guilty. He has been proved guilty and it is now up to him to show that the verdict of guilty was wrong."

"I know him," said Jo. "He'll wriggle out of anything, if he gets the chance. Like he wriggled out of gaol."

"I should hardly call it wriggling," said Lonsdale. "I climbed up a wall, not through a drainpipe."

"Please," said the judge. "This bickering will not help the investigation."

"Did your husband receive any kind of communication from anyone about a week before he was killed?" asked Broadwater.

"He did," said Jo. "He did indeed."

"What was it?"

"He received a threatening letter warning him that, unless he immediately withdrew the action he had started, the consequences for him might be serious."

"Have you still got that letter?"

"I produced it at the trial, and I have the photostat copy which Mr Broadwater has handed to me here."

"Before you produce it, tell me this, Mrs Barnwell. Did your husband withdraw the action?"

"He did not—neither immediately nor at all."

"What happened next?"

"My husband received a large parcel."

"What was in it?"

"It was a road sign which had been dug up."

"What sort of road sign?"

"It had 'YOU HAVE BEEN WARNED' on it."

"Did your husband pay any attention to it?'

"He did not."

"What happened next?"

"He was murdered."

"You mean he was run over by a car," said Broadwater, his customary fairness as a prosecutor getting the better of him.

"I mean he was murdered," said Jo, "by being run over, and that man paid the driver to do it."

"That is a lie," said Lonsdale, getting very red in the face.

"It is the truth, and you know it," said Jo.

"It is a lie, and you invented it," said Lonsdale.

"Once and for all," said the judge, "I really cannot be of the slightest use, if this is the way you're going to go on."

"She started it," said Lonsdale. "She has no respect whatever for the truth."

"You have no respect for anything except yourself," said Jo, "but that respect is unjustified."

"Will you please control yourselves," said the judge. "If this experience does nothing else, it shows the necessity for the Court's power to maintain order. Nothing useful can be done if these interruptions continue. Surely you can see that?"

The judge looked at Lonsdale as he said that.

"Yes, of course," said Lonsdale, "but I cannot stand listening to lies."

"If your case is right," said the judge, "you will have to listen to a lot of them before this inquiry is over. How can I tell whether they are lies or not unless I hear them?"

"I will try to control myself," said Lonsdale, "but this woman deliberately tries to bait me."

"If that is so," said the judge, "why do you give her the satisfaction of seeing her shafts hit the mark?"

"There are some matters on which I cannot conceal my feelings, but I will at any rate try to keep quiet until it's my turn to speak."

"You kept Adolphus quiet all right," said Jo.

This time Lonsdale said nothing.

Broadwater then resumed his examination.

"Now, Mrs Barnwell," he said, "a few minutes ago you said that you had a photostat copy of the threatening letter, which you say your husband had received. Will you be good enough to produce it?"

Jo handed to the judge the document. It was plain that the original consisted entirely of words and letters cut out of a newspaper or several newspapers and gummed together with transparent sticky tape. The sender was obviously taking no chances. Even the envelope, which was of a cheap kind obtainable in hundreds of shops, was addressed in the same manner.

"Had you any idea who had sent that letter?" asked Broadwater.

Charles intervened.

"I don't quite know what course you want to take, Judge,"

he said. "If this were an ordinary trial I should, of course, object to such a question, which is plainly inadmissible, but in the circumstances perhaps you would prefer me not to object?"

"Well," said the judge, "there has been quite enough interrupting so far, I think; and in any event, when the procedure was laid down by our captor, he said that he did not want the rules of evidence to be observed. On the other hand, I really don't see how her answer is going to help me. We all know what she will say. But her saying it won't help to prove her statement or her belief true."

"Very well," said Broadwater. "I won't press the question."

"But I'd like to answer it," said Jo. "I knew perfectly well who had sent it. He had."

And she looked hard at Lonsdale, with the obvious intention of provoking him to an outburst.

"Now——" said the judge warningly to Lonsdale, and Lonsdale remained silent.

"Was there anything which made you think that?" asked Broadwater.

"The substance of the letter," said Jo. "No one else had any reason for sending it. Although, of course, he had his lieutenants and associates—a lot of sycophantic sheep—none of them would have done such a thing, except on his orders. He was the real person who had an interest in threatening my husband. I must admit I didn't think he'd have the guts to go through with it. But he must have sent the letter, and we know from the other evidence that he did."

"Don't let's worry about the evidence for the moment," said Broadwater. "Let us confine our attention to the letter itself. Can you conceive by any stretch of your imagination any other person who could have wanted to send such a threat to your husband?"

"I cannot," said Jo. "And if I were twice as intelligent, and thought for ten times as long, I still couldn't. He sent it all right."

And she again challenged Lonsdale by looking at him as she said it.

This time the judge said nothing, but merely looked at Lonsdale to see if he would rise again; he did not.

"I don't think I've anything else to ask Mrs Barnwell," said Broadwater.

"Very well," said the judge, and invited Charles to cross-examine her.

"Mrs Barnwell," he began, "it is obvious that you have the most profound dislike of Mr Walsh."

"I haven't," said Jo. "I know him for what he is, that's all."

"It is certainly obvious," went on Charles, "that you think he murdered your husband."

"I don't think it—I know it," said Jo.

"Well, you didn't see him do it, did you?"

"He didn't do it himself. He got someone else to."

"You didn't see the other man do it, did you?"

"You know I didn't."

"Nor did you hear him tell someone else to murder your husband."

"The fact that I didn't hear him doesn't make it any the less certain."

"How long have you been so sure that Mr Walsh was, if not the actual murderer, responsible for it?"

"From the very beginning."

"So, from the time your husband was killed, you were satisfied that Mr Walsh was the culprit?"

"I was. And I was right."

"When did you first learn that your husband had been killed?"

"Within a few minutes of his death."

"At that time you had no evidence except that he had been knocked down by a car which did not stop?"

"I had the threatening letter."

"Yes, of course, and the road sign. But, apart from those facts, you had none of the evidence which was given at his trial."

"Of course not. What difference does it make? The evidence is there now and was given at his trial."

"Well, that isn't quite right, is it, Mrs Barnwell? One of the witnesses is dead, isn't he?"

"That's not my fault."

"Of course not. But, coming back to what I was saying, at the time of your husband's death you were quite satisfied that

Mr Walsh was responsible, although you had no evidence against him whatever, except the threats which you believed he sent?"

"I knew he sent them."

"Don't let's quibble about that. You felt sure in your own mind that he was the murderer from the very start. Is that right?"

"It is."

"Now, Mrs Barnwell, will you listen to this question very carefully? You felt sure that Mr Walsh was guilty. You're a highly intelligent woman and you knew quite well that the mere production of the threatening letter and road sign would prove nothing whatever against Mr Walsh. You knew that, didn't you?"

"I never thought about it. I knew he was responsible."

"But you also knew that he wouldn't ever be arrested, let alone convicted, if there were no other evidence against him."

"I never thought about it. I assumed that the police would do their duty and bring the murderer to justice. And they did."

"Did you know that all the witnesses we're going to hear about called on the police?"

"What d'you mean? I don't understand."

"I mean that the police didn't find those witnesses. The witnesses came to the police."

"What's wrong with that?"

"Nothing—if they were honest witnesses. Were they, in your opinion, honest witnesses, Mrs Barnwell?"

The judge intervened.

"What does it matter?" he said, "whether she thought them honest? The jury obviously did."

"I agree," said Charles, "that the jury believed them, but I assure you that it is material to ask this lady if she believed them."

"All right," said the judge. "If you say it's material, ask her."

"Did you believe the witnesses, Mrs Barnwell?" said Charles.

"When do you mean? In the witness box?"

"When else had you seen them?"

"I hadn't."

"Then what else could I mean?"

"You ask so many stupid questions I've no idea what you mean sometimes. Of course I believed them. They were obviously telling the truth."

"Were they?" said Charles. "Are you sure?"

"Of course."

"You would have done anything to bring the person you believed to have murdered your husband to justice, would you?"

"Of course I wanted him brought to justice."

"That isn't what I asked. You'd have done anything to bring him to justice, wouldn't you?"

"The situation never arose. He was brought to justice."

"Without your help?"

"I gave the evidence you know about."

"Did you do anything else?"

"Nothing that I can remember."

"You didn't by any chance see any of these other witnesses before you went to the police?"

"See any of the other witnesses?"

"That's what I asked."

"Not to my knowledge."

"Are you sure of that?"

"Of course I am. I may have seen you walking in the street before today, but I didn't notice you."

"So that before these witnesses went to the police you had never spoken to any of them, so far as you know?"

"I spoke to Mr Allwinter."

"But none of the others?"

"How could I? I didn't know of their existence, did I?"

"Didn't you?"

"I haven't got second sight."

"But you knew, you knew—not thought but knew—that Mr Walsh had killed your husband?"

"You don't call that second sight, do you? That was a logical and obvious deduction."

"And then," went on Charles, "without any prompting from you, the witnesses came along and proved you right?"

"Without my prompting them!" she repeated indignantly. "Are you suggesting that I . . ."

"I'm not suggesting anything," said Charles. "I am merely asking you questions. Did these witnesses have any prompting from you?"

"I've already told you, I didn't know them."

"The answer to the question may be easy," said Charles, "but I should like it none the less. Did those witnesses have any prompting from you?"

"Of course not," said Jo.

"You lie," said Lonsdale.

"Really," said the judge, "we were getting on quite well till then."

"I'm sorry," said Lonsdale. "I tried to bite my tongue, but I just couldn't. This woman is an arrogant liar."

The judge sighed.

"She says you're a murderer, and you say she's a liar. Do you really think that's going to help me to form a view as to whether there was anything wrong with the jury's verdict? I'd better warn you that, at the moment, I have no reason whatever to believe that justice was not done at your trial."

Jo looked triumphantly at Lonsdale.

"But, while I'm here, I will certainly go on enquiring into the matter. So do let there be an end of these silly interruptions. Now, Southdown, is there anything else you want to ask?"

"Not at the moment," said Charles. "But I may want this witness back."

"She will be available," said Lonsdale.

The next witness was Miles Hampton. He described how he had been sitting on a bench in Hyde Park, about a week or so before Adolphus was killed. A man, whom he took to be a down-and-out, was sitting on the same bench. While they were sitting there, a man of about the same height and build as Lonsdale, dressed in a morning coat and grey top hat, walked past them smoking a cigar. A little farther on he stopped at a litter basket and threw something into it. The down-and-out (who was in fact Herbert Adams) got up immediately and went to the litter basket. Shortly afterwards he came back with a newspaper and the remains of a cigar. Miles could not say positively that Lonsdale was the man they had seen, but, from his general appearance, he might have been. Adams asked Miles for a light and proceeded to smoke the rest of the cigar and to read the paper which he had brought back with it. Miles noticed that the paper was curiously mutilated. It was not torn, but had many holes in it of different sizes where parts of it had been cut out. He thought nothing about it at the time, but remembered being slightly puzzled. After Adams and he had been sitting there for a further few minutes, they both suddenly noticed a grey glove which the well-dressed man had apparently dropped. Adams got up and fetched it.

"You can 'ave it for a bob," said Adams.

"And what d'you think I could do with it?" Miles answered.

"Find the other 'arf," said Adams, "I'll make it a tanner."

"No thanks," said Miles. "If I were you, I'd wait here for some time, in case he comes back looking for it. He might give you more for looking after it for him. Nothing more annoying than losing one glove, even if you're made of money."

"Thanks, mate," said Adams. "I ain't got nothing special to do. I'll wait. Wot d'you bet 'e gives me? Is it worth 'arf a crown?"

"It's worth a good deal more than that," said Miles. "They're expensive gloves. But what he gives you is another matter. Some rich men are rich because they never give away anything."

"I'll 'ave something to say if 'e don't."

"I hope you get the chance," said Miles.

But the well-dressed man never returned, and eventually Miles got tired of doing nothing in the park. So he got up and went to do it somewhere else. He had pretty well forgotten about the incident when he read in the newspapers about the death of Adolphus. The paragraph referred to the threatening letter and said that a man had brought to the police a newspaper and a glove which, it was hoped, might throw light on the matter. Miles, having nothing better to do, went to a police station and asked if he could help. It was soon established that the man who had brought in the paper and glove was Adams. Shown both articles by the police Miles had said that, as far as he could tell, they were the identical articles which he had seen Adams pick up.

All this evidence was elicited from Miles by Broadwater, and Charles then proceeded to cross-examine him.

"Have you ever seen this lady before?" was his first question, and he pointed to Jo.

"Oh, yes," said Miles.

"When did you first see her?"

"When did I first see her?"

"Yes."

"I can't be absolutely sure, but I believe it was at the police station. I think she was there, but I can't be quite sure. It may have been the police court."

"Had you ever seen her or spoken to her before you went to the police station about this case?"

"Had I seen or spoken to her before?"

"That's what I asked," said Charles. "And what is the answer?"

"Before I first went to the police you mean?" asked Miles.

"That's right," said Charles. "Hadn't I made my question plain?"

"I just wanted to be sure," said Miles. "No, I'd never seen her before."

"Or spoken to her?"

"Well, you can't speak to a person without seeing them."

"What about the telephone?"

"Oh, of course, I'm sorry," said Miles. "No, I hadn't spoken to her on the phone."

"Or communicated with her in any way?"

"I didn't know her."

"Or communicated with her in any way?" repeated Charles.

"No," said Miles. "I didn't know of her existence before this case."

"That may be," said Charles. "The case started with a man being killed, and what I want to know is, how soon after he was killed did you speak to Mrs Barnwell?"

"I don't know that I ever have spoken to her."

"Do you say that you never have?"

"Well, I can't be absolutely sure. We were at the police court and possibly the police station together, and you know how it is when witnesses in a case are waiting in the same room. They may speak to each other. I may have done. I expect I did. But I can't be certain."

"You do a little acting, don't you?" asked Charles.

"Yes, occasionally."

"Are you doing any now?"

"Acting?"

"Yes."

"Well, I haven't any engagements at the moment."

"I didn't mean that," said Charles. "I meant are you acting at the moment—in this room?"

"Acting what?"

"Acting a part?"

"What sort of part?"

"The part of an apparently honest, entirely independent witness."

"That's what I am," said Miles.

"You really saw all this happen in the park?"

"Naturally, or I wouldn't say I had seen it. I may have made a mistake about a detail or two, but the substance is right."

"What is your present financial position?"

"I can manage."

"How much have you in the bank?"

"I don't use my account much."

"Is that because the bank won't let you?"

"Well, they do prefer me to have a balance before I draw a cheque."

"When did you last draw a cheque?"

"I couldn't say. Some time ago."

"What have you been living on during the period since Mr Barnwell was killed?"

"Oh—one thing and another, you know. I have managed."

"Did you have a bit of luck, by any chance, just before or just after Mr Walsh's conviction?"

"A bit of luck? How d'you mean? What sort of luck?"

"Any kind of luck. Did you have a lucky bet on a horse, for example?"

"What horse?"

"Any horse. Is it a fact that at or about the time of the trial your financial position improved, if only temporarily?"

"My financial position always improves," said Miles. "It can't do anything else. Rather a pleasant position to be in really. Things can never get worse with me. They can only get better. How few people can say that. I find it very reassuring."

"I gather from that," said Charles, "that there is no time when you would not find a present of £50 or so most welcome."

"Well," said Miles, "there are about forty million people in this country, aren't there? There must be darned few of them who wouldn't find £50 useful at any time."

"I take it you are not one of the few?"

"No," said Miles, "I could always find a use for £50."

"Then you would have found a use for it at the time of the trial?"

"I tell you, I would have found a use for it at any time."

"Did you in fact get some kind of payment at or about that time, either £50 or more or less?"

"From whom?"

"From anyone."

"I can't recall it."

"But, if it had happened, you could certainly have recalled it?"

"Indubitably."

"Then why didn't you simply say you hadn't had it?"

"I did."

"You said you couldn't recall it."

"Precisely, because it didn't happen. If it had happened, I should have recalled it. As it didn't happen, I didn't."

The judge looked at his watch.

"I don't know how long I'm expected to sit," he said, "but d'you think we could have a short adjournment now?"

"Of course," said Lonsdale. "I ought to have thought of it. Refreshments will be available in the drawing-room."

CHAPTER THIRTEEN

INTERLUDE

" 'Ow d'yer think it's going, guv?" asked Spikey, after they had left the court room.

"It isn't going at all yet," said Lonsdale, "but then I never expected it would. But I like that young man who's appearing for me. I fancy he's shown two of the witnesses anyway a red light."

"But 'ow are you going to show that they're telling a pack of lies, guv?"

"It'll come with a rush, Spikey. You'll see. They're telling lies and they know it, and they know we know it. One false step by one of them and we'll break the whole thing wide open. You wait, Spikey, you just wait."

Meanwhile the judge was having a quiet word with Charles and Broadwater.

"There was a wind this morning," he said, "and with luck someone'll pick it up."

"I sent one too," said Broadwater.

"Good," said the judge. "This farce has gone on long enough."

"Judge," said Charles, "I'm not absolutely sure that it is a farce."

"You're not at the Old Bailey now, old boy," said Broadwater. "No need to keep up appearances."

"I'm not," said Charles, "but I shouldn't have gone half so far as I did today, if I hadn't thought that there mightn't be something in it. Admittedly, if this were a real trial I should have felt pretty uncomfortable at some of the questions I put, but I should have had to put them just the same. Something my client—I beg your pardon, Judge—something Walsh has told me has made me think very hard."

"Don't overdo it, old boy," said Broadwater.

"Oh, well," said the judge, "we shall see. And it's certainly good practice for you. How long have you been called?"

"Nearly seven years, Judge."

"Have you really? Wish I showed my years as little. But you can't be thirty yet."

"Not quite."

At about that moment a small boy about a mile away from the judge's house had just picked up a piece of paper. It said in block capitals—SEND POLICE AT ONCE TO MR JUSTICE HALLIDAY'S HOUSE, HOWARD HOUSE.

It was signed by the judge himself. The small boy could not read but he entertained himself by tearing the small piece of paper into very much smaller pieces. Then, like Mr Justice Halliday, he threw them to the winds. Meanwhile, the piece of paper sent by Broadwater had stuck in a hedge in a lane.

Miles approached Jo while she was having a drink.

"How am I doing?" he asked.

"Don't ask silly questions," she said sharply. "There's no reason to suppose every word everyone says here is not being listened to. Not that it matters in the least. But it wouldn't take any time to secrete microphones here. Lucky we've clear consciences."

"I see," said Miles, rather abashed. "I only meant . . ."

"Have you been to any good shows recently?" said Jo.

"Well, as a matter of fact, I don't go out a great deal," said Miles. "I find that as I get older I get more and more critical. Things that would have amused me ten years ago either bore me or irritate me now."

"Theatre tickets are expensive," said Jo.

"Yes, I suppose they are," said Miles.

"I sometimes get free seats given to me," said Jo. "If they'd be of any use to you, I might let you have a couple from time to time."

"That would be most kind."

"I'll give you my address before we leave, that is, if we're ever allowed to go."

A few minutes later a car drove up to the house and the Boss arrived. He did not always pay visits to the site, but on this occasion he felt he should do so. He sent a message to Lonsdale to announce his arrival. Lonsdale excused himself from his guests and went to see him.

"Everything all right?" asked the Boss.

"I should like to congratulate you on the efficiency of your service," replied Lonsdale. "It has all gone like clockwork. Not a hitch from beginning to end."

"Delighted to hear it," said the Boss. "Perhaps you can recommend me to some of your friends, if they ever have any delicate matters to be attended to."

"Well," said Lonsdale, "I won't promise to do that. But I'll certainly keep you in mind myself."

"Is there anything else I can do about this?"

"I don't think so," said Lonsdale. "The only possible danger now is from a stray caller, but I think your people have got that pretty well taped."

"That's splendid," said the Boss. "I'll go home then. Spikey knows how to get in touch with me if I'm wanted. No casualties so far, I hope?"

"None at all, thank you," said Lonsdale.

"Good," said the Boss. "I hate a messy job."

CHAPTER FOURTEEN

DIRECT EVIDENCE

WHEN the hearing was resumed Charles said that he did not want to ask any further questions of Miles for the moment. Herbert Adams was the next witness. He gave similar evidence to that given by Miles, and he identified photostat copies of the newspaper he had rescued.

"You will see from these pictures," said Broadwater, "that the threatening letter sent to Mr Barnwell fits exactly into the spaces in the newspaper. At the trial an expert was called, who demonstrated this beyond doubt. But really an expert isn't required. If one looks at it carefully it is reasonably plain to anyone."

"Well, Southdown," said the judge, "you've seen the two exhibits. Do you agree that they're an exact fit?"

"Yes," said Charles. "I'm prepared to admit that."

"What above the glove?" said the judge.

"You'll see about that from the evidence of the police inspector who interviewed the accused. I gather it was not considered necessary or politic to have the inspector here today. At least I take it he isn't here?"

"No, he's not," said Charles.

"Well," said Broadwater, "in that case I might as well deal with his evidence now. He said that, when he interviewed the prisoner, he produced the glove which Mr Adams had found, and asked him if he had any like it. The prisoner produced a right-hand glove but said that he had recently lost the left. It was the left glove which Mr Adams and Mr Hampton had seen the man drop and which Mr Adams took to the police station. No one could, of course, say that it was the prisoner's missing glove, but he himself admitted that it was exactly like his own. He also admitted that he had lost it on the same day that Mr Adams found the glove. He did say that he had not lost it in the park but, he thought, at his club."

"What d'you say about that, Southdown?" asked the judge.

"It's substantially correct, Judge," said Charles. "Mr Walsh did lose his glove and the one found was exactly like the missing one. I don't admit that it was found by Mr Adams in the way he suggests, but it may very well be the missing glove."

"Very well," said the judge. "You'd better ask Mr Adams some questions about it. Because, if it is, your cl . . .—if it is Walsh's glove, it seems pretty clear that he was the man who threw away the newspaper from which the threatening letter was cut out. And if that is so . . ."

"Mr Walsh strongly denies that he threw away any newspaper into the litter basket. But he was dressed in a morning coat and grey top hat."

"Then you'd better question Mr Adams about it," said the judge.

"What time did this happen?" was the first question.

"'Arf past two," said Adams.

"Why are you so certain? Had you a watch?"

"I asked this gentleman," and he indicated Miles, "what time it was."

"Why did you want to know what the time was?"

"It's important, the time is."

"Why? You had nothing to do, had you? You were

going to wait to see if the gentleman came back for his glove."

"I like to know the time, see. Always 'ave. Not so important in the day as at night, but you gets the 'abit."

"What d'you mean—not so important in the day as at night? You're not a housebreaker by any chance?"

"No, I ain't. But my brother was, if you want to know. And 'e taught me to be careful about the time. It was important to 'im. D'you want to know why?"

"Well, why?"

"Well, it's like this 'ere. My brother didn't like being pinched, but, when they found 'im on the job, that was a fair cop."

"What's that got to do with it?"

"I'm telling yer. What 'e didn't like was to be pinched for nothink."

"I can understand that, but what's that got to do with noticing the time?"

"Well, it's like this 'ere. My brother might think of a job ter do while 'e was dressing 'isself in the morning. But you can't pinch a man just for thinking, can you? Well, you can't anyway. I know that much meself. It's a free country. You can think what yer like. Now, if you 'appen to be carrying a jemmy or a screwdriver or some skellington keys or somethink wot might be useful on a job, they can't pinch yer for it before nine at night, see? You can go up to a copper at half-past eight and wave them in 'is face and say 'see these, chum?' and he can't do nothing to yer except tell yer to move on. Unless he can read yer thoughts, and it ain't come to that yet. But if it's arter nine o'clock 'e can pinch yer for carrying 'ousebreaking implements by night, see? And my brother didn't like that. 'E didn't see why 'e should be pinched a mile away from the job 'e was going to do, any more than 'e could be pinched while 'e was dressing 'isself in the morning. It stands to reason, don't it? 'E 'adn't done nothing wrong by carrying the things. 'E might change 'is mind on the way to the job and go 'ome. No, my brother didn't 'old with being pinched for nothing. On the job was one thing, but on the way to it was another. So 'e acted thoughtful, my brother did. 'E made up 'is mind when 'e was going to do the job, and then 'e'd take up the old instruments and 'ide 'em near the place at about 'arf past eight. So they couldn't do nothing to 'im, unless they caught 'im on the job. And that suited 'im. 'E didn't like being pinched for nothing, my brother didn't. So you see, guv, if you want to be sure you're before nine o'clock, you've got to make sure of the time. Guessing won't do. You got ter know. And, once you get used to knowing the time, you sort of always know it."

"But this was your brother, I thought, not you?"

"Yes, but I used to have to find out the time for 'im, and that's 'ow I got into the 'abit. So that's 'ow I knew it was 'arf past three when I saw the gentleman."

"I thought you said half-past two."

"You got me all muddled. Yus, it was 'arf past two."

"Sure it wasn't half-past three?"

"I just told yer. It was 'arf past two."

"Where's your brother now?"

"Dunno."

"Sure you had a brother?"

"Course I'm sure."

"Just the one?"

"Yus."

"Any sisters?"

"No."

"When did you last see your brother?"

" 'Ow should I know?"

"What time of the day was it when you last saw him? Before or after 9 p.m.?"

"I think," said the judge, "we're wandering rather a long way from the subject. It's the glove you're challenging, not the time, I gather."

"Well," said Charles, "we have strayed a bit, I agree, but my suggestion is that the whole of this episode has been invented, glove and all."

"But a glove was produced," said the judge. "You admit that."

"I agree," said Charles, " and I expect it was Mr Walsh's glove."

"Then I don't quite see where this is getting you."

"Suppose," said Charles, "this was a plot. The simple way of doing it would be to steal Mr Walsh's glove, while he was at his club or somewhere. Not very difficult for determined people."

"You're assuming a most diabolical plot," said the judge, "and at the moment there is not the least evidence of it."

"Perhaps not at the moment," said Charles. "Perhaps there wasn't one at all. But, if my instructions are right, there was such a plot. And, if there was, there's at least a reasonable chance we shall be able to prove it."

"All right," said the judge. "Have you anything more to ask Mr Adams?"

"Not at the moment," said Charles.

"The next witness," said Broadwater, "is dead, but I can read his evidence from the shorthand note. His widow is present in case my opponent wants to ask her anything."

Broadwater then read the evidence of the late Kenneth Meadowes. He admitted that he was a man of bad character with many previous convictions. He said that he was approached by Lonsdale three days before Adolphus was killed, and asked if he could drive a car. He said he could. He was then asked if he'd do a job for Lonsdale, a job for which he would be very well paid. He asked what sort of a job it was. Lonsdale, he said, replied that it was easy enough and would only take a few seconds, adding that it meant "driving a car and not stopping." "He told me," Meadowes had sworn, "that I was to wait round a particular corner with the engine running and that, as soon as a man whom he would identify to me walked into the road, I was to drive straight at him hard and then drive on until I was well out of the area. I was then to drive to a lonely spot in the country, to examine the car for blood or any other marks, clean it up as far as possible and do any first aid touching up necessary, and then leave it. He would arrange for it to be picked up. I did what he told me, ran over the man and drove away as he'd said and left the car in the country. I was paid £50 by the accused. I didn't take the number of the car, but it was a large blue car. It might have been a Humber. I was too taken up with the job I'd promised to do to notice much about it."

In reply to further questions, Meadowes had said that he realized he was committing murder, and that anything he said might be used in evidence if he were charged with the murder.

"Meadowes died a few days after the trial," said Broadwater. "Does my friend want to ask Mrs Meadowes any questions?"

Charles said that he did.

"I'm sorry to have to ask you these questions, Mrs Meadowes," he began. "I hope they won't distress you too much."

"I never wanted to come 'ere," said Mrs Meadowes. "I'm supposed to be getting married next week."

"Well, I hope we'll have finished in time," said Charles.

"Well, I hope so, really I do," said Mrs Meadowes.

"Now, tell me, Mrs Meadowes," said Charles, "your husband died of cancer, didn't he?"

"Yes."

"Which he had had for some time?"

"Yes."

"Had he been attending hospital?"

" 'E 'ad 'ad treatment, but they said there was nothing more they could do for 'im. So they sent 'im 'ome."

"He could still walk about?"

"Oh—'e could walk about."

"When did he finally take to his bed?"

"About a week afore 'e died."

"They told him at the hospital that he was a hopeless case?"

"Yes, they told 'im."

"Is that why he went to the police and confessed?"

"I don't rightly know. I didn't know nothing about it."

"But you knew he went to the police?"

"Oh, I knew that."

"And when he went to the police he was a dying man?"

"Yes."

"So he had nothing to fear from any confession he might make?"

"I don't know about that."

"Did anyone pay him anything to go to the police?"

“ ’Ow d’you mean, pay ’im anything?”

“I mean what I say. Did anyone pay him anything to go to the police?”

“I shouldn’t think so.”

“Did this lady ever call on you?” and Charles pointed to Jo.

“’Oo, ’er?”

“Yes. Did she ever call on you?”

“I don’t think so.”

“You don’t *think* so. Don’t you know?”

“We ’ad visitors from the ’ospital.”

“But she wasn’t from the hospital.’

“Oh—wasn’t she?”

“Then she did call on you?”

“Not as I knows of.”

“Mrs Meadowes, I’m sorry to have to ask you this, but your husband had a dreadful character, hadn’t he?”

“’E was all right to me, when ’e wasn’t in the drink.”

“If someone had wanted a man to commit perjury, they couldn’t have made a better choice than your husband, could they? He was a hardened criminal and he was dying.”

“A good man to commit a murder for you,” commented Broadwater.

“Had he ever been convicted of any crimes of violence?” asked Charles.

“Only for bashing me. But ’e was in the drink then and didn’t rightly know what ’e was doing.”

“So, apart from a conviction for knocking you about, he’d never been convicted for violence?”

“Not really. There was ’is mother of course, but ’e only got three months for that.”

“Well,” said Charles, “is it fair to say that he never hit anyone, except members of his own family?”

“Yes, that’s right,” said Mrs Meadowes. “I don’t know if you count me sister-in-law as family. It was when ’e was in the drink. ’E was ever so kind when ’e was sober. Unless ’e was in one of ’is moods.”

“Oh, he had moods too, did he?”

“Well, not to say moods, but it didn’t do to speak to ’im when ’e was in them.”

"So, apart from his family, including sisters-in-law, whom he sometimes hit when he was in a mood or drunk, was he ever violent to anyone?"

"Not wot you'd call violent. It didn't do to argue with 'im, of course, but a lot of men are like that. 'Is brother was just the same. Didn't like a argument. Now, I like one, all friendly, if you see what I mean. But 'e didn't. 'E couldn't abear a argument. 'E didn't say much, though. But if there was something lying 'andy 'e'd use it all right. No, 'e was a good 'usband as they go, but it didn't do to argue with 'im. Least, not if 'e was in a mood or in the drink."

"And how often was he in a mood, or drunk?"

"Week-ends mostly—and Thursdays. I 'ad my 'arf day Thursdays. So we used to go to the boozer. 'E was all right for the first four pints. But after that 'e used to turn difficult. Couldn't please 'im no 'ow. Seemed to want you to argue and, when you did, 'e bashed you. But 'e didn't mean any 'arm. Didn't know 'is own strength."

"I hope your new husband will be gentler," said the judge.

"'E'd better be," said Mrs Meadowes. "'E only comes up to 'ere," and she indicated her shoulder. "I chose 'im special," she added. "Laid 'im flat a week ago, if yer want ter know. Not taking any chances this time. But 'e wasn't a bad man, my Kennie, not to say bad. I known plenty worse. It takes all sorts, don't it?"

"I'd just like to get this clear, Mrs Meadowes," said Charles. "Your husband was violent to his family when he was drunk or in a mood, but not otherwise?"

"Only to the police," said Mrs Meadowes. "'E didn't 'old with them."

CHAPTER FIFTEEN

THE STABLE DOORKEEPER

WHILE Mrs Meadowes was being cross-examined by Charles, Colonel Pudsey-Pease, the governor of Northwall prison, was investigating Lonsdale's escape. The governor was a man who was never at a loss for a word. As far as quantity was concerned, he was a born small-talker. Some people dread cocktail parties. "What shall I talk about?" plaintively asks the wife of the husband or the husband of the wife, as the case may be. Colonel Pudsey-Pease never had to ask such a question. He was equally at home with his convicts, his warders and the ladies and gentlemen at the Lord-Lieutenant's garden party.

He would have chatted cheerfully to the Prime Minister about Britain's policy in the Far East or the problems of inflation, about which subjects he knew practically nothing. He once met a distinguished author of fiction. Almost immediately he said: "I've got a plot for you."

Wearily the author looked, not too obviously, for escape to some other part of the room, but, finding none, he said as politely as possible: "Oh, really?"

"Yes, this should interest you," the Colonel went on enthusiastically. "There's a woman in my mother-in-law's road who only goes out on Thursdays. At least they've never seen her out on any other day. They call her 'Mrs Thursday'. And what d'you think her real name is?"

"Mundy?" ventured the distinguished author, who was fast becoming as distinguished for his good manners as for his good books.

"No," said the Colonel. "Thursby. You could do something with that, I fancy. It's all yours. No charge."

"That's most kind," said the author, "but you really ought to use it yourself. I'm sure you'd do much better with it than I should."

"Well, I don't really write," said the Colonel. "Just a few scribblings. Not that I haven't had a lot to write about. Some of the fellows under my care are a book in themselves. Had a chap the other day who couldn't read or write. What d'you think he was in for?"

"Bigamy," suggested the author. "You don't require the G.C.E. for that."

"Forgery," said the Colonel. "Would you believe it? Couldn't read a word, couldn't write a word. But, when it came to mere imitation of someone else's writing, he took a lot of beating. And bank-notes! I'd have fallen for them. Brilliant fellow. Such a pity. And some of the confidence tricksters I've had. You wouldn't believe some of the things they've done. Mark you, the public's gullible—and greedy. Or they wouldn't fall for it. But he thought up some pretty artful ones, I can tell you. Nearly fooled me once, but I just remembered in time who I was talking to."

The Colonel would have been equally at ease discussing education with the headmaster of a public school, law with a judge or ballet with Ninette de Valois.

But he was very worried by Lonsdale's escape.

"I'm determined to get to the bottom of this," he said to his new deputy. "When a man escapes, somebody in the prison knows where he's making for and I'm going to find out—if I have to put them all on bread and water."

He had not the slightest intention of acting in this illegal manner, but he wanted to show how strongly he felt on the subject.

"We've got to get this fellow back," he said. "There've been too many of these escapes. And the trouble is, unless the fellow's dangerous, the public don't want him to be caught. Sentimental idiots. But just let them think that the wanted man might bump them off and they'll howl their heads off at the wicked prison authorities for not keeping him inside. I tell you, Maitland," he went on, "if you took a Gallup poll today, to find out how many people wanted Walsh caught, you'd find ninety per cent against it. But if we published that, since coming to prison he'd become dangerous, had knocked out two warders, half-killed a third and was believed to be carrying a revolver, it would be the other way round quick enough. Blithering lot of idiots. They're only sentimental when they're not afraid for their own skins."

"I quite agree with you," said Maitland. "Who are you going to see first?"

"Well, the fellow we really want to see is a chap who was released not long before Walsh escaped. He shared a cell with him. Spikey they called him. I've told the police about him, but apparently they can't find him at the moment.

So I think I'll see Jimmy Simpson first. If there's any mischief going on, he'll know about it."

So Simpson was brought before the governor. He was offered a seat.

"Let me see," said the governor, "how much longer have you got?"

"You should know, sir," said Simpson, "better than me."

"Come now," said the governor, "don't be foolish. Politeness costs nothing, but impertinence can be expensive here."

Simpson said nothing.

"Another five years, isn't it?"

Simpson still said nothing.

The chief warder was about to tell Simpson to answer, when the governor held up his hand.

"The other day," he said, "the Home Secretary ordered the immediate release of a man who had still five years to go. Why d'you think he did that, Simpson?"

"Ask him, sir," said Simpson.

"You——" began the warder.

"That's all right," said the governor. "I understand. We understand one another, don't we, Simpson? You think I'm going to ask you for information and that I'm hinting that you might get some remission if you gave it to me, not promising, mind you, but hinting. That's what you think, isn't it, Simpson?"

"I don't think anything at all, sir."

"And you don't think it's right to split on your pals. That's it, isn't it? Well, think it over, Simpson. Five years is a long time. All right, you can take him away."

As soon as they were alone, the governor said:

"Gently does it, you see, Maitland. I've had that type before. He's got plenty of time to think about what I've said. I believe in sowing the seed. But don't force it. Now let's see Everton."

Everton was of a very different type and was not offered a seat. He would have talked as much as the governor, if given a chance.

"You won't tell anyone if I tell you, sir, will you? Because, if you did, I'd be for it."

"You will be fully protected, Everton."

"Well then, sir, I can tell you where you'll find him. Ireland. That's where he is. He was going to lie low in London for a few days, and then off to Ireland."

"Whereabouts in Ireland? It's quite a large place."

"Well, of course, he may have moved, but he was starting in Dublin."

"Any kind of address?"

"Oh no, sir. Don't suppose he knew it himself, sir."

"And what was he going to do in Ireland? Any idea?"

"Now you have me, sir. Lie low, I suppose. He didn't need to work."

"So you think that, if we look for someone lying low in Ireland, we might find him."

"I was only trying to help, sir."

"Then who told you all this?"

"Just prison gossip, sir."

"Very well, thank you, Everton, you may go."

Methodically the governor interviewed every prisoner who might have known something.

"I don't have to answer, do I, sir?" asked one. "I don't lose marks if I refuse?"

"No," said the governor, "you don't have to answer."

"Then what'll I get if I do tell you something, sir?"

"I can make no promises."

"Well, what's the inducement, sir?"

"The inducement," said the governor, "is the possibility —only possibility, mind you—of remission if you give me really useful information."

"Possibility isn't much, sir. Would you make it probability?"

"I can't make it anything. You know perfectly well I've no power to do so. I can only tell the Home Secretary that you've been of use—if you have been. It's entirely up to him then."

"What are the chances, sir?"

"I simply can't tell you, but, if what you tell me does really help, I'll certainly do what I can for you. I can't say more than that, and you'll have no right to complain if you get nothing out of it."

"Very well, sir, I'll take a chance. I think you'll find he's staying with one of the judges."

"What?"

"That's what I heard, sir. He's going to stay with a judge. No one will look for him there."

"Don't be ridiculous. Take this man away," said the governor. He had had a fruitless day, and he was really angry.

CHAPTER SIXTEEN

A DIFFERENT LIGHT

"Look, Bert," said Bert's young woman. "Look what I've found," and she showed him the piece of paper which had got stuck on the hedge. "D'you think it's real?"

"Send the police to Howard House," read Bert aloud. "It's a joke, I expect. That's where his nibs lives. What'd he want with the police? Give us a kiss."

She obliged.

"No, a proper one."

She obliged again.

"But suppose it was real, Bert," she said. "Shouldn't we take it to the station?"

"Well," said Bert, "it wouldn't do any harm, I suppose. But there's no need to hurry ourselves. I like it here."

"So do I, Bert."

"We'll take it in when we go home then. That'll suit everybody."

And Bert turned his attention again to what to him and his young woman on their half-day off were more important matters.

Meanwhile Charles, having finished for the moment his cross-examination of Mrs Meadowes, was inviting the judge to look at the evidence which had so far been tendered.

"All I can say," said the judge, "is that I can see no reason for disagreeing with the jury's verdict. It is perfectly true that the most important witness is dead, and was a man of bad character, but he did say on oath that he killed the dead man and was paid to kill him by the convicted man.

Now it's obvious, I should have thought, that Meadowes had no personal reason for killing Mr Barnwell. Indeed, as far as I know, the only person who would have benefited from his death is your . . . is the convicted man. Well, now, of course, it's possible that Meadowes told a cock and bull story and was paid to do so. But there's no evidence of that at all. It's true that it is unusual for a man to confess to a murder in this particular way. But it would be equally unusual for a man to commit perjury in this particular way. Obviously the jury had to be warned that Meadowes was an accomplice and that his evidence ought not to be accepted without corroboration, but, of course, they were so warned. And now look at the corroboration. There was abundant evidence not only that your . . . that Walsh benefited by the killing of Mr Barnwell, but that he had sent the threatening letter and the road sign. Well, now, if the jury accepted that evidence, and I see no reason why they should not have done so, the position is that the convicted man threatened the deceased with unpleasant consequences if he didn't discontinue his action for slander, that the deceased continued his action, that he was thereupon run over and killed, and the man who killed him said the convicted man paid him to do it. That was the evidence at the trial. What more do you want? As far as I can see, it was a perfectly proper conviction. Your suggestion is that the whole thing was a fake. I can only say that, at the moment, there is no evidence of that whatever."

"I quite understand your present views, Judge," said Charles. "I propose to call Mr Walsh to see if he can change them."

Lonsdale went to the witness chair and sat down. He described his financial affairs, in so far as they were relevant to the dispute with Adolphus Barnwell. He referred to the slander action and admitted that it was a grave annoyance to him.

"I go further than that," he said. "My solicitor told me that, unless Mr Barnwell died, the slander action would continue. I thereupon wished Mr Barnwell dead."

"And he died," put in Broadwater.

"And I agree," went on Lonsdale, "that, before he died,

I sent that threatening letter and the road sign. But I didn't throw the newspaper into a litter basket in the park. I burned it in a grate in my house."

Jo, who had been looking more and more triumphant as she saw the complete failure of Lonsdale's plan, could not resist a cry of triumph.

"I knew it," she said. "I knew it."

The effect upon the judge of this uncontrollable outburst was remarkable. He turned towards Jo and asked immediately:

"What did you know, Madam?"

"You heard him yourself, Sir George," said Jo. "You heard him admit sending the letter and burning the newspaper in his grate. He's admitted it."

For the first time since the enquiry had begun, the judge began to take a real interest in the proceedings. Up till that moment he had listened to the evidence and considered everything put before him with a fairly strong preconceived idea that there was nothing in it at all. Lonsdale appeared to him to be one of those self-righteous megalomaniacs who, though obviously guilty, almost think themselves into believing in their own innocence. In the judge's experience he would certainly not have been the first plainly guilty man who protested his innocence throughout his life. As the judge was compelled to investigate the trial, he had done so with reasonable care and, indeed, his judicial training had compelled him to conduct the proceedings as though he really wanted to enquire into the matter. But, until Jo's outburst, he had had no idea at all that there might be something in Lonsdale's allegation that he had been framed. He was glad that it was not a formal trial and that he could turn his attention to Jo at once.

"Mrs Barnwell," he said slowly, "why was it a surprise to you that the witness admitted sending the letter? You knew he'd sent it. You'd heard all the evidence."

"I never thought he'd admit it," said Jo.

"But he didn't admit the evidence given against him. He said that he burned the newspaper in his own grate. Whereupon you said: 'I knew it, I knew it.' And you said it in a tone of obvious delight."

"Of course I was pleased," said Jo. "I want this man back in prison."

"That you have made clear enough," said the judge, "but was not your pleasure at your *guess* that he sent the letter being right?"

The judge looked hard at Jo as he asked this question, and she could not continue to look at him. Nor could she immediately answer the judge's question.

"Now, Mrs Barnwell," he went on, "if what the convicted man says is true, those two witnesses who told this elaborate story about the park are telling lies. And there could be no possible reason for their telling lies unless they had been paid to do so. Of that there can be no doubt. So, if he burned the newspaper in his grate, someone persuaded those two men to put up their story. And someone cut out a newspaper so as to fit the letter which was in your possession."

The judge paused and then added:

"And I suppose someone could quite easily have stolen his glove first."

The whole atmosphere in the room had changed and everyone waited for the judge's next words.

"Mrs Barnwell," he said, "can you suggest anyone except yourself who might have persuaded those men to tell this story?"

"I certainly didn't," said Jo.

"I didn't ask you that," said the judge. "Can you suggest anyone else who might have done so?"

"No," said Jo, "and I don't know why you should assume that they're not telling the truth."

"It was you, madam, who first did that," said the judge, "when you said 'I knew it' on hearing the witness say that he had burned the newspaper in his grate—the newspaper which was produced in court."

"Does it matter how he did it?" said Jo. "He sent the letter all right."

"We shall see if it matters," said the judge. "I can imagine it mattering a great deal. Well, we'd better continue with your story, Mr Walsh."

Lonsdale was not the only one to notice the "Mr".

"Tell me, Mr Walsh," said Charles. "Did you ever ask Meadowes to run over Mr Barnwell?"

"I did not," said Lonsdale.

"Had you in fact ever seen Meadowes before you saw him in Court?"

"To the best of my belief I had never seen him before."

As soon as he had said that, Jo started to look feverishly in her bag. After a short search she obviously found something in it which pleased and surprised her. She at once got up and went across to Broadwater and whispered to him. Meanwhile Charles was still cross-examining.

"Did you attend a wedding one day in Bayswater?" he asked Lonsdale.

"Yes, I did, and Mrs Barnwell knew that I did. She also knew that it was at a church near to Hyde Park, and that I might easily have taken a stroll in the park before or after the ceremony. I probably did."

"What about your glove? Did you lose it in the park?"

"I did not. I first missed it in my club. That was before I went to the wedding. I had not been near the park at that time. When I missed it I assumed that I had dropped it in the street and, of course, I may have. But now I believe it was probably stolen from the cloakroom in my club. It would be easy enough for a stranger to appear to walk in with a member. Indeed, for all I know, the thief walked in with me."

"What about the road sign?"

"Yes, I sent that too. I wanted to scare him. I may add that I sent appropriate compensation to the Council to whom it belonged."

"There's only one other thing I want to ask you," said Charles. "Why didn't you give evidence at your trial?"

"I wanted to, but my counsel was very frightened of the effect of the admissions I should have to make about the threatening letter and road sign. And he persuaded me not to. I can't pretend that I tried very hard to alter his view. If you employ an expert, you take his advice. He told me that it was safer to rely on the fact that Meadowes was not only a party to the crime on his own confession, but had a very bad record as well."

"Thank you," said Charles. "That is all I wish to ask."

Broadwater then started to cross-examine.

"I think you said that you'd never seen Meadowes before you saw him at the Magistrate's Court?"

"That is correct."

"You're sure of that?"

"Certainly, so far as I know."

Broadwater handed him a photograph which he half covered over.

"Is that a picture of you?" he asked.

"Yes," said Lonsdale. "Not a very good one, but it's me all right."

Broadwater then showed him the rest of the photograph.

"And who are you talking to?" he asked.

"Good God!" said Lonsdale. "Some people are never satisfied."

"What on earth do you mean?" asked the judge.

"I mean this," said Lonsdale, "and, if anything will convince you of this woman's dishonesty, this will. This is a picture of me talking to the late Kenneth Meadowes."

"I thought you said you'd never seen him before?" said the judge.

"I did," said Lonsdale, "and I meant it. And, in the sense I said it, it was true. I said I had never seen him before, as far as I knew. But, of course, one has seen all sorts of people in trains and in the street and in theatres and so on. And one doesn't remember them, any more than one remembers the man who stops you and asks for a light or to know the way. But people do ask for lights and do ask you the way. And I cannot tell you what Kenneth Meadowes was asking me when that photograph was taken. But I can say that I had never seen him before then—in the same sense as I've just mentioned—and I can say that I was not then asking him to murder Mr Barnwell; and I can say that it is very, very extraordinary that someone should have thought it worth taking a photograph of the two of us, and even more extraordinary that the photograph should be in the possession of that woman."

"Yes," said the judge, "but there is something even more important than that. Why was this not produced at the trial? You were in the case, Broadwater. Do you know why?"

"Very simply," said Broadwater, "because the prosecution had no idea of its existence."

"I see," said the judge. "Why didn't you give it to the police at that time, Mrs Barnwell?"

"I didn't think it important. I don't know why I've kept it so long. I only looked in my bag on the off-chance."

"You didn't think it important," said the judge, heavily underlining the words.

At that moment one of the guards came in hastily and spoke to Lonsdale. He thought for a moment and then said:

"Sir George, there's a police car coming up the drive. A real one, I mean."

"I see," said the judge, and he, too, thought for a moment. As a judge and a lawyer he knew that, from the point of view of arriving at the truth in Lonsdale's case, it was vitally important that he should go on with the enquiry without interruption. Although he could, no doubt, ensure that a further enquiry would be held later, the witnesses would have had time to think by then. If, as he was now beginning to believe, Lonsdale's complaint that he had been framed was justified, now was the psychological moment to go on with the investigation. Any serious delay might be fatal to the ascertainment of the truth.

"May I be allowed to go and interview the police myself?" he asked.

"Yes, Sir George," said Lonsdale without hesitation.

The judge got up and went to the front door. The car had just arrived. An inspector and sergeant got out.

"I'm so sorry to trouble you my Lord," began the inspector, "but we've just had this brought in to the police station. I thought I'd better come down myself."

The inspector handed to the judge the note which Bert and his young lady had found.

The judge laughed.

"Well, it's nice of you to come, Inspector. I'll let you know if I want you. Good afternoon. Forgive my rushing off, but I'm just in the middle of something."

The judge went in.

The inspector looked puzzled.

"Extraordinary old boy," he said to the sergeant. "Didn't want to know what it was all about or anything. Practical joke, I suppose. Oh well—off we go."

As they drove off, the inspector said to the sergeant:

"What's one of our chaps doing up here?"

"We haven't got one," said the sergeant.

"Well, I'm sure I saw one going round the house as we drove up. Seemed to be in a hurry."

"Must have been a mistake, inspector," said the sergeant. "There's no one up here."

"It's all very odd," said the inspector, "I could have sworn I saw one."

"Helmet or cap?" asked the sergeant.

"Helmet," said the inspector.

"Perhaps the judge is playing charades, inspector," suggested the sergeant.

"From the way he behaved he might be playing anything," said the inspector. "Now what on earth are we going to put in the report book? Don't want to be had up for contempt of Court. It'll take a bit of thinking out. Any bright ideas?"

"I'd be an inspector if I had any," said the sergeant.

The judge had meanwhile hurried back to the enquiry. There was a very different atmosphere prevailing. Lonsdale was full of expectancy. Jo was extremely worried but was grimly determined to battle on. The other witnesses were only dimly aware of what was happening or what might be in store for them.

"Now, Mrs Barnwell," said the judge briskly, as soon as he had returned, "you had this photograph in your possession at the time of Mr Walsh's trial, but you didn't think it important enough to show to the police. Is that the truth?"

"Yes," said Jo.

"Did you expect the accused to plead guilty or not guilty to the charge?"

"Not guilty, I suppose."

"Did you expect him to deny his guilt in the witness box?"

"He didn't go into the witness box."

"You didn't know that he wasn't going to give evidence, did you?"

"No."

"Then, before the trial started, you must have thought it at least possible that he would go into the witness box?"

"I'm not sure that I thought about it at all."

"Are you saying that, before the trial, you never visualized the man you believed to have murdered your husband, and whom you accordingly and very naturally hated, going into the witness box and telling his story? Surely you must have thought about it? You're an intelligent woman."

"Thank you," said Jo, "but I'm not a judge or even a lawyer. And we think about things differently from lawyers. You always think about things in terms of witnesses and evidence and so forth. Ordinary folk are different."

"I dare say, Mrs Barnwell," said the judge, "but ordinary folk like you have their passions and one of the things you wanted was to see the man you believed to have murdered your husband brought to justice. That at least is right, isn't it?"

"Yes, that is right," said Jo. "And he was. He was brought to justice. He was found guilty—as he was."

"I'm beginning to have grave doubts," said the judge, "if he was brought to justice. He was tried, certainly, but the question of justice is another matter. Whether or not you considered the possibility of the accused giving evidence, you surely must have realized the possibility that he would deny having asked Meadowes to run over your husband?"

"I tell you, I never thought about it. I told the police all I knew, and there it ended."

"Might I interpose a question, Judge?" said Charles.

"What is it?" asked the judge.

"Well, Judge, she was at the Magistrate's Court, and must have heard the police officer, who interviewed Mr Walsh, give evidence that he denied ever having spoken to Meadowes."

"Yes," said the judge, "thank you. Well, Mrs Barnwell, you heard what Mr Southdown said. It's right, isn't it? You knew before the trial at the Old Bailey that the prisoner was denying ever having spoken to Meadowes?"

"It's a long time ago now," said Jo, "but I suppose I heard it."

"Then why on earth did you not at once produce this photograph and prove that his denial was false?"

Jo did not answer at once.

"Here was this man who had murdered your husband calmly saying that he had never seen or spoken to the man who actually did the murder. And here were you with a trump card in your possession. Why did you not produce it?"

"I can't really say," said Jo. "I didn't, that's all."

"Where had you got this photograph from, madam?" asked the judge.

"I'm not sure. I think Mrs Meadowes gave it to me," said Jo.

The judge immediately turned to Mrs Meadowes.

"Is that right?" he asked, "did you give this to Mrs Barnwell?"

Mrs. Meadowes looked blankly at the photograph.

"That's 'im," she said.

"Yes, we all know it's your late husband," said the judge, "but have you ever seen this photograph before in your life?"

"I couldn't rightly say," said Mrs Meadowes, "but I'd know 'im anywhere. 'E was a 'andsome man, until the drink got 'im. But I've known worse nor 'im," she added. "And sober, too."

"No doubt," said the judge, "but you don't remember ever giving this photograph to Mrs Barnwell, do you?"

"It wasn't the one on the mantelpiece. I wouldn't 'ave given 'er that. That was took on our wedding day."

"Quite so," said the judge.

"I'm keeping it there when I'm married again."

"Yes, yes," said the judge impatiently.

"That's all arranged. 'E didn't take to the idea at first, but 'e liked the frame. So that's settled," said Mrs Meadowes happily.

"But this photograph was never in a frame, was it?"

"I never sold it, straight I didn't. 'E did all that sort of thing 'isself."

"Mrs Meadowes," said the judge, "will you please try to follow what I'm asking you. Have you ever seen this photograph before?"

Mrs Meadowes looked at the photograph critically.

"'Ave I ever seen it before?" she asked.

"Yes, have you?"

"Where?"

"Anywhere."

"Ask 'er," and Mrs Meadowes pointed to Jo, adding, "'ave I ever seen it before?"

"You know you gave it to me," said Jo.

"That's right," said Mrs Meadowes.

"Please don't interrupt," said the judge.

"Why shouldn't I?" said Jo. "This seems to be a free for all, with the police being sent away and everything."

"That's my responsibility," said the judge.

"I'll see that it is," said Jo. "Here am I, an ordinary citizen, kidnapped by a lot of thugs and, when I have the chance of being freed by the police, a High Court judge prevents it."

"We'll deal with one thing at a time," said the judge evenly. "You can make any complaint you like later."

"You can be sure of that," said Jo. "It's outrageous."

"I'm not going to let your threats deter me from investigating what I believe may have been a grave miscarriage of justice," said the judge.

"It was nothing of the kind," said Jo.

"Mrs Meadowes," said the judge, "I suppose you couldn't tell me who took the photograph?"

"That I couldn't," said Mrs Meadowes, "but it's 'im all right. There weren't two of 'im. There aren't any of 'im now, but it takes all sorts, don't it?"

"Mrs Barnwell," said the judge, "when do you say Mrs Meadowes gave you this photograph?"

"It's too long ago—I couldn't say."

"And how did you happen to be seeing her?"

"I was sorry for her. I bore her no ill will. I knew her husband was dying, and I'd lost mine. There was a sort of bond between us."

"Did you by any chance make enquiries at the hospital which he attended?" asked the judge.

"What d'you mean, make enquiries?" asked Jo.

"I mean 'make enquiries.' Did you make enquiries to find out how long Meadowes was likely to live? It may be possible to check that, you know."

"I may have at some time."

"Did you know that Meadowes had a very bad criminal record?"

"Of course I did at one stage."

"Did you arrange for him to approach Mr Walsh in the street, and to have a photograph—this photograph—taken?"

"Of course not. It's ridiculous."

"And did you keep the photograph in reserve for use if necessary?"

"Absurd. Why should I want to do that? If I'd had it taken specially, I would have produced it, wouldn't I? That's what you suggested yourself."

"I asked you why you didn't produce it, and you've not given any satisfactory answer about that yet. Let me suggest a possible reason. Perhaps you thought that, if you added that piece of evidence, it might make the case too good to be true?"

"Nonsense."

"Let us just see," said the judge, "and I warn you, Mr Hampton, and you, Mr Adams, to listen carefully to what I'm going to say. Mrs Barnwell felt sure that Mr Walsh had murdered her husband. But she had no evidence of any kind that he had done so. She had a threatening letter, which she felt sure he had written. And that was all. Now, I'm going to suggest what she might have done. I am not saying at present that she did it, but just that she might have done it. She makes enquiries to find out the name of a hardened criminal who is suffering from a fatal disease. That would not be difficult to ascertain under the guise of charity. She persuaded him, under promise of a payment of money either to him or his wife or both, to go to the police and make the statement which he in fact made. But, first of all, she arranges for the photograph to be taken. She then arranges for someone to steal Mr Walsh's glove. She next finds two characters who are prepared to commit perjury for money. She has the original threatening letter and cuts out a newspaper so that it will marry up with the letter. Now that may not be exactly what happened, it may not be what happened at all, but, if it did, it would account for the whole of this evidence, would it not? Can you suggest any flaw in my reasoning, Mrs Barnwell?"

"If you choose to assume that everyone's committed perjury, I can't stop you," said Jo. "But you could say the same in any case."

"In other cases you don't find photographs withheld by a witness for the prosecution, nor do you find such a witness giving that extraordinary exhibition which you gave when Mr Walsh admitted sending the threatening letter. Which reminds me. Tell me, Mr Walsh, what did you intend by that letter?"

"I intended that Mr Barnwell should fear for his life. I wanted to frighten him out of his wits, so that he should not go on with the slander action. I do not seek to justify my action, but that is what I intended."

"It's a great pity you didn't give evidence at your trial," said the judge. "I should have thought your frankness, as compared with the hedging and show of indignation by Mrs Barnwell, would have stood you in good stead with the jury."

"It is a great pity," said Lonsdale, "but, as I said, I had to abide by the advice given to me."

"And do you still say that, apart from being asked for a match or something of the sort, you had never spoken to Meadowes in your life?"

"I do," said Lonsdale. "Mrs Barnwell knows me well, and she knows that I never lie."

"I know nothing of the kind," said Jo. "He's a liar and a humbug."

Lonsdale went very red in the face. He must have realized that everyone was looking at him.

"I'm sorry, Sir George," he said, "but I find it difficult to contain myself when such a deliberate untruth is told. Mrs Barnwell knows as well as anyone that I have never told her a lie in my life."

"Do you still say that you never—either by letter or telephone or face to face or through a third party—requested Meadowes to run over Mr Barnwell?"

"I do. The whole story is a concoction from beginning to end."

"Very well," said the judge. "I think the time has now come to ask Mr Hampton some more questions."

Miles had now begun to realize what was happening.

"As a matter of fact, I was going to ask if I could be excused. I don't feel terribly well."

"What's the matter?" asked the judge sharply.

"I just don't feel very well."

"In what way?"

"Don't bully the man," said Jo. "He said he feels ill. Have you never felt ill? You don't have to have a pain or a temperature to feel ill."

"You seem a little anxious that he shouldn't be questioned, Mrs Barnwell. Why?" asked the judge.

"I'm nothing of the kind. You just twist everything I say. I wonder they made you a judge. You won't be one much longer after I get out of this. It's an absolute scandal. I think I'm going."

And Jo got up to go out of the room.

"I'm sorry, Jo," said Lonsdale, "you're not leaving here until this is over."

"You'll be sorry for this," said Jo. "You're all going to be sorry for this."

She went back to her seat.

"What about Mr Adams?" asked the judge. "Is he feeling quite well?"

"I'm all right," said Mr Adams.

"Good," said the judge. "Tell me, Mr Adams," he went on, "do you know what is meant by perjury?"

"Not exactly."

"It's telling lies on oath."

"Oh," said Mr Adams, "that's bad."

"Have you ever done it?" asked the judge.

"Wot me?" said Mr Adams, with a reasonable show of astonishment.

"Yes, you," said the judge.

"Wot should I want ter do that for?"

"Money."

"Oh."

"What does that mean?" asked the judge. "Why did you say 'oh'?"

"I dunno. I just said it. It's all right, ain't it?"

"Have you ever been given money for telling lies?"

"That's asking something, ain't it?"

"I know it is. And what's the answer?"

"That'd be telling, wouldn't it?"

"Yes," said the judge, "and I want you to tell me."

"Oh," said Mr Adams.

"Well," persisted the judge, "when were you offered or given money to tell lies?"

"What'll 'appen to me if I tell?"

"Nothing," said the judge. "Nothing that anyone says at this enquiry can be used in evidence against him—or her—as the statements will have been made under duress."

"What does all that mean?" asked Mr Adams.

"It means you can't get into trouble for what you say here."

"Oh," said Mr Adams. After a pause, he went on:

"But what about what I said any other time?"

"What you say now can't be used in evidence against you."

"Why should it be?"

"It can't be."

"Oh."

"Well, now, Mr Adams, tell me the last time you told lies for money."

"The last time?"

"Yes."

"I don't rightly remember. I can tell you the time before, though."

"What! Has it happened so often?"

"Has what happened often?"

"Have you told lies for money so often?"

"Not to say lies. I did 'elp my brother once or twice."

"How did you help him?"

"With the time like."

"The time?"

"Yes. I said 'e was at 'ome."

"And he wasn't?"

"'E might 'ave been. I was asleep."

"So it comes to this, that you used to give your brother an alibi every now and then?"

"That's right. But I stopped it in the end."

"Why was that?"

"They didn't ever believe me."

"You must have found it a refreshing change to be believed at Mr Walsh's trial?"

"Wot's that?"

"The jury believed you about the glove and the paper."

"Oh."

"D'you think they should have?"

"'Ow should I know? That's their job, ain't it?"

"But you know if you were telling the truth."

"It ain't so easy as that. I once said my brother was in bed at 'ome all night and 'e was. You could 'ave knocked me down."

"They believed you that time then?"

"They didn't 'ave to. 'E'd 'ad the doctor in the night, but I didn't know. I wasn't there. They let 'im go that time, though. Stands to reason. 'E'd 'ad the doctor. It was someone else, as a matter of fact."

"Not you by any chance?" asked the judge.

"They never found 'oo it was," said Mr Adams, "but it weren't my brother. 'E'd 'ad the doctor."

"Did you tell the truth about the glove and the newspaper? Did you really see anyone drop a glove and throw a newspaper in the litter basket?"

"Wot would 'appen if I said I didn't?"

"Well, for one thing, Mr Walsh would probably be let out of prison."

"'E's out now, ain't 'e?"

"He'd be let out properly, through the gate, not over the wall."

"And wot about 'er. Would she go in instead?"

"No," said the judge. "I doubt if anything could be done to any of you."

"So nothing can't 'appen to me whatever I say?"

"Nothing."

"All right," said Mr Adams. "I'm ready. What's the question?"

"Is what you said at the trial true?"

"Nothing can't 'appen to me?"

"No."

"Right. Well," began Mr Adams, "I don't feel all that good. Feel queer like."

"Was the evidence you gave at the trial true?"

"Near enough."

"Near enough to what?"

"Well mostly."

"What wasn't true?"

"It was near enough."

"You leave it to me to say if it was near enough. How much of it wasn't true? Did you ever sit in the park at all next to Mr Hampton?"

"Oh, yes, I sat next to 'im all right."

"And did a gentleman come along and drop a glove?"

"Oh, yes, 'e did that all right."

"And put a newspaper in the litter basket?"

"Oh, yes, I saw 'im."

"And you went and took it out?"

"Yes."

"And picked up the glove?"

"Yes."

"And later took it and the newspaper to the police?"

"Yes."

"Well, everything you said at the trial was true then?"

"I said near enough."

"You said it was a gentleman like that one there. Was it?"

"It was about 'is heighth."

"But you wouldn't say it was him?"

"No, I couldn't say that."

Charles then intervened.

"Might I make a suggestion, Judge? If my case is right, this was an elaborate plot and it would be much easier for these witnesses to give evidence, if the thing really took place as far as possible. There was nothing to stop Mrs Barnwell from arranging for these men to be on a bench in the park, and from sending someone of Mr Walsh's height, dressed in a morning coat and grey top-hat, armed with Mr Walsh's glove and the cut-out newspaper. It's much easier for witnesses to give evidence of something that really happened than to have to invent it."

"Yes, I see," said the judge. "And that would fit in with Mr Adams' answers 'near enough.' But they'd have to be primed as to what was going to happen and what they must do afterwards, or it might all go wrong. So, if it was a fake, they'd have to be a party to it."

"Yes, Judge, I think so," said Charles. "Perhaps you might care to ask them about it—if they're well enough?"

"Well, Mr Hampton," said the judge, "I don't know if you heard what Mr Southdown said—but was the whole thing a play in which you'd agreed to take part?"

"Well," began Miles.

"The man's not well," said Jo, "leave him alone."

At first when Jo had started to behave like this everyone had been very startled. Although the judge was not in robes and the room was not a Court, everyone knew he was a judge and the idea that he could be spoken to with impunity as Jo was speaking to him had not occurred to anyone. Nor did anyone else feel like trying it. But Jo proposed to use every weapon at her disposal.

"I don't believe there's anything the matter with him," said the judge.

"You're not a doctor, not even a bad one—you're supposed to be a judge, though no one would guess it."

"Mrs Barnwell," said the judge, "when this enquiry first started and when it appeared to me that Mr Walsh had been properly found guilty, you behaved yourself perfectly, just as though this were a Court. Do you not realize what a bad impression your altered behaviour is bound to make upon me? Don't you realize that it is likely to confirm my belief that you were party to a grave conspiracy?"

"That's no more than what I should have expected," said Jo. "As long as everyone licks your boots and says 'Yes, my Lord' and 'No, my Lord' they've got a splendid case. But, as soon as they speak their mind or hurt your dignity, you say they're guilty of conspiracy. I'm sorry for the people who have their cases tried by you."

"Mr Hampton, do you feel well enough to answer a few questions?" asked the judge.

Miles hesitated.

"It rather depends on the questions," he said eventually.

"I see," said the judge. "It's that sort of illness."

"That's right," said Jo, "twist everything he says."

"Well, then, Mr Hampton," went on the judge, ignoring Jo, "try this one. Before you went to sit in the park did you know that someone was going to come along and drop a glove and put a newspaper in the litter basket?"

"Well, I had an idea," said Miles apologetically.

"And who gave you that idea?"

"It's rather a long time ago."

"Yes, I know. But it must have been rather an unusual occurrence for you to go and sit in the park and wait for something which you knew was going to happen?"

"Yes, it was unusual," conceded Miles.

"Then you should be able to tell me who asked you to do it. Such a thing has presumably never happened to you before or since?"

"I can't say that it has."

"Well, then, can't you help me? Was it a man or a woman?"

"It's a little difficult."

"It must have been one or the other."

"Yes, I suppose so."

"Then which was it? Come, Mr Hampton, I'm sure you want to help me."

"The velvet glove," sneered Jo. "Come along, my dear little man, no one's going to hurt you. Just say what I want you to say and then you may go. It's lucky everyone doesn't know how judges behave."

"Well, Mr Hampton," said the judge, "a man or a woman?"

"I really don't feel terribly well," said Miles.

"You're quite well enough to answer that question."

"I'm going to faint," said Miles—and fainted.

"Well done," said Jo. "Now you can hit him on the head. He won't feel it."

Miles was soon restored with a little cold water and,

while he was resting, the judge questioned Adams again.

"Well, Mr Adams, did you know it was all going to happen and, if so, who told you?"

"Well, it was like this 'ere," said Adams. "A bloke came to me and asked if I'd like to make a bit. Naturally, I wanted to know what it was all about. First of all I asked 'im if 'e thought I was me brother, because I wasn't in that line. 'E said no, 'e knew me brother and it wasn't in 'is line. So naturally I said: 'Wot's in it for me?' and 'e said 'Fifty nicker'. So naturally I said: 'When do I get it?' and 'e said 'When you've done it.' So naturally I said: 'When I've done wot?' and then 'e told me."

Mr Adams relapsed into silence.

"What did the man tell you?"

"I told yer."

"No you didn't. You just said he'd pay you fifty pounds when you'd done it."

"That's right. I told yer. That's what 'e said."

"But what did he tell you you were to do for the fifty pounds?"

"'E said it was dead easy. There wasn't nothing to it, 'e said. So naturally I said 'if there ain't nothing to it, why do I get fifty nicker?' So 'e said: 'Cos that's the price; ain't it enough?' So I said: 'All right. Wot is it?' and then 'e told me."

"But what did he tell you?"

"Wot I 'ad ter do."

"But what was that?"

"Wot I did."

"You mean he told you to go and sit in the park and that a man would come along and drop a glove and throw a newspaper into a litter basket, and that you were to go and take them to the police?"

"That's right," said Jo. "Put the words into his mouth. Is he telling the story, or are you?"

"Is that what happened, Mr Adams?" persisted the judge.

"Near enough," said Adams.

"And did you get your fifty pounds?"

"Oh, yes, 'e played fair all right. 'Arf on the day and 'arf later. Oh, yes, 'e paid all right. Still don't know why 'e paid as much. But naturally yer can't turn down fifty nicker, can yer? 'E was quite right. It was dead easy."

"Who was this man who paid you £50?"

"I dunno. 'Adn't seen 'im afore."

"How did he get hold of you?"

"I dunno. 'E just came. Expect 'e 'eard that I did odd jobs for people."

"This was about the oddest, I expect," said the judge.

"I wouldn't say that," said Adams, "but it was paid the best."

"Well, Mr Hampton," said the judge, "I don't know whether you heard any of that, but may I ask how much you got for sitting in the park and telling about it afterwards? All right, you needn't answer," he went on hurriedly, as he saw that Miles was changing colour again.

"Now, Mrs Barnwell," said the judge, "are you still prepared to deny that, apart from the evidence of the man who was present when your husband was killed and the police evidence, you procured the whole of this evidence against Mr Walsh?"

"Of course I am," said Jo. "You can't bully or cajole me, as you have these other witnesses. I've never seen such a disgraceful performance. Witnesses fainting all over the place, evidence given at the pistol point, the police turned away, and then you have the impertinence to ask me if I deny having concocted a case which has been believed by a jury, believed by the Court of Criminal Appeal and believed by the Home Secretary. My case is the only true one, but your methods would twist any case, however true. You can do what you like about it, but so shall I. The newspapers and Members of Parliament and the Lord Chancellor will be told all about this. And there are too many witnesses here for you to deny it. You're almost worse than he is," and she pointed to Lonsdale. "After all, he has got himself to look after. You can't so much blame a man for doing that. But you—you're so puffed up with your pride in being a judge that you love to interfere in other people's affairs, which are nothing whatever to do with you. The case has been decided. It's over. There was only one thing for you to do—hand this man and his confederates over to the police as soon as possible."

"Mr Walsh," said the judge, "I shall have to consider most carefully what I am to do about this, but it is right to tell you now that, in spite of the unorthodox, unofficial manner in which this enquiry has come before me . . ."

"Unorthodox!" sneered Jo, interrupting.

"Unlawful, if you prefer it," went on the judge. "In spite of all that, I am quite satisfied that there was a gross miscarriage of justice at your trial. I am quite satisfied that the whole of the main evidence against you was fabricated by or at the instigation of this woman. I am quite satisfied that, had the true facts been known to the jury, they would unhesitatingly have acquitted you. I shall write to the Home Secretary to that effect, and give him my detailed reasons for my opinion. Unfortunately, as far as I can see, no proceedings whatever can be taken against Mrs Barnwell or any of her witnesses. They were brought here by force or by a trick, and their evidence has unquestionably been procured by threats and duress. What is to happen to you and your confederates for the methods you have seen fit to adopt, it is not for me to say. But, criminal though those methods have been, you are at any rate entitled to say that, as far as I can see, unless you had adopted them, your innocence could not have been made known. In these circumstances it may be that the Home Secretary will be able to take a different view of your behaviour and of that of your colleagues than seemed possible a day or two ago. But I must make it plain that that does not lie in my hands and that all I can do is to make the report which I have just indicated. I now call upon you to keep your promise to allow the police to be summoned and to give yourself up to them."

"Certainly," said Lonsdale, "but, first of all, I am going to give those who have assisted me an opportunity of getting well out of the way. I see no reason why they should take any unnecessary risks, whatever view the authorities may eventually take. Spikey, tell everyone who wants to be off to go as quickly as possible. Anyone who wishes may remain. I suggest we wait a quarter of an hour before summoning the police. Perhaps Spikey would produce some drinks for those who would like to wait. Forgive me for continuing to act as host for the moment, Sir George. I will hand over to you as soon as my assistants have left. And I should make it plain that we have brought our drinks with us."

"I take it I may leave now?" said Jo.

"Certainly, Jo," said Lonsdale.

"Just a word in your private ear before I go," said Jo.

She took Lonsdale aside and whispered:

"Don't think you'll get away with this. I'll get you yet."

"Perhaps we shall get each other," said Lonsdale.

"I loathe you," said Jo.

"You don't," said Lonsdale and, much to the judge's surprise, he kissed her good-bye.

"You wait," said Jo, and went hurriedly out of the room.

"All right boys, beat it," said Spikey. "I'll 'op it after the drinks."

Within ten minutes no one was left in the judge's house except the judge and his staff, Lonsdale and Angela, Charles, Mr and Mrs Broadwater, Mrs Meadowes, Miles, Adams and Allwinter.

"I'm most grateful to you, Sir George," said Lonsdale, "for the trouble you have taken over this matter, and I do apologize for any inconvenience you and your staff have been caused. I would also like to thank Mr Southdown and Mr Broadwater for their help and to apologize to them and Mrs Broadwater. I should include in my apologies Mr Allwinter, against whom I have no complaint."

"Well," said the judge, "I don't think we'd better discuss the matter any further. It will obviously be the subject of a further enquiry by the Home Office. It will certainly give the newspapers something to talk about."

In a corner of the room Broadwater chatted to his wife.

"What a bit of luck I insisted on coming," she said. "This is better than anything I could have hoped for. Think of the publicity."

"My dear Mary," said her husband, "you're entirely wrong. Certainly I shall have something for my reminiscences but, if you think that the publicity in this case is going to advance me one foot nearer to the Bench, you're very much mistaken. Judges are not appointed by the number of times they appear in the paper or the number of cocktail parties they attend. In the old days undoubtedly politics had something to do with it, but fortunately today they hardly enter into it. I'm not saying there aren't some bad appointments sometimes. There are. And that gives me a chance."

"Don't be modest, darling," said Mary, "you'd be a very good appointment."

"That's a thing which no one can say. That's why there are bad appointments. You get a man who's first-class at the Bar but makes a rotten judge. And you get a man who isn't much of an advocate and only has a moderate practice who'd make a first-class judge, if only they knew it. On the whole, of course, you can get a fair idea of whether a man is likely to be a reasonably good judge. In most cases you might say it's a pretty safe bet. But there are always the exceptions. Surprise appointments which turn out well and expected appointments which turn out badly."

"I don't mind which you are, darling," said Mary, "so long as you're appointed."

Angela was in the meantime chatting to Charles.

"I think you were wonderful," she said. "No, I really mean it. Mark you, I take great credit to myself for having picked you out. You fitted into the scheme of things so well. I'd no notion why father wanted a barrister, but I can see now all right why he insisted on the qualifications he mentioned. How right he was. And how right I was both in my judge and my counsel."

"I'd like to think I was your counsel," said Charles.

"Would you really?" said Angela. "You don't know me very well. And my father's in gaol, or will be very soon."

"You don't know me very well," said Charles, "but I can put that right, if you'll let me."

"You can start right now."

"Will you dine with me this evening?"

"I'd love it. It's such a shame I shan't be able to dine with daddy. But it won't be long now."

"I think I ought to warn you," said Charles, "that it may take a little longer than you think."

Angela became anxious.

"You're not suggesting . . ." she began.

"Oh, no," said Charles. "I'm sure they'll give him a free

pardon. But a thing like this must take time. They don't just have a drawer with free pardons in it, and take one out. Don't forget, the Home Office knows nothing of all this, and though, with the weight of Halliday's authority, I'm quite sure everything will be all right, they've got to enquire into the matter. And that must take some time."

"What do you mean by 'some time'? How long?"

"Well, of course, I can't say with any certainty. But days at the least. Possibly weeks. I don't think more. But suppose the Home Secretary orders an enquiry. First of all he's got to appoint someone to preside at it. Then they've got to arrange about the place where to hold it, the witnesses who are to be summoned, counsel who are to be briefed. You can't rush important things like this. After all, your father has been convicted and his appeal dismissed. You can't scrub that out in a couple of minutes. Indeed, it's very fortunate for you that you've got someone like Halliday on your side. If it were one or two of the other judges I know, well, first of all, you might never have got to this stage; and secondly, even if you had, there would be less alacrity on the part of the Home Office to jump to it. No, you couldn't have had a better choice than Halliday."

"You really chose him for me, but I chose you. I can take full credit for that."

Mrs Meadowes, Miles and Adams had a little conversation with each other.

"Wot's it all about?" said Adams.

"Blessed if I know," said Mrs Meadowes. "When do we go 'ome? And 'ow do we get there? I'd come 'ere to win a football pool. Shan't go in for them any more, if this is wot 'appens. I don't know what my Ernie will say. 'E ain't all that partial to judges."

"Personally," said Miles, "I wish I'd never had anything to do with it."

"We'll get our names in the papers," said Adams. "And our pictures, I shouldn't wonder."

"Yes," said Miles, suddenly remembering his B.B.C. interviews, and brightening a little at the thought. "Yes, there is that. Look," he added suddenly, "the three of us might give an interview on TV."

Miles had originally thought of having a solo appearance but it occurred to him that the contrast between him and Mrs Meadowes and Adams might show him up to advantage.

"What d'you say?" he asked. "You leave it to me, and I'll try and fix it up. We ought to get £10 apiece for it. What about it?"

"I don't mind," said Mrs Meadowes, "so long as they don't ask me a lot of silly questions."

"I'm afraid that's inevitable," said Miles. "It's a very difficult job, you know, interviewing someone. People think it's dead easy. But it isn't, not by a long way. Suppose you were interviewing me now, how would you begin?"

"Well, I know that one," said Adams. "I seen it. I'd say 'Good evening, Mr whatever your name is.' That's right, isn't it?"

"Yes," said Miles, "that's all right so far, but how d'you go on after that?"

"I know that too," said Adams. "So good of you to come tonight."

"Jolly good," said Miles. "And after that?"

"Now you've got me," said Adams. "But then it ain't my job. But I didn't do so bad, did I?"

"It was just like the real thing," said Mrs Meadowes. "We got a new one coming when we're married. Ernie says 'e can't abide those small screens. Can't see enough of the girls."

"My brother made ours," said Adams.

"He's a TV expert, is he?" asked Miles.

"E knows where to find 'em," said Adams.

At this point the judge went to the telephone.

"Well, Mr Walsh," he said, "I think time's up. Your chaps have had ample time to get away now."

"It's very good of you to have waited," said Lonsdale. "Which reminds me that I've never thanked you for sending the police away."

"Well," said the judge, "I can't pretend I'm very happy about having done that. But it seemed to me that, if I didn't get to the bottom of things there and then, no one might ever do so. I took a chance. I hope I was right."

"I'm sure you were," said Lonsdale. "But then, of course, I suppose I'm prejudiced."

"Hullo," said the judge on the telephone, "can I speak to the inspector, please? This is Sir George Halliday speaking."

"Hold the line, please, sir," said the sergeant. "Can you beat it," he said to the inspector, "it's the old boy on the telephone. I wonder what he wants."

The inspector went to the telephone.

"Inspector," said the judge, "I have an escaped prisoner here. His name is Lonsdale Walsh."

"Lonsdale Walsh!" said the inspector incredulously.

"That's right, inspector. Will you send for him at once? I don't think he'll run away, but come at once, please."

"I *can* beat it," said the inspector to the sergeant. "He's got Walsh up there with him. If you ask me, he's had him there all the time. Now why on earth should he do that?"

"I'd be a superintendent if I knew," said the sergeant.

CHAPTER SEVENTEEN

PUBLIC ENQUIRY

THE same day Lonsdale was taken back to prison. He was almost immediately taken before the governor. The judge had given Lonsdale a letter addressed to the governor, who had read it before the interview.

"This is all very well," said the governor, "but you can't do this sort of thing. This letter says that in Mr Justice Halliday's view you were wrongly convicted. Well, I'm not a judge. I'm just a prison governor. There's no doubt you were lawfully committed to my prison and unlawfully broke out. As far as I'm concerned, everyone here is guilty."

"I quite understand, sir," said Lonsdale, "but what else could I do? I had tried all the lawful channels, the Courts and the Home Secretary and my Member of Parliament. If you remember, I came before you, sir, and asked what I could do. You told me to wait ten years."

"So you should have," said the governor. "It's unlawful to break out of prison."

"It was a choice of evils, sir," said Lonsdale. "I had to break the law in order to have my conviction set aside. If I'd done nothing, no one else would. I should have rotted here."

"Rules were made to be kept," said the governor. "There are a lot of people here who say they're innocent, but, if we let them all out to try to prove it, we'd have no one left in the end. They'd all say they wanted to prove their innocence."

"Mine is rather an exceptional case, sir," said Lonsdale.

"Exactly," said the governor. "Hard cases make bad law. You can't provide for every exceptional case. You've put everyone to an enormous amount of trouble and expense. D'you know that I personally have interviewed nearly every man in the prison to see if I could find out where you were going?"

"I'm extremely sorry, sir," said Lonsdale, "but, if you'll put yourself in my position, what else was there to do?"

"I refuse to put myself in your position."

"At least I gave myself up when I was satisfied that something would be done about my case."

"Most considerate of you," said the governer. "D'you realise how much you've cost the country up till now? I'm a humane man, I hope. But I won't stand for lawlessness. How did you get out anyway?"

"I climbed over the wall."

"Oh, you did, did you? That was an outrageous thing to do."

"I couldn't very well walk out of the gate, sir."

"Don't be impertinent. You had outside help, I suppose."

"Oh, yes," said Lonsdale. "They threw a rope ladder over to me."

"Then you needed some inside help as well."

"Only one," said Lonsdale.

"I imagine you're not going to tell me who he was."

"No, sir."

"Well, I don't grumble at that, but it'd be better for you if you did. You've committed a number of offences now, whatever the truth about the original charge. And you can be punished for them."

"I must take a chance on that, sir,"

"Very well," said the governor. "I shan't deal with you myself. I shall wait for the visiting justices, but I should make it plain that personally I'm against you. What's the good of a prison if people can escape from it because they want to prove they're innocent? It's ridiculous. Take him away."

The first announcement of Lonsdale's recapture was given some prominence in the newspapers, but there was no hint in the first news of the sensation which was to follow. At first there were only rumours, and passages began to appear such as:

"It is said that there will be surprising developments when the facts surrounding Walsh's escape are made public. It has been suggested that for a time he hid in a High Court judge's house."

Eventually there were so many semi-accurate and inaccurate statements made that the Home Office issued an official pronouncement. But even this was in somewhat guarded language.

"Lonsdale Walsh, who recently escaped from prison and was subsequently recaptured, during his period of freedom gave certain information to Mr Justice Halliday, as a result of which a report from the judge is now being considered by the Home Secretary. Certain other persons also gave information to Mr Justice Halliday."

A crop of rumours then began to circulate as to the nature of the information given to the judge and the names of the people, in addition to Lonsdale, who gave that information. Finally, Miles went to one of the television authorities and offered to tell his story at an interview. The persons responsible for authorising such an interview immediately communicated with the Home Office and asked if there was any objection to this story being published, to which the reply was received that the Home Secretary would much prefer that nothing was said in public pending a further official statement, which was being issued. The note added that the responsibility for any inaccuracies or mis-statements would be that of the television authorities. "It is also possible," added the note, "that questions of contempt of Court might be involved."

So Miles had to wait. But his visit certainly speeded up things.

Three days later the Home Office announced that the Home Secretary was proposing to appoint three Supreme Court judges to enquire into the circumstances surrounding the escape and recapture of Lonsdale Walsh, including any matters which might throw light on the question whether there was a miscarriage of justice at his trial for murder.

Soon after, Lord Justice Manners, Mr Justice Swann and Mr Justice Tennant were appointed, and the public waited with interest to hear and read what would transpire.

The result was beyond their wildest expectations, because one of the chief witnesses at the enquiry was Mr Justice Halliday himself. The whole of the circumstances of the house imprisonment of the judge and the kidnapping or enticing of the witnesses was made known. There were two main questions to be answered. The first was whether Lonsdale had been wrongly convicted and, if the answer to the first question was Yes, the second question was what was to be done about the methods adopted by him to prove his innocence.

The tribunal decided to go into the first question first.

"It is true," said Lord Justice Manners, "that in point of time the escape and kidnapping came first, but the unanimous view of the Tribunal is this. If we are not satisfied that there was any miscarriage of justice, then there is no real point in our enquiring into the other matters. The law must take its course and those responsible for breaking it, including, of course, the escaped prisoner, should be proceeded against for such crimes as they have committed. If, however, we are satisfied that Walsh's conviction for murder was procured by perjured evidence and ought not to stand, we must then proceed to consider what, in our view, in the public interest ought to be done about these other offences."

Lonsdale was represented at the enquiry by Charles, while the Attorney-General appeared for the Crown with a Treasury junior. All the other people concerned were represented by counsel. In opening the case the Attorney-General said:

"Although this is not a rehearing of the case tried at the

Central Criminal Court, I have considered it desirable, subject to the view of the Tribunal, to have present all the available witnesses who gave evidence there, and, of course, everyone available who was in Mr Justice Halliday's house. One thing I should make plain. It is the view of the Crown that nothing said in Mr Justice Halliday's house could be used in evidence against the person who said it, at any subsequent criminal proceedings against that person. They were detained by force in that house and undoubtedly that threat of force to some extent at least compelled them to make their statements. On the other hand, anything said now by any witness can, of course, be used in evidence for or against that witness in any subsequent proceedings. Accordingly, the Tribunal may wish to warn some of the witnesses that they are not bound to answer any questions which might incriminate them. Unless, of course, the Tribunal take the view that they should be compelled to answer such questions. In that case, of course, the answers would not later be available against them."

Lord Justice Manners, after consultation with his colleagues, then announced that they were proposing to treat the proceedings for that purpose as a court of law and that no witnesses would be compelled to incriminate themselves.

The first witness to be called was Mr Allwinter. He gave similar evidence to that which he gave to Mr Justice Halliday and Charles was then asked if he wished to cross-examine. Before doing so he thanked the Tribunal for allowing him to appear at all.

"As I am a witness to what took place before Mr Justice Halliday, I should, of course, normally have refused this brief. Indeed, I should automatically have refused it had your Lordships not indicated that, in view of my client's very strong desire to have my services on this occasion, it would be proper in the exceptional circumstances for me to appear."

He then proceeded to cross-examine Mr Allwinter.

"Mr Allwinter," he began, "a lot of water has flowed under the bridge since I last questioned you, has it not?"

"It has indeed."

"And you yourself saw it first trickle and then burst into flood."

"If you like to put it that way, yes."

"Now, Mr Allwinter, all you actually saw of this occurrence was a vague impression of a car moving and then a man left dead after having been struck by it, and the car moving off swiftly afterwards?"

"Something like that."

"When I questioned you last time, you were obviously of the opinion that it was a case of murder."

"I was."

"And when I pointed out the possibility of it being a hit-and-run driver, you referred to the 'other evidence'."

"That is correct."

"By the 'other evidence' you meant the witnesses who made statements to Mr Justice Halliday, and the man Meadowes who died?"

"Yes."

"You have now had the advantage of seeing their performances before Mr Justice Halliday?"

"Yes."

"They were rather different from their performances at the Old Bailey, were they not?"

"They were indeed."

"Are you still of the opinion that this was a case of murder or was it not just as likely, or indeed much more likely, the case of a hit-and-run driver?"

"I feel quite sure now that it was a hit-and-run driver."

"Thank you," said Charles, and sat down.

"But I gather," said Lord Justice Manners, "that previously you were convinced that it was a case of murder."

"That is so."

"That was because you had heard other evidence?"

"Yes."

"And now you are convinced that it was a case of a hit-and-run driver?"

"Yes."

"So the truth of the matter is surely this, Mr Allwinter. As far as your own eyes and ears at the time of the occurrence are concerned, you haven't the faintest idea whether it was murder, manslaughter or no offence at all by the driver, except that he or she failed to stop?"

"I suppose that's right, my Lord," said Mr Allwinter.

"That shows the danger of paying attention to other people's statements when you are supposed to be saying only what you saw and heard yourself."

"It is only fair to Mr Allwinter," said Charles, "to mention that he didn't in the first instance say anything except what he had seen and heard. It was only when I questioned him that he showed what his views were."

"In other words you say, Mr Southdown, that, as far as his actual evidence about the occurrence is concerned, Mr Allwinter did not allow it to become coloured by his opinion."

"That is quite correct, my Lord."

"Then I should congratulate Mr Allwinter," said Lord Justice Manners, "rather than criticize him. In most accident cases witnesses who have formed a view as to the cause, allow their evidence to become violently coloured by their views. Such evidence is pretty well valueless."

"Please don't think I intend to be offensive to Mr Allwinter," said Mr Justice Swann, "but his evidence, dispassionately given as it is, is also pretty well valueless. We all know that the unfortunate man was killed by a car. And that is all he can tell us. Presumably his injuries and position in the road were such that this could have been deduced quite simply by his body being found in the road. That the car did not stop was plain because it was not waiting by the body."

"It might have been a horse and cart," put in Mr Justice Tennant.

"Or an omnibus," said Lord Justice Manners.

"Or a motor cycle," continued Mr Justice Tennant.

"Or van," said Lord Justice Manners. "We have to thank Mr Allwinter for telling us that it was a car."

"Does it help us much to know that it was a car?" asked Mr Justice Swann. "What we want to know is whether the person in charge of the vehicle ran the man over deliberately or by accident. As far as Mr Allwinter's evidence is concerned, the man might just have been found dead."

"Surely," said Lord Justice Manners, "what we want to know is whether the vehicle, whatever it was, was driven by Meadowes. If it wasn't, that's an end of the first question we are invited to consider. Meadowes himself cannot tell us, and we have to find out from all the other evidence whether he was driving. Mr Allwinter, admirable witness though he is, doesn't help us in the least about that."

Mr Justice Swann leaned back in his chair with an air of finality. His point had been established.

"Perhaps then, Mr Allwinter can be allowed to go home," suggested Lord Justice Manners. "Does anyone in the case want him to remain? Do you, Mr Attorney?"

"No, thank you, my Lord," said the Attorney-General.

"Does counsel for any other party wish him to stay?"

One by one, counsel got up and said that his client did not require any further evidence from Mr Allwinter.

"Very well," said Lord Justice Manners. "Thank you, Mr Allwinter. We shall not want you any more. You may go away."

"Do I have to?" asked Mr Allwinter. "I'd like to hear what happens."

The next three witnesses were very simply disposed of. They were Miles, Adams and Mrs Meadowes. One by one their respective counsel got up and said they had taken the responsibility of advising their clients not to give evidence. That is to say, they would, of course, go through the formality of going into the witness box and being sworn but, when it came to answering any material questions, they would claim privilege on the grounds that the answers might incriminate them.

"You talk of the formality of being sworn," said Mr Justice Swann. "From what you are saying, it suggests that your clients considered it a very unimportant formality."

"If your Lordship pleases," said counsel for one of those witnesses.

"I don't please at all," said Mr Justice Swann. "Your clients, having given vital evidence upon which a man was convicted of murder, now, if you please, haven't the courage to try to put right any wrong they may have done by their original evidence."

"I don't please at all either, if I may say so," said counsel, "but, in all the circumstances, I think it the proper course for my client to take, and my learned colleagues take the same view."

"This is tantamount to an admission that their original evidence was false," said Lord Justice Manners.

"I cannot make any admissions," said counsel.

"We are not asking you to do so," said Lord Justice Manners. "But, before we can relieve your clients of the obligation of answering the material questions, we have to be satisfied that, to force them to answer, might reasonably result in their incriminating themselves. You have not merely to admit that, but to assert it."

"We all assert it, my Lord."

"Very well, then. The only way in which your clients could incriminate themselves is by admitting that they had committed perjury at the original trial."

"That is not the only way, my Lord," said counsel. "They might have to admit other offences as well."

"You mean such offences as conspiring to defeat the ends of justice?"

"That is so, my Lord."

"And you all claim privilege for your clients on the grounds that, if we compelled them to answer, they might render themselves liable to be indicted not only for perjury but for another offence or offences as well?"

"That is so, my Lord."

"And you each make this claim of privilege on behalf of your clients, bearing in mind your responsibility to the Court as counsel and after careful consultation with your respective clients?"

"Yes, my Lord."

"Very well, then," said Lord Justice Manners. "I repeat that this is tantamount to an admission by these witnesses that they endeavoured successfully to swear away a man's liberty by perjured evidence."

"I am not in a position to say anything as to that," said counsel.

The three judges conferred for a few moments. Then Lord Justice Manners said:

"We know that we can completely trust counsel neither to mislead the Court nor to make a dubious claim for privilege of this kind without disclosing the circumstances giving rise to the doubt. All three counsel have made it quite plain that, if their clients were compelled to answer the questions material to this enquiry, they might well find themselves prosecuted criminally. No one is required to give evidence himself in this way and we accordingly allow the claim of privilege in reliance on counsel's statements and, of course, on what we know of the case. But the witnesses will remain within the precincts of this building until the enquiry has been completed."

The next witness was Jo.

"I gather from your silence," said Lord Justice Manners to Jo's counsel, "that your client does not wish to claim privilege."

"She does not, my Lord."

Jo then went into the witness box and gave much the same evidence as she gave at the trial. She stoutly denied that she had procured any of the witnesses and she repeated her explanations, such as they were, for not producing the photograph earlier and for her sudden exclamation before Mr Justice Halliday. In view of the refusal of the other witnesses to give evidence, hers was an impossible task and she knew it. But at least she stuck to her guns and made no admissions of any kind. When her evidence had been completed, Lonsdale went into the witness box.

He gave his evidence well and frankly and appeared obviously to be telling the truth. When he had finished, the judges consulted for a few minutes and then Lord Justice Manners said:

"We have without difficulty come to a clear conclusion on the first question we have been asked to consider. We will put our reasons into writing, but it is right to say at once that we are all firmly convinced that there was a gross miscarriage of justice when Mr Walsh was convicted. We must now, therefore, consider the second far more difficult question, which really comes to this. To what extent are a man and his collaborators free from criminal responsibility when they break the law in order to remedy an injustice? It is an extremely difficult problem. And perhaps I was wrong to put it so generally. For example, it is plain that if a man charged with capital murder is acquitted and subsequently confesses to the crime, it would plainly be murder for someone to kill him, even though he ought to have been executed. I think I must revise what I said. We have to consider whether the steps taken in this case were morally justified and whether, although amounting to crimes, they ought or ought not to be visited with the normal consequences of committing a crime."

"There is, my Lords, a further question which I am instructed to raise," said counsel for Jo. "I do so with some embarrassment, but I am quite sure that it is my duty to refer to it, in view of my instructions."

"What is the point?" asked Lord Justice Manners.

"It is the conduct of Mr Justice Halliday," said counsel. "With the greatest possible respect to the learned judge, he appears to have rendered himself liable, certainly to a civil action. Whether or not his actions amounted to a crime I leave it to your Lordships to say."

"What on earth are you talking about?" said Lord Justice Manners, with some heat. "The learned judge was in effect kidnapped, like your client, and forced to act as he did. He appears to have acted in a most courageous and balanced manner in very difficult circumstances."

"My Lord," said counsel, "I don't dispute that for a moment. And up to a certain stage in the matter the learned judge was completely blameless."

"When then do you say he incurred some kind of liability for his actions?"

"My Lord, when he deliberately sent away the police."

"When he sent away the police? What are you talking about?" said Lord Justice Manners.

"My Lords, you have not yet heard the evidence, but the learned judge will himself tell you, I am quite sure, that at a fairly late stage in the proceedings, if I may so term them, the police arrived at the house and he sent them away again."

"To prevent a pitched battle, no doubt," said Lord Justice Manners.

"No, my Lord. It is perfectly true that only two police officers arrived and that they would have been heavily outnumbered and outgunned, but the learned judge did not send them away to get reinforcements, he sent them away so that he could proceed with the enquiry he had been forced to start. And the police will tell you, my Lords, that he gave them the impression that nothing was wrong but that he was busy."

"Is that correct, Mr Attorney?" asked Lord Justice Manners.

"Substantially, yes, my Lord," said the Attorney-General.

"Well," said Lord Justice Manners, "you have brought the matter to our attention and no doubt it falls within the scope of our enquiry. We had better wait until we hear exactly what happened."

The Attorney-General then called Mr Justice Halliday to give his account of what happened. When he had finished, Lord Justice Manners conferred with his colleagues.

"We are a little troubled, Sir George," he said, after a short consultation, "about this matter of the police being sent away. As we understand the position, until that moment you were all held prisoner in your house?"

"That is so, my Lords."

"But then you were permitted to interview the police inspector and sergeant and you could have asked them to bring help to release you. Is that right?"

"That is quite correct, my Lords."

"In fact, however, you did nothing of the kind but put off the police as though nothing were the matter and went back to continue your enquiry."

"Quite true, my Lords."

"Well, Sir George, whatever the motives or reasons which prompted you to act in this way, didn't your behaviour identify yourself, to some extent at any rate, with your captors as far as the other captives were concerned? For example, Mrs Barnwell wished to leave the house but was prevented from doing so by the threat of force. If you had asked the police to bring up reinforcements, that would not have happened. May it not, therefore, be said that by your deliberate abstention from seeking help, when help could have been obtained, you became party to the false imprisonment of Mrs Barnwell?"

"My Lords," said Mr Justice Halliday, "while I am making no formal admission on the subject, I recognize that, as a pure proposition of law, that may be right. I had a very difficult choice to make. Shall I tell your Lordships why I acted as I did?"

"If you please, Sir George."

"At the precise moment when the police arrived I had reached a critical stage in the enquiry I had been compelled to make. Your Lordships have now held that there was a gross miscarriage of justice at Mr Walsh's trial. At the time the police arrived I had come to the conclusion that that might have been the case, but I also realized that, unless I could pursue the enquiry at once, it might well be that it could never be satisfactorily concluded. It was a case of striking while the iron was hot. Three witnesses have before your Lordships refused to give evidence on the ground that they might incriminate themselves. Had the enquiry come to an end at the time the police arrived, it is at the very least possible and, in my view, probable, that those witnesses would have sufficiently recovered themselves and received sufficient advice and encouragement from other sources to prompt them to continue the conspiracy to defeat the ends of justice, which your Lordships have held they have impliedly admitted. Of course, my view may have been wrong, but I do not think it was. The position was, therefore, in my opinion, that, if I called for help from the police, it might never have been possible to establish the innocence of this man, and he would have had to complete his sentence of life imprisonment. The view which I held then, and which I respectfully adhere to, was that in such circumstances the sanctity of human liberty for such a length of time was more important than the comparatively short time for which our imprisonment would continue. If by my conduct I have rendered myself liable in damages to Mrs Barnwell or anyone else, if anything more than a nominal sum should in the circumstances be paid to them, I consider the money well spent. But I hasten to add that I think the Treasury ought to pay it. As far as crime is concerned, I entirely dispute that my action in failing to ask for police help amounted to any crime known to the English law. If it did, the law ought to be altered."

"No doubt, Sir George," said Lord Justice Manners, with the suspicion of a smile, "the Attorney-General will address us on the law if necessary. Thank you for your explanation. Does anyone want to ask Sir George any questions?"

Jo's counsel got up. "Sir George," he said, "you agree that Mrs Barnwell wished to leave the house and was prevented from doing so?"

"I have already said so."

"Did she not protest in the strongest possible terms about your conduct in sending the police away?"

"She did so, as you have said, in the strongest possible terms."

"So that, in effect, you deliberately kept her in the house against her will."

"I did not actually keep her, but I put it out of her and my power to get released."

"Presumably you realized that you were doing this—that you were unnecessarily prolonging Mrs Barnwell's and your own imprisonment?"

"I did not consider that aspect of the matter at the time, I confess, but I agree that it was implicit in what I did. Perhaps I ought to add that it is possible that by my action I saved injury or life. I should make it plain that that was not the object of my sending the police away. I believed that, as soon as the enquiry was over, Mr Walsh would keep his word, send his men away and surrender to the police. But I also believed that he and his assistants were quite determined that the enquiry should be completed before his recapture. It is at least possible, therefore, that, had I called for help, there would have been a pitched battle between the police and our captors. I repeat that I had not that in mind. But your client may care to consider that it is possible that I saved her from injury or even death. Nor was she kept a prisoner for a moment longer than was necessary to complete the enquiry. I cannot conceive that the same thing will ever happen again, but, if it did, I think I should feel obliged to act in the same way."

The judge completed his evidence and then Lonsdale gave evidence about his escape and the reasons for it. He refused to divulge the names of his associates and was not pressed to do so. Again he gave his account well and with obvious sincerity.

"The governor of my prison suggested that I ought to have waited in prison until I was released," he said. "I quite understand his point of view. No governor can view escapes with equanimity or, if I may say so, without bias. It was his job to keep me inside. It was my job to get outside. Had there been any legal method of achieving my object, I should, of course, have pursued it, but I had exhausted all legal methods. What else was there for me to do?"

That indeed was an unanswerable question. In order to have his case reviewed, he had not only to escape but to take the other illegal and dangerous steps which he had taken. When Lonsdale had finished his evidence, Charles took up the burden on his behalf.

"Your Lordships have now proclaimed my client to have been the subject of a disgraceful conspiracy and to have been wrongfully convicted. We know that occasionally such cases may occur, but this one has only come to light by reason of my client's illegal activities. It would, in my respectful submission, be an outrage if he were now prosecuted for the crimes he was forced to commit. I agree that there is less to be said for his accomplices who took on the job as one of business and for which they have been well paid. But my client has particularly asked that your Lordships should hold that no proceedings ought to be taken against any of them who can be found or identified. For certain it is that without their help my client would never have been able to do what he did. Their moral guilt may be rather more than my client's but, even in their case, they knew they were assisting in an attempt to prove my client's innocence. Whether or not they believed in it I do not know, but they may well have been impressed by the amount my client was prepared to spend on the undertaking."

"Mr Southdown," said Lord Justice Manners, "I gather

that most of your client's accomplices could not be identified, as they were masked."

"That is so, my Lord."

"Speaking for myself only, I must say that I should at least think it rather bad luck on anyone who was not so disguised being charged, while his associates get off scot free."

"The same remark could apply to any burglary," said Mr Justice Swann.

"Of course it could," said Lord Justice Manners, "but this is very different from a burglary. Indeed, the main object was not a felonious one at all. It wasn't a crime at all. The object was to procure an enquiry. That is all. The methods used to procure it were, of course, criminal, but no one was injured or more than inconvenienced as a result, and, as the object was a good one, I should have thought that the pursuit of the perpetrators would not be particularly desirable. Although public feeling is by no means always the right guide in these matters, there is no doubt whatever but that the public would be very much against the prosecution of any such proceedings. The only proceedings which, in my personal view, ought to be taken are proceedings against those who successfully sought the conviction of Mr Walsh by a criminal conspiracy. But there is obviously in law insufficient evidence to bring them to trial, however loudly the facts speak for themselves."

Eventually the Tribunal completed its hearing and, in due course, its findings were published. They completely vindicated Lonsdale and recommended that no proceedings should be taken against anyone. Lonsdale had been released immediately after the public hearing. He received many letters of congratulation, including one from Jo.

"You've done very well," she wrote, "and I congratulate you. But don't think I'm going to let it rest at this. Love, Jo."

Lonsdale smiled, and threw the note into the fire.

A little later on he had a visit from the Boss. He had asked him to call.

"How nice to see you again," he said, after the Boss had been shown in. "I do want to tell you how grateful I am for all you did."

"Not at all," said the Boss. "It was a real pleasure and paid for handsomely. I wish all my customers were as forthcoming. D'you know, I've almost felt like retiring. But I should get bored, you know. I shall take a holiday, of course."

"Why don't you write a book?" suggested Lonsdale. "That's quite a recognized profession for retired crim . . . retired people to take up. I expect you could tell a few interesting stories. Change the names, of course, and alter them about."

"I'm not much good with a pen," said the Boss. "I wasn't at school. My essays were dreadful. Always getting into trouble over them."

"Oh, well," said Lonsdale, "it was only a passing thought. I'd hate to see anyone, who's been as useful to me as you, languishing in prison. I gather that they do catch up with you sometimes."

"It has been known," said the Boss. "It's my own fault really. But I like to see a job's done really well, and that does mean paying visits to the site from time to time. But, after all, I shouldn't have got my practice together if I hadn't done that. So I can't really complain."

"But you'll have to retire some time," said Lonsdale. "Why not make it now? You're still young enough to enjoy life."

"That's the trouble. When I'm older I may not want the excitement I need now. You've no idea how thrilling it is to watch a well-prepared plan carried out. I got a terrific kick out of arranging yours. No mountaineer retires until he's past it. He just can't give it up. It'll be the same with me. However, let's hope I'm lucky. They haven't had me for some time."

"They'll be on the look-out for you now," said Lonsdale. "I expect they know you were behind this."

"I'm sure they do," said the Boss. "They know that no one else could have done it so well."

CHAPTER EIGHTEEN

COUNSEL'S OPINION

Two days after Lonsdale's release from prison, Jo walked into a solicitor's office. She had an appointment to see Mr Manage of Streak & Manage. As soon as she had sat down she came to the point.

"Mr Manage," she said, "would your firm have any objection to bringing an action against a High Court judge for conspiracy?"

Mr Manage brightened perceptibly.

"Mrs Barnwell," he said, "subject only to considerations of professional propriety, my firm would be delighted to bring an action against a High Court judge for conspiracy, bottomry, barratry or even for plain straightforward negligence. I personally should welcome the opportunity. Shall I tell you why?"

"By all means," said Jo.

"I am only a humble solicitor, as you know. But in my humble capacity I have had the inestimable privilege of supplying barristers with briefs. You may or may not know that briefs are as necessary for a barrister as water for a fish. Neither can survive without a sufficient and continuous supply of, in the one case, briefs, in the other, water. Perhaps you knew this already?"

"I had some idea of it," said Jo.

"So you know, too, that the legal profession in this country is divided into two branches. The superior, that is the Bar; the lowly and inferior, that is the solicitor's profession. But, humble and lowly as we are, we do have the great honour of being allowed to supply the superior branch with their necessities of life, briefs. Naturally we count ourselves most blessed to be allowed to nourish such an admirable body of men and women as the Bar with their main source of existence. We do this from the moment the barrister is qualified. We help the young man, we bring distinction to the older man and, in a very large measure, we are responsible for the promotion to the Bench of the most distinguished members of the Bar. For you must know that judges are selected only from the Bar. You might have thought that, in the circumstances, there would be a measure of gratitude shown by the judge to the solicitor. Without his briefs, he would never have become a judge. Indeed, while he is still practising at the Bar, he usually treats solicitors not only with the utmost courtesy and consideration, but you might almost say that at times he shows actual signs of fawning on the hand that feeds him. You must forgive this rather long introduction."

"Certainly," said Jo, "if it means that you want to help me."

"I certainly do. And I will now tell you why. As soon as many of these courteous, polite barristers are elevated to the Bench their attitude towards their humble brethren, the solicitors, appears to undergo a marked change. 'Where is the solicitor in the case?' they say. 'How comes it that he has done so-and-so and not done so-and-so? While I am not trying an issue between him and his client as to whether he has been guilty of negligence, I feel bound to say that I can't see what answer he would have to such a claim.' On another occasion he will go so far as to make the solicitor pay the costs personally, a horrible thing to do. In other words, he turns and bites the hand that fed him. All our loving care goes for nothing. Gone is the 'Good morning, Mr Manage. How are you, my dear fellow? So glad to see you. Thank you so much for your instructions in the Wallaby case. They were, if I may say so, admirably drawn.' Instead, we have: 'It's outrageous that this notice wasn't given or this document not produced. What's a solicitor for?' When they ask that last question I always want to say, 'To brief the barrister and that was once you, my Lord.' But I don't. I should be sent to prison for contempt of Court. So I must be content with muttering to myself and telling my counsel to get up and stand up for me. Now, I think it was a charge of conspiracy you wanted to bring. That sounds admirable. I'd charge the whole lot of them with it, if I got the chance. But, of course, I must first be satisfied that you have a reasonable case. What's it all about?"

"Presumably you have read all about it, Mr Manage," said Jo. "Why shouldn't I sue Mr Justice Halliday and Mr Walsh for conspiracy to detain me against my will? The judge knew that by letting the police go I would be detained by Mr Walsh and he intended that I should be."

"It's a nice idea," said Mr Manage, "a very nice idea indeed. My only regret is that I can't say that Mr Justice Halliday has ever made me pay the costs personally. Indeed, he has been rather an exception to the rule I was mentioning. However, that can't be helped. It should be an example to the others. Let me think."

Mr Manage was silent for a short time. Then he said: "As a mere solicitor, my opinion on a matter of this delicacy is of little value. We shall have to approach the superior branch. In other words, we shall need the opinion of counsel. Do you mind the expense?"

"Not if it will get me anywhere," said Jo.

"Very well," said Mr Manage. "We will approach the most suitable of these learned gentlemen who is available. My first choice would be Mr Trent. He is quite intolerable, but so are most of them in their different ways, as a matter of fact. At the same time, he appears to me to know his law as well as any of them. Not that that means very much. The standard of lawyers at the Bar gets lower and lower."

"Well, if the Bench is recruited from the Bar," said Jo, "you can't think much of the Bench."

"I don't, Mrs Barnwell," said Mr Manage. "I don't. Between you and me there are only six decent lawyers in the country. Three are in the House of Lords, one's an ecclesiastical lawyer and the other two are dead. Mr Trent I consider to be the best of the extremely bad bunch which is available for your matter."

"Then why don't you rely on your own opinion, Mr Manage?"

"That's quite simple, my dear Mrs Barnwell, quite simple. If I'm wrong, you could sue me. If I get counsel's opinion, you can't."

"Even if he's careless?"

"Even, my dear Mrs Barnwell, if he is negligent to a degree which would justify the vituperative epithet of gross. The position is that, when your professional adviser, be he doctor, accountant, architect or humble solicitor, gives you the normal careless advice which the public have come to expect from him, you can take him to the Courts and his insurance company will pay you. But when the barrister is careless, far beyond the normal degree expected of him, you have no remedy against him and, of course, no remedy against the solicitor instructing him."

"I must say it seems odd," said Jo.

"It not only seems, but it is odd. I must make one qualification about my own position. If I took you now to a barrister who was a patent specialist and knew nothing about such things as judges conspiring with escaped convicts and, if he were foolish enough to accept the instructions and gave you advice which might have been admirable if you had just invented a machine for making the tea and shaving you at the same time, but which was completely off the rails in relation to a claim for false imprisonment, then indeed I might be liable to you for going to an obviously unsuitable man. I am taking no such risk in going to Mr Trent. That he is intolerable, I have already told you. That he may insult you, I add now, but he certainly practises in those courts where judges who conspire with escaped convicts would be brought, if such cases were in the normal run of things."

"Very well," said Jo. "Let us go to Mr Trent."

So a conference was arranged with Mr Trent's clerk and, at the appointed time, Jo and Mr Manage arrived at his chambers. They were not kept waiting.

"On the dot, you see, Mr Manage," said Mr Trent cheerfully, as he welcomed them in. "I see no reason why a barrister, however busy he may be, should not keep his appointments punctually. I expect you to be here on time. You have a right to expect that I am ready."

"That is most kind," said Jo.

"It is not intended to be," said Mr Trent. "It is intended to be good business. Members of the Bar don't like referring to the word 'business.' They consider that it lowers their prestige. In my view, nothing lowers a barrister's prestige except inefficiency. And I venture to think you will find none of that here, Mrs Barnwell. You see, I don't even pretend not to know your name. I have taken the trouble to memorise it. You will find no affectation here either."

"What we hope to find," said Jo, "is the answer to my problem."

"That goes without saying," said Mr Trent. "I have read these papers and come to a clear conclusion in the matter. That's something I deprecate in many of my colleagues. They give you so many alternatives in their opinions, so many 'ifs' and 'buts,' that you don't know what they really are advising you. My advice may be wrong—it isn't, but, of course, you can't tell that—but it is always definite. The other day we won a case in the House of Lords. We had lost it before the judge of first instance. I had said that we should win it. 'Should,' mark you, not 'would.' I naturally cannot guarantee the correctness of every decision of a judge of first instance, even if I am appearing in the case. Some judges are so dense that you cannot penetrate their minds with any but the simplest propositions. I am not saying that was the case in the action I was telling you about. The judge was an excellent one, but unfortunately I was unable to accept the brief. The case was done by a very worthy and fairly able colleague, but, quite frankly, he wasn't up to it. So my client had to go to the Court of Appeal. There I would have appeared but, unfortunately, I was taken suddenly ill and had to return the brief. The case was lost again. You can imagine that at that stage my client must have been doubting the correctness of my advice. Four judges had now decided against my opinion. However, he came to consult me again and I advised him to go to the House of Lords. My advice was not that he 'should' win there but that he 'would' win. Provided, of course, that I was able to argue the case. I must say, my client took a lot of persuading to go on with the appeal. But, fortunately for him, in the end he agreed. I argued the case in the House of Lords and we won by a majority of three to two. The legal journals pointed out that that meant that six judges of high standing had decided in favour of my opponent and only three in favour of my client, and yet my client won. I pointed out, in a short and apt letter, that justice does not always go to the big battalions. I offer no apology for telling you all this. Mr Manage knows my reputation. That, no doubt, is why he comes to me. But you don't, Mrs Barnwell, and I always consider that the lay client—that is you, Mrs Barnwell—should get a fair idea of the man she is consulting."

"I think you've given me an excellent idea," said Jo. "Apart, however, from what you have told me yourself, Mr Manage gave me a very good description of your qualities."

"Did he?" said Mr Trent. "He probably told you, then, that I was quite intolerable."

Mr Manage blushed.

"So I am, Mrs Barnwell," said Mr Trent, "to most solicitors. Their abysmal ignorance and inefficiency is sometimes beyond bearing. I am not particularly referring to Mr Manage's firm, which is as good as any. Though, I am bound to say, that isn't anything much. Now, most members of the Bar don't talk like this, Mrs Barnwell. They flatter their clients, usually without the slightest justification. You will gather that I don't. I tell them exactly what I think of them, and I am bound to admit that some of them don't come back for more. Indeed, if it were not for the fact that fortunately nature had endowed me with certain qualities which peculiarly suit me for this profession—I claim no credit for it, any more than one claims credit for having been born—if it were not for that fact, I don't suppose I should have a single client. I should have had to give up the Bar years ago. Fortunately, as you can see from the briefs on the table, that lamentable event did not occur. Solicitors have to come to me, whether they like it or not. I don't suppose Mr Manage likes it any better than most of the others. Now, shall we proceed?"

"Yes, please," said Jo.

"You want to know whether you would have a reasonable chance of succeeding in an action for conspiracy against Mr Justice Halliday and Mr Walsh, the conspiracy being to imprison you falsely. The answer to that question is, quite simply, yes. If the action were tried by a judge, he would, in my view, if the case were properly argued in front of him, be bound to find in your favour. If the case came before a jury, I cannot predict with the same certainty what they would say. But, even if they decided against you, you would have a fair chance of upsetting their verdict on appeal."

"Well, that's very good hearing," said Jo. "We'll start at once."

"Wait a moment," said Mr Trent. "The two questions which would arise in your action are whether the claim is legally justified and, secondly, what are the damages. If, as I think it would be, the first question is decided in your favour, the second question arises. What are the damages? Now normally they might be heavy. But I am bound to say that, in the very peculiar and exceptional circumstances of this case, I think you would be lucky if you were awarded more than £5. That amount the defendant would certainly pay into court and, if you recovered no more, you would have the pleasure of paying the costs of both sides. Of course, you could accept the £5, but I rather think that would not appeal to you."

"£5!" said Jo indignantly. "Can decent citizens be imprisoned by judges without justification and only recover £5?"

"No," said Mr Trent, "I didn't say that. But I feel quite sure that any judge or jury would hold that you were not a decent citizen, and that you were only detained in order that a wrong for which you were responsible could be remedied."

"Are you on their side or mine?" asked Jo.

"I am on no one's side yet," said Mr Trent. "I am advising you to the best of my ability, which, as I have already indicated to you, is considerable. In the light of the Tribunal's report, any judge or jury would take the view that Mr Walsh was wrongly convicted and that you were in all probability responsible for that conviction."

"He's a murderer," said Jo. "He murdered my husband."

"Fortunately," said Mr Trent, "what you say to me is privileged and will, of course, be treated by me in complete confidence, but, if you are wise, you won't make statements like that outside these chambers."

"That is where I am going anyway," said Jo, "and I shall say and do what I please there," and she left the room abruptly.

"I'm sorry," said Mr Manage to Mr Trent, "but she feels strongly on the subject."

"It is quite unnecessary to apologize," said Mr Trent. "I

have only proved you to be right—in your advice to your client about me, I mean."

"It's nice to be right for once," said Mr Manage.

"I hope you won't have to wait too long for the next time," said Mr Trent.

CHAPTER NINETEEN

ALL SQUARE

MILES HAMPTON never had his interview on television. The best he could get was a ghosted article in one of the Sunday newspapers. It was called: "Why I Refused To Give Evidence," and Miles received £100 for being a party to it. He read the article he was supposed to have written, and, though he could not fully understand the reasons, as stated, why he had not given evidence, he enjoyed seeing his name and photograph in the paper. He enjoyed the £100 almost as much. And, in the circumstances, he considered that, all in all, he had not done so badly. Instead of receiving anything up to seven years for perjury he had had an interesting experience, received a good deal of publicity and been paid for it.

Mrs Meadowes duly married her new husband and both of them were good value, in the public houses which they frequented, for some months.

Herbert Adams went back to his bench in the park and waited for something else to happen.

Mr Allwinter went back to his art and had several ideas for pictures which he put into execution. One, a large canvas, called "Mr Justice Halliday at home" and showing accurately the scene at the judge's house during the enquiry, was shown in the Academy. The judge bought it quickly. Mr Allwinter began another.

Angela and Charles began to see more and more of each other, with Lonsdale's entire approval.

Lonsdale himself, after taking a short rest, began to consider fresh financial ventures. About six weeks after his release he was taking, as he often did, a stroll in the evening near his London house when a large blue car ran into and over him in the middle of the road. He was fatally injured, though not killed on the spot. The car endeavoured to drive on, but somehow the collision had affected the steering and it swerved into a lamp-post. In the result, the police, who were quickly on the scene, were able to take a statement from the driver, after Lonsdale had been rushed to hospital. There were no independent witnesses but the driver explained that the injured man had suddenly rushed into the middle of the road in front of the car, giving it no chance. The police might have had no difficulty in accepting this statement as true, but for the fact that the driver was Jo Barnwell.

As soon as they discovered her identity, they did all they could to get a statement from Lonsdale before he died. A policeman sat by his bed the whole time, night and day.

It was obvious that he would die, but a day after the accident he recovered consciousness sufficiently to speak. He was asked how the accident happened. Before he answered the question, he asked:

"Did the driver stop?"

He was told that she couldn't help it.

"Then you know who she is?" he asked.

"Yes," said the police officer.

"What was her version?" asked Lonsdale.

The officer told him.

"Absolutely correct," said Lonsdale, and closed his eyes.

"Nurse," called the officer. "Quick. He's gone almost purple."

Later, recovering consciousness again for the last time, he asked to see Jo alone. She knew by then that he had confirmed her story.

"Why did you tell a lie?" she asked. "You know I did it on purpose."

"I know," he said, "but I've a great regard for you, Jo, and I didn't mind that sort of attack. That was quite straightforward. I ought to have thought you might try it. After all, it's only what I did to Adolphus myself."

"Then it was you, and you managed to lie about that too."

"I didn't, Jo. I didn't have to, though I would have, if necessary."

"You must have told your daughter you were innocent. I'm sure she said you had."

"I only told her and everyone else that I'd been convicted by perjury. That was true enough."

"So the only lie you've ever told was to save me?"

"Yes, Jo. I'm not sure that you deserve it. Fancy suggesting that I'd let anyone else run over Adolphus for me. He'd have been sure to make a mess of it. But I did better than you, Jo. I killed him outright."

"I did try, darling," said Jo apologetically.

ALIBI FOR A JUDGE

CHAPTER ONE

ON ALIBIS

WILLIAM BURFORD's defence was an alibi and the judge who presided at his trial was Mr Justice Carstairs. The alibi was not one of the best alibis and the judge was not one of the best judges. It may perhaps help to an understanding of the case and its curious consequences to consider first the nature of an alibi and then the nature of a judge.

From time immemorial the alibi as a defence has been popular with criminals. And not only with criminals. Most people remember Mr Weller senior's despairing cry, "Oh, Sammy, Sammy, Vy worn't there a alleybi?" when Mrs Bardell won her action against Mr Pickwick. It is logical enough. The charge against William Burford was safe breaking on a pretty large scale. It was alleged that, with the help of another or others, he had not only blown open the safe but removed about £80,000 as well. No doubt William said to himself: "If I can prove I was elsewhere when the safe was blown, I'm bound to be acquitted." And he was quite right; it was a cast-iron defence—if it succeeded.

That is the trouble with alibis. They are at the same time the best and worst defences. They are the best because, if you weren't there when the man was murdered, you couldn't have murdered him. They are the worst because, once you raise an alibi, no other defence is usually open to you. In the case of murder, for example, you can't rely on self-defence, accident or extreme provocation. You say you weren't there. So you can't have been provoked; you can't have been threatened by the man and picked up a weapon with which to defend yourself; he can't have slipped on a piece of orange skin and fallen accidentally on to the knife with which you were peeling the orange. You were nowhere near the man at the time. Or so you say. And, if the jury don't believe you, that's an end of the matter.

Criminal cases are not like civil cases in this respect.

Judges and barristers are quite used to inconsistent and alternative defences in civil matters. Says the plaintiff in the County Court:

"Your Honour, the defendant owes me £50 for goods sold and delivered."

"What do you say?" says the judge to the defendant.

"Oh, your Honour," says the defendant, "I never agreed to buy the goods."

"An excellent defence," says the judge. "Any other?"

"Oh, yes, your Honour. He never delivered them to me."

"Better and better," says the judge. "Any more?"

"Oh, yes, your Honour. They were no good and I couldn't re-sell them."

"Yes," says the judge. "What's the next one?"

"He agreed to take them back."

"Fine," says the judge, "and now he refuses to do so?"

"Exactly, your Honour," says the defendant. "And I've one further defence."

"I felt sure of it," says the judge. "Keep the best till the last. What is it?"

"I've paid for them, your Honour."

"As I thought," says the judge. "How many children have you got?"

"Five, your Honour."

"Very well, then. Pay £2 a month."

Well, perhaps it isn't quite like that, though, according to a current story, that is how it seemed to an American lawyer who was visiting the English Courts.

But, though this sort of thing can be done in a civil court, where the only issue is usually whether A should pay B and, if so, how much and when, it is quite impossible in a criminal court. For example, in William's case it was alleged that he was seen running from the scene of the crime. Having sworn that at the time he was some miles away in bed with his wife, it would have been impossible for him to rely alternatively on the inconsistent defence that he was a customer of the bank and he had gone to sleep while waiting in a queue of people all of whom were paying in vast numbers of cheques and notes, which had to be counted and re-counted; that, when the bank closed, he was somehow or other forgotten and locked in; that he was disturbed by the real thieves, that when he realized the position, he thought he might find himself in a compromising situation if he remained and so he bolted down the street. Nor, if that story seems anyway rather fantastic, could he have said more simply, as an alternative to his alibi, that he was certainly seen running from the scene but that it was a pure coincidence; he happened to be in the neighbourhood at the time and was in a hurry to get home.

No, once you've committed yourself to an alibi, that is your only mode of escape, and, if that breaks down, you must wait, as composedly as you can, for the sentence. In consequence the wise criminal thinks carefully before he relies on an alibi. And the wisest prepare it in advance, as in a military operation, with watches synchronized and excellent reasons arranged for the supporters of his alibi being able to remember the time when the accused was supposed to have been with them. Up to midnight the wireless is a most useful asset. The supporter listens to the programme and (provided the accused doesn't get arrested on the spot) primes him with it later.

Many people are rather sceptical of alibis and, indeed, some cynics say that they are never genuine. They argue that, if the accused really was somewhere else at the time the crime was committed, he would never have been charged with it. But this implies that no innocent person is ever charged with crime, and, though it is a very rare occurrence, it does occasionally happen. William passionately declared that it had happened in his case.

CHAPTER TWO

ON JUDGES

It should perhaps help to an understanding of Mr Justice Carstairs' behaviour after the trial of William Burford to have some appreciation of a judge's position in England.

How are they appointed, what qualities do they require to make them satisfactory judges, how and why do some of them fail to be satisfactory and what is the effect upon themselves and upon the public of such failure?

Mr Justice Carstairs had been appointed in the normal way, that is to say, he had had a substantial practice at the Bar, was looked upon as a sound lawyer and a person of complete integrity; he was offered the appointment by the Lord Chancellor, and he accepted. There was no surprise at his appointment and no expectation that he would either be very good or very bad.

In some countries there is a judges' profession and, if you want to become a judge, rather than an advocate, you must join that profession. If you do join it, you no doubt start off in some administrative capacity with no judicial duties, but you see how the judges do their work. Then, in due course, you will be given some very minor judicial post, and your progress thereafter will presumably depend upon how you acquit yourself in that post and in any more important posts which you may be given.

The result is that no one in those countries is appointed to high judicial office unless he has proved himself to possess not only the qualities necessary for a good judge but the ability to make full use of those qualities as well. In consequence, the public in those countries can be almost certain that, unless the extra power suddenly goes to a man's head, the judge holding high judicial office will be patient and fair-minded, intelligent, a good lawyer and, perhaps most important of all, not an advocate on the Bench. It can also be reasonably sure that he will not be a person who worries excessively. No one can, of course, be quite certain of that matter, as a judge may carry on his worrying entirely in private and never disclose it to any superiors, colleagues or subordinates, but this does not often happen.

It is, of course, possible that preferment to high judicial office will suddenly go to a man's head, but, if he has been having continuous preferment for many years, it is fairly certain that he is not a person whom power corrupts.

The position of a High Court Judge in England is extremely important and there is, therefore, obviously something to be said for ensuring that no one is appointed to that office unless he has proved himself to be fitted for it. A man may be a brilliant lawyer and a brilliant advocate and an appallingly bad judge. And you cannot tell for certain what sort of a judge he will make until he is on the Bench. If a mistake has been made, it is then too late to correct it.

In spite of this danger the English system of the appointment of judges entirely from the Bar has worked, on the whole, extremely satisfactorily, but undoubtedly it has fallen down from time to time. It was a mistake to appoint Mr Justice Carstairs, though neither he nor anyone else realized it at the time. But the advantage of the system is that the judge, having been at the Bar most of his working life, understands all that has been happening before the case comes into Court and all that is happening from the advocate's point of view in Court. This knowledge is of the greatest value and is only available to judges in those countries where they are appointed from the Bar.

The one case where the English system has in the past been known quite unnecessarily to fail has been in the appointment of the Lord Chief Justice. His position is of the greatest importance, both to the judges and to the public, but until comparatively recently there was a practice by which he was appointed direct from the Bar, the Attorney-General of the day being considered to have some kind of moral right to be so appointed. The strong probability is that this practice is now defunct and that no Lord Chief Justice of England will ever be appointed except from among the judges themselves. It would seem elementary that no one should be appointed to such high office unless he has proved that he is a judge of the highest quality. The unfortunate result of appointing as Lord Chief Justice an Attorney-General, who was a man of brilliant ability in many respects but whose judicial qualities had never been tested, and were in fact dreadfully deficient, is well within the memory of many lawyers, and it is unlikely that such a risk will ever be taken again. It was necessary to take a risk in appointing Mr Justice Carstairs a judge of the Queen's Bench Division. It would have been ludicrous to take the risk of making him Lord Chief Justice. How ludicrous this story will show.

No little handbook entitled *Do's and Don'ts for Judges* is

issued to barristers on their appointment to the Bench. Most of them realize instinctively what is required of them. Even those who do not turn out to be particularly good judges try to act as particularly good judges do act. This has the advantage that on the whole litigants feel that justice has been done, even if it hasn't, and apparent justice is the next best thing to justice itself. Nor do newly-appointed judges attend a short course of lectures with the object of receiving helpful advice from their more experienced brethren.

All the same, a class for new judges is a pleasant idea.

"Now, Toothcombe J., what would you do in a case where the plaintiff said, etc., etc.?"

Toothcombe J. remains deep in thought.

"Come along, Toothcombe J., one of the things a judge has to do is to make up his mind."

Still no answer.

"Very well then. Next. Next. Next. I see your hand is up, Blinkers J. What is your answer to the problem?"

"I was just stretching, I'm afraid."

"Oh, very well. So long as it was a genuine yawn, I don't think it matters very much. But never do it on purpose."

But, although handbooks and lectures are quite unnecessary for the average judge, it would have been a good thing if Mr Justice Carstairs could have had the advantage of both. For, although in private life he was a kindly and generous man, he was one of the few judges who did not appreciate instinctively his responsibilities, or realize how easy it was to abuse the power vested in him.

An omnibus conductor has considerable authority in his omnibus. He can't tell people to take their hands out of their pockets or to stop sucking sweets but he can order people about to a substantial extent. Few conductors abuse this power but some do. Such abuses cannot do much harm, although they can start an unfortunate train of events moving. If a conductor is rude to a businessman, it may rankle until he reaches his office. He may find there that a clerk has made a mistake. Normally he would have overlooked it, but, unconsciously, in order to be avenged for the conductor's rudeness, he creates a fuss about it all and makes some unwarranted remarks to the clerk. Eventually the clerk is provoked into answering back and is given a week's notice. This may lead to all sorts of domestic complications.

"Lost your job, have you? What am I going to use for housekeeping, tell me that?"

"It wasn't my fault, really, Mary."

No, it wasn't. It was the conductor's.

So, even the abuse of authority on that very small scale can have serious effects. And, conversely, good manners and helpful conduct, even on a small scale, can start a chain reaction of a happier kind.

But abuse of power by a judge may very well have serious effects. It is one thing for a man to be told in public to get off an omnibus, it is quite another for a judge to say of him in public, with the probability that it will be reported in the press:

"I have never seen such a nauseating spectacle as Mr X in the witness box. He is incapable of telling the truth except when it suits him and he tells his lies in a sanctimonious and self-righteous manner which I find utterly repulsive."

When Mr Justice Carstairs, on his way home from Court, read in the newspaper "*Mr X . . . a nauseating spectacle.* Judge," he entirely failed to appreciate that in speaking of Mr X in that way he had simply satisfied his own personal dislike of the man. For the purposes of his decision it was quite unnecessary for him to do more than to say that he did not accept Mr X's evidence and why: for example, that some of his evidence was contrary to letters which he had written or that he contradicted himself in the witness box or the like. But to describe him as a nauseating hypocrite was to indulge in mere abuse. Perhaps the judge was right in this view, perhaps he was not, but, though his judgment could be reversed in a higher Court, his words could never become unspoken.

And, after all, he had seen the man in the box for perhaps an hour. It may be that in the unaccustomed atmosphere of the Court Mr X went to pieces and did not do himself justice. It is indeed surprising that so many witnesses are able to control themselves sufficiently to appear outwardly calm. Justice can never be perfect and, if a man is a bad witness, he may lose his case, but he should not have to suffer the sort of treatment which Mr Justice Carstairs handed out. And unfortunately no one who knew the judge well enough ever told him of this defect in his behaviour. It was as bad as that of a judge who said to an acquitted prisoner:

"You're discharged. You're very lucky in your jury."

In saying that, the judge had endeavoured to cast doubt upon the jury's verdict in order to satisfy his own sense of annoyance at the prisoner being acquitted.

A further serious fault of Mr Justice Carstairs was his complete inability to restrain himself from intervening during the course of a case. Everyone knows the man who can't refrain from taking the lead in private conversation. If a story, which he happens to know, is being told, he can't resist interrupting and finishing it off. So with Mr Justice Carstairs in Court. It has frequently been said that a judge should hold himself aloof from the struggle going on in Court between the advocates. Of course sometimes he has to blow his whistle when there has been an infringement of the rules, or when someone has been hurt, but otherwise he should leave the battle to the advocates. Mr Justice Carstairs, however, girded himself for war and joined lustily in the fight.

Another of his serious faults was to have carried his advocacy to the Bench. That is one of the prices of the system of appointing judges solely from advocates. But it is impossible to tell whether a man will do this until you see him at work on the Bench. It by no means follows that, because a man has been a fierce and determined advocate, he will not be completely fair-minded on the Bench. One even finds such an advocate, on appointment to the Bench, having difficulty in coming to a decision. But the judge who carries his advocacy to the Bench makes up his mind (often much too early) as to what in his opinion the result of the case should be and proceeds to press that point of view, just as though he were the advocate whose duty it was to press it. A judge cannot help forming a view about a case as it goes on; that is what he is there for. But, as far as possible, he should keep it to himself and in no circumstances should he try to steer the case to the result which he considers it should have. A judge who apparently seems to procure a particular result in a case must invariably appear unfair.

It was unfortunate that Mr Justice Carstairs should have these faults but by themselves they would only have resulted in his being a bad judge. It was the combination of these faults with two other faults which caused him to act so strangely. He was a worrier and he indulged in self-deception.

It is important for a judge, both for his own peace of mind and for the quality of his decisions, that he should not worry about them. He should do his very best to get them right, but, having done so and delivered his judgments, he should not be tormented by doubts about their correctness. A judge should be able to make up his mind and, having done so, he should give his decision and go to the theatre.

There was once a judge who had many admirable judicial qualities but he worried so much about his cases that he actually died within a comparatively short time of his appointment, because his mind and body could not stand the strain any more. Mr Justice Carstairs did not die from worry but this can only have been because his mind and body were both able to stand the strain better than the judge who died. But he tormented himself unmercifully when he had any doubt about a decision he had given.

He also indulged in self-deception. Most young barristers have done this in their early days. The young man loses a case in a County Court, and on his way back from the trial suddenly thinks of something which he failed to do and which might have altered the whole situation. For a moment he feels quite sick, and then he starts to convince himself either that his new idea was not in fact a good one, or that it would really have made no difference if he had put it into effect. Before he has got back to chambers he has decided that no one else could have won the case, although in his heart of hearts he knows this is not true. Most young men grow out of this habit, and start to learn to profit by their mistakes. They still find on the way back from Court that they've forgotten to ask an essential question or something of that kind, but they no longer try to convince themselves that it would have made no difference. In other words they seek to profit from holding a post-mortem and they resolve to try to do better in the future.

In its strict sense an alibi means a claim that you were elsewhere at the time something happened. But the word is also used loosely and inaccurately to mean simply an excuse. In that sense Mr Justice Carstairs had from the start of his career at the Bar used alibis and on his way home from Court, after having given judgment in a rather difficult case, he would suddenly think of some point that he thought he might have overlooked. Thereupon the worrying side of his mind and his power of self-deception would have a fine struggle and by the time he reached home he would have decided that he was right after all. That, however, would not prevent him from having a very bad night through worrying about it all over again.

But for the explanation of how judges are appointed readers might have wondered how this particular judge came to be appointed. But he was quite a good lawyer and some of the faults which made him unqualified to be a judge were not appreciated when he was only an advocate. They were not even appreciated by the judge himself. Had they been, he would never have accepted the offer. There is a considerable strain on a judge imposed by the mere concentration which he has to maintain throughout the case. But, if he has serious difficulty in coming to a conclusion on any but the simplest cases, and if he continually worries after most of his decisions and is only stopped by having to concentrate on the next case, the burden is too great for him.

A man once said to a judge:

"If you make that order I shall commit suicide."

The judge made the order and the man committed suicide. Had such an event occurred to Mr Justice Carstairs he might conceivably have committed suicide himself, but, even if he had refrained from taking that drastic step, he would have undergone torments. In fact the judge had no alternative but to make the order. He reported the threat to all the responsible authorities and there was no more that he could do. If a judge were to yield in any way to such a threat, any litigant could win his case by making it, as no one could ever tell whether he really meant it. Of course it wouldn't last very long with that particular judge, as very soon both sides would make the same threat and it would become common form for counsel for the plaintiff, having asked all the relevant questions material to the case, to add this last one before sitting down:

"And now, Mr Y, will you kindly tell the learned judge what you will do if he does not decide in your favour?"

"I shall commit suicide."

"Thank you, Mr Y. That is all I have to ask."

Then counsel for the defendant would do exactly the same and the threats would pretty well cancel out. Of course it might be awkward when there was a claim and a counter-claim and the judge dismissed them both. No doubt in such a case he would warn both plaintiff and defendant that it would be a serious contempt of Court to put their threat into practice within the precincts of the Court.

Fortunately for William Burford he had no idea of the nature of the judge who was going to try him. He had indeed asked his counsel what the judge was like and had received the assurance:

"Don't you worry about the judge. It's the jury that matters."

CHAPTER THREE

TRIAL

It was more comforting for William to be told that than to be told: "He's the very devil and will get you convicted if he possibly can."

And that was the only reason that William's counsel, Mr Empton, said what he did. He was an able and experienced practitioner in the Criminal Courts and he knew perfectly well that in a difficult case, like William's, he would have the judge against him. It follows from what has been said earlier that a judge should not be "against" anyone when a man is being tried by a jury. And, even when he is trying a civil case alone, he should not appear to be against either side until he gives his judgment. But Mr Empton knew well that, unless he were extremely lucky, Mr Justice Carstairs would run the case against him from start to finish, and that, though the verdict would be the jury's, it might well be difficult for them in a case of this kind to withstand the pressure from the Bench. But there was no point in worrying his client unduly in advance by telling him this. He had enough to worry about as it was.

It is well known among lawyers that, when something starts to go wrong with a case, it often happens that nearly everything seems to go wrong. Usually, though not quite always, this is because the case is a bad one. William's case began badly and got worse as it went on. It started with a bad judge, it was dependent on a poor alibi, something happened in the course of the case which made the alibi even worse, and throughout the case the judge and Mr Empton were at loggerheads. William soon became like a passenger on a sinking ship. The captain (Empton) was on the bridge doing his best but the waves were battering the boat unmercifully, it was taking in water all the time and, though, of course, a rescue was always possible, it appeared to William at almost every stage of the trial that he was going down. The captain, of course, would not have to go down with his ship.

The first witness against William was a policeman. At about 11.30 p.m. he had been on beat duty near a branch of a well-known bank when he heard what sounded like a muffled explosion. He stopped and listened but heard nothing more, and saw nothing. He thought it must have been the sound of a collision in the distance. After standing still for a minute or two, he continued on his beat. About twenty minutes later he heard a sound of someone running. Turning round a corner he saw a man running and carrying a suitcase. He called on him to stop. The man glanced round and increased his pace. The policeman followed, but lost him. Later he identified William as the man he had seen.

Mr Empton had a difficult decision to make when he rose to cross-examine the policeman. The witness had admittedly only seen the man's face for a moment, but he had unquestionably picked him out at an identification parade. As far as William could tell, this parade was a perfectly fair one. But—and it was a very big but—some eight years previously William had unfortunately served a sentence of six months' imprisonment for receiving goods knowing them to have been stolen. Since his release from prison he had apparently gone straight. He had married a charming girl and taken a steady job and, as far as was known, had avoided the bad company he had been keeping at the time of his conviction.

In consequence of this conviction, however, the police had a photograph of William. If the witness had been shown this photograph before the identification it would be easy enough for him to pick out William. It might have been shown to him perfectly properly with other photographs, *before* William's arrest, to see if he could spot the man. On the other hand, it might have been shown to him *after* William's arrest, in an excess of zeal by the police who, believing that William was their man, wanted to secure a conviction. On the whole it was most unlikely that it was shown to the witness before the arrest, as William had never been concerned in safe blowing or anything of that sort. But Mr Empton's difficulty was that any cross-examination by him to suggest that the witness had seen a photograph of the accused might very well lead an intelligent member of the jury to realize that William had a previous conviction for crime. Mr Empton did not consider that this was one of those rare cases where it was desirable to rely upon the fact that the accused had a criminal record, and accordingly he was in a dilemma. The policeman positively identified William. It was no use simply shouting at him that he was a liar or asking if he had made a mistake. The policeman would politely deny such suggestions. On the other hand, the only method of making an inroad on the identification was by referring to a matter which might gravely prejudice his client's chances of acquittal. He also had to bear in mind that, if the witness had been deliberately shown a photograph of William before the parade, it was most unlikely that he would admit it. So that all he might get for his pains would be a statement that there was such a photograph in existence—which would be a pointer to a previous conviction—and a denial that the policeman had ever seen it.

Such a situation requires the most delicate handling and even the most brilliant and intelligent advocate might take a wrong course or come to grief when taking the right one. Mr Empton's cross-examination went as follows:

EMPTON: You only caught a glimpse of his face, Officer?

WITNESS: I saw it, sir.

EMPTON: I know you saw it, but it was only for a moment, wasn't it?

WITNESS: It was only for a moment but I saw it plainly.

EMPTON: Have you a good memory for faces?

WITNESS: Average, I suppose, sir.

EMPTON: You didn't see the prisoner in the police station until five days after you saw the man running?

WITNESS: That is correct.

EMPTON: Had you been trying to memorize his face in the meantime?

WITNESS: Yes, sir, I had.

EMPTON: How d'you do that?

WITNESS: Well, I just did it, sir. It struck me as very suspicious that a man carrying a suitcase refused to stop when called upon by me, and I tried to keep his face in mind.

EMPTON: Not an easy thing to do?

WITNESS: I don't know, sir. I've never really tried to do it before.

EMPTON: When did you first give information about this man?

WITNESS: I reported it immediately on the telephone, sir. And later that night, when I heard of the bank robbery, I made a further report.

EMPTON: Did you have any difficulty in identifying the accused at the parade?

WITNESS: I had to look along the line of men twice, sir, and then I felt sure.

EMPTON: Did you have any help in identifying him?

JUDGE: What d'you mean—have any help?

EMPTON: My Lord, I would respectfully ask your Lordship to allow me to ask the question without intervening.

JUDGE: But the jury and the witness and I must know

what you mean by the question. You say "did he have help?" Help could be given in a variety of ways.

EMPTON: My Lord, I'm sure your Lordship must realize the difficulties which counsel sometimes have in this type of cross-examination.

JUDGE: Some cases are very difficult.

EMPTON: My Lord, I do most respectfully protest at that observation, and I ask for a new trial before a fresh jury.

JUDGE: Certainly not. Go on with your cross-examination.

EMPTON: Well, Officer, did you have any help?

JUDGE: What d'you mean by "help"? Do you mean—was the prisoner pointed out to the witness before he went on the parade? Is that what you mean? I'll ask the officer myself. Did that happen, Officer?

WITNESS: No, my Lord.

JUDGE: Is that what you meant, Mr Empton?

EMPTON: No, my Lord.

JUDGE: Then kindly explain what you do mean.

EMPTON: I wish your Lordship would let me ask the question.

JUDGE: It's no good you asking the question unless the witness knows what it means. Do you know what it means, Officer?

WITNESS: No, my Lord.

It would have taken a particularly scrupulous and courageous policeman to reply to that last question: "Yes, perfectly, my Lord." Whether such a witness would have become a Chief Constable, Commissioner of Police, or have eventually been dismissed as unsuitable for the police force, is a matter for conjecture.

So Mr Empton's difficulties, which were very great anyway, were increased by the judge. Before he started his cross-examination he had thought for a moment that he had a brainwave. His client was not an athlete but he had done a little running, and Mr Empton had ascertained that a picture of him had once appeared in a local paper when he was running with the Loamshire Harriers. Mr Empton considered a cross-examination on these lines: "Now, Officer," he thought of saying, "my client has done a certain amount of running and has had his picture in the papers. I suppose you hadn't by any chance seen a photograph of my client before the identification parade?"

Mr Empton felt he could rely on the witness playing the game. The police know all about the danger of a prisoner's past bad character being made known to the jury, and never voluntarily refer to it. Mr Empton felt that he and the police officer could have a complete understanding about what he meant by a photograph, but the jury would have been misled (though, for once, perfectly properly) by the reference to the local paper.

At first, when Mr Empton had, without much hope, enquired of his client whether he had ever had his picture in the paper, he had been delighted at the reply, but he eventually decided it was not worth it. To pray in aid that the accused was a bit of a runner when it was alleged that he had outrun the police officer, seemed tantamount to suicide.

So Mr Empton continued cross-examining the witness as best he could, having regard to the actual difficulties of the situation, increased as they were by the interruptions of the judge. And Mr Justice Carstairs did not simply interfere with his mouth. He interfered with his eyes, which turned towards the jury with a look which said pretty plainly:

"I'm sorry, members of the jury, that your time has to be wasted like this. But that is one of the misfortunes of our present situation which we each have to bear. This man is obviously guilty but we have to humour the public conscience, which likes to go through the motions of trying him."

In other words Mr Justice Carstairs indulged in all the tricks of the lesser and least judges, who, entirely forgetful of the true role they should be playing, deliberately try to steer a case in the direction which they themselves think it should take. Although they know perfectly well that the verdict should be the jury's they do all they can to see that that verdict shall coincide with their opinion. Occasionally, even, they are hypocritical enough to say something like this:

"Members of the jury, the verdict in this case is yours and yours alone. And, if you think that inadvertently I have expressed my own opinion, you should entirely disregard it unless it happens to coincide with your own."

Such advice, given genuinely when a judge has not acted as Mr Justice Carstairs was acting, is sound and fair enough —and often given by judges of the highest distinction. It is only when it is said by a judge who has deliberately tried to procure the verdict he wants that it is objectionable.

That Mr Justice Carstairs should form an opinion during the case was only to be expected. No one with the intelligence of a judge, however mediocre, listening attentively to the whole of the evidence in a case, could fail to do so. But he should have kept his opinion to himself. It is true enough that 99 out of every 100 people who stand in the dock are guilty, but, if one is to take account of that fact, one might as well give up trying them altogether, and explain to the luckless 1 per cent that it is far cheaper to convict everyone and that they are suffering in the cause of the national economy.

It is important to bear these considerations in mind. Otherwise it might be difficult to appreciate the extraordinary behaviour of Mr Justice Carstairs after the trial.

After Mr Empton had unsuccessfully tried to attack the evidence of the police officer he sat down. There was no re-examination and the next witness was called. This was a detective-sergeant who, in company with another police officer, had called on William five days after the robbery. The effect of his evidence was this. As a result of information given to him, he went to the house where William lived with his attractive wife, Lesley. The detective-sergeant did not state that she was attractive but later she came into Court and everyone could see it for themselves.

William had opened the door to the officers and had seemed very ill at ease when they told him who they were.

"Mr Burford," the sergeant had said, "are you prepared to tell us where you were at 11 p.m. on the 23rd of this month?"

William had thought for a moment and then said that he had gone for an hour's walk, as he did not feel sleepy enough.

"By yourself?"

"Yes."

"So no one can confirm your story?"

"My wife can say I went out."
"But she can't prove where you went?"
"No, of course not."
"D'you mind if we look round your flat?"
William had hesitated. Eventually:
"I suppose not," he had said, "but I'd like to know why you want to."
"We'll tell you later."
The officers looked round the flat and soon became most interested in a bundle of £1 notes they discovered in a desk.
"D'you often keep money like this in the house?"
"No."
"D'you mind telling us where you got these?"
Again William hesitated.
"A man gave them to me."
"That was very nice of him. Would you tell us his name?"
"Thompson."
"Where does he live?"
"I don't know."
"Where did you last see him?"
"Here."
"Where is he now?"
"I don't know."
"How long have you known him?"
"Oh, for years. We were at school together."
"What school?"
"I forget."
"You forget?"
"I'm sorry. I made a mistake. We weren't at school together. I meant I'd known him since my schooldays."
"An odd mistake to make. Where were you at school?"
"What does that matter?"
"It doesn't really. So you've known this man Thompson for years, and he gave you these notes. What else can you tell us about him?"
"Nothing, really."
"That's strange. What does he do for a living?"
"I don't know."
"Why did he give you these notes—£25 worth?"
"I don't really know."

"You're sure there is a Mr Thompson?"

"Of course. My wife has seen him."

"Is that correct, Mrs Burford?"

"Of course it is," said Lesley. "He's tall, and fair, with a straight nose."

"So is your husband as a matter of fact," the sergeant had said.

"Yes," said Lesley, "they are rather alike."

"Extraordinary," said the sergeant. "You're quite sure that they're not so alike as to be one and the same person?"

"Of course not," said Lesley indignantly.

"You've seen the two together, Mrs Burford, have you?"

"Certainly I have."

"Well, that proves it, doesn't it, unless you were seeing double—or you're not telling us the truth."

"Well, I wasn't seeing double and I am telling the truth."

"How many pairs of trousers have you got?" was the next and unexpected question the sergeant had asked.

"What on earth d'you mean?"

"Just answer the question, please. How many?"

"Three. No, four."

"It's five if you include an old pair of white flannels," said Lesley.

"May we see them?"

"If you really want to."

"We do."

William and Lesley brought out the four pairs of trousers, and the police officers proceeded to turn down the turn-ups of each and place a sample of the dust into little boxes. They repeated the process with the pair he was wearing.

"Which were you wearing when you went for that little evening walk five days ago?"

"These."

The officer made a special note on the label of the box into which he had put the dust from those trousers.

"Mr Burford," the sergeant had said, when they had finished, "I should like to take away these notes. I'll give you a receipt for them, but I have reason to believe they were stolen from the bank which was robbed five nights ago. You may have read about it."

William had gone white.

"You're not suggesting . . . ?"

"I'm not suggesting anything at the moment, but I may want to call back and see you again."

That was the substance of the sergeant's evidence relating to his first interview with William, and there was no real dispute about it. Naturally the sergeant did not state in evidence that he did not believe the story about Mr Thompson. He was so used to such stories. William's version was merely a slight variation of a well-known theme, which runs as follows:

"Where did you get this?"—"this" being some article which was known to have been stolen.

"From a man."

"What's his name?"

"Fred."

"What is his other name?"

"Dunno."

"Where does he live?"

"Dunno."

"Where did you meet him?"

"At the market."

"Is that where you usually see him?"

"Yes."

"Will he be there now?"

"Shouldn't think so."

"Tomorrow, then?"

"He never goes Tuesdays."

"Well, the day after—or the day after that. Tell us when you will be able to show him to us?"

"As a matter of fact I think he's left London. Talked of going abroad."

William's story of Mr Thompson was not, in the sergeant's view, far removed from this classic model. The sergeant's story continued with his second interview with William and Lesley. On this occasion he was able to inform them that the notes had been positively identified—by cashiers' writing on them—as notes which had been taken in the bank robbery. And worse than that, from the Burfords' point of view, he also informed them that dust from William's trousers had been identified as precisely similar to dust from the bank's strong room. William was then asked to attend an identification parade, where he was identified by the first witness.

It was after this identification parade that William produced his alibi. He said that he was mistaken in saying that he had gone for a walk by himself. That was the night before. On the night of the bank robbery he was in bed with his wife and she could corroborate his story. William also now became rather more confiding about Mr Thompson and, after he had been charged with the robbery, he said that he had been to race-meetings with him and that it was as a reward for his services during those meetings that the money had been paid to him. He had no idea that it was stolen.

Asked to account for the dust in his trousers, William was unable to give any explanation.

"Your suggestion is," the sergeant had said to him, "that this man Thompson must have been the thief. You didn't lend your trousers to him I suppose?"

No, William had not.

So the case against William was a very strong one and his last-minute alibi obviously shaky. Even a better judge than Mr Justice Carstairs would have felt pretty certain of his guilt. But a better judge would not have shown it.

CHAPTER FOUR

VERDICT

Eventually the time came for William to give evidence. He said that he had had nothing to do with the robbery, and insisted that he was in bed with his wife at the time. He had not seen Thompson since before the war until he called on him a week or so before the robbery. They went to a few race-meetings together and he assisted Thompson by putting money on horses for him. If they won, Thompson gave him a present. That accounted for the £25, which had been given to him the morning after the robbery when they had gone to a race-meeting near London. They had come home from the meeting and Lesley had given them a cup of tea. That was the last he had seen of Thompson. It was just a mistake when he said he had been at school with Thompson. He was upset by the police officers and made a slip. As to the alibi, he had simply got the days wrong when he was first asked to account for his movements. The policeman who identified him must be mistaken. The dust in the trouser turn-ups was either a coincidence or Thompson must have put it there.

"Thompson," repeated counsel for the prosecution, "Thompson is the villain of the piece, you say?"

"Yes," said William.

"I gather that you agree that he looks something like you?"

"I can't really say, but I agree my wife said so."

"And she should know?"

"Presumably."

"Now, Burford, you're an educated man. You were at a public school, weren't you?"

"Yes."

"Which?"

"Must I say?"

"Of course you must say," said the judge. "No doubt they've produced some useful citizens in addition to yourself" he added.

"Really, my Lord," said Mr Empton, "I must respectfully protest at that remark."

"Indeed?" said the judge. "Do you object to my classing your client along with others as a useful citizen? So he is, unless and until the jury decide otherwise," and the judge gave the jury one of those looks. He was in fact rather overdoing it, a dangerous thing for a judge who wants a conviction. It sometimes so inflames an intelligent jury that they acquit, even somewhat perversely.

"Well," went on prosecuting counsel, "what was the school?"

"St. James's."

"A very excellent school, no doubt."

"Naturally I think so."

"Then why did you at first tell Sergeant Brown that you'd forgotten the name?"

"I was muddled."

"But I don't understand," said the judge. "I suppose it's possible that by accident you said a man had been at school with you, when you really meant that you had known him since your schooldays, but personally I cannot for the life of me follow why you should say you'd forgotten the name of the school."

"I didn't want to bring the name of the school into it."

"You mean you thought it might bring disgrace on the school?"

"Well, I did not know . . . I didn't see what the school had got to do with it."

"Well—you mean that, for one reason or another, you didn't want to tell the police officer the name of your school —and so you said you'd forgotten it?"

"Yes."

"Then why did you answer counsel a moment ago and say that the reason you said you'd forgotten the name of your own school was because you were muddled?"

"Did I say that?"

"You know you said it."

"Well—I was muddled."

"But that wasn't why you said you'd forgotten the name of your school?"

"I suppose not."

"Then it was a lie?"

"I didn't mean to lie."

"Then why say something that isn't true? It's very difficult for the jury, you know," went on the judge, "unless you pay some attention to the oath you took not so very long ago."

"I'm sorry, my Lord."

"There's no need to apologize. I was just warning you for your own good."

The judge then invited prosecuting counsel to continue.

"So you were in bed with your wife when the missing Mr Thompson robbed the bank?"

"I suppose so."

"You suppose so? I thought that was your case."

"Well, I didn't see him rob the bank, did I?"

"Quite right, Burford, you didn't see him rob the bank. I'm obliged to you for the correction. You merely assumed, from his presenting you with the money and dust which came from the bank that he was the thief?"

"Yes."

"And unfortunately the policeman identified you and not him."

"You've already said we're alike.'

"No—it was your wife who said that. And I suppose that, if there were no Mr Thompson and it really was you all the time, it was quite a good idea for your wife to say that?"

"She said it because it was true.'

"So you say. But suppose it wasn't true—it would have been a sensible thing to say, wouldn't it?"

"I've never thought about it."

"Well think about it," said the judge. "Everyone can make mistakes, can't they, but unless the police officer's evidence is a mistake, it's pretty damning, isn't it? So it makes it much easier to persuade someone—the jury, for example—that it is a mistake, if you and Mr Thompson are alike, doesn't it?"

"I suppose so."

"And you had a good deal in common, hadn't you," went on counsel, "the money and the dust?"

William made no answer.

"And—for a moment or two anyway—until the mistake was discovered—the same school? No don't bother to answer." And counsel for the prosecution sat down. There was no re-examination.

"Your next witness, Mr Empton, please," said the judge.

"That is the case for the defence, my Lord."

"No other witnesses?"

"No, my Lord."

The judge sighed.

"Oh, very well," he said. "Do you propose to address the jury?" and he turned to counsel for the prosecution, plainly indicating that the case was so clear that no such address was necessary.

"Very shortly, my Lord," said counsel, and, keeping his word, he made a five minute speech in which he effectively ridiculed William's alibi and referred tellingly to the undisputed facts of the case. Mr Empton then did the best he could in reply.

Empton's best point was that fingerprints had been found on the scene of the crime which were proved not to have been William's; but this was evidence of a very negative type. It was obvious that more than one man must have been involved in the affair and accordingly the fact that another man's prints and not William's were found was little help. But Mr Empton was grateful to have even this point to urge. He had wondered whether to suggest that the prints might have been those of Mr Thompson, but there was a feeling in the court—which he shared—that Mr Thompson did not exist. And so he left out this suggestion. He could not risk the smile which he felt the point might raise on the faces of some members of the jury.

When Mr Empton had finished his speech, the judge proceeded to sum up.

"Let me first of all say," he began, "that it is not for the accused to prove his innocence but for the prosecution to prove his guilt. And they must prove it beyond all reasonable doubt. Counsel for the prosecution submits that has been done. Mr Empton contends that it has not. It is for you, and you alone, to say which of them is right."

The judge then went on to deal with the facts. Eventually he came to William's alibi.

"Or should I say alibis?" he said, "for you will remember that it is common ground that at first the accused said he was walking alone in the streets. Later on he improved on that by saying he was with his wife. I say improved because two witnesses to an alibi are no doubt better than one. That is, they are better if you believe them. Of course, one witness whom you believe is better than fifty—or even two—whom you don't. But in fact you've only seen one witness for the defence. It is certainly a matter for you to decide but, if Mr Thompson really does exist, you might have thought that the prisoner's wife would have gone into the witness box to confirm it. We are told that she is in the precincts of the court. So the walk into the witness box should not have been too far for her. Why is she silent? You have heard counsel for the prosecution, in cross-examining the accused, pour scorn on this story of a Mr Thompson, this evanescent person, resembling in looks the accused and even in what he keeps in his trouser turn-ups. If you had been the wife of the prisoner, and had seen this Mr Thompson, could you have resisted the urge to add the weight of your word to that of your husband? She too was the other witness to the alibi. No, witness is the wrong word. She is said to have been with the prisoner when the crime was committed. She is said to have seen this Mr Thompson—but she is not a witness. What you have to ask yourselves, members of the jury, is why not? Why not?" The judge paused. In the middle of the pause there was a sensation.

"I want to give evidence, my Lord," shouted Lesley from the gallery.

"Silence," said the usher.

"One moment," said the judge. "Was that your client's wife, Mr Empton?" he asked.

"Yes, my Lord."

"Did I understand that she now says she would like to give evidence?"

"Yes, my Lord."

"D'you make any application for leave to call her?"

Mr Empton thought for a moment. He then decided that, having regard to the way the case had gone and was going, he had nothing to lose by applying.

"Yes," he said, "yes, my Lord, I do."

"Can you satisfactorily explain why she was not called before?"

"No, my Lord," said Mr Empton.

"You could have called her, but you decided not to?"

"That is correct, my Lord."

"And now, in the middle of my summing up, you apply for leave to call her?"

"Yes, my Lord."

"Your application is refused," said the judge, and thought for a few moments. "Let the prisoner's wife be accommodated with a seat in the well of the court," he said, "where she would have been, had she given evidence," he added.

There was a few minutes' delay while Lesley was brought

down from the gallery. When this was done the judge addressed her.

"Do you wish to remain in court during my summing up," he asked her.

"Yes, my Lord, please."

"Well, you must keep quiet then."

"I want to speak for my husband."

"You have had the chance and not taken it. It is too late."

"But, my Lord. . . ."

"Be quiet, madam. If you interrupt again I may have to deal with you for contempt of court."

Lesley sat down and the judge continued his summing up.

"Members of the jury," he said, "no doubt you have wondered what has been happening in the last few minutes. And well you may. And let me tell you, so have I. I may also tell you that never since I came to the Bar, let alone became a judge, have I heard such a piece of gross impertinence offered to judge and jury in charge of a case. Here was a man who was afforded the entire rights of an accused person. He was defended by counsel. That counsel was briefed by a solicitor. The case took several days in front of a magistrate before the accused was committed for trial, and this is the second day on which you and I have heard it. During all that time the accused and his wife and their legal advisers have known perfectly well that Mrs Burford was or could be an important, even a vital witness for her husband. They have had an opportunity for weeks, not to say months, to make up their minds whether she was to be called as a witness. Even right up to Mr Empton's closing his case she could have been called. You remember—and but for this extraordinary incident I should not have reminded you—I asked counsel for his next witness. I assumed, wrongly as it turned out, that Mrs Burford would be called. When Mr Empton said that the accused's evidence completed the case for the defence, I actually went so far as to help him—in so far as I properly could—in case he had forgotten, by saying 'No other witnesses?' It will be within your recollection that Mr Empton said there was no other witness to be called for the defence. And now—now that in my duty as a judge I comment on the fact that she was not called, the woman has the effrontery to say that she wishes to be called, and counsel has the . . . what shall I call it—I think temerity is the best word—counsel has the temerity at this stage of the proceedings to apply for leave to call her. You may not have been surprised at my rejecting the application out of hand. What shall we have next indeed? An application to call such evidence after the jury's verdict perhaps? Would that be much more outrageous? I will say no more about it, except that you should not allow this matter to prejudice you against the accused. He is to be tried on the evidence alone, though, of course, in coming to your conclusions, you are entitled to consider any lack of evidence too."

The judge then continued his summing up and, when it was over, the jury retired. They discovered almost immediately that they were all of the same view. They would all have liked to acquit William because of the judge's bias against him, but nevertheless, having sworn to try the case according to the evidence, they did not see how they could let him off.

"Perhaps we could add a rider," suggested one of them.

"What sort of a rider?"

"Oh, by saying we'd have had less difficulty in coming to our conclusion if he'd had a fairer trial, or something of that sort."

"He'd send us all to gaol."

"Well, that wouldn't suit me," said a housewife. "My husband's expecting me to cook his dinner. No, I'm sorry in a way for the young man but he shouldn't break into banks. I vote we just say that."

So in the end the jury somewhat regretfully gave their verdict of guilty, but most of them found it difficult to stomach the judge's smile as he beamed at them and told them that he entirely agreed with the verdict. And one of them could not contain himself:

"My Lord," he said, "I nearly said 'not guilty,' because you were so unfair."

"What did you say?" said the judge.

But the juryman did not reply. He had got it off his chest, and did not propose to do any more. Indeed, the anger he felt was swiftly being replaced by fear.

The judge spoke to the clerk, who went very red in the face as he replied.

"What is your name?" asked the judge of the juryman.

"Thomas Honeyman."

"That was a most improper observation."

Mr Honeyman said nothing.

"Mr Honeyman," said the judge, "I am addressing you."

Mr Honeyman got up. "Yes, my Lord," he said.

"I said that your observation was most improper."

"Yes, my Lord."

"You agree?"

"Yes, my Lord."

"Do you wish to express your regret?"

"Yes, my Lord, for having said it."

There was a slight emphasis on the word "said," which implied that Mr Honeyman was not apologizing for having thought it.

"Very well," said the judge. "I had considered sending you to prison for contempt of court, but in view of your apology I shall overlook the matter."

"Thank you, my Lord," said Mr Honeyman, and felt mightily relieved. He was a man of some moral courage but it is doubtful if he would have qualified for a monument at the Old Bailey, as did the twelve jurymen who in 1670 refused to do as the judge wished, although they were locked up without food or water for two nights.

The judge then turned his attention to the question of sentence. A police officer referred to William's previous conviction ten years before.

"What were the circumstances?" the judge asked.

"My Lord, I understand that the prisoner, who was then only twenty-one years of age, went into the motor trade and got mixed up with some highly undesirable characters. He was eventually charged with conspiracy to steal and receive motor cars. The ringleaders got heavy sentences and the prisoner received six months. As far as is known, since then he has gone straight until this offence."

"Bad company again?"

"I expect so, my Lord."

"Not Mr Thompson by any chance?" asked the judge, smiling.

"I don't think so, my Lord," said the officer with a grin.

William was finally asked if he had anything to say. All he said was this:

"I may have behaved stupidly when the police called on me, but I didn't do this thing. You think there isn't a Thompson. Well, there is. I swear it. And he's the man. Not me. That's all I have to say, my Lord."

"William Burford," said the judge, "you have been convicted on the clearest possible evidence of a very grave crime indeed. Hardly a month passes without something of this kind happening. None of the money has been recovered with the exception of the £25 which was found on you. I disregard your previous conviction, which was of a different kind and which you appear to have lived down. Whether you committed this crime as a result of sudden temptation, or because you are a criminal at heart, I know not. But it must be made known to all persons who contemplate this sort of crime that the punishment, if they are caught, must inevitably be severe. It must be shown conclusively that it does not pay. What may be considered heavy sentences have been passed in recent years but they do not seem to have checked these outbreaks. In consequence the price must go up and in my view it ought to continue to go up until it is a sufficient deterrent. And I publicly warn any persons who may be minded to go in for the same kind of law-breaking that, if they come before me, even heavier sentences will be passed than that which I am about to pass on you. You will go to prison for ten years."

William seemed stunned by the sentence and the warders ushered him away before he could fully appreciate its reality. Lesley, sitting in court, sat absolutely motionless, her lips tight together and her eyes staring in front of her. The solicitor had to touch her on the shoulder and to guide her out of the court. She saw the whole life which she and William had built up together spirited away. All she could think or see was "Ten years—ten years."

Mr Empton went back to his chambers in the Temple.

"We went down," he told one of his friends. "I shouldn't so much have minded that. I expected it. He was guilty all right. But Carstairs was a real so-and-so. Never gave us a run. But there was one good thing. One of the jurymen had a poke at him. You'll read about it. And he got away with it too. Stout fellow."

Meanwhile Mr Justice Carstairs was walking home.

CHAPTER FIVE

RETROSPECT

It was the most uncomfortable walk he had ever had. Any judge might have been troubled by the juryman's remark, but for one of Mr Justice Carstairs' temperament it was almost as stunning a blow as the sentence was to William. It had only been by extreme self-control that he had managed to appear outwardly calm in Court and to pass sentence as though nothing had happened. Nor was the severity of the sentence any result of the juryman's remark. He would have passed that sentence in any event and, severe though it was, it was difficult to say that it was not justified in the prevailing circumstances. Criminals must be taught that robbing banks does not pay and that the enjoyment of the loot may be too far off in time to make the risk of capture worth while.

But the judge was not at first worrying about William or Lesley or what the conviction and sentence meant to them. He was thinking about himself. At first he tried dismissing the whole affair.

"Ridiculous!" he said to himself. "It isn't true anyway. I was as fair as the nature of the case allowed. I always am. Anyway it was only one of them who said it. He must have been mad or he wouldn't have dared to speak. I suppose I should have sent him to prison. That shows how fair I am. I didn't."

This conversation satisfied him for about a minute. Then the doubts began to recur.

"Unfair! It's absurd. I gave the man every chance. He hadn't a hope anyway. Then not calling the wife! I wonder if it was that which worried the chap? But what else could

I have done? No one would have allowed the application at that stage."

This satisfied him for another minute.

"I've always been particularly careful not only to be fair but to appear fair. And I was in this case. What was the man getting at? What had I done? Nothing. It was a plain case and the jury had to convict. Unfair! Ridiculous!"

And so it went on all the way home, and, by the time he reached home, he was already telling himself that—even if occasionally he had been unfair—it would have made no difference. Well, man's verdict showed it.

He took hours to go to sleep that night and, when at last he succeeded, he dreamed about it and the word "unfair" kept coming into his dreams. In one dreamlet he found himself talking to himself.

"You weren't unfair," he said. "You were just yourself."

That woke him up. What an appalling thing to say! He *wasn't* unfair. There were lots of judges much more unfair than he was. It was intolerable. He ought to have sent the juryman to prison and kept him there for months. That would have taught him to tell lies about a judge. Now he could go home to his family and tell all his friends and acquaintances:

"I told a judge he was unfair, and nothing happened to me."

But he did apologize. Of course, I'd forgotten that. He withdrew and apologized. Well, did he actually withdraw? What were his actual words? "I'm sorry I said it." That was surely a withdrawal. It must have been. He didn't realize what he had said. He didn't mean it—that's why he withdrew it. But then there had been a slight emphasis on the word "said." "I'm sorry I *said* it." How easy it is to imagine an emphasis where there isn't one. I'm probably too sensitive. The man was withdrawing and apologizing unreservedly. He was just overwrought. Perhaps he had domestic or business worries. It must be very difficult to be a juryman in such circumstances. Could I write and ask him if he really meant it, and explain why? Don't be absurd. Who ever heard of a judge writing to a juryman? I must be mad even to have thought of it.

And then for a moment, as he was considering his own unhappy position, he thought of the Burfords. Well, they're much worse off than I am. They certainly are. But it's not my fault. I had to give the sentence. And he was certainly guilty. I wonder why she didn't give evidence, and why she wanted to later? Of course it might have been something to do with that idiot Empton. I never have liked him. He's an oaf, if ever there was one. He could never be a judge. What a ridiculous thought! But why didn't she give evidence? She was an extraordinarily attractive-looking girl and might well have made a good impression on the jury. But, all the same, no one would have believed her. Anyway a wife counts for nothing when supporting her husband. Most of them do—even if they don't really like them. But what am I to do? This is driving me mad. You can't go mad just like that. There has to be something wrong with your brain to go mad. There's nothing wrong with mine. But what am I to do? What am I to do?

The judge had had such soliloquies on a minor scale before, but he had never had anything like this. He remembered judges who could be classed as opponents on the Bench. He remembered having complained about them himself. Perhaps he hadn't been entirely fair to Burford. Perhaps he *had* run the case against him. Dammit, he knew he had. He always did. He just couldn't help it. When he saw a man was guilty, he had to get him convicted. But it wouldn't have made any difference. The fairer the judge, the more certain the conviction. Why was it he always had to run a case as he did? He didn't mean to. He'd go on the Bench determined to be fairness personified and, before he knew where he was, he was making some sarcastic remark, quite unnecessarily, at the expense of one of the parties. Just like too talkative judges who, knowing their weakness, determine not to say a word unnecessarily during a case—and then never stop talking from the time they sit on the Bench.

But it wouldn't have made any difference, surely? Thompson didn't exist. If the man was with his wife, why didn't she come and say so? And that ridiculous statement about forgetting the name of his school. Yet why did a man who was happily married and in a decent job suddenly rob a bank? Suppose there had been a mistake? What a terrible thing to happen. Ten years! I couldn't bear ten days—but ten years! And for something you haven't done! But he had done it. Of course he had. But a man must be tried fairly. It isn't a trial at all if he isn't. "I nearly said 'not guilty' because you were so unfair." That showed the juryman was satisfied of his guilt anyway. Or there'd have been a disagreement. But why did the prisoner protest his innocence at the end? And it certainly sounded genuine. But lots of them do that. No good appealing otherwise. A good actor, that's all. But he certainly wasn't much of an actor in the witness box. Ten years! And that girl without him all that time.

Well he gets a third off for good conduct. That means only six and three-quarters. That doesn't sound quite so bad as ten. If he'd only given him seven years he'd have only had four and three-quarters to do. Perhaps the Court of Criminal Appeal would knock something off. He didn't like appeals being allowed against anything he had done. But he began almost to hope so. But even then—nearly five years in prison. "I nearly said 'not guilty' because you were so unfair."

The words continued to echo in his ears.

CHAPTER SIX

INTERVIEW WITH A JUDGE

A FEW days later Mr Empton was surprised to receive a note from the judge asking him to be kind enough to come to see him.

"I wonder what I've done now," he said to a friend. "I had a few dust-ups with him but they were all over, I thought."

"Perhaps," said his friend, "he was so impressed with your performance that he wants to ask you if you'll take a pupil for a friend of his."

"He's seen my performances often enough before," said Mr Empton. "Somehow I don't think it's that."

Later that day he went to see the judge in his private room at the Law Courts.

"Oh, Empton, come in and sit down," said the judge affably. "Nice of you to come over."

Empton sat down and waited.

"You must be pretty busy at the moment," said the judge, after a pause.

There is a tradition in the Temple, observed by most of its inhabitants, that, if you have a lot of work, you make light of it, and, if you haven't, you put on a show of being grossly overburdened.

"Oh, it's not too bad," said Empton. "Just jogging along, you know."

I wonder if he is going to ask me to take a pupil, he thought. That might well be the opening gambit.

"Good of you to take the time off to see me."

"Not at all, Judge."

There was another pause.

"Now, don't answer this question if you'd rather not," said the judge eventually, "but I have a special reason for asking it which you may find not unhelpful."

The judge stopped. Mr Empton broke the uncomfortable silence with:

"Of course I'll answer it if I can, Judge."

"It's nothing very alarming," said the judge, trying to get the interview on to a less constrained level. "I just wondered what you'd put in as your grounds for appeal against conviction in the Burford case."

"He's not appealing against conviction, Judge, only sentence."

"What on earth are you talking about?" said the judge sharply.

Mr Empton was so surprised at this sudden outburst that he waited for a moment or two before replying.

"He's not appealing against conviction, Judge."

"He must be mad."

"I've advised him it's hopeless."

"*You've* advised him that? Then *you* must be mad."

"Really, Judge, it *is* my business. He's got quite a chance of getting a year or two knocked off on sentence, but to my mind it's hopeless to appeal against conviction."

"What have you to lose by appealing against both?"

"Time and money. If we only appeal against sentence the case will come on much sooner and he won't have an extra month or two in prison."

"What's a month or two extra, compared with getting off altogether?"

"Nothing, I agree, Judge, if there were any chance of his getting off. But in my view there isn't."

"You utterly amaze me," said the judge. "Now, let me tell you this. I sent for you because I thought that you might have been embarrassed to put in your best ground of appeal. I wanted to tell you not only that I didn't mind but that I should support it in my note to the Court of Criminal Appeal."

"I'm sorry, Judge, but I couldn't think of any grounds."

"You're still in time for appealing?"

"Yes, Judge, we've a couple of days more."

"If I tell you two good grounds for appealing, will you put in an appeal?"

"Well, of course, Judge, I'd have to take the client's instructions, but, if I'm able to tell him what you say and that it comes from you, I don't suppose he'll want any more encouragement."

"Well," said the judge, "if you must tell him, you must, but I should prefer you just to advise him to appeal after all—that's if I can convince you you've got good grounds."

"I'll certainly do that if I can, Judge."

"Good," said the judge. "Now I'll tell you your two grounds of appeal. I don't care which order you put them in. First—the judge rejected an application to call further evidence, without first properly considering it. In other words, he never exercised his discretion in refusing the application—he rejected it out of hand."

"But really, Judge, with respect," said Mr Empton, "if I had the temerity to say that to the Court, I'd be blown out in two seconds, *and* they wouldn't be very nice about it."

"I tell you," said the judge, "that I didn't exercise my

discretion. I shall tell the Court the same. That's cast-iron, isn't it?"

Mr Empton thought for a few minutes.

"Well, Judge," he said, "it's very good of you to tell me this, and it certainly puts a new complexion on the matter. But I shouldn't like to say it was cast-iron."

"My dear Empton, just think. Here was the wife, the only other witness to the alibi, the only other person who could say Thompson existed, and you applied for leave to call her to give evidence. Of course you were late in applying; or rather, you wouldn't have had to apply at all if you'd called her before you'd closed your case. But she was a very important witness and, before the case was in the hands of the jury, you applied for leave to call her. The judge ought at least to have considered your application. He didn't. He rejected it out of hand. Who can say what the effect of that additional witness might not have been on the jury?"

"Well, I am most grateful, Judge," said Mr Empton, "and I see how you put it. I'll put it to my client and I expect he'll agree. I'll certainly advise him to. But you said there was another ground."

"Yes," said the judge, "there is. It's just this."

He stopped, as though not quite certain whether to go on, but in fact he had made up his mind that he would go on and was only considering the form in which he should put it. There is no greater protagonist of a religion than a convert. And equally there was no doubt that when Mr Justice Carstairs went into reverse he went backwards all the way.

"The second ground," he went on, "is that the trial was conducted unfairly by the judge from start to finish."

"But really, Judge, I couldn't put that in."

"Of course you can, if I support you."

"But it was no different from any other trial I've had before you."

The judge smiled a little bitterly.

"I hope that by that remark," he said, "you do not intend to be offensive."

Mr Empton became confused.

"I'm sorry, Judge," he said, "I didn't mean for a moment —I mean . . . I shouldn't have dreamed of. . . ."

"All right, all right, I understand," said the judge. "Let's forget the other trials. We're only concerned with this one. You can rely on all my interruptions for one thing."

"But you were entitled to intervene, Judge."

"Look, Empton, d'you want to win this appeal or not?"

"Really, Judge," said Mr Empton rather angrily, "I want to do the best I properly can for my client, but I'm not going to make a fool of myself in the Court of Criminal Appeal for nothing."

"You won't make a fool of yourself. I tell you, my note to the Court will state that I have read your grounds of appeal and agree with them. Now, let me see, you can not only rely on my actual interruptions and the prejudicial remarks I made, the scorn I poured on your client's case, but you can refer to the way I looked at the jury."

"There is a limit, Judge. I couldn't possibly do that."

"Why not?"

"Well, for one thing, it's not in the shorthand notes. How did you look at the jury, anyway? How am I to describe it?"

"There is a point there. Let me think. I must cast my mind back."

He thought for about half a minute.

"You're quite right. It's extraordinarily difficult to describe it in words. I tell you what. I'll do it now and we'll see what we can make of it."

By now Mr Empton was convinced that the judge was out of his mind, and he decided that he would humour him in every way.

"That's an excellent idea, Judge. Shall I be the jury?"

"Don't be silly. I want you to watch me. The jury are over there—by the window."

"Very good, Judge."

The judge turned towards the window, but, not being a particularly good actor, was not able to assume any particular expression.

"How's that?" he said.

"Jolly good, Judge," said Mr Empton.

"How would you describe it?"

Mr Empton paused.

"It's not too easy is it, Judge?"

"Perhaps it would be better if I said something, to get into the part. Yes, I know. Something like this. Ah, yes—Mr Thompson . . . you were speaking of Mr Thompson—although I don't think we are going to have the privilege of seeing him—if, indeed, anyone ever has had that privilege."

Inspired by these words the judge was able to give one of his famous looks to the window.

"How's that?" he said.

"First class, Judge."

"I'll tell you how to describe it. Take this down."

Mr Empton took out a pencil and the judge gave him a piece of paper.

"Ready?"

"Ready, Judge."

"Right. 'From time to time the judge looked at the jury in a manner which plainly said to them that the accused's story of Mr Thompson was not to be believed, thereby usurping the jury's function.' Got that?"

"Splendid, Judge. Yes. I've got that."

"Well, if you go through the shorthand notes you'll find lots of examples of that sort of thing. Put them all in and say at the end that it all adds up to an unfair trial."

"All right, Judge, I'll do it," said Mr Empton, "and perhaps I could add at the end what the juryman said. That would lend weight to it."

"What the juryman said has got nothing to do with it," said the judge with some asperity. "It's I who am saying it."

"Yes, of course, Judge. I'll leave out the bit about the juryman."

"Put in what you like," said the judge, "but I should have thought that, if a judge himself says that he's been unfair, it doesn't matter in the least what a twopenny halfpenny juryman thinks."

"No, of course not, Judge. Well, I really am most grateful."

Mr Empton got up and turned to go. Just before he left, he could not resist saying:

"What a pity you won't be able to lead me on the Appeal, Judge!"

"I hope you're taking this seriously, Empton," said the judge. "I meant every word I said."

"Of course, Judge, thank you so much," said Mr Empton hurriedly, and managed to get out of the door and down the judges' corridor and out into the Strand before he broke into laughter. Strangers seeing him walk across the road might well have thought him as mad as he believed the judge to be.

As soon as he got back to his chambers he burst into the room of the first available person and told him what had happened.

"It isn't really funny, because the poor old boy's as mad as a hatter, but oh—good Lord!—if you could have seen him. And heard him."

After he'd repeated the extraordinary story to as many of his friends as he could find, Mr Empton became calmer. He now had to consider what was to be done about it. Suppose he made all the allegations suggested by the judge and his note did *not* support them? How could he rely upon the word of a man who was mad? And anyway, if he was mad, what possible weight could his note have? It was a difficult problem and he decided to consult another judge whom he knew quite well, and who would not be sitting in the Court of Criminal Appeal when the case came before it. The judge whom Mr Empton consulted agreed to see Mr Justice Carstairs without saying anything about the case, to ascertain if he appeared normal in other respects. He was able to report that he saw nothing out of the ordinary about him.

"I think you'll have to put in the appeal," was the advice he gave. "After all, it's your client you have to consider. If this gives him a chance of getting off, it's your duty to take it, isn't it?"

So, after a great deal of thought, and an interview with William and his solicitor, Mr Empton arranged for an appeal to be lodged against conviction as well as sentence. He worded the grounds of appeal as tactfully as possible, so that, if things went wrong, he would have a reasonable line of retreat.

Meanwhile, Mr Justice Carstairs prepared his note for the

use of the Appeal Court, and anxiously looked in the list of Criminal Appeals to see when the case would be coming on for hearing. At last it came into the list and the night before it was heard was a very anxious one for the judge.

CHAPTER SEVEN

COURT OF CRIMINAL APPEAL

It was obvious to Mr Empton after he had started to open William's appeal that the three judges had read Mr Justice Carstairs' note and were not a little embarrassed by it. Judges had been known to admit mistakes in the past (though not as often as they made them) but this admission of wholesale unfairness was quite unique. And it was particularly difficult for the Court, as the judge had done little more and little less than some of his colleagues of similar calibre did from time to time.

Mr Empton stated the facts and issues in the case, and then came to the first ground of appeal.

"My Lords," he said, "I approach this first ground with some hesitation, and wish to assure your Lordships that I should not have raised it in its present form were it not for the fact that I understand the learned Judge agrees with the way in which the case is put in my notice of appeal."

"That is quite true, Mr Empton," said the presiding judge, "but the fact that the learned judge agrees with your submission that he did not purport to exercise his discretion on the question of calling the prisoner's wife is not conclusive of the matter."

"But, my Lords," contended Mr Empton, "if he might have exercised his discretion either way, he might have exercised it in my client's favour, and, therefore, his failure to exercise his discretion at all surely amounts to a miscarriage of justice?"

"In certain cases that might be so, but I'm not at all sure that the learned judge in his report to this court does himself justice. He says that he never exercised his discretion at all, but dismissed the application out of hand. But was he really doing more than saying that it was a very bold application which no judge could possibly have acceded to?"

"For myself," said Mr Justice Grain, "I should have refused the application."

"And so should I," said Mr Justice Pantin. "In my opinion no judge could have done otherwise. I don't agree with the learned judge that he never exercised his discretion. In my opinion he exercised it very quickly, that is all."

"And with such an application," said the presiding judge, "it couldn't have taken any judge very long to make up his mind. Here you had the opportunity of calling the witness. No doubt for good and proper reasons you elected not to call her. Then, in the middle of the judge's summing up, just because he comments unfavourably on your failure to call Mrs Burford—as he was perfectly entitled—and I, for one, think almost bound to do—just because he makes those unfavourable comments, you ask to be allowed to change your mind. Really, Mr Empton, the proposition only has to be stated to show what the inevitable answer must be."

In the face of these opinions, it was not long before Mr Empton had to proceed to his second ground of appeal.

"My Lords," he said, "again I should make it plain to your Lordships that I should not have raised this ground of appeal if the learned judge's note did not support it."

"There's no need to apologize, Mr Empton," said the presiding judge, "furthermore, even if the learned judge's note had not supported your submission it would have been your right and duty to raise it if, in your considered view, the conduct of the trial had been unfair. Counsel must, of course, act with a due sense of responsibility and with due care but, subject to those qualifications, it must not be thought that there will be any animadversion on his conduct from this Court or, I venture to suggest, from any other Appeal Court, because he criticizes, however strongly, the conduct of the judge in the court below. Subject only to the qualifications I have mentioned, it is counsel's right and duty fearlessly to make such criticisms as he properly thinks are in the interests of his client. Fortunately, it is very rarely that the question arises."

"I am much obliged to your Lordship," said Mr Empton,

"but I repeat that in this case I should not have made these criticisms if not, in fact, invited to do so by the judge's note."

"Well, let us see what they amount to," said the presiding judge. "First you complain that the judge intervened too often, and always contrary to your client's interests."

"That is so, my Lord."

"But a judge is entitled to intervene, is he not?"

"Of course, my Lord."

"And, if there is a strong case against the accused, his interventions may sometimes—and even always—appear against the accused's interest?"

"Yes, my Lord."

"Do you agree that there was a strong case against your client?"

"Yes, my Lord, there was."

"Then personally I don't quite see what all this amounts to. Of course, a judge should not intervene too often, and he should never come down into the arena and join in the fight. But, subject to that and to the ordinary rules of evidence and procedure, every judge must try a case in his own way."

"Justice must always appear to be done, my Lord."

"Indeed, yes, Mr Empton. And does it not appear to have been done in this case? What other verdict could the jury have returned? Even the juryman who made that most improper observation, so leniently regarded by the learned judge, felt he was bound to convict the prisoner."

"I see," said Mr Justice Grain, "that you even complain of the way the judge *looked* at the jury. Have you by any chance any complaint to make about the way I am looking at you now?"

"Of course not, my Lord."

"It is new to me," said Mr Justice Pantin, "that a judge's face is to be a ground of appeal. I tremble to think how many appeals there might have been from my judgments on that ground."

"It is not the face, my Lord, but the way he used it of which respectful complaint is made."

"Well, how am I using mine now, Mr Empton?"

"My Lord, there is no jury to be influenced. That is the gravamen of the complaint, the effect on the jury."

"Which do you prefer, an ugly judge or a good-looking one?"

"Either, my Lord, provided he doesn't use his ugliness or good looks unfairly to influence the jury."

"And how can he do that?"

"Well, my Lord, there are various ways. By a wink, for example."

"Are you suggesting that the learned judge in this case winked at the jury?"

"No, my Lord."

"Then what did he do?"

"He looked at them in a manner which suggested that the accused was telling lies."

"Are you sure you're not getting mixed up, Mr Empton? Was it not perhaps the accused himself who looked at the jury as though he were telling lies?"

"No, my Lord, it was the judge."

"But apparently it was the accused as well. At any rate, that is what the jury showed they thought by their verdict."

"I'm interested in this look," said Mr Justice Grain. "Can you help us at all about it by giving an imitation?"

"I'm not a very good actor I'm afraid, my Lord."

"Try, Mr Empton. Suppose we were the jury. Show us how the judge looked at them."

"I can't, my Lord."

"But it's you who are making the complaint. Surely it's up to you to make your complaint good, or abandon it?"

"I've carried it as far as I can, my Lord," said Mr Empton.

"I think you have," said the presiding judge, who then proceeded to give judgment.

"We cannot help feeling," he said, in the course of it, "that the learned judge has, since the trial, been affected by quite unjustifiable doubts as to his own conduct of the case. For ourselves, we can see nothing in the criticisms which have been made. The case against the appellant was a very strong one and, on such occasions, it is inevitable that remarks of the judge may appear to be against him. We are not saying that every interruption by the judge was necessary or desirable, and it may perhaps be true that he did give a little too much the appearance of favouring the prosecution at the expense of the appellant. That appearance should, of course, be avoided, and, no doubt, the learned judge, if he considers that he made errors of judgment in his conduct of the trial, will, as we all do, profit from a realization of those errors, but we see nothing in his conduct of the trial which amounts to a miscarriage of justice. The appellant was convicted because the jury felt sure of his guilt. So apparently did the judge and so do we. The appeal will be dismissed."

The court then went on to consider the question of the sentence but in all the circumstances they decided that, although severe, it should not be reduced.

"Why did I listen to the old fool?" said Mr Empton on his return to chambers. "All I've done for my wretched client is to get him an extra three months in prison."

"There's a message for you from Mr Justice Carstairs," said his clerk. "He'd be grateful if you'd go and see him as soon as possible."

CHAPTER EIGHT

AT THE HOME OFFICE

Mr Empton went to see the judge but not very willingly. The appeal had gone off much as he expected, it had been against his better judgment to allow his client to appeal and he had been over-persuaded by the astonishing behaviour of the judge. But, while that was all very funny and made a good story among his friends, he was annoyed with himself for giving way, and he could not help thinking of his client who had not only paid for it but got an extra few months in prison as well. In consequence he was not particularly in a mood to humour the judge, however mad he might be.

"I'm absolutely amazed," was the first thing he said, as Mr Empton came into the room. "I wouldn't have believed it possible. Tell me exactly what happened."

Mr Empton told him.

"I just don't understand it," said the judge when he had

heard the sad story. "It's not your fault, of course. I'm sure you did all you could. It just shows what an unsatisfactory court it is. If civil appeals go to a higher court, so ought criminal appeals. There should be three extra Lord Justices to try them. However, we can't go into that now. We'll have to try to get this to the Lords. You can put in a formal application to the Attorney-General at once and we can formulate the precise grounds later."

"The House of Lords, Judge? The Attorney-General's *fiat*?"

"Certainly. There's no time to be lost."

"I'm extremely sorry, Judge. I have to sign the certificate that it's a proper case to go to the Lords, and I'm very sorry, Judge, but I'm not prepared to do it."

"Not even if I back you up and say that in my view it is a case for the Lords?"

"I'm afraid not, Judge. You backed me up before the Court of Criminal Appeal, but it didn't prevent my making a blithering idiot of myself and my client getting an extra few months."

"But applying for the *fiat* won't add to his sentence."

"I dare say not, Judge, but I'm afraid I'm not prepared to take the responsibility of applying for it. In my view there are no sufficient grounds."

"I suppose you think your client guilty too?"

"I don't care whether he is or he isn't, Judge. I'm responsible for giving the certificate and I'm not prepared to give it."

"Would you have any objection to my going to see your client and suggesting that he should find other counsel who would certify?"

"Judge, really!"

"Would you have any objection?"

"Yes, Judge, I would. I would have every objection. In my view, for one thing, it's not fair to the man or his wife to hold out more hope to them. The case is as dead as mutton. The Attorney would certainly refuse his *fiat*, and, if he went mad and granted it, the House of Lords would dismiss the appeal and make some rude remarks about the Attorney-General for granting a *fiat*. No, Judge, I'm very sorry to have to talk like this, but I've done enough in this case, quite enough—too much in fact."

"I'm only trying to help, you know," said the judge.

"I know, Judge. I'm sure you are. But quite frankly, if you'll forgive my saying so, you're not succeeding. Naturally I can't stop you approaching my client if you think it's a proper thing to do, but in my opinion it'll do no good to anyone. And, if you get anyone to sign a certificate, it'll either be someone who doesn't understand what he's doing, or someone with a reputation I shouldn't care to have."

"I'm afraid I've annoyed you, Empton. I'm sorry," said the judge, "but I feel strongly about this case."

"So do I," said Mr Empton.

When he had gone, the judge decided that Mr Empton was probably right. An appeal can only be made to the House of Lords on a criminal matter if the Attorney-General certifies that an exceptionally important point of law is involved and that it is in the public interest that an appeal should be brought. In a civil matter it is enough to get leave from the Court of Appeal or from the House of Lords itself, if either Court think that the justice of the case makes a further appeal reasonable. No important point of law need be involved. But, if the question is whether you should be hanged or sent to prison for life, only the Attorney-General can send you to the House of Lords, and even he can't do so unless your case involves an exceptionally important point of law. This looks almost as though pure law is considered more important than life and liberty.

Mr Justice Carstairs on further consideration had difficulty in seeing how it could be fairly said that a point of law of exceptional public importance arose. So he had to abandon the idea of a further appeal. But he was not beaten yet. He asked to see the Home Secretary and an interview was arranged between the two of them. The Permanent Secretary and the Chief Legal Adviser to the Home Office also attended. Naturally, before doing so, they had studied all the particulars of the case.

"How nice to see you, Judge," said the Home Secretary. "I don't know if you know Reynolds and Batey."

They all shook hands and sat down.

The Home Secretary started the conversation.

"I do think it good of you, Judge," he said, "to have taken so much trouble over this case. I wish Mr and Mrs Burford could know. I don't think people always realize how much goes on behind the scenes."

Having said that, the Home Secretary paused. He was not sure that his last sentence was a very sensible one. Nothing like this had ever gone on behind the scenes before.

"Thank you," said the judge. "Having ruined two people's lives I don't claim much credit for trying to put the matter right."

"Oh, come, Judge, isn't that putting it a little high? I'm sorry for Mrs Burford, and all wives of criminals, but surely Burford ruined his own life when he broke into that bank?"

"Home Secretary," said the judge, "I don't believe he did."

There was complete silence in the room after this bombshell. They could all believe that the judge had a bee in his bonnet about the way he'd conducted the case, but that he should now really think the man innocent had not been expected.

"But is there some more evidence we haven't heard of?" asked Batey, the legal adviser.

"I know of none," said the judge.

And there was silence again. The Home Secretary broke it.

"Look, Judge," he said, "I'm only a poor layman. I read science, as a matter of fact. What am I doing at the Home Office? Well, that's another story. But I have to be guided by the lawyers in these matters. And I'm bound to tell you that everyone who's touched the case in the legal department, from Batey downwards—though, with his natural modesty I'm sure he'd prefer me to say upwards (and I must say he has some pretty bright legal chaps in his office)—everyone—all of them haven't the least doubt of this man's guilt."

"They weren't at the trial," said the judge.

"But the jury were."

"Their verdict was my fault."

"But you yourself appear, if I may say so, from your summing up and . . ."

"Yes, yes, I know," said the judge. "I certainly formed too hasty a view at the trial. I'm not saying there wasn't a strong case against the man. But that's no reason for a judge making a jury return his verdict."

"But, Judge, I'm sure you're unfair to yourself there. All the members of the Court of Criminal Appeal said the same."

"That's because I may be sitting on appeal on them one of these days. No, I don't really mean that, but I do think the system's a bad one. However, I haven't come to talk about that. The point is that I just have a feeling about this case. And I can't exactly tell you why. And I'll admit this —that if I hadn't been so grossly unfair, the possibility of the man's innocence would never have occurred to me. It was while I was considering my own shortcomings and the result of them—before I'd really considered the question of guilt or innocence—that I suddenly thought: just suppose he is innocent! And then I cast my mind back to the man in the witness box and in the dock. He was a bad witness I grant you. Personally I believe he was keeping something back but I can't rid myself of the feeling that, in spite of the facts against him, he's innocent."

"You think Thompson exists?"

"I do."

"Well, they may have been in it together. Has that occurred to you? There was at least one other person besides Burford involved."

"Of course it's occurred to me, and of course he may be guilty. All I'm telling you is that I, the judge who tried the case, have a doubt about it; I have a feeling that a grave injustice may have been perpetrated and naturally, as I feel in large measure responsible for that injustice, I want it remedied. I want you to recommend a remission of sentence."

"But Judge, how can I? Naturally I pay the greatest respect to anything said by you, and so do Batey and Reynolds and everyone else, but, if the Court of Criminal Appeal didn't think your report sufficient to justify interfering with conviction or sentence, how can I? I should be usurping the prerogative of the Courts."

"Yours is the prerogative of mercy. I cannot now ask for justice. There is no means open to me. I tried to get Empton to go to the Attorney-General for a *fiat,* but he wouldn't. And I suppose he was right. So justice is out. But mercy knows no bounds or rules. You only have to make a recommendation and the thing's done. There are no precedents in these matters. I, the trial judge, tell you a mistake may have been made. That should surely be enough to invoke the prerogative of mercy?"

"But, Judge," said the Home Secretary, "I'm sure you'd be the first to understand that this prerogative of mercy, although, as you say, it is available in every case, is not to be lightly or capriciously used."

"Capriciously!" said the judge. "That's an odd word to use when the trial judge asks for mercy."

"It was a wrong word. I'm sorry, Judge. I apologize. What I meant was that there must be some concrete ground for exercising the prerogative. Some doubt, for example, on the evidence as it stands. Some additional evidence. Even evidence which was available to the accused at the trial and which, therefore, couldn't be called on appeal, can be considered by me. If there were something you could say which would create a doubt, or suggest that there might have been a miscarriage of justice, I could consider that. But there must be something that so far has not been considered, unless the case as it stands itself raises doubts—and I gather you don't suggest it does?"

"*I* have doubts."

"Yes, Judge, but so might counsel for the defence or prosecution, so might the clerk—so might anyone in Court. Please don't think I'm equating you with them, except in this sense that, if a consideration of the whole of the evidence suggests no doubts, the mere fact that someone at the trial —even the judge himself—has a doubt, is not enough. At least, so I am advised and, as I told you at the first, being a mere layman I must take advice."

"You're not bound to act on it."

"Certainly not, if I think it wrong. But I'm afraid in this case I don't."

"You implied that a statement by Mrs Burford might affect your mind?"

The Home Secretary scented danger.

"I don't want to mislead you, Judge. If she could produce something concrete which showed that her husband might be innocent that would, of course, be most carefully considered. But the mere fact that she repeats her husband's story that they were in bed together at the time of the robbery, and that she says there is a Mr Thompson—those mere statements themselves wouldn't help very much. Of course, even they would be considered, but it wouldn't be right to suggest that her mere say-so would be likely to make me change my decision."

"Then you've already decided?"

"There I am, a layman all over," said the Home Secretary with a laugh. "No wonder I need these wise men to guide me. No, of course I've made no decision. I was waiting for your help, and am most grateful to you for having given up so much of your valuable time."

On his way back from the Home Office the judge spoke to Mr Empton on the telephone.

"Empton," he said, "I've just been to the Home Office to see if I could obtain any remission for your client. It might help if I could see his wife. Have you any objection?"

"No objection at all, Judge. It's very good of you. You can see the Queen and the Lord Chancellor and the Archbishop of Canterbury, if you like, as well, as far as I'm concerned," he added, but only after he had replaced the receiver.

CHAPTER NINE

UNUSUAL CONFERENCE

It must be at any rate unusual for a judge who has sentenced a man to seek an interview with his wife. Even in the bad old days when there were corrupt judges it is doubtful if a judge ever had a man hanged in order that he might lay siege to his widow. The bad example of David and Uriah the Hittite has, it is believed, seldom been followed.

But, if Mr Justice Carstairs' motives had been improper and corrupt—and they were certainly not—he could not have chosen a more attractive young woman than Lesley

Burford. By nature she was in the best sense of the word average. She was ordinarily intelligent, had the usual likes and dislikes of a happily married young Englishwoman. Anyone who has all these qualities to an average degree is a pretty satisfactory person. It means that she was very far from perfect. She was, for example, normally truthful, but no more than that, and she would, if, in her view, circumstances demanded it, lie as the average person does lie. There is a substantial minority of persons who tell lies to the Inland Revenue and cheerfully deceive the Customs authorities, but (one hopes) they are a minority. Lesley was not in that minority. She did not consider it was necessary, or desirable, to cheat the Government or public institutions. But she was not in the least prudish about it. She just did not do that sort of thing. But, had it been necessary to lie to save her husband, she would certainly have done so and suffered no remorse in the process, like most average wives.

Anyone seeing her in Court for the first time could naturally not have been aware of her general character, but he could not have failed to be aware of her exceptional physical attractions. Mr Justice Carstairs had noticed them at the trial, but they had made no impact upon him, and accordingly it gave him quite a shock when he was introduced to her by William's solicitor, Mr Sinclair Hunt, in his office.

Mr Hunt was the best type of solicitor. He had one partner and two managing clerks and a practice which they could conveniently manage between them. He was careful but not absurdly cautious and was prepared to take a great deal of trouble himself over his cases. He never went to counsel for advice when he felt he was capable of finding the correct answers to a problem himself. In consequence, at his own risk, he saved his client time and money, for a solicitor who takes competent counsel's opinion is always protected against an action for negligence as a result of the opinion being wrong, whereas a solicitor who gives a wrong opinion himself, without going to counsel, is liable to be sued if his advice is wrong. The action will only be successful if the advice was given negligently, but it is a great temptation to a solicitor to avoid that risk where there is the least uncertainty about the answer to a legal problem, and quite often when there is not.

But Mr Hunt was a person of character and independence and he was able and prepared to form his own conclusions on matters of law. He was confident and inspired confidence in his clients. He had, too, a pleasant and comforting manner, and he combined an air of efficiency with sympathetic understanding.

Before the judge arrived at his office he had had a chat with Lesley.

"What do you think he wants?" she asked.

"I've no idea but it can only be to your advantage."

"It wouldn't be trying to see if I was involved in the robbery too?"

"Good Heavens, no!"

"But he was so prejudiced against William, I'd believe anything of him."

"My dear Mrs Burford, no judge would dream of doing a thing like that. I can guarantee that that is quite impossible. No judge would dream of playing the detective."

"Well, I believe you," said Lesley, "but, if you hadn't said so, I'd have thought him capable of anything."

"I can assure you that, if a judge once did such a thing, he would not remain a judge long. As far as I know, no High Court Judge has ever been removed but he certainly would be for that. No, such a possibility is quite inconceivable. I've heard and said some harsh things about certain judges from time to time, but they'd no more think of going themselves to catch somebody out than of taking a bribe."

"Well, what is it then?"

"Any suggestion I make can only be a guess. So why not wait till he comes and know for certain?"

"It'll help to make the time go. Tell me your guesses."

"Well, for one thing, he may be sorry for you and want to see if he can help."

"*Him* sorry for *me*? Never."

"You can't be so sure. I quite agree he was a pig in court but that wasn't because he disliked you or your husband. It was just because he was convinced your husband was guilty. Such a judge might well be sorry for an attractive young wife. And don't forget, he saw you in Court. I'm not saying it's a likely thing but it is possible. Judges have been known to help the families of men who have been sent to prison, but usually it's done anonymously or at least by correspondence. Having seen you, however, and being a man after all, he may have wanted to have a look at you at closer quarters. It's most unlikely but it is just conceivable."

"How beastly. I won't touch a penny of his money."

"I told you I was only guessing. And anyway you mustn't be too hard on him. I can't pretend it is very meritorious in a would-be benefactor to want some return for his money, if it's only an interview with an attractive girl in the presence of her solicitor, but at least it's human."

"Well, I don't want his help. What else can it be, d'you think, if it's not that?"

"Well, again, I'm only guessing. I suppose it is possible he's got second thoughts about the ten years."

"D'you mean that?"

Lesley became quite excited.

"I'm sorry. I shouldn't ever have suggested it. I'm just using my imagination. Supposing he thought ten years was a bit hot he might want to make a representation to the Home Office, as the Court of Criminal Appeal hasn't done anything about it."

"Then why come and see me?"

"To find out more about him. If I wanted to make a report about a man, I'd certainly think it a good idea to find out as much as I could from his wife."

"If he should make a report would it do any good, d'you think?"

"On the whole I think it would. After all he's the judge who sentenced him."

"How wonderful! How much will they take off?"

"Now you're jumping again. He may be coming for some completely different reason. Ah! there's the buzzer. It should be him. Good luck."

A few minutes later their interview with the judge began.

"I know this is very unusual," he said, "and I need hardly say I spoke to Mr Empton before asking for this interview. I am very grateful to you both for seeing me."

"Not at all, Sir Gerald. It's extremely good of you to come to my office. We would willingly have come to see you."

"Thank you, but I think it's better here. Mr Hunt, do you mind if I ask Mrs Burford some questions?"

Lesley looked quickly at Mr Hunt. "I told you so," her glance said, "he's come to pump me."

"On what subject, Sir Gerald?"

"There's only one subject we're all interested in, as far as I am aware," said the judge.

He had been so wrapped up in his own increasing desire to help the Burfords that it had not even occurred to him that there might be a hostile atmosphere at the meeting.

"Perhaps I should make it plain that my object is to help your client and nothing else."

It was Mr Hunt's turn to look "I told you so" at Lesley.

"I felt sure of that, Sir Gerald, but I do hope you'll understand my natural anxiety to protect my client."

"Of course, Mr Hunt, very natural and very proper."

The judge waited for a couple of moments before going on.

"Mr Hunt," he said finally, "can you advise your client to answer my first question, if she answers it at all, with absolute truthfulness. Her husband's trial is over, his appeal is dismissed. She can do him no harm by telling the truth. She may do him no good by doing so, but there is a chance, however faint, that, if she really tells the truth, I may be able to help. It is only a small chance, but without the truth I can do nothing."

"I understand, Sir Gerald, and the question is?"

"Before you answer it, I should also say this. I had a feeling that your husband was keeping something back in his evidence. I may be quite wrong but I had that feeling."

"You had a feeling," said Lesley, "that he was telling nothing but lies."

"That's perfectly true," said the judge. "And you can now help me to know whether that feeling was right or wrong."

"Sir Gerald," said Mr Hunt, "it occurs to me that the information you may be seeking is what has happened to the money or who were my client's confederates. That is the information that is usually asked of a convicted man in these circumstances. If that is what you are seeking, I can only say at once that my client absolutely denies that he had anything to do with the robbery. The only part of its proceeds he knows anything about is the £25 which was given to him by Thompson."

"No," said the judge. "I was not going to ask about that. May I now ask the question?"

"Very well, Sir Gerald."

"And will you advise Mrs Burford to tell me the complete truth?"

"May I have the question first, Sir Gerald, please?"

"You are suspicious," said the judge, "but I suppose you're quite right. The question is simply this: What is Mr Thompson's full name?"

No one said anything.

"Would you now advise Mrs Burford to tell me the whole truth, Mr Hunt?"

"Certainly," said Mr Hunt. "Mrs Burford, I advise you to answer that question truthfully."

"And the whole truth, Mrs Burford."

"You really think you can help, Sir Gerald?" asked Lesley.

"I can only say I want to do so."

"Well his full name is . . . as a matter of fact he'd changed it."

"Then it wasn't Thompson?"

"That's what he called himself."

"Then that was his name," said the judge. "But what had he changed it from?"

"Wilson."

"Wilson to Thompson. Why?"

"Why does any crook change his name?"

"Did you know he was a crook?"

"Not till William was arrested."

"Why didn't your husband say that his name had once been Wilson?"

"I don't really know. I suppose because it didn't seem to make any difference what his name was if no one believed he existed."

"Do you know what his full name was?"

Lesley hesitated for a moment.

"Forgive my asking," said the judge, "but are you hesitating because you're trying to remember or because you're not sure whether to tell me?"

"There's a third possibility, Sir Gerald," said Lesley, "I might be hesitating because I was making it up."

"Well," said the judge, "do you mind telling me what was the reason?"

"As a matter of fact," said Lesley, "it was the first two. He had one rather odd name and I had to try to remember it, and secondly I wasn't sure whether to tell you anyway."

"Why not?"

"Well, Sir Gerald, you can surely understand that, after the way you conducted the trial, it's difficult for me to follow why you should now be on my side."

"Yes. I understand that," said the judge, "but I'm much more interested in the rather odd name. What were his Christian names?"

"Cedric Mattingly."

"Cedric Mattingly Wilson? How d'you happen to know them?"

"Because he was at school—I mean because he'd known my husband since they were at school."

"The same school?"

"No."

"And it was Cedric Mattingly Wilson, later Thompson, who came to your house and gave your husband those twenty-five notes?"

"Yes."

"And you would know him again?"

"Oh yes, certainly."

"And it must have been he who put the dust in your husband's turn-ups?"

"Yes."

"And at the time of the robbery you were in bed with your husband?"

Lesley hesitated before saying:

"Yes, I was."

"Why did you hesitate?"

"Have I got to give a reason for the way I talk?"

"Of course not. But, if you are wise, you will."

"There was no reason. I simply hesitated. I'm not used to being questioned like this."

"And this man Thompson or Wilson looks rather like your husband?"

"Yes, he does. They're not doubles or anything like that. But my husband said that, when they were at—that, when they were boys together, people would comment on it."

"Have you any idea how we can trace him?"

"The only place I can think of is a race-course."

"He goes there a lot?"

"Yes."

"I see."

The judge got up.

"I think that is all I want from Mrs Burford, but I think I should like to see her husband. If I can arrange that with the Home Office, will you consent?"

Mr Hunt thought for a few moments.

"Subject to my client's consent, yes."

"Do you wish to be present?"

"If my client wants me to be, but not otherwise."

"Well, thank you both for seeing me," said the judge and very soon afterwards he left.

That evening he sent a personal letter to the Home Secretary in which he stated what had taken place at the interview. He added:

"Having questioned Mrs Burford myself I am satisfied that this man Thompson, previously Cedric Mattingly Wilson, exists and I shall be obliged if you will arrange for the police records to be consulted to see if he is known to them. Although I still feel that I do not know the whole truth I am satisfied that further investigation of the matter is plainly necessary. I no longer think that this is a case where the prerogative of mercy should be invoked, but that it is one where serious efforts should be made to find the man Thompson. I shall be glad to hear that the police are prepared to take steps to try to find him. I am told that he is a frequenter of race-courses."

He had a formal reply to this letter, and, a week later, was informed that neither Cedric Mattingly Wilson nor Cedric Mattingly Thompson had a prison record. There were, the letter added, a good number of Thompsons and Wilsons all with different Christian names. Nothing was said about trying to find the man. The judge waited a week and then wrote to ask what steps were being taken to try to trace him. He eventually received a reply that the police had taken such steps as were open to them but without result.

Angrily the judge sought and was given another interview with the Home Secretary.

"But, Judge, really," said the Home Secretary, "let us assume that the man does exist. There are only a limited number of police, you know, and if we employed the whole force on every race-course how would they find him? They could not question every man who answered his description, could they? And you must appreciate, Judge, that much as I should like to help you, crime is so prevalent at the moment that the police force, which is already inadequate, must be used for the prevention of crime and for the detection of unsolved crimes."

"This one is unsolved in my view," said the judge.

"But not in the jury's view, nor in that of the Court of Criminal Appeal, nor, I am afraid, Sir Gerald, in mine."

"But at least something could be done. Have the police been on one race-course?"

"Certainly not, Sir Gerald. They wouldn't know who to look for."

"They could take Mrs Burford with them."

"Even then they could only go to one course at a time and I am afraid that in my view the time and manpower involved is not justified by the facts at present before me."

The Home Secretary was getting a little tired of the persistent judge, and, though he remained polite, he took less pains to be conciliatory.

"I am sorry, Sir Gerald, I am afraid you will have to accept my decision that there is nothing further to be done. Unless, of course, some new evidence is forthcoming. Naturally that would be considered immediately."

The judge left the Home Office and bought a newspaper. Ten minutes later he telephoned Mr Hunt.

"I would like to take your client's wife to the races tomorrow," he said. "Have you any objection?"

CHAPTER TEN

THE VIEWS OF BROTHERS IN LAW

THE judge dined in the hall of his Inn that night. As he came into the room where they have sherry before dinner, he could tell at once that they had been talking about him.

"Go on," he said, "don't stop for me."

Thus encouraged, one of the Benchers enquired:

"Tell us what it's all about, Gerald."

"Certainly, if you're interested," said the judge.

The Benchers of an Inn of Court consist of both judges and barristers, and constitute the cream of the profession. There is probably no profession where there is a greater friendliness between its members. At all legal gatherings judges and barristers mix on terms of easy familiarity and between contemporaries Christian names are the order of the day. So when Benchers are together, views and confidences are exchanged with complete freedom. It was, therefore, an ideal opportunity to tackle the judge, if he was prepared to be tackled. But it is doubtful if anyone would have mentioned the subject if the judge had not pretty well invited it.

"Tell me just for my own amusement what is the wildest rumour about me."

"They say you've threatened to resign unless this fellow what's-his-name is let out at once."

"Well, I can put paid to that. I'm not such an ass."

"What is the truth about the matter? That was an extraordinary report you made to the Court of Criminal Appeal. Criticizing yourself for unfairness. Now, if you'd been criticizing someone else, I could have understood it. But this is a sort of hara-kiri."

"I suppose it is really," said the judge, "and, oddly enough, I didn't behave very differently from some judges I've known."

"You can't have been as bad as Sammy," said another judge.

"I don't know," said Sammy. "I think I'm rather fair. So

long as they don't make me late for bridge in the evening I don't mind what they do. And, after all, I let those two fellows in the car case get away with it, and they were as drunk as lords."

"Why?"

"A fellow feeling, I suppose. There but for the grace of God. . . . No, as a matter of fact I summed up dead against them, but the jury let them go. Always do. Now, if the penalty for driving when drunk was an award of a couple of dozen Bollinger, a jury might convict a few of them. As it is, there's all this ridiculous business of being frightened if a policeman smells your breath after an accident. Every juryman who drives a car sees himself in the dock. A chap has to be senseless before they'll convict and even then they're just as likely to say he was ill as drunk."

"Aren't we getting away from old Gerald's case? I want to hear about it from the horse himself," put in a Bencher.

"Well, what do you want to know?" asked the judge.

"Everything. Tell us from the start."

"Is she a pretty girl?"

"What made you take such a strong line?"

"Don't you really think he's guilty?"

"What did the Home Secretary say?"

"One at a time," said the judge. "Yes, she's a very pretty girl, and I'm taking her to the races tomorrow."

"What!"

"Why?"

"Oh, you mustn't ask him that. It isn't a fair question."

"Yes, you may," said the judge. "It's really a very simple story. In my view, I made a so-and-so of trying the case and, having gone into it a bit further, I have strong doubts as to the justice of the matter. If he'd only got fifteen months or something, I'd probably have left it. But ten years is no laughing matter even with the remission. Now I believe there is a villain in the piece."

"You?"

"Well . . . yes . . . me . . . but only in the second instance. The first villain got away with it but nobody believes he exists. I'm not a 100 per cent sure but I've got enough belief to want something done about it. Nobody will do a thing. So I've just got to."

"But what on earth can you do?"

"Not much, but something. The wife says this fellow Thompson is a racegoer. Well, the least the police could have done is to go to the races with her once or twice and see if he shows up, but they won't even do that. So I'm going to."

"Can I lend a hand?" said a voice. "I'm quite prepared to take an attractive girl to the races once or twice. Might even pay for it myself."

"If you're serious," said the judge, "I'd value your help. It may be quite a job doing it all myself."

"But you aren't really going around to race-meetings with the wife of a convict?"

"Who's going to stop me?" said the judge.

The absolute seriousness of the judge suddenly got home to all of them.

"Really, Gerald," said the Lord Chief Justice. "Why don't you have two or three months' rest? You've been overdoing things and the case is preying on your mind."

"The case is certainly preying on my mind, but I've not been overdoing things. And I'm perfectly sane. Or as sane as I ever am. Are any of us, when you come to think of that? We sit up there pontificating and making rude remarks and sending people to prison and how often do any of us look at ourselves and say 'aren't you overdoing it a bit?' and I don't mean it in the sense you mean, either."

"Don't be angry with us, Gerald."

"I'm not in the least angry, I'm just explaining myself, as I thought you wanted me to. And coming from the general to the particular, suppose this chap is innocent—or, if you like, not so guilty—suppose there is a Thompson and suppose any of you believed that to be the case—will you tell me—any one of you—what on earth I could do, except what I am doing—or nothing? What would you do, Charles?"

"What would I do? To begin with, the problem would not have arisen. I'd have summed up fairly."

"Never mind the summing up. Suppose there were a case

in which you believed in a man's innocence and he'd been sent to prison for ten years and you'd done all you could along the usual lines and nobody would do anything about it, what would you do?"

"Well, if it's a serious question and you want a serious answer, I'd do what you've done up to the moment, report to the C.C.A. and, if that failed, I'd go to the Home Secretary. And if that failed, I'd mind my own business."

"You mean you'd do nothing?"

"I shouldn't feel called on to do any more."

"But wouldn't you want to?"

"I don't know whether I'd want to or not, as the situation has never arisen, but I know what I'd do—and that's nothing. It's not our job to do any more."

"But suppose you felt strongly about it?"

"I feel strongly about a lot of things, capital and corporal punishment, drinking offences and so on, but I don't sit down and write to the papers about them, because it isn't my job. My job is to try cases and that is what I do. Indifferently, if you like."

"Well, supposing you wanted to do something about it, what else could you do except what I propose to do?"

"I've no idea. All I can say is that, having exhausted the usual channels, I shouldn't do anything about it."

"Look," said another, "I'm very fond of animals and I can't bear to see dogs straying in the street. It isn't fair to them or to motorists, but I can't stop every time I see a stray dog, can I?"

"No, of course not," said the judge. "But you can stop once in a while, or at any rate once in a lifetime, and that's just what I'm going to do."

CHAPTER ELEVEN

UNDER STARTER'S ORDERS

THE judge decided to make at least one visit to the races before seeing William. For one thing he had never been to a race-meeting before and he wanted to see the sort of chance there would be of identifying Thompson, if he existed and appeared. He realized, of course, that the criticisms of his brethren and the doubts as to the propriety of his behaviour were probably fully justified, but a High Court Judge is answerable to no one for what he does, provided he does not infringe the law and provided, of course, his conduct is not so outrageous as to prompt Parliament to move the Sovereign for his removal. Such a removal has never taken place within known memory and the judge's contemplated behaviour was, at any rate, so far, not such as to make any reasonable person even dream of such a thing. He was simply going to a race-meeting, or maybe indeed several race-meetings to see if his companion could find and identify a particular man. If he were found, the whole matter would be handed over to the police. His behaviour was eccentric, was unwise for a man in his position, but there was nothing disgraceful about it.

He called for Lesley in his car and it did immediately occur to him, as they drove along to the race-course, that a High Court Judge at the wheel and next to him a most attractive girl, who was the wife of a man sent to prison by him, made an odd pair. So odd indeed that just for one moment he contemplated giving up the whole idea. But two things prevented him, first and foremost his real desire personally to take at least some steps to make up for his unfairness, and secondly his pride, which made it difficult for him to run away from the battle in which he had told his colleagues he was going to engage.

At first they hardly talked. Lesley said it was very good of him to take so much trouble, and he said that that was quite all right. That conversation lasted them for a quarter of an hour. Then the judge decided to break the ice.

"You'll have to tell me all about it, you know, I know nothing about race-courses. I don't even know where to go in."

"I see," said Lesley. "Well, it all depends on which enclosure you want to go into."

"Enclosure?" said the judge, "sounds a bit like sheep."

"It is," said Lesley. "That's what makes a favourite—sheep."

"I'm afraid you're talking in a foreign language, but we needn't go into that now. Just tell me where among the sheep we're most likely to find Mr Thompson."

Lesley did not answer.

"Well, where? Which enclosure or whatever you call it?"

"Sir Gerald," said Lesley. "I haven't told you the whole truth."

"That does not altogether surprise me," said the judge. "The sooner you do, the better for both of us."

"D'you mind if I wait till we get there? Then we can sit down quietly and I'll tell you. It's difficult while you're driving."

"Very well then. I hope you're not going to tell me that there's no Mr Thompson?"

"Oh no! Really there is. I swear it."

"I wonder why you didn't swear it at the trial."

"I can tell you that now if you'd like to know."

"I certainly would."

"Well, I was going to give evidence, and then I had a conference with Mr Empton and he decided not to call me."

"Why on earth not?"

"He said he didn't believe me."

"He said he didn't believe you? That's impossible."

"Well, he refused to call me."

"But that's ridiculous. It's not for him to believe or disbelieve you. That's for the jury. Of course there are cases where it's too risky to call a witness, but this couldn't have been one of them. I should never have thought that Empton would do a thing like that. But perhaps I'm judging him too fast. I'd better see what you've been holding back from me. Perhaps that influenced him."

"No, it wasn't that. He didn't know it as a matter of fact."

"Well, I don't understand it. Now tell me which enclosure we should go to."

"If you don't mind the extra expense, I think we should go to the Members' Enclosure."

"But I'm not a member. Are you?"

"No, that doesn't matter. You can become a member for a day."

"Whoever you are?"

"Well, you've got to look respectable and give your name and address and so forth, and they like to have a look at any ladies you may be bringing in, just in case, you know."

They reached the race-course without any further conversation of importance and were soon lunching together.

"Now tell me," said the judge, "what have you been holding back?"

"This man Thompson first came to see William a day or two before the robbery. They hadn't seen each other for a good many years and William was surprised to see him. I ought to tell you that William, whom I love dearly—more than anything in the world—is a weak character. That's how he got into trouble ten years ago. It wasn't really his fault then at all. He thought he knew everything at twenty-one and with a little capital left him by his mother went into the motor car business. He knew nothing about business at all and, when the much older people he was in business with assured him that what they were doing was perfectly in order, he fell for it. Of course, he shouldn't have but there it is, he did, and he paid terribly for it. When he came out it was difficult to get a decent job, but he really tried and tried hard, and he's started to make a decent career for himself. It meant an awful lot of work, and at the moment we have enough to live on carefully but no more. Well, this man Thompson asked William if he'd like to make a bit on the side. He said it was perfectly legal and, as far as I know, William's part in it was. But, when the police called, William became terrified that there was something crooked about it, so he was rather cagey about it at first. Then, when he knew of the bank robbery, he was worried whether the notes were part of the proceeds, and he became cagier still. You see, he knew the police knew of his record and that his previous conviction was for receiving goods knowing them to have been stolen. The same could have applied to the notes, couldn't it?"

"Only if he knew they were stolen."

"Well, of course, he didn't until after the police came, but that, of course, gave him a guilty conscience even though he'd done nothing wrong."

"You still haven't told me what he did for this man Thompson."

"I'm coming to that. It was nothing really. He just bought winning Tote tickets for him."

"You must explain. All I know is that there is a thing called a Totalisator and people can back horses through it. I suppose they're given a ticket and, if the horse wins, they get their money back and something extra."

"That's right."

"And I suppose when they've won, this ticket is a winning ticket."

"That's it."

"Well, I suppose everyone wants to buy winning tickets. I can see that. What's wrong with it? Suppose I bought a ticket and the horse won, I'd have bought a winning ticket."

"Yes, but you'd have to name your horse before you bought your ticket."

"Yes, of course, and that may be difficult. It depends how much you know on the subject, I suppose. But, if you choose the right horse, then you've got a winning ticket. I can't for the life of me see what's wrong with that. I suppose your husband knew something about horses."

"No, he didn't really, but that isn't the point. The point is that he only bought winning tickets."

"That was very clever of him. If everyone did it the Totalisator couldn't exist."

"He didn't buy them from the Totalisator."

"Do bookmakers sell them then?"

"No, they don't. You can back with them at Tote odds, but that's quite different. No, Thompson wanted William to buy winning tickets after a race was over from some of the people who held them."

"Why on earth? But let me see if I understand. A race being over and a horse called Black Polly having won it and a man called Brown having bought a ticket from the Totalisator with that horse's name on it. . . ."

Lesley interrupted.

"It doesn't have a name on the ticket—just the number."

"Does that make any difference?"

"Not really, but I thought it better for you to understand as much as possible."

"Very well then. Brown in other words having successfully backed Black Polly with the Totalisator, holds a winning ticket."

"That's right."

"And your husband was to buy that ticket? How much for? Do winners sell them at a discount? I can't see why, though. To save waiting in a queue or something?"

"Not at a discount. At a premium."

"At a premium? You mean that, if Brown was owed £5 on his ticket by the Totalisator, your husband was to offer Brown, say five guineas, for his winning ticket?"

"That's exactly it."

"But that's simply giving money away. I can't see anything wrong with it, but I can't see any object in it either, unless a man wanted to go bankrupt as quickly as possible. Or unless you wanted to do Brown a good turn. But then I expect there's some subtle point which I don't follow because of my ignorance of racing."

"William didn't know what it was about at first but Thompson told him when he gave him the £25. It's got nothing to do with racing really."

"I'm completely at sea. It seems a most unprofitable transaction but it seems only to do with racing."

"It's to do with taxation."

"Taxation?"

"Yes. As you know, there are a good many people who evade taxation one way or another."

"Yes, indeed, too many, but I don't see how buying Totalisator tickets at a loss can help them in that."

"Well, you will. Now, if I have a winning Tote Ticket, I can either cash it at the window or I can keep it and get cash or a cheque for it at the London office of the Tote."

"Well?"

"Now, if you have a crooked businessman who has had a lot of cash transactions in the way of his business and made a large profit, he can leave the transactions out of his books or fake them but he's got to do something with the cash. He could keep it under the bed or in a safe deposit but that isn't really satisfactory, because a lot of the things he may want to do with the money can only be paid for by cheque. So he has to bank the money. But, if the tax inspector comes to see his bank account, he's got to account for, say £2,000, paid into the bank. If he just says, as some of them do, I won it at the races, there's only his word for it and the tax inspector and later the Commissioners of Inland Revenue may not accept his bare word. But, if he's had a cheque from a bookmaker or the Totalisator, that is pretty well conclusive proof that he did win the money at the races."

"I'm beginning to see," said the judge. "What you're saying is this. If he were disbelieved about his £2,000 he might have to pay taxes of anything from £1,000 to £1,800 on it according to his income for the year. But if he can prove it was won on a betting transaction he won't have to pay any tax at all. So, if the face value of the winning tickets is say £2,000, it's worth his while to pay something more than that for the tickets, provided the extra is well below the tax he'd have to pay."

"That's it."

"So your Mr Thompson employs agents to buy the tickets at a loss and then resells them at an even bigger loss for the purchaser, but really making a profit for everyone. Brown gets more than he could from the Totalisator, Thompson gets the money he's spent and some more and the purchaser from him saves tens or hundreds or thousands of pounds in tax. The only people who lose are the public at large. Yes, it's a swindle all right. And anyone who took part in it knowingly would be guilty of criminal conspiracy. But you say your husband didn't know till the last time he saw Thompson."

"I'm sure he didn't. But he was a bit worried about it. Like you, he couldn't see the point."

"Why are you telling me all this now?"

"Well, you asked me how we could best find Thompson. And I had to explain to tell you. The only way of knowing whether a person has got a winning ticket in the Tote, except by chance, is to stand by the windows where they pay out after a race. You'll see a queue there. We want to follow anyone who goes up to one of the queue and persuades him to come out of it before he's cashed his ticket. Or Thompson might do it himself, of course."

"Well, that certainly means we don't have to wander all over the race-course."

"The obvious place to go is to the £1 and £5 pay-out windows. You'll understand that these tickets aren't worth buying unless they're for fairly large amounts. Occasionally, of course, there's a huge win for the holder of a ten-shilling or even a four-shilling ticket, but obviously in the ordinary way only the higher price tickets are worth considering."

The races began but neither Lesley nor the judge backed any horses. Lesley did ask the judge whether he wanted to try his luck, but he replied that he knew of more satisfactory ways of losing his money. As soon as winners started to assemble at the pay-out windows they went on duty together. Occasionally men came and spoke to a member of the queue but at no time did anything even faintly suspicious occur. Although the judge was able to sit down during and between the races he had to do a good deal of standing and by the time he had waited for the pay-out from six races he was very tired and that was the only result of his first day's racing.

CHAPTER TWELVE

THEY'RE OFF

ALTHOUGH his first day's efforts were fruitless the judge had to admit to himself that he did not find Lesley's company at all unpleasant. He, in turn, set out to be as pleasant as he could be to her. He realized her great unhappiness and the strain of having a husband in prison, which he was, in a way, making worse. If nothing can be done to remedy a situation, an individual must accept it for better or worse. People vary as to how they accept an inevitable situation but the average person somehow adjusts himself or herself to it. But, as long as there is a chance that it may be remedied, hope creates a constant and telling strain on the person concerned and, if in the end, the hope, however slender, has to be finally abandoned, the last state is certainly worse than the first.

Recognizing this, the judge made himself as amiable as he could to Lesley and actually took her out to dinner to make up for the disappointment of the first day's hunt. As the evening wore on, the natural awkwardness between the two began to vanish, and after a third glass of wine Lesley said:

"You know, you're not at all stuffy like one would expect a judge to be."

"We are a bit different," he said, "when we don't have our wigs and gowns on. At least I hope so. Personally I think the uniform's an advantage. It gives us an appearance of complete impartiality. Though, now I come to think of it, I don't imagine that appearance lasted long for you. You must have thought I had a personal spite against your husband."

"Well, you've shown me how wrong I was," said Lesley. "And, whatever happens, William will be thrilled to know that something is being done and that you're the person who's doing it."

"Well, I'm glad," said the judge. "I've been able to convince you of my good intentions. I wish you could convince me that you'd told me everything."

Lesley sipped her burgundy but said nothing.

"There was one thing I ought to tell you—but not yet, please. It might make you lose your belief in our case—and that I just couldn't bear. Will you accept my word that really and truly William is innocent and let me tell you this thing in my own time?"

Lesley then proceeded to take full advantage of the situation, which was that she had large eyes and an appealing mouth and that the judge had also had three glasses of burgundy as well as two glasses of sherry before dinner.

"I don't know," he said, "if you're a very wicked young woman. I certainly hope not. But, when you look at anyone like that, it's difficult to resist you. I imagine you can do anything with your husband."

"I don't have to," said Lesley. "He always does what I want."

"That's what I meant," said the judge. "I think," he added, "we should go and see him soon."

"We?" she said. "Can I come too?"

"I'm sure they'll let you in the circumstances. That's about the only thing they will do—let me get instructions from my client."

At that stage in the evening the judge rather enjoyed referring to a man who had been sent to prison as the client of the judge who had sent him there.

"And I'm sure your presence will be necessary for my purposes."

"Oh—thank you," said Lesley. "I can't tell you what it'll mean to me—to see him so soon. It's wonderful of you. Don't take any notice. I'm going to cry a bit. No, I won't. There. I don't want to disgrace you."

They talked about several subjects, nothing to do with the case—music, pictures, books and swimming. Lesley was an expert swimmer.

"You must look very attractive in the process," said the judge, and suddenly realized that, as he looked at Lesley, he was putting her into a bathing dress, a red one with—but then he stopped himself. This really won't do. He quickly referred to the case again.

"What we must try to do," he said, "if we don't have any luck in tracing Thompson ourselves is to try to find some of the people to whom he has sold tickets and see if they can be persuaded to give some information about him. Your husband might be able to help us there. D'you think he can?"

"He might," said Lesley. "He never mentioned any names to me, but it's possible he knew some."

"What I'm proposing to do," said the judge, "is to devote the whole of the long vacation, which starts next week, to your affairs."

"You're awfully kind."

"I suggest you don't get a job until the next legal term. There's nothing I can really do without your help, as you're the only person apart from your husband who knows what the fellow looks like. First though, tell me once again that he does exist."

"He does exist," said Lesley with every appearance of absolute sincerity.

On the following Saturday they went to the next race-meeting. They followed the same routine, except that on this occasion the judge risked ten shillings on a horse called Lord Justice. It lost. He had just seen the end of the race when a voice he knew called to him. He turned round to see a barrister whom he knew quite well but was not at all pleased to see in the circumstances.

"How are you, judge? Didn't know you patronised this sort of entertainment. May I introduce my wife? Sir Gerald Carstairs."

There was nothing for it, and the judge had to introduce Lesley. In mentioning her surname he can be excused for using a trick which most judges employ when they don't in fact know the name of someone appearing before them. They make some odd noise which might be anything. In this case what the judge said was something like this:

"How d'you do? May I introduce Mrs Borreforth."

Borreforth is the nearest to the sound which letters can give, but, as the word was half-swallowed anyway, what was certain was that it was quite unrecognizable.

"Haven't I seen your picture in the paper recently?" said the barrister's wife, who had been famous all her life for quite unwittingly making tactless remarks.

The judge hastily intervened.

"Now where did we meet last, Mrs Canterbury? It was at the garden party, wasn't it?"

After a few minutes conversation they managed to disengage themselves.

"I'm terribly sorry about that," said Lesley. "It must be awkward for you going around with the wife of a bank robber."

"Never mind," said the judge, and was about to add something when they both saw a doubtful looking character walk up to the £5 pay-out window and engage one of the three people waiting for their winnings in a whispered conversation. The winner remained in the queue but the other man handed him something and then spoke to the next man who waved him aside. The third winner just ignored him. As soon as he had left the queue, the judge and Lesley went up to the doubtful character.

"Excuse me," said the judge, "but do you buy winning Tote tickets?"

The man scratched his head.

"You barmy?" he said and walked away. The judge swiftly realized that, if you want to retain the dignity of being on the High Court Bench, you can't talk to seedy looking individuals on race-courses.

Altogether they went to six race-meetings and drew a blank at each. The judge soon found it extremely tedious. The sport itself interested him not in the least, the standing about he found most tiring, he did not care to bet and, whenever he did, he lost, and generally he was quite unable to understand why such a large number of the population enjoyed a day at the races. It was expensive, it was boring, it was tiring and for the most part it put money into the pockets of some of the most undesirable looking people he had seen outside the dock. Bookmakers on a race-course, he thought, may be and I hope are good husbands and fathers, good rate-payers, good tax-payers and generally good citizens, but for a lot of loud-mouthed, dangerous or shifty-looking thugs they take a lot of beating.

It was while they were coming back from the last of these meetings that Lesley suddenly remembered that William had mentioned a name to her. It was an odd name and she couldn't think why she'd forgotten it, but, she said, she distinctly remembered her husband saying that one of Mr Thompson's customers was a Mr Hanamil Routang.

"There can only be one of those in the telephone book," said the judge. "I'll look him up."

And there they found Routang, Hanamil, 8 Cloister House, W.1. Cloister House was an expensive block of flats in the West End. They decided that a call must be paid on Mr Routang. But who was to pay it, the judge or Lesley, or both together?

CHAPTER THIRTEEN

MR ROUTANG AT HOME

HANAMIL ROUTANG was a mid-European with some Scottish, Irish and English blood in him and not inappropriately he was naturalized British. He looked a little like a gorilla but was far more friendly on first acquaintance. He was obviously destined either for a long entry in *Who's Who*, including a statement of his many benefactions to national art galleries, or for an imposing place in the Rogues' gallery at Scotland Yard, or possibly for both, the former presumably preceding the latter. He was at the moment at the one-yacht-three-mistresses stage but he had hopes of much better things, and he had several ladies in mind for whom he had take-over bids ready when he could afford it.

His purpose was to remain in England until he considered that the various individuals and enterprises he was in the process of milking were running dry. The extent of his success can be gauged by the fact that he actually paid large sums in income tax and surtax, though it should hardly be necessary to add that he evaded paying far larger sums. He looked forward to the time when it would not be necessary for him to reside in England within the meaning of the Tax Acts, but at the moment his activities were so continuous and concentrated that this was out of the question. It will therefore be appreciated that any means, lawful or otherwise, of avoiding payment of tax appealed strongly to Mr Routang, subject only to the proviso that there was no real chance of his being found out. He was prepared to risk imprisonment for a large-scale conspiracy to defraud. That was just a normal commercial risk. But to go to prison for defrauding the Revenue was a horrible thought which he would not even contemplate.

The problem before the judge and Lesley was not a simple one. It was unlikely that Mr Routang would give them any useful information unless he could see an advantage from giving it. Eventually they decided that the best course would be for Lesley to pay him an experimental call. It did not take the judge long to come to the conclusion that it would be impossible for him to make the call himself, and so, while Lesley was calling on him, he waited anxiously and rather impatiently in a near-by tea-shop.

Lesley had a piece of luck at the beginning, because Mr Routang happened to see her as she came to the front door, and, though he would not usually see strangers who came without an introduction, he was nearly always ready to interview attractive women, whatever their business. Even a travelling saleswoman would have a chance of a personal meeting with the great man if she were good-looking enough. So, within a few minutes of her ringing the bell, Lesley had been invited to come in.

"Sit down there, my dear young lady," said Mr Routang. "I know we can't have met before or I should have remembered it. What a charming hat, if I may say so. Cigarette?"

"No, thank you," said Lesley. "It's very good of you to see me."

"It is a privilege. You seem to like that picture?"

Lesley had turned her eyes to avoid the intensity of Mr Routang's gaze and they happened to be opposite an Impressionist picture, though she was not really looking at it.

"Pissarro," he said, "but I won't tell you what I paid for it."

"It's lovely," said Lesley.

"It will be worth twice as much in two years," he said.

"You're fond of pictures?" she asked.

"I'm fond of lots of things," he said. "The great day will be when I'm in a position to get them all."

"Won't that be terribly dull? If you've got everything, there's nothing to look forward to."

"Ah, my dear young lady, I only said when I'm in a position to get them all. There will always be something I want. How nice when I know I shall be able to get it. Window shopping I have never cared for. Would it be embarrassing to say that I was doing some at the moment?"

Lesley pretended not to understand.

"Window shopping?" she said.

"And I don't even know the name of the shop," he said.

A moment later he added:

"And by coincidence I don't even know your name."

"Burford—*Mrs* Burford."

"Ah—you have a husband. All the most charming women have husbands. But perhaps he is a long way away."

"He is as a matter of fact."

"Then," said Mr Routang, "let us drink to his return but not too soon."

He got up and went to a cabinet.

"I have sherry at this time in the morning, but I know some people prefer champagne. Which can I offer you?"

Lesley accepted a glass of sherry.

"This is going to be a good day," said Mr Routang. "It has started so well."

"I expect you wonder why I'm here."

"Please don't tell me for a long time," said Mr Routang. "I shall be no party to accelerating your departure."

They sipped their sherry.

"How charmingly you drink, if I may say so," said Mr Routang. "So few people notice these things. They look at a woman's legs and her face and how she walks, even perhaps how she eats. But seldom how she drinks. There is a queer art in drinking. Personally, I love to watch people and animals drink. Horses, dogs, cats, sportsmen, manual workers—they all have their individual methods. But how few women know how to drink. If I might make only one small criticism, if I dare. It will not offend you?"

"Of course not," said Lesley.

"The eyes," said Mr Routang, "should peer a little more over the glass. Only a little. Don't make it too obvious. Ah! that's perfect. You must forgive me. That's what I am—a perfectionist. I have, of course, never seen you eat. Do you perhaps happen to be free for lunch today?"

"I'm afraid not," said Lesley and smiled slightly. She could not help thinking for a moment of the picture of the judge in the tea-shop, and wondering what he would do and feel, if she left him there and went out with Mr Routang. But she had no intention of annoying the judge. He was much too important to her. But Mr Routang was important too. She was even pleased at the blatant advances he was making. It certainly would not make her task more difficult.

"Perhaps some other day, or dinner perhaps?"

"You are very kind," said Lesley, "but I ought to tell you what I've come for."

"Ah! now you disappoint me. With women business is always first. The weaker sex indeed! Those large seductive eyes conceal a mind which is intent on charter-parties or bills of lading instead of love."

"What is a charter-party?" said Lesley.

"You don't know? Good. Excellent. And a bill of lading, that means nothing to you?"

"Nothing at all."

"Better and better. And love—that has some meaning?"

"Quite a lot," said Lesley.

"Some more sherry?" suggested Mr Routang.

"Thank you," said Lesley. "Tell me if I've improved," she added as she sipped her second glass.

This is too easy, thought Mr Routang. I wonder what she does want. She's not a detective, I suppose. Well, there's nothing she'll be able to get hold of at the moment. If she is from the police, I must say they've got good taste.

"Much improved," said Mr Routang. "I didn't think you could do better, but you must be a perfectionist, too. Well, I suppose," he added regretfully, "putting off the evil moment won't avert it altogether. Let's get it over and then we can chat."

"I've got a friend who might be able to sell you something."

"Sardines?" queried Mr Routang.

"No."

"Silk stockings?"

"No."

"Caviar perhaps?"

"No."

"I give in. Not Indian hemp by any chance? I'm overstocked already."

"Tote tickets."

"Chicken feed," said Mr Routang. "How much?"

"How much could you do with?"

"I'm not really interested. How much have you got?"

"Could you tell me anyone who might take them?"

"You tell me how much you've got."

"I haven't actually got any at the moment, but I can get them. That's why I want to know how much you want."

"I never buy blind. I like to see what I'm getting."

"But if you tell me what you want, you wouldn't be buying blind. I'd show you the ticket, the race-course and the result of the race."

"How could I know who'd printed the ticket?"

"Then you could come with me to the Tote office and pay me when you'd got your cheque."

"But how much can you do? A couple of thousand?"

"Two *thousand*?" replied Lesley.

"I told you I wasn't interested in chicken feed," said Mr Routang. "Suppose we compromise and have dinner tomorrow night."

"All right," said Lesley, "I'd love it. Where shall we meet?"

"I'll send my car for you. Where shall he call?"

Lesley gave him her address.

"But don't bring any bills of lading or charter-parties with you," said Mr Routang. "We shan't have any time for them."

CHAPTER FOURTEEN

A CAPTURE

LESLEY described her interview to the judge in full, "But what is the object of dining with him? That sort of man will tell you nothing."

"I'm not so sure," said Lesley. "He's already pretty well admitted that he buys these tickets. I could threaten to report him to the Revenue if he didn't tell me."

"That's blackmail," said the judge.

"What's the punishment?" asked Lesley.

"Well," said the judge, "it's blackmail all right but it isn't actually an offence."

"Well, that's all right," said Lesley.

"It isn't all right at all. I can't be a party to that sort of thing."

"You won't be. I will do it all myself."

"No," said the judge. "I'm prepared to go on helping you but not if you use methods like those."

"Well, there's no harm in my dining with him," said Lesley.

"I hope not," said the judge, "but if it'll do no good, what's the point? I can't think your husband would be terribly pleased to know of it."

"He'd know it was only to help him—just like my going out with you."

"I'm not sure that I really care for the comparison," said the judge, "but, leaving that aside, I'm very much afraid that unless we get some information soon, I shall have to let things take their course. We've been trailing round race-meetings without finding out anything. I'll go to see your husband, as I promised, but unless we get something to go on soon, I'm afraid we'll have to abandon it as hopeless."

Lesley kept her appointment with Mr Routang. She was as friendly as she could be during dinner, and towards the end of the evening she tried to persuade him to give her at least one name to help them in their search.

"Well," said Mr Routang, "I know one man I can put you on to."

"Oh—please," said Lesley.

"I don't actually know his name—but I can tell you pretty certainly how to find him."

"That would be wonderful."

"What should I get in return for the information?"

"I don't buy blind either," said Lesley.

"Fair enough," said Mr Routang, "you can pay me on receipt of the goods."

"All right," said Lesley. "How do we find him?"

"It's quite simple really," said Mr Routang. "As you may imagine, he spends a good deal of time on race-courses. If you go round race-meetings you're bound to catch up with him sooner or later. Well, there you are. You've got the goods. Pay on delivery."

"I've got a headache," said Lesley, and wondered what on earth she could tell the judge.

Although Mr Routang did not receive any reward for his

pains, he did not count the episode as a waste of time. He considered that he was still attending the night-school of experience. As in commercial dealings, so with women, one must be able to tell at the outset whether an investment is likely to be profitable.

Lesley was glad to find the judge in a less despondent frame of mind. He had worried throughout the night, first that he'd undertaken the adventure at all, and then that, although he had been angry with the Home Office for doing nothing, so far he had only been successful in proving how right they were, and in making a fool of himself into the bargain. The laconic "You barmy?" still rankled a little. So he had decided that he would really try to get some information out of William to set him on the right track and, as there was a race-course on the way to the prison, he thought they might as well have one more attempt there.

While the judge was waiting for a few minutes by himself after the end of the second race, he noticed a man who might have answered to Lesley's description of Mr Thompson behaving in a rather peculiar manner and standing near the Tote pay-out window. The judge kept him under observation. Suddenly the man appeared to realize that he was being looked at. He stared at the judge for a moment and then made off hastily. As soon as Lesley rejoined the judge, they tried to follow in the direction he appeared to have taken but they could not at first see him. They had gone towards the car park when suddenly they noticed a small car with a solitary male driver drawing out of the line of cars.

"Come on, quick," said the judge. "It might be a wild goose chase but we'll follow him."

They reached their car and were able to get started before the man had got out of sight. They were soon in pursuit. They both realized that the probability was that there was nothing in it, but it was something to have a definite object in view. It was, too, undoubtedly odd that a racegoer should leave the course so early and apparently only after he realized he was being looked at. Fortunately the judge's car was faster than the man's, and though they lost him from time to time, they were able to get his number. They were unable to see the man's face and, as he had crammed his hat over his head, it was difficult for Lesley to form any impression of his identity.

"He's got to stop some time," said the judge, "and then you'll be able to see him properly."

But it did not prove to be as easy as that. After some hours they lost him and were beginning to despair of finding him again when to their delight they came across his car outside a hotel in a small town. They stopped and went in, but could not find him in any of the public rooms.

"Perhaps he's taken a room for the night," suggested Lesley.

They enquired at the reception desk and were informed that a Mr Brown with the car number they had been following had taken room No. 1.

"What do we do now?" said Lesley.

"You wait here," said the judge.

He went to room No. 1 and knocked.

"Who's there?" said a voice.

"Might I have a word with you?" asked the judge.

"Who are you?" said the voice.

"I'm a stranger," said the judge, "but I wonder if you could move your car for me?"

"I'm sorry," said the man, "I'm very tired and I've gone to bed. The car's not locked. Would you mind moving it? So sorry."

The judge very gently tried the door. It was locked.

He went back to Lesley.

"Wait here," he said, "I'm going to get the police."

"Is it him?" said Lesley excitedly.

"I've no idea," said the judge, "but I'm going to explain the situation to the police and ask them to send a man over."

The judge went to the local police station and was back again within ten minutes with a constable.

"You will be very apologetic, won't you, officer," said the judge, "as there's probably nothing in it at all."

"Of course, sir," said the policeman.

The two men went to the door with Lesley a few yards behind them.

The policeman knocked.

"Who's there?" The voice was almost a whisper.

"It's a police officer."

"What do you want?"

"Just a word with you, sir."

"Wait a moment, please. I'm not dressed."

"Don't bother to get up, sir," said the policeman, "I'll only keep you a moment."

They heard noises in the room as though he were dressing. Suddenly they heard a window open. The policeman immediately tried the door. It was still locked.

"Open the door," said the policeman in a much louder voice.

There was a noise at the window and then silence.

"Quick," said the policeman. "He's got out of the window."

They rushed round to the back and saw a figure making hurriedly for a near-by wood in the gathering darkness.

"You leave this to me, sir," said the policeman. "He may be dangerous." He started to run.

Lesley and the judge followed. By the time they reached the wood the judge was beaten and had to sit down. Lesley stayed with him. They could hear the policeman making his way through the wood.

"Stop!" they heard him shout.

A few minutes later a figure dashed past them, tripped and fell. The judge immediately sat on him, while Lesley called for the policeman. Fortunately for the judge the man must have been winded and did not struggle, and the policeman was on the scene before any more force was necessary.

"Now, what's the game?" said the policeman. "Who are you, anyway?"

He turned the man over and shone the torch in his face.

Lesley gasped.

"Is it Thompson?" asked the judge excitedly.

For answer Lesley threw herself into the man's arms weeping.

"Bill darling," she said, "I didn't know. Please, officer, don't take him back at once."

"Sorry, madam," said the policeman. "We've only just had news of the escape. Come along now, Burford. No nonsense now."

CHAPTER FIFTEEN

UNUSUAL INTERVIEW

THE judge was given the opportunity of a chat with William at the police station, but William was not at first very communicative. He was very indignant with the judge.

"Not content with giving me ten years for a crime I didn't commit, you have to go and catch me when I escape."

"It was quite unintentional," said the judge. "As a matter of fact we thought you might be Thompson."

"What d'you want with him?"

"We're trying to help you as a matter of fact. Your wife thought that the most likely place to find him would be on a race-course."

"Just what I went for," said William. "But why on earth do you want to help?"

"Because I do," said the judge. "Because I have some doubts of your guilt."

"It's a bit late for that," said William, "but why don't you tell them that at the Home Office? They'd listen to you surely."

"No," said the judge, "they won't. I've tried, tried hard. And so the only thing left was to try to find the man."

"You didn't believe he existed."

"No, I didn't."

"Do you now?"

"Your wife assures me that he does."

"So do I. But you didn't believe me before. Why now?"

"I can't tell you," said the judge. "To be quite candid, I'm not really sure of anything. I think you and your wife are keeping something from me, but, in spite of that, I have a feeling that the man does exist."

"Well, he does, that's certain. What d'you say we're concealing from you?"

"I don't know but your wife told me as much. And there's another thing. If this man exists, you were at school with him, weren't you?"

"No," said William, "I was not."

"Both you and your wife made the same mistake, said that you were and then corrected it."

"I can't help that," said William. "We were not at school together."

There was silence for a moment and then William added:

"You will go on helping won't you? Can you imagine what it's like being in prison for something you haven't done?"

"I can imagine few things more dreadful," said the judge. "It's because I think that's possible in your case that I've been trying to help."

"For God's sake go on," said William.

"Well, don't try to escape again," said the judge. "What do you think you can do by it?"

"I thought I might have spotted the man, that's why I was on the race-course. Then I saw you looking at me and I suddenly recognized who you were. I thought you'd recognized me."

"Now is there any other information you can give me which can help? Your wife has told me of this fellow Routang but she's got nothing out of him. D'you know of anyone else who might have dealings with Thompson?"

"According to him," said William, "it's amazing the number of people who do. I don't know of course if he's telling the truth and he is the sort of chap who's pretty good at shooting a line, but he says he's got doctors, lawyers and even a judge on his list."

"Nonsense," said the judge. "For one thing it's only of use to people who have cash transactions. And we don't."

"Of course when he says a judge he might mean a justice of the peace. They're judges really too."

"I shouldn't take much notice of what a man like that says anyway. But is there no other name you can give us or any place we might come across him? I confess I'm getting a little tired of frequenting race-courses, and the only time anything happened was today."

"Don't I know it?" said William. "But I do really want to thank you for all you're doing, sir. It is most kind."

"You'd better keep your thanks until I've some tangible results," said the judge. "But don't escape again or we might catch you. And that would be such a disappointment for all of us."

After a little further discussion the judge left William, and Lesley was allowed half an hour with him. Then William was put in a cell to await removal back to prison, while the judge and Lesley drove back to London, mostly in silence. Lesley was thinking of William, and the judge was wondering whether he should tell Lesley that he was thinking of writing a letter to her. He had not made up his mind by the time he had reached her home. So the problem was solved for him and, as soon as he got home, he started to write.

CHAPTER SIXTEEN

TO WRITE OR NOT TO WRITE

"Dear Mrs Burford" (he wrote):

"This is a difficult letter for me to write but after careful consideration I see no alternative. When I first undertook to help you to try to find some evidence that your husband was not guilty of the crime of which he was convicted, I must confess that I had little idea of what steps could usefully be taken in that direction. I have now spent some considerable time in taking the only steps which might be of help, with absolutely no result whatever. Nor, unfortunately, can I see what further steps can be taken. You would not, I know, expect me to attend every race-meeting in England (and Scotland, too, for that matter, for I have learned that racing takes place even there) but, even if I were to agree to do so, it might still be of no avail because I have also learned that on some days as many as five race-meetings may take place in different parts of the country. Although I understand that some jockeys hire aeroplanes to take them from one meeting to another on the same day, I should not feel justified in incurring this heavy expense, and, even if I were prepared to do so, it would still mean that on some days there would be meetings which we could not attend. If there were other steps by which I could usefully (and properly) help you I should be prepared to consider taking them, but, unless you are able to suggest any such steps to me, I am afraid that there is nothing further that I can do.

I am sorry to have to write like this, particularly just after the recent shock you must have had in seeing your husband recaptured, but I feel that it is better to say so now than to go on dragging out the matter interminably.

If at any time you receive information which you think may be helpful to your husband's cause I shall be pleased to consider it.

Yours sincerely,

Gerald Carstairs."

Having written the letter he went to bed, but he had a bad night worrying about the matter. He had quite a vivid imagination and he pictured Lesley seeing the post and the letter in a handwriting she did not know. With feminine intuition she might guess who it was from and even what was in it. He could see her opening the letter with apprehension and reading it with something like despair. It must have seemed like a miracle to her to find that the judge who had presided at her husband's trial was on her side and wanted to help. As long as he was doing so, she could feel some hope that the nightmare would come to an end. But if he stopped what was there left? You can't expect two miracles.

And then he looked at the other side of the picture. Suppose her husband really was guilty and there were no Mr Thompson, then she was just playing with him, either in the hope that something might turn up, which, coupled with the backing of a judge, would lead to her husband's wrongful release, or just out of revenge or for amusement. After all, everyone but he had no doubt about the matter. The jury clearly had no doubts. Empton thought their verdict was right and that an appeal was ridiculous. The Court of Criminal Appeal had no doubt when they dismissed the appeal. The Home Secretary and his advisers made their view of the matter abundantly clear. Why on earth should he alone be right? Moreover, even he felt that the Burfords were concealing something. Why shouldn't that fact be the simple one that Mr Thompson did not exist and that Burford was as guilty as everyone else felt. He was a fool even to have contemplated helping the couple.

And then he thought of the few famous miscarriages of justice which had taken place in this country, one even quite recently, when a man had actually been wrongly identified by a policeman. It was eventually proved conclusively that the convicted man was not guilty, but the jury had returned their verdict against him in a quarter of an hour. They had laughed at his defence of an alibi. Yet that man was proved to have been innocent of that particular crime. Such occurences were fortunately very rare but they did happen. Was this one of them? If it was, how appalling for the young couple. No amount of compensation could put matters right for them. If Mrs Burford remained faithful to her husband till he was released in seven years' time she would be wasting all those years of her life when she might be having children. If she committed adultery and Burford divorced her, a happy home would have been broken up.

A judge should be able to see both points of view, but he should also be able to make up his mind between them. This judge was quite unable to do so. He lay in bed alternately satisfying himself of William's guilt and convincing himself of his innocence, assuring himself that there was nothing more he could do and then that it was not fair to take on a job like this and drop it in the middle.

In the middle? Was it in the middle? Wasn't it the end? Hadn't he done all he could do? There was certainly no end to these conflicting thoughts. He got up and took two sleeping tablets.

CHAPTER SEVENTEEN

ON HOLIDAY

When he awoke, he got up at once and read the letter he had written, thought about it and tore it up. Then he decided to say it on the telephone instead. He picked up the telephone and then put it down again because he couldn't think how to begin. He was still undecided when Lesley telephoned.

"I've had an idea," she said. "Why shouldn't I advertise for someone who could give information of Thompson's whereabouts?"

"There's no reason why you shouldn't," said the judge, "but you must be prepared to draw another blank."

"Of course," said Lesley, "but I thought it might be worth trying."

Four days later she informed the judge that a man had answered the advertisement.

"He's a pretty unsavoury specimen," she said, "but he claims to know Thompson and says he's sure he can find him for me."

"Well, that's good," said the judge. "There's no harm in following up any of his suggestions. But the way you speak makes me think there's a snag in it. Is there?"

"Not really," said Lesley. "It's just this, that. . . . Well, I find this awfully embarrassing—you've been so terribly kind and I must have cost you quite a lot of money so far and. . . ."

"How much does this man want?" said the judge.

"Twenty-five pounds, to begin with," said Lesley.

"What do you get for the twenty-five pounds? What does 'to begin with' mean?"

"Twenty-five pounds is for the first try. If it comes off, that'll be that. If it doesn't, he'll want more."

"Well, you say the man's unsavoury; if he's a crook he could run up a whole lot of twenty-five pounds."

"I know," said Lesley. "One's pretty well in his hands, but I thought. . ."

"All right," said the judge. "I'll stand for the first lot."

"You are good," said Lesley.

"Probably only foolish," said the judge.

But in fact he was quite pleased to be able to do this. It solved his problem for the moment. He could easily afford the money, and providing it was a useful compromise between giving the whole thing up and doing futile things himself. So for a day or two he ceased to worry so much about the matter. After all, he was doing all he had been asked to do. For peace of mind it was cheap at the price.

One evening a few days later he received a very odd call from Lesley. He could recognise her voice but she was speaking very softly and in an extremely strange manner, so strange indeed that he wondered if she could have been drunk. She had always treated him up to that moment as he would have expected. She either called him "Sir Gerald" or nothing at all and, though they had become on terms of easy familiarity, she had never taken advantage of that fact. Accordingly he was astonished to hear her say when he answered the telephone:

"Is that you, Gerald?"

He felt pretty certain who it was but none the less he asked:

"Who is it?"

"Lesley, of course," she answered. "Look, Gerald, do come down and join us at the Bear at Esher for dinner."

"I beg your pardon?" he said.

"It's just on the spur of the moment, but I do want you to come. I *want you to come terribly*. The party will be nothing if you don't."

It was quite plain that she was putting something into her words which for some reason she was unable or unwilling to say. For once the judge made a swift decision.

"All right," he said, "I'll come at once. I should love it."

"How sweet of you," she said. "Do be quick or we shall have drunk all the champagne."

So the judge got out his car and was soon on the way to Esher. He was there within three-quarters of an hour. He found Lesley in front of the hotel to meet him. He parked the car and got out.

"What is it?" he said.

"I'm terribly sorry," she said, "it's a washout, but I couldn't think of anything else to do."

"For heaven's sake explain yourself," he said.

"He was here," she said. "Only left twenty minutes ago. I just didn't know what to do."

"Who was here and what did that extraordinary call mean?"

"It was like this. My man was right and I found Thompson at Sandown. I couldn't let him see me or he'd have bolted. I came by coach and couldn't have followed him. After the races he came here. I could just get in and out of the 'phone box without his seeing me, but he could hear every word I said. I don't mean that he was necessarily listening, but he could have heard if he wanted to. If he'd heard anyone ringing the police he'd have been off and away at once. And if he'd heard me speaking to you properly, as I should have done, calling you Sir Gerald and asking you to come quickly, he might have smelled a rat. So I thought you'd understand if I spoke to you as I did. I do hope you didn't mind."

"No, of course, I didn't mind that," said the judge, "but the net result is that I might just as well have stayed at home."

"I'm afraid so," said Lesley, "but I couldn't tell, could I? And it was such a chance."

"Well, next time get on to the police at once," said the judge.

"Well, of course," said Lesley, "I would have this time, but you do see how I was placed."

"I suppose so," said the judge. "And, now, I imagine your doubtful friend will want another twenty-five pounds."

"I'm afraid he will."

"And, as a matter of fact, you ought to have someone else with you and a car on these occasions. You'd better get hold of a private detective. You really did see this man Thompson today—really and truly?"

"Really and truly," said Lesley.

"No doubt of any kind? No possibility of mistake?"

"None whatever."

"All right. I'll pay for the detective. I think perhaps I'd better arrange for one myself. I'll let you know who it is."

So Mr Maclachlan of Hounds Ltd., private enquiry agents, had the privilege of having a High Court Judge sitting in his office. After having appeared himself on innumerable occasions in the witness box before High Court Judges it was a novel and pleasant experience. Mr Maclachlan had in the past been told by different judges that they believed every word he said and also that they believed nothing that he said; that he was an admirable witness "as different from the normal enquiry agent as it would be possible to imagine", and that his evidence was "almost a classic example of evidence which had long been recognized by the Courts as being of the most unsatisfactory nature." Judges had said to him "So you expect me to believe that, do you?" and "Thank you very much, Mr Maclachlan."

Hounds Ltd., which was in effect Mr Maclachlan's other name, had a considerable practice and a reputation for getting things done. Praise and blame came alike to Mr Maclachlan. So long as it was one thing or the other, he felt that his firm had pulled its weight. What he would have considered a danger sign would have been if his evidence or that of his employees had simply been ignored. As long as it was described as "obviously truthful" or stigmatized as "near-perjury" he was perfectly satisfied.

The judge explained to Mr Maclachlan what he required. He was to supply an agent to go with Mrs Burford and act under her instructions at any time of the day or night in order to ascertain the existence of a Mr Thompson, formerly Cedric Mattingly Wilson. As soon as he could be definitely identified the agent was to communicate with the police. The judge would finance the transaction up to an extent of a sum not to exceed £100, including expenses.

"That raises a point, my Lord," said Mr Maclachlan, who, not being sure how to address a High Court Judge out of Court, was taking no chances. "Suppose my employee was in the middle of tracking Mr Thompson when the £100 ran out?"

"You must use reasonable discretion, of course," said the judge. "Naturally, in the circumstances, I would pay any reasonable additional charges."

"Thank you, my Lord," said Mr Maclachlan. "With my experience of the Courts I think it as well to clear up these little points before we start."

"I quite agree," said the judge. "Now is there anything you're not clear about?"

"I think not," said Mr Maclachlan, "but, if I may have your telephone number, perhaps I may be allowed to telephone you, if necessary."

The judge told Lesley to call on Hounds Ltd., and make the necessary arrangements so that she could be supplied with an agent at short notice. He then went on holiday in a happier frame of mind, but he gave Lesley his telephone number in case she needed him.

For the first couple of days at his hotel the judge was much happier. Since he had lost his wife many years previously he enjoyed holidays on his own. Oddly enough he liked his own company, though it is perhaps not really so odd, when one considers that, if you are a worrier by nature, it is much easier to worry when you are by yourself. The judge used to choose a comfortable hotel and spend part of his time reading, part talking to his fellow guests and part listening to some of them complaining how uncomfortable the comfortable hotel was.

He found, for example, Mr and Mrs Sugden-Placey quite a tonic, though, after listening to them for a week abusing each other and everything else in the hotel, he became rather sorry for them in a way. The husband was an indifferent shot, and an unkind guest, who had seen his performances on the moors and in the hotel, put forward the opinion that Sugden-Placey only hit a bird if he imagined that it was his wife who had risen. Then he let fly with both barrels and scored with each, but on the same bird.

There was usually some entertainment at meal times.

"Now I don't want to make a point of this," Sugden-Placey would begin.

"Well, don't then," said his wife.

"I haven't started yet."

"I said 'dont'."

"It's too bad they always put the toast on the table before we come down. I like mine fresh. If I've mentioned it once, I've mentioned it a hundred times. It's not as though we were only here overnight. We're here for a month."

"You should come down earlier," said his wife.

Little realizing that he played very much the same game with himself, the judge took an unkind pleasure in listening to their bickering. He also observed how the staff, while maintaining an almost exaggerated air of politeness, saw to it that they were usually served last and that, if any inconveniences had to be suffered, it should be the Sugden-Placeys who suffered them. The simple moral, unintelligible to Sugden-Placey, is that, the less you complain, the less you have to. If, as soon as you arrive, there's something wrong with the door of your lock-up garage, your luggage isn't taken off the car quickly enough, the girl in the office is on the telephone and doesn't attend to you at once, your room isn't as large as you thought it was going to be and faces the wrong direction and there are no face towels then, if you howl at the top of your voice about every one of these disasters, you can be pretty sure that they will be followed by many more. It is not very easy to find a good hotel but it is almost certain that the Sugden-Placeys will never find one.

Such people are, however, useful members of society if, for no other reason, than that they give the other guests something to talk about. The judge never criticized other guests but he listened cheerfully to them criticizing each other. He was quite a popular figure in the bar of the hotel. High Court Judges usually are. One reason is probably the fascination of evil. It is a great thrill for most people to see a man in the dock. The more serious the crime, the greater the thrill. And, if you have the luck to see a man charged with capital murder, and have a good imagination, you can picture to yourself what is going to happen to the unfortunate prisoner, if convicted. But few people get this opportunity. So it is a good substitute to meet a judge whose duty it is to pass sentences of death or even long terms of imprisonment.

"Forgive me asking you, Judge—I expect you get asked this question a lot—but what does it feel like to pass a death sentence?"

"It's always unpleasant to sentence anyone, but one shouldn't take on the job if one isn't prepared to do what is required," was the judge's usual reply.

He had spent a week in this sort of way without hearing a word from Lesley or Hounds Ltd. and he was beginning to feel and hope that he had perhaps heard the last of the affair, when to his surprise Mr Empton and his wife arrived at the hotel.

"Why, Judge," said Mr Empton when they first saw each other, "what a coincidence! How nice to see you."

"How are you, Empton?" said the judge.

For the first day they kept clear of the subject but it was obvious that this could not go on for ever. When they did start to discuss the case the judge could not help saying:

"One thing that puzzled me was your failure to call Mrs Burford."

"And well it may, Judge," said Mr Empton. "I intended to call her."

"Yes, I understand that," said the judge, "but she told me that later you said you didn't believe her and refused to call her."

"That I didn't believe her?" said Empton. "The little liar. I didn't call her because I *did* believe her."

"I don't understand," said the judge.

"Well, I suppose that, strictly speaking, I shouldn't tell you, but the case is all over now so far as we are both concerned and it can't really do any harm. I'll tell you why I didn't call her."

"Why was it?"

"Well, you know that when the police first interviewed him, Burford said that at the time of the robbery he was going for a walk by himself. They didn't say they were asking about the robbery, they just asked him where he was at such a time on such a day. But, later, when they charged him with the robbery, he said he was in bed with his wife. And she confirmed it at first. So, of course, I was going to call her, first to prove Mr Thompson's existence and secondly to prove the alibi."

"And then what happened?"

"Well, for reasons which don't matter, I thought this was a case where I ought to have a conference with her. During it she let slip that her husband wasn't in bed with her but that the case seemed so strong against him that they thought they'd better say they were together, so that they could have two witnesses instead of him alone."

"Go on," said the judge.

"Well, naturally, I put the point to him. He obviously didn't know what to do. He either had to stick to his guns or admit that both he and his wife were liars. He decided to stick to his guns and said his wife's correction was a mistake. So what was I to do? I obviously couldn't call her after that, could I, Judge?"

"No, of course not," said the judge. "You're quite sure of all this, I suppose. There's no possibility of a mistake?"

"None at all. She explained to me that, when they saw the evidence piling up against him and there appeared to be only his word against so much, it seemed to be the only thing to do."

"Then why did she admit it to you?"

"It was an accident, I think. She let something slip, and I cross-examined her about it. And then it all came out."

"This fellow Thompson—do you think he exists?"

"Do you, Judge?"

"Well, I confess that, until you gave me this last bit of information, I was inclined to think he did. But now it's a very different situation."

"What always annoys me about these absent villains is that they always call them by such obvious names. It's always Brown or Jones or Thompson, or something of that kind. Why can't they say Montgomery?"

"Or Sugden-Placey," said the judge. "A name like that would certainly carry conviction. I don't mind telling you, Empton, that I've made a complete fool of myself over this case. Even more than I thought a few minutes ago. Heavens, what a fool!"

"I'm sure you haven't really, Judge. It must be very worrying to think you've made a mistake if a man's life or liberty depends on it. I'm very glad to have been able to relieve your mind on the subject."

"You certainly have in one way," said the judge, "but you've raised another problem at the same time."

He was now wondering whether he should get on to Maclachlan and tell him to cry off the search immediately. He also had to decide what he was to tell Lesley. He couldn't in fact tell her what he'd heard, as Empton shouldn't have given away to anyone what Lesley had said to him. It was a very awkward problem, and, as usual with the judge, the worry began to multiply itself. He had just told Lesley in effect that he believed her story that Thompson existed. How could he suddenly tell her that he didn't without saying why? And, if he simply wrote that he'd changed his mind and was not prepared to help any more, that would be tantamount to doing the same thing. He would like to have consulted Empton on the subject but he did not feel he could.

He had still not made up his mind what to do when he went to the bar for a drink before dinner.

"That was an odd case," said a fellow guest, "when you helped to recapture the man you'd sentenced."

"Yes," said the judge. "It was odd."

"How the fellow must have hated you."

"What surprises me," said another, "is that judges never seem to be attacked by criminals whom they've sentenced. You hear occasional threats from the dock when a man is sentenced, but, when the chap comes out, he never tries to do anything about it."

"That's as well for us," said the judge. "But I suppose it's because they appreciate that we're really doing our duty and that we're quite impersonal and simply representing the public."

"But," said another guest, "one might have thought the relatives of a chap would have a go. Some of them believe passionately in their husband's or father's innocence. This fellow Burford's wife, for instance, has she ever written to you an anonymous threatening letter?"

"Well, if it was anonymous," said the judge, "and the handwriting carefully enough disguised, I couldn't tell, could I? But in fact I've had no threatening or abusive letters from anyone about the case."

At that moment the receptionist came into the bar.

"Oh, Sir Gerald," she said, "there's a lady to see you, a Mrs Burford."

CHAPTER EIGHTEEN

INTERRUPTIONS TO A HOLIDAY

WITHOUT a clear idea of exactly what he was going to say, the judge went out to see her. One thing he was determined to do and that was to finish the thing off there and then. Embarrassing as her call was, at least it enabled him to deal with the matter at once.

He found her in the hotel front lounge looking excited and almost happy.

"Sir Gerald," she said, "I've some wonderful news. I had to come over at once."

"You have wasted your time," said the judge, "and mine."

She saw how angry he seemed to be.

"I'm terribly sorry to have disturbed you at your hotel," she said, "but I really did think it was justified. Do please forgive me."

"Please say what you want and then go."

"But Sir Gerald, I don't understand. We've found the man and Mr Maclachlan is keeping an eye on him at the moment."

"Now, look, Mrs Burford," said the judge. "I've had just about enough of this. You've lied to me from the start and I've no doubt you're lying now."

"I'm not, Sir Gerald, really I'm not."

"But you have lied to me, haven't you? About your husband's alibi?"

"How do you know?"

"Never mind how I know. It's enough that I do. And that's an end of the whole matter. I wash my hands of it."

"But Sir Gerald, you must let me explain. We've really found him again. It would be too dreadful if we had to let him go."

"You can go to the police."

"But I have and they say there's nothing they can arrest him for. They won't do anything without your backing."

"You've had all the help I'm prepared to give."

"But let me explain, Sir Gerald, about the alibi. I did tell you a lie about that. I didn't give evidence because I wasn't with William. I know it was wrong of us to make it up, but everything was being made up against William and, if evidence is faked on one side, it doesn't seem so bad to do a little in return."

"Are you suggesting the police faked evidence against you?"

"No, not the police—Thompson."

"Oh, Thompson," said the judge. "I'm a bit tired of him."

"But do listen to me, Sir Gerald. You've done so much and been so kind. I'm sure you wouldn't let me down now. My husband's in prison for ten years, and there he'll stay without your help. Now that I really have found the man, surely you'll give just that one extra piece of help."

"You found him at Esher, I believe," said the judge.

"Yes, I did," said Lesley. "Don't you believe me?"

"How can I?" said the judge, "you lie whenever it suits you. I ought to have realized it from the start."

"Sir Gerald, I had to lie to you. I was terrified if I told you the truth about the alibi you wouldn't go on helping. Can't you see that? My husband is doing ten years for a crime he didn't commit. I tell you that within six or seven hours I can show you the man who actually committed the crime and planted the evidence on my husband. Are you just going to throw me out because I told a lie? Was it so dreadful to tell that lie? Of course, we shouldn't have done so, but no one would believe William about anything and there seemed no alternative. You've never had a case faked against you, Sir Gerald, you can't know what it means."

"I'm not sure that I don't," said the judge.

"Please, Sir Gerald," said Lesley, "I will do anything in the world to try to convince you."

"I believe you'd *say* anything in the world," said the judge.

"This is our last chance," said Lesley. "Please give it us. Surely you give everyone a last chance."

"Where do you say the man is at the moment?"

"He's at a hotel in Doncaster."

"Why didn't you telephone?"

"Because I wanted to fetch you."

"What do the police say?"

"They say there's nothing they can do without some evidence."

"All right," said the judge, "I'll miss my dinner and come with you. I'm probably a fool. In fact I know I am. But you ask for a last chance and you shall have it. I'll get some things. I suppose I shall have to stay the night there."

The judge went to collect some clothes and on the way back from his room he ran into Empton.

"Hullo, Judge, you going out before dinner?"

"I've been called away suddenly—just for the night."

"People in the bar were saying that a Mrs Burford had called to see you."

"People in the bar can say what they like," said the judge. "I'm in a hurry."

But he wondered what they would say when he was away and what he could say when he came back.

He was just about to leave the hotel when he was summoned to the telephone. It was his clerk. A judge who was to have sat in the Court of Criminal Appeal next morning had been taken ill. The Lord Chief Justice would be most grateful if the judge could possibly take his place. It was anticipated that the appeals would only take a day.

"Very well," said the judge, "I'll do it."

A few minutes later he explained to Lesley what had happened.

"I'm sorry," he said, "but this must come first. Keep your man under observation the whole time and I will come tomorrow night if the list is finished. You can telephone me at the Law Courts."

Before he left to catch the last train he saw Empton again.

"In case the people in the bar want to know what I'm doing, I'm going to London to sit in the Court of Criminal Appeal tomorrow."

"Are you really, Judge?"

"Yes, I am," said the judge almost angrily. "You'll probably see a report of it in the papers."

"Burford isn't appealing again, I suppose—but, no, of course, that would be impossible."

"Burford and Mrs Burford haven't got anything to do with it," said the judge.

But they had a good deal to do with the judge on his way to London. It seemed impossible to believe that Lesley wasn't telling the truth this time, and yet once you know people to be liars can you have any trust in them? But what could her object be in getting him to go to Doncaster if she hadn't found the man? What could her object have been in getting him to Esher? She had certainly lied to him, but wasn't there something in her explanation? If she'd admitted having lied, from her point of view, she might have lost the interest of the only person who was prepared to help. Yes, he must give her this last chance.

CHAPTER NINETEEN

THE LAST CHANCE

THE last chance is what most criminals get when they appeal to the Court of Criminal Appeal, for, as Mr. Justice Carstairs complained, when Mr Empton refused to try to get the Burford case to the House of Lords, a further appeal to that House is impossible in most cases, and the Court of Criminal Appeal is their final fling. And in the bad old days of that Court it was not much of a fling. All that has fortunately now been changed, but in those days it was a nice point whether it took longer to have an appeal dismissed or to obtain a decree in an undefended divorce or *vice versa*.

An appeal would start, somewhat unpropitiously from the point of view of the appellant, with the presiding judge saying in an audible whisper to his neighbour:

"There's nothing in this, is there?"

The other judge would shake his head and then the appeal would begin. It was a little discouraging for counsel who had to open the batting on such a wicket. The question was, perhaps, whether a man should hang or go to prison for many years and an appearance that the appeal was going to be heard, before the judges had made up their minds to dismiss it, would have been some comfort to the appellant. But in those days there usually presided over the Court a judge who had made the solemn pronouncement that justice must not only be done but must manifestly be seen to be done. He was much praised for this admirable and well-worded declaration of the rights of those who come before the Courts. It was just unfortunate that of all the judges who functioned at that time he was himself the one who paid the least attention to the maxim. It is doubtful if the criminals whose appeals were dismissed by his Court took much comfort from the fact that the language of his judgments was exquisitely chosen. He used few and simple words, admirably arranged and easily understood. It was a delight for those unconcerned in a case to listen to him, and even counsel who suffered under him remembered with respect the brilliant choice of language with which he tore them to pieces.

The trouble, of course, was that, as he was Lord Chief Justice, other judges were inclined to take their tone from him. He was a first-class example of the danger of making a man Lord Chief Justice until he has proved himself as a judge. It is an example which, it is hoped by many, will be remembered for ever.

In those days, after the discouraging preliminaries between two of the judges to which reference has been made, the appeal would be opened, and it would proceed something like this:

COUNSEL: This is an appeal from a conviction before Mr Justice So-and-So at the Central Criminal Court. The appellant was convicted of murder. The facts which the prosecution alleged were—

LORD CHIEF JUSTICE: You may take it that we have all read the evidence.

COUNSEL: Thank you, my Lord. My Lord the grounds of appeal are as follows—first——

LORD CHIEF JUSTICE: Which is your best ground?

COUNSEL: Well, my Lord, I would respectfully submit that the judge never put the appellant's case to the jury. In support of that, my Lords. . . .

MR JUSTICE SPEER: One moment, Mr. Hoop. If that's your best point, why have you put it third in the written notice of appeal?

COUNSEL: Oh, my Lord, the grounds weren't formulated in order of merit.

LORD CHIEF JUSTICE: Did you say merit, Mr. Hoop?

COUNSEL: My Lords, I should prefer, if I may, to point out to your Lordships. . . .

MR JUSTICE BLENKIRON: Do you really say that the judge never put the appellant's case to the jury? Look at the passage on page 123. "Now the accused says that he was not there at the time. If you believe that, members of the jury, that is an end of the matter."

LORD CHIEF JUSTICE: Mr Hoop, do I correctly understand that you settled this notice of appeal?

COUNSEL: Yes, my Lord.

LORD CHIEF JUSTICE: Then will you kindly explain how you came to make that wholly unfounded criticism of the learned judge in view of the passage which my Lord has just read.

COUNSEL: My Lords, you should have heard the way the learned judge said it.

LORD CHIEF JUSTICE: That is a most improper observation for which you will apologize immediately.

COUNSEL: Oh, my Lord, I didn't mean to. . . .

LORD CHIEF JUSTICE: You will apologize immediately.

COUNSEL: My Lord, I'm extremely sorry.

LORD CHIEF JUSTICE: Very well then. Have you anything else to add in support of this appeal?

The Lord Chief Justice then ostentatiously picks up the Law List and looks in it. By this he successfully conveys to the lawyers in the Court without saying a word: "Who is this fellow Hoop?"

Within a further five minutes the appeal is over, the Lord Chief Justice remarking that the only reason the appeal was brought was because it was a case of murder, as though it were rather insulting to their Lordships to have to consider the dull question whether a man should be hanged or not.

Such an unenviable tradition does not die easily, and it was some time before the Court became what it is now, a Court for *hearing* as well as determining appeals.

The cases which came before Mr Justice Carstairs and his brethren were a varied lot, but they were all considered on such merits (if any) as they had. They included a gentleman who had actually been convicted by a jury of being too much under the influence of drink while driving a car, two cases of bigamy, three of false pretences, a robbery with violence and two burglaries.

The Court was presided over by Mr Justice Fairweather, and the third member of the Court was Mr Justice Dalmunzie. He was a Scotsman who had somehow or other found his way on to the English instead of the Scottish Bench. He used to show considerable annoyance when his name was incorrectly pronounced. This could never happen when he was sitting alone as then he was invariably called "my Lord." But, when he was sitting with other judges, it might be necessary for Counsel in addressing the Court to say "as Mr Justice Dalmunzie had said" or something of that kind.

Experienced practitioners knew that the "z" was pronounced more like a "g" but young and inexperienced barristers could not at first make out why the judge in question spoke tartly to them after they had pronounced his name. He felt as strongly about his name, as many judges feel when the late Mr Justice Lopes' name is pronounced as one syllable to rhyme with ropes instead of two syllables to rhyme with Tropez.

It was quite a relief to Mr Justice Carstairs to have to apply his mind to his ordinary work, and, although it was impossible for him in the intervals of thinking about an appeal not to wonder whether Lesley really had found her man, he was able to concentrate on the matters in hand pretty well.

One of the cases of false pretences was by a Mr Green who conducted his appeal in person.

"I'm not appealing against sentence this time, my Lords," he began. "The sentence was very fair as sentences go."

"What are you appealing against?" asked the presiding judge.

"The whole bags of tricks, if you'll forgive the expression, my Lords," said Mr Green.

"Now, Green," said the presiding judge, "you must behave yourself."

"I'm sorry, my Lords," said Mr Green, "that was a false start, shall I begin again?"

"We shan't hear you at all, unless you talk sense," said Mr Justice Dalmunzie.

"I see," said Mr Green gravely. "Then, if your Lordships will forgive me while I pull myself together—which normally at this stage I've already been told to do—as Mr Justice Dalmunzie has just said. . . ."

He pronounced the name with absolute correctness, and he repeated it just to show it wasn't a mistake.

"As Mr Justice Dalmunzie has just said, I must talk sense and that takes a bit of doing, as your Lordships must well know."

Mr Justice Dalmunzie was so pleased at his name being correctly pronounced from such an unlikely quarter that he decided for himself that he was prepared to let Mr Green have quite a bit of rope. How many counsel, he reflected, took the elementary precaution to ascertain in advance how a judge's name was pronounced?

"Well," Mr Green continued, "I'm not saying that the facts didn't look black against me. They did. And, as I've done the same thing before, it was difficult for the judge not to think I'd done it again."

"Had you?" asked Mr Justice Carstairs.

"Now, my Lord," said Mr Green, wagging a forefinger towards the judge, "that would be described by some ignorant people as a leading question. But I know better. It isn't leading at all. It's a perfectly proper question if I may say so with respect. But awkward, my Lord, awkward. But then you wouldn't have been one of the leading cross-examiners in the country if it weren't awkward, would you, my Lord?"

"Talk sense or be quiet," said Mr Justice Fairweather, who was the only judge Mr Green had not so far done his best to please.

Mr Green, who had in fact far more experience of the criminal courts than many members of the Bar, had made the most careful enquiries about his judges before he appeared. He was delighted to find the key to Dalmunzie's heart, as he never appealed more than once to the vanity of the same judge. He had found nothing for Fairweather, and had decided to wait for an inspiration.

"I'm sorry, my Lord," said Mr Green, "I mustn't abuse my position. A fair hearing's all I want. And it's the one thing I know I'll get here. I wouldn't say that to everyone, my Lords."

"Now, come along, Green," said Mr Justice Dalmunzie, "what's your complaint about the trial?"

"It went wrong from the beginning, my Lord. My defence never got going."

"But what was it?"

"You may well ask, my Lord," said Mr Green. "If I hadn't been there myself, I wouldn't have believed it."

"Wouldn't have believed what?"

"That such a good defence should vanish in front of my own eyes."

"What was your defence?"

"It was cast-iron, my Lords. It couldn't fail. Only it did. That's what I'm complaining about."

"But I don't follow," said Mr Justice Carstairs. "What was wrong with the trial?"

"Oh, my Lord," said Mr Green, "a cast-iron defence shouldn't fail, should it, my Lord? There must be something wrong, if it does."

"Perhaps what was wrong was that it wasn't cast-iron."

"That's a point," said Mr Green. "That's quite a point. I should like to chew that over, my Lord."

"Well, we have chewed it over," said Mr Justice Dalmunzie, "and I'm afraid it seems to me at any rate that you hadn't any defence."

"That's how it strikes you, my Lord?" said Mr Green.

"I'm afraid so."

"And what about you, my Lord? You didn't think that, did you?" said Mr Green, addressing Mr Justice Fairweather.

"Yes, I did."

"And that only leaves one of you in my favour," said Mr Green. "That's terrible."

"You mustn't make that assumption," said Mr Justice Carstairs. "For the moment I'm against you too."

"Oh dear!" said Mr Green, "then I'll have to begin all over again."

It was not long, however, before the Court felt compelled to dismiss Mr Green's appeal. He thanked them all for a most courteous hearing.

"Better luck next time, Green," said Mr Justice Dalmunzie.

"Next time, my Lord?" said Mr Green, with affected pain in his voice. "I'm going straight in future—if I can remember which direction that is."

During the lunch adjournment they were discussing Mr Green's case, when Mr Justice Dalmunzie said to Mr Justice Carstairs:

"You know, it's a pity about that chap. There's a lot of good in him and he's got a great sense of fun. Most criminals are dull dogs. If someone could have given him a helping hand early in his career he might have had a very different life."

"Could very well be."

"Have you ever followed up a case and tried to help the fellow?"

"I can't say that I have," began Mr Justice Carstairs. "Well, not in the sense you mean. As a matter of fact, I have been trying to help a man get rid of a conviction."

"Oh, Burford—yes, I've heard all about that," said Mr Justice Dalmunzie.

"What's your view?" said the judge.

"D'you really want it?"

"Of course."

"Well, I'm a dour Scotsman, but I think you must be mad. Haven't I heard that you've been up and down the country staying in hotels with the man's beautiful wife?"

"Certainly not," said the judge. "I've been to a few race-meetings with her—that's all. And I did once go on a wild goose chase to Esher, and as a matter of fact I'm going on another tonight."

"Well the rumours weren't so far wrong then. But, if you want my advice, you'll get out of it quick. Women like that can be very dangerous. She might even try to blackmail you."

"Whatever for?"

"Oh, nothing, of course. But if I were you I should keep my bedroom door locked when you go on one of your wild goose chases."

"But, if you thought a man was innocent, wouldn't you do anything about it?"

"Of course I would. But it wouldn't entail going out with the innocent man's wife. We'll all be inviting Mr Green to dinner at the club at this rate."

"That's completely different. He's just a comic crook. This man Burford's doing ten years and may be innocent."

"May be?"

"Yes, of course, it's only 'may be' but wouldn't that be enough for you to want to do something?"

"I've already said 'Yes'—but not what you're doing. However, as I said, I'm a dour Scotsman, and we're rather inclined to keep our energies for causes which haven't been lost. They're more productive."

It was this kind of conversation which strengthened the judge in his determination to give the Burfords this one final chance. Although he felt far from certain in the matter having regard to the lies which Lesley had told him, he couldn't really see how she could just be pretending this time. He hoped the list would end early so that he could get to Doncaster as quickly as possible and get things over one way or the other. For that reason he personally would not have given Mr Green as much latitude as his colleagues were prepared to give.

In the afternoon they dealt with the motorist. His complaint was a simple one.

"My Lord," said counsel on his behalf, "when my client was first examined by the doctor at the police station, he asked for a blood test. It was refused."

"Why was that?" asked Mr Justice Fairweather.

"I cannot do better than give the doctor's own answer. 'Because,' he said, 'the accused was obviously drunk and it wasn't necessary'."

"How do you know that a person is obviously drunk?" asked Mr Justice Dalmunzie.

"Exactly, my Lord," said counsel. "That was my point. The doctor said he applied the usual tests and the appellant failed every one of them. He couldn't walk straight, he couldn't spell properly, his speech was slurred, his eyes were glazed, his tongue furry and his breath smelled strongly of alcohol. In addition he insisted on calling everyone 'darling', though he was not an Irishman. I put to the doctor that any one of his symptoms, with a single exception, could have been due to causes other than drink. The doctor agreed. He even added that it was possible, though not likely, that they could all occur at the same time in the same person. The one reason that he refused to apply a blood test was because, in addition to the symptoms which could theoretically have been accounted for by something other than too much alcohol, his breath, so it was said, smelled strongly of alcohol."

"Well, so far," said Mr Justice Fairweather, "I don't know what you're complaining about."

"My client said then, and he maintains now, that his breath nearly always smells of alcohol even though he has taken none for twenty-four hours. He is even ready to prove it to your Lordships now. He has been in custody for the past twenty-four hours and he would like to demonstrate to your Lordships that his breath smells strongly of alcohol now."

"Perhaps he took in such a quantity before surrendering to his bail that it is still effective," said Mr Justice Fairweather.

"Well," said Mr Justice Dalmunzie, "I for one am not going to smell the appellant's breath."

"I certainly cannot smell anything from here," said Mr Justice Fairweather, turning his head towards the prisoner who was about seven yards away.

"You should have offered the jury the opportunity," said Mr Justice Carstairs.

"We did," said counsel, "and that is one of the grounds of appeal, that the judge would not permit it. He said that he could not allow evidence to be given to the jury which was not also given to him. And the learned judge took the same view as Mr Justice Dalmunzie." Counsel pronounced the "z" as he spoke the name of the judge.

"The learned judge was perfectly right," said that judge, showing a trace of annoyance in his voice. "A judge is not a witness, nor is a jury."

"But they have a view sometimes," said counsel. "Why not a smell?"

"At any rate," said Mr Justice Carstairs, "the judges at the Central Criminal Court would have an advantage over us. They have nosegays. Did you suggest to the learned judge that one of the Sherriffs' nosegays might be passed round the jury after the test? The judge could have used his own."

"I'm afraid not, my Lord."

"Did you call evidence to prove that the appellant's breath always smelled of alcohol although he had not been drinking?"

"His wife and two children, my Lord."

"Poor things," said Mr Justice Fairweather. "But I suppose they get used to it. But did you not have tests made before the trial to prove your point?"

"No, my Lord."

"Why not? It was the obvious thing to do. If you could

have shown that, although a test would prove that the appellant had no alcohol in his blood, his breath nevertheless smelled strongly of alcohol, that would have gone some way to make good your point."

"Well, my Lord, if your Lordships would allow further evidence, that could still be done," said counsel.

"But how can we?" said Mr Justice Fairweather. "We cannot make ourselves into a jury. And even your test, if successful from your point of view, would not prove your case conclusively. Your client's breath could have smelled of alcohol for one of two reasons, either the usual one because he had recently taken some or because he had some special affection or whatever you like to call it which caused the smell to linger about him long after the liquid itself had left his blood stream. Now the jury could—I only say could—have given your client the benefit of the doubt if satisfied by the test, but we couldn't possibly do so."

"You should have prepared your case better," said Mr Justice Dalmunzie. "Before you go into Court there are several things that a wise advocate should do—for example, learn how to pronounce the names—the names of any cases he may be going to cite and so forth. But, if he fails to take any of these precautions, that is not a good ground of appeal."

"But, my Lord, it could have done no harm for the doctor to make the test," said counsel.

"No doubt," said Mr Justice Fairweather, "you urged that on the jury."

"My Lord, it's true that I did. But I do urge on your Lordships the undesirability of this case being finally decided without my client being given a proper chance to prove this point. Would your Lordships not even let the usher smell the appellant's breath, or better still the warder sitting next to him."

"Well," said Mr Justice Fairweather to the warder, "does the appellant's breath smell of alcohol?"

The warder went very red in the face.

"I'm afraid, my Lord," he said, "I've only just come on duty and I had a glass of beer with my lunch."

Shortly afterwards the appeal was dismissed and the Court

went on to consider the case of the next appellant whose name, unfortunately for Mr Justice Carstairs, was Thompson. It pulled him up with a jerk and he looked at the clock. The appellant had been charged with burglary and his defence was an alibi.

"Just up your street," whispered the presiding judge to Mr Justice Carstairs. The judge gave a slight grin but it was not a happy one. He hoped it looked better than it felt.

There was ample evidence against the accused, but he claimed, just as William had claimed, that he was in bed with his wife.

"Why is it," whispered the presiding judge to Mr Justice Dalmunzie, "that burglars are always so affectionate?"

"Because they work at night," replied his colleague.

It transpired that the short ground of appeal was that, although in this case the wife had given evidence to support her husband's alibi, the judge's summing up had hardly referred to the matter, and had then done so in a manner most prejudicial to the appellant.

"It is true," he had said, "that the prisoner's wife has said on oath that the prisoner was with her at the material time but one can have some sympathy with a wife who feels compelled to support her husband's story in such circumstances."

"I must say," said Mr Justice Carstairs, "that, for myself, I think that was a most unfortunate way in which to refer to the woman's evidence. It was a clear suggestion that she was committing perjury. That was for the jury to say."

"I respectfully agree, my Lord," said counsel. "Her evidence was entitled to as much consideration as anyone else's, and it was pushed aside with what I hope I may term, without disrespect to the learned judge, a sympathetic sneer."

"Your trouble," said Mr Justice Fairweather, "is this, isn't it? Had the evidence of the appellant's wife been put properly to the jury, as I agree with you it ought to have been, could the jury in the light of the rest of the evidence have returned any other verdict? Although I think we all agree that the learned judge was in error in treating her evidence as he did, were not the jury bound, or almost bound, to come to the conclusion they came to in view of the case for the prosecution?"

"If your Lordship says 'almost bound', that is surely sufficient for my purposes," said counsel. "Unless they were bound to find my client guilty the judge's summing up may have unfairly led them to a verdict which they might not otherwise have given."

"We think we should like to hear what the prosecution says about this," said Mr Justice Fairweather.

"What I say is this," said counsel for the prosecution. "The case against the accused was about as formidable as such a case can be. The accused was questioned twelve hours after the burglary and was found to be in possession of articles which were undoubtedly stolen at the time of the burglary. At first he would give no explanation. Then he said he found them. Found a bicycle pump, a spanner and a spare bicycle wheel in good condition. Of course, my Lords, if the word 'found' is used in the sense in which I believe it has sometimes been used in the Army, I do not criticize the appellant's answer. Later, however, he said that he had not found them but that they'd been sold to him by a man whose name he didn't know, for a price he couldn't remember. Apparently he wanted to buy a bicycle pump and a spare wheel when he hadn't a bicycle. He said he was thinking of getting a bicycle."

"But you say he stole them," said Mr Justice Fairweather. "What *did* he want them for?"

"Oh, my Lord," said counsel, "it must have been in your Lordship's experience that, if you burgle a place, there may unfortunately be nothing worth taking but you don't like to have nothing for your pains, so you take whatever you can, even if you have no real need for it."

"I can assure you I don't," said Mr Justice Fairweather.

"I apologize, my Lord. I put it badly."

"You put it very well," said Mr Justice Fairweather, "but in the wrong direction."

"Thank you, my Lord. And I may add that those articles, although not of much use, could be sold. You would get—I mean he could get, my Lord, a few shillings at least for them."

"What troubles me," said Mr Justice Carstairs, "is the lack of appearance of justice in this case. I agree that there was a very strong case against the appellant, but, unless we abolish trials in such cases, the accused must be tried fairly. It becomes little more than the pretence of a trial if a judge simply laughs a defence out of Court. The whole object of a trial is to put the matter into the hands of the jury. Naturally they may be greatly affected by what the judge says, and, if he says in effect that evidence can be disregarded, I imagine that most jurymen might say to themselves—well, the judge is used to these cases, if he says 'disregard it' it's better to do so. That's possible, isn't it?"

"Yes, certainly, my Lord."

"Well, then, isn't it making a farce of the trial? You offer the prisoner the right of going into the witness box and calling his wife to support his case and you then tell the jury to take no notice of what they say. It's true that the learned judge didn't say that about the appellant's evidence, but the principle is just the same if he says it about his wife's."

"In my submission the jury were bound to convict anyway, my Lord, whatever the judge said," urged counsel.

"Then he might just as well not have been tried," said Mr Justice Carstairs.

"My Lord," said prosecuting counsel, "there must be a lot of cases where, having regard to the evidence, no jury could properly acquit, but nevertheless the man must be tried if he pleads not guilty."

"Precisely," said Mr Justice Carstairs. "He must be tried and tried fairly. Who am I, or who are you, to say that a jury *must* convict? That is usurping their province. It is perfectly true that there are such things as perverse verdicts but that isn't the right way to approach the conduct of a trial. Should a judge say to himself: 'In case this jury is perverse, I will sum up unfairly so as to make sure of a verdict of guilty'?"

"Of course not, my Lord."

"Then, I confess, I don't know why in this case the learned judge did not put the defence and *all* the evidence in support of it fairly before the jury. He put the evidence for the prosecution fairly enough. It's true this appellant has a very bad record and, if I had to give my personal opinion, I should think he was probably guilty of the crime with which he was charged, but he was entitled to plead not guilty and have the case proved against him and he was entitled to be tried fairly."

It will be seen that there is no stronger critic of some other judge's unfairness than a judge who is himself normally unfair. In view of the harassing mental experiences which he had recently had, it did cross Mr Justice Carstairs' mind, as he belaboured the judge who had presided at the burglar's trial, that he was perhaps expressing himself more freely because of his own shortcomings. And for one brief moment he wondered whether the judge in question would suddenly have a revulsion of feeling as he had had. But, no doubt quite rightly, he soon dismissed the notion. "What are they worrying about?" the other judge would say. "The chap was as guilty as he could be." But those, he thought, are just the cases you have to watch. Everyone watches the doubtful cases. It's the "clear" cases where injustice may be done. Cases where a man has many previous convictions, like the burglar, or perhaps one only, like William Burford. Yes, this case was an object lesson to him. No doubt the burglar was guilty but you can't try people like that, or occasionally someone, who has all the appearances against him, will be convicted when he should be acquitted.

"For my part," he said aloud, continuing his thoughts, "I do not see how you can successfully urge that there has been no miscarriage of justice. The appellant swore he did not commit the crime and that he was with his wife at the time. His wife confirmed that story. That defence ought to have been put fairly and squarely to the jury without what I may describe as a judicial smirk."

The other two members of the Court said something to themselves about pots calling kettles black, but they felt, as Mr Justice Carstairs felt, that this summing up just would not do. They allowed the burglar's appeal and set him free to burgle again until he was caught again. But they did not put it that way to the burglar.

"You have a deplorable record," said Mr Justice Fairweather in announcing the judgment of the Court. "See that you take full advantage of what has happened today."

"I will, my Lord," said the burglar and almost meant it. It

is not often that you get clean out of a seven-year sentence.

As Mr Justice Carstairs hurried to the train he thought he caught a glimpse of the burglar and his wife hurrying into a tea shop to celebrate. He was quite wrong in fact, as he should have realized. Burglars seldom celebrate on tea. But it made him for a moment think of the joy that would be in Lesley's face if her William were let out of prison. He caught the train without the slightest hesitation.

CHAPTER TWENTY

MR THOMPSON AGAIN

But on the way in the train the judge began to have doubts again. What was it that Dalmunzie had said? Blackmail? Keep your bedroom door locked. Ridiculous. Yet was it? What did he know of the Burfords? A previous conviction for receiving stolen goods wasn't much of a reference. And now he had actually started to give her money. Not very much it was true and the larger expense he was paying direct to Hounds Ltd. No, he was being too suspicious. Anyway he would soon know now.

Then he thought about the trial again. Had he really been so unfair? Not as bad as the judge who tried the burglar. That was rather a nice phrase he'd used about him—"a judicial smirk." And yet wasn't he regularly guilty of the same kind of thing himself? He knew he was. Much better to admit it and turn over a new leaf. It was not too late. It was a tremendous responsibility being a judge. He'd always realized it in a way, but obviously not sufficiently. It was certainly Burford's case which had brought it home to him, and, oddly enough, this burglar's as well. One mustn't be too sentimental about it but it was a satisfying thought to see the man reunited to his wife. Even if it were only for a few weeks.

Yes, one thing was certain. Whatever the result of his journey now, he would be a very different judge in the future. Patient, tolerant, quiet and above all fair. How easy it should be, now that it was brought home to him. And, apart from the good which it would do, he would be so much happier himself. And, of course, he would find everything much less worrying. Probably it was his unconscious instinct that he was a bad judge which made him worry so much. Well, that was all done with. With these comforting thoughts he went to sleep and only woke up shortly before his arrival at Doncaster.

Lesley was there to meet him.

"How good of you to come," she said.

"I'm not too late?" he asked. "The bird hasn't flown again?"

"No, it's all right—I think."

"You think? Then something has happened."

They were standing by a taxi.

"No. Please jump in."

Her tone was urgent.

"Very well."

They got in the taxi and it drove off.

"Hadn't we better call at the police station and fetch an officer?" he suggested.

Lesley hesitated.

"Yes, I suppose we'd better."

He spoke to the driver:

"Go to the police station first, please."

As soon as they arrived there the judge got quickly out and was soon interviewing a police inspector. He explained who he was.

"Yes, sir, we've already been told about this matter," said the inspector, "but I'm not exactly sure what you want us to do."

"The situation is this," said the judge. "This man Thompson is said by Burford and his wife to have planted the evidence on him. Pound notes handed over, dust somehow put in his trouser turn-ups. Now I must confess that at the trial I didn't believe the man existed and the jury didn't believe it either."

"Quite so, sir."

"Now, if it can be proved that he does exist, that fact by itself is material in which the Home Office may be interested."

"But that could be ascertained by Mrs Burford looking at him, sir, couldn't it?"

"Really, Inspector!" said the judge, "Mrs Burford is the wife of the convicted man. Naturally her identification of the man should be corroborated by an independent police officer."

"Yes, I see that, sir. Well, that's easily arranged."

"And apart from that, it is highly desirable that the man should be questioned. If he is completely innocent in the matter, he will come to no harm. If he was a party to the robbery you are perfectly entitled to question him."

"But he isn't bound to answer, sir."

"I dare say not, Inspector," said the judge, "but how many times have I read in the paper that a man has been taken to the police station for questioning?"

"But, if you'll forgive my saying so, sir, I have also read that judges have condemned this procedure as totally illegal. No one, I understand, sir, is bound to answer questions and no one is bound to go to a police station unless he is arrested."

"You may take it I know the law, Inspector," said the judge. "I also know the practice of the police. If you are not prepared to help when I tell you the matter may be of the greatest importance, please say so."

"Of course, I'm prepared to help, sir, and I'll send an officer with you right away. I was only very respectfully pointing out the limitation of our powers in the matter."

Ten minutes later the judge and Lesley and a policeman were on their way to the hotel. Mr Maclachlan was standing outside when they arrived.

"I'm terribly sorry about this, Sir Gerald," he said, as soon as the judge got out.

"What d'you mean?" said the judge.

"Hasn't Mrs Burford told you?"

The judge looked at Lesley.

"So he's gone again, has he?"

Lesley said nothing for a moment.

"If you'll come inside, I'll explain. I suppose the police officer had better go back to the station."

"I suppose so."

"Very well then," said the judge. "Thank you, officer. I'm

sorry you've been troubled. Please apologize to the inspector for me for your wasted journey."

The policeman returned to the police station and the judge and Lesley and Mr Maclachlan went into the hotel.

"It's most unfortunate," said Mr Maclachlan. "I had to go off duty for five minutes and left Mrs Burford watching him. And if he hadn't to go and pay his bill and leave in that five minutes!"

"Did you see him yourself?" asked the judge.

"Of course."

"What did he look like?"

"Much as you'd told me."

"What name is he using at the hotel?"

"Warren."

"Not Thompson or Wilson?"

"No, Warren."

"Where's he gone?"

"We don't know."

"Has he left no forwarding address?"

"No."

"Why didn't you tell me this at the station?" the judge said to Lesley.

"I was afraid you'd go straight back. I wanted to prove to you the man existed."

"You've proved nothing. Why even the police have never seen the man. They haven't have they?"

"No. They wouldn't do anything without you. But Mr Maclachlan has seen him."

"Mr Maclachlan has seen a man you pointed out to him, a man whose whereabouts are unknown and who registered here under the name of Warren. That proves precisely nothing. You might have pointed out any man, as far as Mr Maclachlan could tell. That man over there, for example. That's right, isn't it, Mr Maclachlan? All you know is that you were watching a man whom Mrs Burford pointed out to you. That's right, isn't it?"

"Yes, sir, I'm afraid it is."

"Well, I'm sorry you've had so much trouble for nothing, Mr Maclachlan. I'm sorrier still that I have."

"I'm afraid it isn't for nothing," said Mr Maclachlan.

"No, of course not," said the judge. "It's not your fault and of course you'll be paid. Now I'm going home."

"I'm afraid the last train has gone, Sir Gerald."

"Damnation!" said the judge. "I'm sorry, but I'm really angry. I suppose I shall have to get a room here."

He walked up to the desk followed by Lesley and Mr Maclachlan.

"Have you a room for the night?" he asked the receptionist.

"Twin-bedded, sir?"

"Certainly not, I want a single room."

"I'm so sorry, sir, I thought madam was with you. Yes, we have a room, sir."

"I'd like to go to it at once, please."

"Certainly, sir. The porter will take you."

"Good night," said the judge curtly to Lesley and Mr Maclachlan. "Please send your bill in in due course," he added to Mr Maclachlan.

He went angrily to his room, undressed angrily, got into bed angrily and actually went to sleep angrily. He was awakened by someone coming into his room.

"Who's that?" he called.

It was Lesley and she said so.

"Go away at once, please," he said.

"I must speak to you," she said and turned on the light. She was in pyjamas and a dressing-gown.

"I couldn't sleep," she said.

"Well, I could. Please go away."

He suddenly remembered Dalmunzie's advice. He wished he'd taken it.

"You must please listen to me. I'm so terribly unhappy."

"I dare say you are, but I can't help you any more."

"Are you being quite fair?" said Lesley. "Everything I've told you has been true."

"It's been nothing of the sort. You deliberately lied to me at the station."

"Oh, that," said Lesley, "yes, I'm sorry about that. But I had to do it or you'd have gone home."

"I certainly would. Now will you please leave me or I shall ring the bell."

"Please listen to me first. I am sorry about lying to you

again but it's not my fault that the man went off. If it hadn't been for that beastly Court you went to, he'd have still been here."

"He always has to wait till I'm about ten yards off. Then he disappears."

"That really isn't my fault. We found him at Doncaster races and followed him here. We've kept him under observation between us ever since. But you must realize I couldn't let him see me, or he might take fright and go abroad for a bit. He can't know he's being followed at the moment and it's vital he shouldn't. Can you imagine my feelings when I had to let him go, knowing you were on the way up here?"

"Can you imagine mine when I was told he'd gone?"

"Of course, I can, but is it fair of you to blame me for it? I thought judges were always fair. You came up to Doncaster because you believed you might see the man and get the police to make enquiries about him, didn't you?"

"Yes," said the judge grudgingly.

"Well, what has happened to make you decide that that can't still happen? We've been to the police and Maclachlan saw the man himself. Why should I go to all that trouble unless it were true? What possible object could I have?"

"How can I tell what are the objects of a person who deliberately lies to someone who is helping her?"

"Oh, please, please, Sir Gerald, don't give us up. You're our only hope."

And Lesley burst into tears and put herself in the judge's arms. For a moment the judge wondered if the door would suddenly open and a man demand what he was doing with his wife. Blackmail. Keep your door locked.

But the door did not open and Lesley remained sobbing on his chest.

"There, there," he said and patted her back.

It was a silly thing to do because at the third pat his hand stayed there for a moment or two and, being a normal man, he could not help realizing even more than he had before that Lesley was an extremely attractive young woman. And she was in his room. On his bed. At the same moment he realized that High Court judges did not usually receive the wives of convicted felons on their beds, even fully dressed. And Lesley wasn't.

"Now, please," he said. "This won't do. You must sit up."

Lesley sat up and for a split second the judge almost regretted it.

She looked him full in the eyes and said:

"Please."

Usually in such circumstances it is the man who is saying: Please.

"I'm sorry," he said. "I quite see your point of view, and I was annoyed and perhaps a little hasty. But I really can't go running up and down the country any more."

"But if I find him again? And I'm sure we shall now. He obviously feels things have blown over and that the police have got their scapegoat in William. He thinks they won't be looking for anyone else. He'll turn up again."

"Then you must go to the police. Tell them everything you know and ask for their help."

"We won't get far without you to back us."

The judge remembered that even with his help the police had not been particularly co-operative.

"I suppose," he said, "it is the same man as you saw at Esher?"

"Of course it is. Do you still disbelieve the whole story?"

"To be frank, I just don't know what to believe. What address did Warren register in the hotel book?"

"Another hotel. In Blackpool."

"Well, enquiries can be made there."

"I expect it'll be hotels all the way along and he won't have stayed at the last one. Or just a non-existent address."

"You seem to know all about this sort of thing."

"I'm only using my imagination. Isn't that what a crook would do?"

"I thought you said he didn't think he was being followed."

"Even so, he wouldn't give away anything unnecessarily. You may not think you are being followed, but you don't advertise how you can be found, do you?"

"As he's going round race-meetings so much surely there must be people who know where he is. Bookmakers or people like that?"

"I expect he does any betting in cash."

"Tell me something completely different. Why did both you and your husband at first suggest that this man and your husband had been at school together, St. James's wasn't it?"

"It was just a mistake."

"It was St. James's, wasn't it?"

"Yes, but you're not going there, are you?"

"Why are you so anxious that I shouldn't?"

"Oh, nothing, really. There's no point in it. Besides we naturally didn't want William's second conviction advertised too much."

"But they must know of it?"

"I suppose so, but don't go there, will you? It can only hurt us."

"At the moment," said the judge, "I don't propose to go anywhere—except to sleep, if you'll let me. But I'll see you in the morning. Now go back to your room, there's a good girl. I really am sorry for you, and, if there's anything I can do to help which doesn't entail wild-goose chases up and down the country, I will. For instance, if you find him again I'll speak to the police on the telephone. That should be just as good. They can check the authenticity of the call."

"Oh, you are good," she said and kissed him quickly on the forehead. Then she left.

But the judge did not sleep this time. His worrying apparatus came swiftly into action. There was no doubt that Lesley lied when it suited her but, on consideration of everything that had happened, he could not think of any motive for her behaviour except possibly revenge. And that really seemed futile. So he finally decided that he would help her in the way he had indicated but that he would not undertake any further long journeys and he certainly would not stay again at the same hotel as Lesley. He also decided that he would pay a visit to the headmaster of St. James's, which was quite near London, but he did not propose to tell Lesley of this intention.

CHAPTER TWENTY-ONE

INTERVIEW WITH A HEADMASTER

ABOUT a fortnight later he wrote to the headmaster for an interview and was given an appointment. Henry Sprout, the headmaster, was a remarkable man. He had left school at the age of fourteen completely untaught. Always near the bottom of his class, he had failed in every examination which he had taken, however simple. So far from complaining at his behaviour his parents encouraged him. The sooner he was out and earning, the better. There was always a danger that, if a boy did well, they would keep him at school, like Henry's elder brother Alfred. Alfred was always held up to Henry as an example of what not to do. Alfred had been forced to go into a Grammar School and even to a University. He ended up as a librarian with £600 a year at the age of twenty-four. Eight or nine years wasted when he might have been earning an average over the years of at least £9 or £10 a week. Several thousand pounds lost to the family. It was like failing to post a winning line on a pools coupon. Horrible.

So Henry was the blue-eyed boy of the family and his parents gloated over such reports on his progress as: "Might do a little better if he tried." "Good boy," his father would say, "there won't be no flippin' grammar schools for you."

But as soon as he left school and started to earn £4 a week as a boy in a garage Henry acquired a thirst for knowledge. It was not simply his parents' encouragement which had prevented him from learning at school. It was the method of teaching which he could not stand. He was an obstinate person and resisted strongly anything to which he objected. But, as soon as the shackles were removed, the qualities in his mind which had shown themselves to a limited degree in his brother Alfred began to make themselves felt and at a very rapid rate. He began to read voraciously. And the more he learned the more he wanted to learn. The boy who resisted all efforts to teach him at his elementary school voluntarily attended night school. And not only that. He soon started to show himself to be head and shoulders above the other students in his capacity to learn. There were still, of course, huge gaps in his knowledge, and he would sometimes startle his teachers as much by his ignorance as by his memory.

His parents had now no objection to his attending school. Henry was earning and it was much better in fact to know that he was at night school or reading at home than to wonder whether he might become involved with young hooligans or, almost as bad, whether one day he might inform them that unfortunately by pure accident and without really meaning it his girl friend Elsie was going to have a baby. No, Henry remained the blue-eyed boy, earning steadily and increasingly and leading a quiet, respectable life.

About ten years after he had left school Henry was lying under a car in the ordinary course of his work when it suddenly occurred to him that he was wasting his time. He was now a very well-educated young man, though still with occasional odd gaps in his knowledge which were even rather attractive, like one untidy curl in exceptionally pretty hair.

His parents were at first alarmed when he told them his plans, but, as the plan included a period of intensive work at the garage during which he proposed to save enough to enable him to give up work for the purpose of getting a degree, they did not make too much fuss about it. And indeed, they knew it would be useless, for Henry was twenty-four and quite capable of looking after himself.

At the age of thirty Henry, complete with the necessary qualifications, obtained his first teaching job. He at once showed himself to be a born teacher. He applied the methods which he would have liked to have been applied to himself. He had a complete mistrust of examinations, but he realized that, as long as the system of examinations continued, he would have to get his pupils through them. But, as far as possible, he concentrated on creating in his pupils a desire to know.

Henry's father and grandfather had come from Bermondsey and Henry had been brought up to talk as they did. As he began to associate with more educated people he started to acquire a more cultured accent and method of speech, and, as he had a particularly musical ear, it was only a few years before he could talk almost perfect English. On the other hand, he could relapse, whenever he wanted, into his original dialect, just as many Scotsmen who can speak perfect English without a trace of Scottish accent can also speak the broadest Scotch. Henry could speak rhyming slang and back slang, and he had a complete Cockney vocabulary at his command, and on occasion he found it was most effective with his class. He would, for example, sometimes introduce a subject like this:

"Yer put the *x*'s up on the board and yer put the brackets arahnd 'em."

It was not long before Henry's flair for teaching made itself felt and he gradually acquired better and better jobs, ending up with the headmastership of St. James's. He was immensely successful as a headmaster and his sense of mischief, which sometimes induced him to shock some of the parents, was an asset rather than the reverse. On one occasion, for example, when the parents were attending some school function immaculately dressed, many of them in morning coats and grey top hats, Henry greeted them in his shirtsleeves. "Sorry," he said. "Forgot me tie."

This sort of behaviour would never have been tolerated in a lesser man, but parents whose sons were guaranteed as good an education as you can get in the country could afford to be amused at some of his antics and to leave their sons quite confidently in his charge.

One of Henry's pet aversions was pomposity, and it was dangerous to give yourself airs in his presence, either as a parent or a pupil.

"Wot's yer farver, Spriggs?" he said one day when he thought the form needed a little uplift.

"A schoolmaster, sir."

"Tell 'im to come in a bowler 'at next time. The monkey should stick to 'is tree. Now we'll do some 'omer. 'Ow many of you don't know the first three books of the *Iliad by* 'eart?"

All the boys' hands went up.

"Well, yer will by the end of term or there won't be no end of term."

It was on this remarkable man that the judge called.

Unfortunately for him Henry Sprout had a particular dislike for judges. This was partly due to his dislike of pomposity, which he always associated with the judiciary. Partly also it was probably due to an innate dislike of the successors of men who had sent some of his forbears to prison. The judge, however, was wholly unaware of the character of the man whom he was going to interview. He drove up to the school and, as he got out of his car, the headmaster in his shirtsleeves, approached him.

"I've an appointment with the headmaster," he said.

"Well, yer late."

"I am not," said the judge, "and, even if I were, there's no need to be rude about it."

"Do yer know 'oo yer talking to?" said the headmaster.

"I'm afraid not, except that it's someone who ought to learn some manners."

"It's you wot's going to learn. This wye."

The headmaster led the judge into the school and along several corridors. On the way they met some of the boys who appeared to treat the judge with the utmost deference. "Nice-mannered boys," he thought, "they can't know who I am. If the teaching is as good as their behaviour it must be a first-class place."

Eventually they reached a room. The headmaster opened the door.

"In yer go," he said, "and sit down. People say make yerself at 'ome, but 'ow you do that with a 'ard uncomfortable chair like this one I just dunno. Still it's all yours."

The judge sat down opposite a desk and to his amazement the headmaster went and sat in his own chair facing the judge across the desk. Well, it was not his business how the school servants behaved, though he certainly proposed to report this man for his rudeness.

"Will the headmaster be long?" he asked.

"Not longer than I can 'elp," said Mr Sprout. "Wotcher want?"

"I'll tell that to the headmaster."

"That's wot I've arst yer to do."

The judge decided that silence was the only dignified weapon he could use.

"Come on," said Mr Sprout, "cough it up."

"Will you kindly tell the headmaster that I'm here," said the judge angrily.

" 'E knows," said Mr Sprout. " 'E's a-looking at you at this werry moment."

The judge looked around the room to see if there were any hatchways or spyholes but could not see any. There was another door to the room and he could only imagine the headmaster was looking at him through the keyhole. Extraordinary behaviour, he thought.

"You're a judge, ain't yer? Don't seem very quick off the mark."

"I shall report you to the headmaster," said the judge.

"That's just wot you're a-doing of."

"Don't be absurd," said the judge.

" 'Oo d'yer think this room belongs to?"

"The headmaster."

"Right. And this chair?"

"The headmaster."

"Right. Go up top. And wot am I doing in it?"

"I haven't the faintest idea," said the judge.

"Go down again," said Mr Sprout.

"Now, look," said the judge, "I've had enough of this tomfoolery."

"That's O.K.," said the headmaster. "If you've 'ad all yer want, yer know yer way out."

"Where is the headmaster?" said the judge loudly and angrily, in the faint hope that, if he were anywhere near, the headmaster would hear him.

"Yer 'oped 'e'd 'ear that, didn't yer? Well 'e did, if yer wanter know."

"Please tell me where he is."

" 'Ere."

"What d'you mean?"

"It's me. D'yer mind?"

The judge thought for a moment or two.

"Are you telling me that you are the headmaster?"

"I am. And sober, too," he added, anticipating the judge's next question, which he could not quite stop.

"Are you. . . ."

"I just tole yer. Stone cold sober. Never touch a drop before the eleven break."

"You're the headmaster of this school?" asked the judge incredulously.

"Look, chum," said the headmaster. "I ain't taking no offence at the presink. A lotter people don't reckernize me first go. Now I only 'ave to tell my boys a thing wunst. I won't say blokes like you don't need it twice. And I won't say no to wunce more. But if yer ask again after three times, them's fighting words in these 'ere parts."

And the headmaster jumped up, got into a fighting position and, after sparring for a moment or two, knocked out an imaginary opponent. "One, two, three," he began. "Out," he added. "Satisfied?" he asked while the judge was still trying to take in this astonishing performance.

"I suppose you're saying to yerself, 'ow can a bloke like 'im run a school like this. It don't make sense. Well, yer wrong, it do. Take a dekko at this."

The headmaster went across to a wall and pulled up a blind which disclosed a table.

"O level," he announced proudly. "A 'undred and fifty entrants. A 'undred with eight subjicts, thirty-seven with seven, eight with six, four with five and one little basket with only three. No failyers. Can they beat that at 'Arrer? Not, mind yer, that I think a lot o' this way of eddication. I don't 'old with it at all. I didn't 'ave no O and A levels. I learned 'cos I wanted to. And that's the only way. I could teach 'em so that they really 'eld the knowledge and wanted more. 'Course, yer got to 'ave a system. But this crammin' ain't it. Got yer breaf back yet, Dad?"

The judge was still gaping.

"Orl right," said the headmaster. "Take it easy now. 'Ere's A level. Wotcher think o' that?"

He went to another blind on the wall and raised it.

"Seventy-eight candidits, no failyers. One with four subjicts, sixty-five with three, eleven with two and one with one. 'E was the brother of the other little basket. I'd boot 'em out, only it ain't their fault. They're both the same. Their 'eads is like leaky tins. Yer can push in as much as yer like but it all comes out again."

The judge had at last found his voice and from utter stupefaction was becoming interested.

"How did you get them through at all?" he asked.

"Found yer voice, eh? Good. I'll tell yer. Well, I tole you their two 'eads were like tins with 'oles in 'em. So it's no good trying to fill 'em up. So wot I do is this. I fill 'em up just below the first 'ole, see."

"How d'you do that?" asked the judge.

"Concentrate on one subjict only. That's something. That means they'll get one O and one A at least. Better than none of either. Oh, they won't be eddicated. I can't 'elp that. It's the fault of the system. If I 'ad my way, my boys would learn a good bit less but they'd learn it good. It'd stick and they'd ask for more. That's the way to teach. A level and O level! Pah!"

And he pulled both blinds down sharply, as though to emphasize his disgust.

"Well," said the judge. "Thank you for this exposition. First of all, I should like to apologize for not realizing who you were."

"No 'ard feelings, mate," said the headmaster. "Shake." And he held out his hand. The judge shook it.

"How d'you do?" he said.

"Nicely, thanks," said the headmaster.

"What subjects do you teach personally, may I ask?" said the judge after a short pause.

"I do a bit of each mostly," said the headmaster. "Greek, Latin, Maffimatics, Physics and all that stuff."

"English?" queried the judge.

"No, yer got me there, mate. My English is orl right mind yer, just for ordinary talking. But when it comes to Shakespeare and such I can 'ear myself that there's something missing."

He then proceeded to recite in violent Cockney several extracts from *Hamlet* and *Macbeth* and finally wound up with the whole of the balcony scene from *Romeo and Juliet*.

"Don't sound so good, do it?" he said.

"You've a remarkable memory," said the judge in genuine admiration.

"Not bad," said the headmaster modestly, for the first time

speaking in his ordinary voice. The change of voice was almost as great a shock to the judge as the shock of finding that this was the headmaster.

"As a matter of fact," went on the headmaster, in his normal voice, "I could give you six books of the Aeneid and the whole of the Iliad if you'd like it. But I mustn't keep you. Did you just want to have a look round or was there something else?"

The judge sat back in his chair. "Well really!" he said eventually. "I can hardly be blamed for my mistake. Do you play this game on all your visitors?"

"No," said the headmaster, "I choose them most carefully. I've never been called on by a judge before. It was an opportunity I couldn't miss. Please forgive me."

"Very well," said the judge. "If the performance is over, perhaps I can tell you why I've called."

"Look, chum," said the headmaster, "don't come the old acid. It's you wot wants something outer me, ain't it?"

"You're quite right," said the judge. "I apologize."

"O.K., guv," said the headmaster. "And now what can I do for you?"

"I'm making enquiries about an old boy of yours. He wasn't here in your time, I imagine. Before the last war, as a matter of fact."

"I bin 'ere four years come Christmas," said the headmaster. "Or I should say I shall have had this appointment four years next Christmas."

"Please don't exert yourself for me," said the judge. "I can understand you very well."

"Back slang and all?" asked the headmaster.

"I know what it is," said the judge, "but I couldn't follow it if you talked quickly."

"I must admit I'm a bit rusty on that," said the headmaster.

"Well, if I may get down to business," said the judge. "The name is William Burford."

"Oh, we know all about him. 'E's in the nick, ain't 'e? I should say that——"

"You needn't translate," said the judge. "Yes, he's in prison. I sent him there."

"Breaking into a bank or something. Well, it's better than picking pockets. Must take some guts. All the same, we don't actually teach it here. Well, what can I tell you about him?"

"To tell you the truth," said the judge, "I don't really know. But, since the case has been over, I've taken an interest in the man and his wife and it's possible I can help them."

"Well, he doesn't come back to the school," said the headmaster, "and, from what I read, he isn't likely to for some time. But I'll send for his record. We try to keep up with all the old boys."

He pressed a bell and shortly afterwards there was a knock at the door. The headmaster's secretary came in. She was an efficient-looking middle-aged woman.

"We've an enquiry for an old boy. Can you bring his record, please, Pimple?"

"The confidential one, sir?" said Miss Pimple in an ultra refined voice.

"Under our system," the headmaster explained, "we keep two cards. One we can show to anyone and one with the truth, what he was like at school, who his friends were and so on."

"It would be most helpful if I could see the confidential card," said the judge. "I should particularly like to know who his friends were."

"Right," said the headmaster. "We've a customer, Pimple, let's hope the system works."

"And the name, sir?" said Miss Pimple. "The system would not work without a name."

"Wot's in a name?" said the headmaster. "No, you say it, Pimple," he added. "Sounds better from you."

"That," said Miss Pimple, "which we call a rose by any other name would smell as sweet. And the name is, sir?"

"William Burford," said the judge. "I should imagine that he was here between 1934 and 1939. Something like that."

"Thank you, sir," said Miss Pimple. "I'll get it at once."

" 'Stand not upon the order of your going'," began the headmaster. "There I am, off again."

Miss Pimple left, and the judge continued his chat with the headmaster. He decided to take full advantage of meeting this remarkable man.

"To what do you attribute the present increase in crime?" he said.

"Keeps you busy, doesn't it?" said the headmaster. "Lack of education in the right subjects mostly. I might have been a burglar or something for all the education I had. It's all this O level, A level and eleven-plus. First you've got to teach the parents. Then you won't have to teach the sons and daughters. But who is teaching the parents? Here I have four hundred and thirty-two future parents and how many hours a week can I teach them the things that really matter? Two. Two flippin' hours a week, that's all. I beg your pardon. Two solitary hours. Mind you, that's better than most places where they don't have it for two flippin'—two solitary—minutes. I'm not saying knowledge is a bad thing. On the contrary. But no amount of knowledge is any good wivout you understand wot you've got to do wiv it, that is to say—but you understand, I see. Well, I take every boy in this school on How to Live. If they don't learn that, all the Shakespeares and Homers and binomial theorems won't do them any good."

"How do you teach them to live, may I ask?" said the judge.

"By example, mostly. ''Ere, Spriggs,' I say, 'you're a married man with two children and you meet a beautiful girl in your office wot gives yer the orl right signal.' That's for the older boys, of course. But similar with the younger ones. Cheating the railways, and so on. Oh no, it isn't a lot of pi jaw. It's business, that's what it is. Here, I'll show you. I'll turn on Smith minor."

He went to a tape recorder and set it going at the place he wanted. The judge immediately heard the voice of the headmaster talking to a small boy.

"Now, Smith, what is meant by telling the truth?"

"Not telling lies."

"Why not tell lies?"

"Because it doesn't pay."

"Why doesn't it pay?"

"Because no one would ever trust you."

There was a noise at the door and Miss Pimple came in with two cards.

"Thank you, Pimple," said the headmaster.

"I'll have ready the cards of this boy's friends, sir."

"I'll ring twice if I want them, Pimple, thanks ever so," said the headmaster, and Miss Pimple went out without the trace of a smile. She was obviously used to the headmaster's little ways and she simply ignored them. Oxford or Bermondsey was all the same to her.

They looked at the cards.

"This is the chap all right," said the judge looking at one of the cards. "Married Lesley Elizabeth Rogers, September 1950."

"This is the one you want," said the headmaster. "Six months for receiving, February 1947. Now let's see him at school."

The headmaster looked at the card. "Not a bad chap really. Rather easily led. Weak character: all right in the right company."

"Had he a friend called Wilson?"

"What initials?"

"C. M."

"Yes he had. This will interest you. This fellow Wilson was a gambler, borrowed money and didn't pay it back. Not enough proved to expel. Bad influence on Burford. We'd better send for Master Wilson's card."

He rang the bell twice and after a very short while Miss Pimple appeared with several cards.

"Confidential on C. M. Wilson, please, Pimple."

"I opined you'd want him, sir. It's at the top."

She brought out the card.

"Do you wish any of the others, sir?"

"Leave them with us, Pimple, please."

Miss Pimple put down the cards. "Anything else before I go for my beer, sir?" she said.

"No thanks, Pimple. Keep half a pint for me."

"Very good, sir. Mild or bitter?"

"The usual, Pimple, please."

Miss Pimple went out.

"Irreplaceable," said the headmaster. "Lots can do shorthand and typing and the rest. But how many can take their beer?"

"This man Wilson," said the judge, "his Christian names are?"

"Cedric Mattingly."

"That's the man," said the judge. "I knew there was something in it. But why on earth didn't they want to say that he was at school with him? I suppose he's got some convictions against him, or something."

The headmaster suddenly looked more serious.

"He might have, if he'd lived, poor chap," he said, "but he's dead, killed in the war. Paid his debts all right."

"Dead, did you say?" asked the judge.

"Yes, killed in action in the desert—1943. It's funny, you know. He was a bad hat all right, judging from his report. But because he was killed, we wipe it all out. He may have been called up and been a bad soldier. But he was killed. And that balances the lot. Oh well, I suppose it's right. Life's the thing we all want most, and Cedric Mattingly Wilson hasn't got his any more. We've got ours, though."

"And his full name again?"

"Cedric Mattingly Wilson."

"There can't be two people of that name. Wilson's common enough but there couldn't be more than one Cedric Mattingly Wilson."

"There aren't any of him now, poor fellow," said the headmaster.

"I wouldn't have believed it," said the judge. "And yet somehow I knew."

"What is it? You seem to have had a shock. What about a glass of beer? It's gone eleven."

"No, thank you," said the judge. "Yes, indeed, I have had a shock. I may tell you, Mr Sprout, that I have been going up and down England looking for this man Wilson."

"That's hard," said the headmaster. "He couldn't very well be here. You couldn't call England heaven or hell. Purgatory, perhaps, though."

"I'm afraid I don't find it a joke," said the judge.

"No, I'm sorry. But have you really been looking for a dead man?"

"Yes," said the judge, "I have."

"Who told you he was alive?"

"Burford and his wife."

"They did, did they? Well, they picked the wrong man to say that to."

"I'm not sure that they did, Mr Sprout. Because I believed them. Do you know that that woman has actually sent for me twice because she has said she had the man under observation?"

"What for?"

"You may well ask. It's one of two motives. Either to get money out of me—and she has, a little—or to revenge herself on me for sending her husband to prison."

"In other words, mate, you've been 'ad for a sucker?"

"Yes," said the judge. "That's exactly what has happened. When I think what I've done to try to help her find Wilson—they said he was going under the name of Thompson, but that his real name was Wilson, Cedric Mattingly Wilson—when I think of all she's persuaded me to do, I feel—well, to tell you the truth, Mr Sprout, I hardly know how I do feel. All the time I've felt there was something else about the case, and she's even told me lies which she's later admitted were lies. And then each time she's persuaded me that there were reasons for her lies and that the substantial truth lay on her side."

"What has Wilson got to do with it? Why do you want to find him?"

"He's supposed to be the man who committed the crime for which her husband went to prison."

"Well, he can't have, can he?"

"No," said the judge, "he can't."

"What are you going to do about it?"

"I must think it out," said the judge, "but I think I ought to prosecute her."

"I should hope so. We can't have judges being made more fools of than they—we can't have judges being made fools of, can we?"

The judge was so used to Mr Sprout by now and so entirely devoted in his mind to his appalling discovery that the sally passed unnoticed.

"I confess I don't like the idea of the publicity," he said, "but I can't really see any alternative. I shall go and consult the Director of Public Prosecutions immediately. Thank you very much for your help."

"Glad to have been of help but sorry it's been such a knockout."

He led the judge from the room towards the entrance. They passed the War Memorial. The judge looked at it and with unpleasant fascination saw in its expected place among those killed in the 1939-45 War, Private Cedric Mattingly Wilson.

CHAPTER TWENTY-TWO

A PLAIN CASE OF FRAUD

THE next day the judge interviewed the Director of Public Prosecutions and disclosed the main facts to him.

"Undoubtedly," he said, "I've made a fool of myself and it will appear so to the public, but all the same I personally think the public interest requires that the woman should be prosecuted."

"Presumably for obtaining money by false pretences," said the Director.

"Yes," said the judge. "All the ingredients are there. One way or another she's had about £150 out of me. Whether, strictly speaking, the money I paid direct to the detective could be made the subject of a charge, I'm not sure. I should think not. But the money she got for paying the man she said was her informant certainly can. I don't suppose for a moment that he exists. But, even if he did, she got the money from me to pay him by pretending Thompson was alive when she knew he wasn't."

"But how can her informant exist?" queried the Director. "She knew the man was dead. So she couldn't possibly have asked someone to find him."

"I agree," said the judge, "that must be right. But there's no point in putting that in the charge. We've got a straightforward pretence that Thompson was alive."

"Oh, certainly," said the Director. "There's just one thing and, as far as I can see, only one. I know it's in the highest degree unlikely—particularly having regard to the reluctance of both Burfords to admit that the boys were at school together—but theoretically, I suppose, there could be two Cedric Mattingly Wilsons. The coincidences would be incredible but I think we've got to stop up that hole before we proceed."

"How do you suggest doing so?"

"If you don't mind, Judge, I would like you to go with a police officer and interview the lady. You can state in her presence what has happened and she can be asked under caution whether she says it is another man and that it is pure coincidence that her husband was at school with someone of exactly the same name with whom he apparently consorted a good deal. If she admits it's the same person or refuses to answer we can go ahead, because we'll know for certain that it is the same person. In the unlikely event of her saying that there is another person the officer must get as much information as he can from her and we must then see if the evidence is sufficient. I shall be very surprised if she tries that, though."

"I shall not be surprised at anything," said the judge. "After the way that woman has pleaded with me on—on—" He was about to say "on bended knee," when he suddenly realized that she had done so on his bed and he saw no reason why he should make a present of that to the Director. "After the way she has pleaded with me to believe her and assured me that Thompson had only gone away a short time before I arrived—and twice, mind you—I'd believe her capable of anything."

"Well, you'd like to go ahead, Judge, then?"

"Yes, I'm afraid so," said the judge. "It'll be great fun for the public and most unpleasant for me, but I think it's my duty."

He thought for a moment and then added:

"Yes, I can see no alternative."

"Very well, Judge, I'll arrange for a superintendent to call for you and take you to see the lady. I'll tell him to come and see you first to be briefed and then you can arrange any time that's convenient to you."

The judge thanked the Director and walked home from his office. It was only on the way home that a horrible thought struck him. He was kicking himself for being such a fool when he remembered Dalmunzie's warning, "Lock your bedroom door." It pulled him up short in his thoughts. This woman was plainly a dangerous woman. Her exact object might never be known, but she was prepared to lie her head off. He had, in fact, behaved with perfect propriety when she came to his bedroom but whose word was there for that except his? If she alleged that they were lovers and, for example, that the Thompson business was just a fiction between them to cover up their relationship and that he only prosecuted her when she refused to comply with his abnormal sexual demands!

They were horrifying thoughts. It was not that his friends would disbelieve him but at the best, even if the woman's story was not entirely credited, some members of the public would feel that there was something in it. And then another terrible thought struck him. Suppose Burford petitioned for divorce on the ground of her adultery with him. Again, his friends would believe him and in view of her lies about Thompson, most of the public would believe him too, but some might not. And then, again, who was to prove the lies except himself?

Mr Maclachlan, she can say, was just part of the scheme, in case her husband found out. And, after all, he would have to admit that he, a High Court Judge, had attended six race-meetings with the woman and stayed the night in the same hotel. He would also have to admit that she had come to his bedroom in her nightclothes while he was in bed and thrown herself in his arms.

"Oh, my God!" he said to himself. He had done nothing wrong and everything from a good motive, and yet it was not absolutely impossible that not only would the woman be acquitted but he himself found guilty of adultery. And, of adultery in the worst possible circumstances—with the wife of a man he had sent to prison. He had done things which can never have been done before and, from the public's point of view, if a judge—a widower—did such very odd things, was it so unlikely that he would also do a very natural thing and sleep with an exceptionally attractive woman?

He could now see himself completely ruined by the affair.

Why on earth had he embarked on it? Well, it was no good thinking about that. The question was, what was he to do now? Just nothing? Perhaps that was the best solution. But, then, suppose the woman did try to blackmail him or suppose divorce proceedings were brought against him, he would have to explain the delay in taking action after he first learned the truth about Thompson. What answer could he give except that he was frightened of the consequences? That was the truth. But why frightened if he had done nothing wrong? How could he successfully explain to a judge or jury or the public the motives which prevented him taking action with a certainty of being believed? If he had not done such extraordinary things in the first instance the matter would have been very different.

By the time he reached home he was drenched with sweat. He had a bath and changed and thought about the matter again. He called up his resources on the other side. He had an absolutely clear conscience, he had acted solely to see if an injustice had been done. His reputation was of the highest. It was surely very odd that such a judge should suddenly stoop to behave in such a scandalous manner. And he could certainly prove that he had tried to get the man off and out of prison. That was quite inconsistent with adultery.

Then he became angry with himself. Here he was almost hounding himself out of society, when he it was who had been the victim. He was the wronged person. Why should he be so frightened?

And then the forces of fear came into play again. What about the woman who committed suicide when the charge of rape she had made was dismissed? May she not have had a clear conscience and been unable to stand the verdict of acquittal which reflected guilt on her? Everyone is nearly always on the side of the person in the dock. He gets all the sympathy. They don't think of the chief witness for the prosecution whose reputation may be gravely damaged by an acquittal, with no possibility of redress.

Then he fought back again and the first weapon he used was his recollection of Lesley's face. She did not look like a blackmailer. She undoubtedly had a very sweet face. Surely she couldn't be capable of doing what he was imagining.

And yet she was capable of the most genuine looking tears and protestations of telling the truth when in fact the whole thing was a pack of lies from beginning to end.

After a pause in the battle he pulled himself together. He must decide what he was to do. Cry the whole thing off or prosecute? He came to a decision for two reasons. First, he was in the right and he would not yield to the forces of wrong, whatever the consequences; and, secondly, if he did nothing, he would never know whether the woman was going to make allegations against him. He was not prepared to wonder about this. She would have to make her allegations almost immediately if they were to be believed. Indeed, perhaps it would be as well if in the presence of the superintendent he recited what had happened at the hotel. Not as though he were defending himself at all, but, on the contrary, as evidence against the woman of the lengths she went to deceive him.

He made up his mind only just in time, as the superintendent telephoned and asked when it would be convenient for him to call and have a chat about the matter.

CHAPTER TWENTY-THREE

THE PROBLEM

THE superintendent was punctual for his appointment and they proceeded to discuss the case immediately. The judge told him everything except that Lesley's final plea at Doncaster had been in the bedroom. He was to regret not having mentioned this almost immediately. When he had finished his story, punctuated by a few questions from the superintendent, the judge asked him if there was anything more he would like to know. The superintendent thought for a moment and then coughed before asking his first question. The slight cough before starting a cross-examination is a normal sign of nervousness in an advocate and the superintendent's cough had the same significance.

"Sir Gerald," he said, "this woman, we know, is a consummate liar. She may be dangerous too. It's important that I should know in advance, if possible, what truth, if any, there is in what she says."

He stopped and the judge said in perhaps a slightly testy voice, which did not lessen the Superintendent's nervousness:

"Well, what else is there that you want to know?"

The superintendent coughed again. The judge noticed it and was not pleased.

"Have you a sore throat, Superintendent?" he asked. "If so, I can provide you with a lozenge."

The superintendent, after a moment's thought, decided to accept the invitation. The conversation was, therefore, slightly delayed while the judge fetched a box of lozenges.

"Thank you, sir," said the superintendent, "it is most kind."

"Not at all," said the judge. "Now we can get on. You were saying something."

"It was just this." The superintendent just managed to repress a cough and took a vigorous suck at the lozenge instead. The judge winced. It was a sound he could not bear, and he regretted his impetuosity in offering the lozenges. He knew from experience that the awful noise would continue through their conversation. Noisy eaters and sweet suckers who take an audible suck at least once every half minute were two of his abominations. There was an awful fascination about it too, like water dripping at long intervals from a tap. You never knew when the next suck was coming.

"You might find it rather too strong, Superintendent," said the judge hopefully. "If you'd like to get rid of it, please do. Here's an ashtray."

"No, indeed, thank you, Sir Gerald," said the superintendent. "I like it very much. It's more like a sweet really," and he took a vigorous suck.

"Might I perhaps know what they're called?" he added.

"The name's on the tin," said the judge and pushed it rather grudgingly across the table.

"*Succaroles,*" read the superintendent. "I've never heard of them before. I must remember the name."

And he sucked again.

"Now," said the judge, "perhaps . . ." and he waited for the superintendent's question.

"It's just this, Sir Gerald. There may have been trifling things which you haven't thought worth mentioning. Names, for example."

"What do you mean?" said the judge.

"Well, I don't want to alarm you, Sir Gerald, but we may be dealing with rather desperate people. And they're certainly quite unscrupulous."

"I quite follow that," said the judge, "but I wish you wouldn't beat about the bush. Ask me in plain English what you want to know about names."

"Well, Sir Gerald, what used you to call her?"

"Call her? By her name, of course, Mrs Burford."

"You never used her Christian name?"

"No, certainly not."

"I'm sorry to annoy you, Sir Gerald, but. . . ."

"You're not annoying me in the least," said the judge angrily. "Kindly ask any further questions you wish."

"You see, Sir Gerald, supposing, when we went in, she greeted you by your Christian name, I should know, as you weren't on Christian name terms, what she was up to."

"What would she be up to?"

"Well, Sir Gerald, I've had pretty good experience of this sort of woman. Even if she isn't a blackmailer by profession, with her back against the wall she may try anything. Now, if you had been on Christian name terms, the mere fact that she called you by your Christian name wouldn't mean anything. As it is, it will be an immediate danger signal and we'll know the sort of thing to expect."

"Such as, Superintendent?"

"Oh, anything. Forgive me putting it this way, Sir Gerald, but she might allege anything—absolutely anything."

"Do explain, Superintendent. What do you mean by anything?"

"Well, Sir Gerald, we're men of the world and you'll forgive this, I'm sure, but if it starts off that way she might allege—she might suggest—she might imply or actually say—she might treat your relationship with her as though . . . as though . . ."

"As though we'd slept together. If that's what you mean, Superintendent, for Heaven's sake say so."

"Well, of course, it would be incorrect, but it's the sort of thing those women do. In so many cases it's most difficult to refute, and they know it. It's just word against word and, as men do sleep with women, they hope they may be believed. Of course, in your case, no one would believe it for a moment. You did unfortunately stay in the same hotel together—I don't mean together, of course, but on the same night. But I expect your room was nowhere near hers."

"I've no idea where it was."

"Anyway she was never in your room and you were never in hers. She'll lie about that, of course, if she's the sort of woman I'm referring to, but no doubt your word would be accepted. The difficult cases are where the parties have been in the same room and it's just a question of what happened when they were there."

"As a matter of fact," said the judge, "she did come to my room."

"She came to your room?"

"Yes, I'm afraid so."

"You hadn't asked her to do so?"

"Of course I hadn't. She came and woke me up in the middle of the night."

"Oh, I see," said the superintendent, "so you weren't both fully dressed."

"Of course we weren't, Superintendent. I was fully undressed. I was in bed and asleep in my pyjamas."

"And she?"

"She was in pyjamas and a dressing-gown."

"I'm afraid this looks serious, Sir Gerald. This looks like the real thing. It's an old game. Did . . . er . . . er . . . anything take place between you?"

"Of course something took place between us," said the judge angrily.

The superintendent gaped.

"If you didn't waltz around the matter, Superintendent, we'd get on quicker. If you were woken up in the middle of the night by a woman, she wouldn't just stand there saying nothing and you wouldn't lie there doing nothing.

Something would happen, wouldn't it? If it was only that you told her to get out, as I did."

"Is the woman . . . er . . . good looking at all?"

"Yes, she is . . . very," said the judge.

"I see," said the superintendent. "And all that happened was that you told her to go and she went."

"No," said the judge, "I told her to go and she didn't."

"So you rang the bell and had her turned out?"

"No," said the judge, "I didn't. I threatened to and she pleaded with me to go on helping."

"She didn't by any chance throw her arms round you while she was pleading with you?"

"Well, she did, as a matter of fact."

The superintendent thought for a moment.

"This is going to be extremely awkward, Sir Gerald. This looks to me pretty well like a typical case. These women are the very devil. They'll allege anything, and particularly with someone in your position. She'll know that you won't want the publicity. And she may do it out of pure vindictiveness, even if she's got nothing to gain by it for herself."

"What are you leading up to, Superintendent?"

"Well, sir, she may not be a blackmailer in the first instance. Some of these women who get money by fraud simply keep this sort of thing as an avenue of escape. In other words, they won't blackmail you for money, but, if a prosecution is threatened, they'll try and head it off by threats of this kind, and, if you call their bluff and prosecute, they make good their threats out of pure spite."

"I still ask you, Superintendent, what all this is leading up to."

It was no comfort to the judge that the superintendent was saying what had been thought of by him the day before. He was indeed horrified to find how right he was.

"I was only wondering, Sir Gerald, if in the circumstances you wanted to prosecute."

"I've discussed the matter with the Director and we've decided that it's the only proper course."

"Then the Director knows all you've told me, Sir Gerald?"

"Not quite," said the judge a little uncomfortably. "I

didn't mention the bedroom scene. It didn't seem to be relevant at the time. But I do now see its importance."

"It looks so premeditated, Sir Gerald. That's what troubles me."

"But, if she's going to try blackmail, surely she'd have started by now."

"Not necessarily, Sir Gerald. And anyway, as I said, she may not intend to use blackmail except as a defence."

"Well, I don't see how I can leave the matter as it is," said the judge. "This woman has obtained money from me by blatant persistent fraud. I have, in fact, done absolutely nothing wrong. I have simply, no doubt unwisely, been rather foolish in letting myself get into this position. In those circumstances it seems to me that it would not only be cowardly but contrary to my duty as a judge if I let the matter go, just because I am frightened of the possible consequences to myself. One might just as well have a bachelor High Court Judge refusing to prosecute a burglar because it was suspected that entirely false allegations would be made by the burglar. In my view I'm under a duty to prosecute or rather to set the wheels of prosecution in motion. Of course the Director will prosecute. I shall simply be the chief witness. Besides," he added, "there's always the possibility that she is a blackmailer, and would have to be prosecuted for that later. If that happened, the failure to prosecute now would make it look as if I had something to hide, and lend colour to the allegations she would no doubt make on her prosecution."

"I see your point, Sir Gerald. And also, of course, you would always have it hanging over your head, and you may prefer to know the worst now rather than wait for it."

The judge did not at all relish the way in which the superintendent was voicing his doubts of the day before. He had hoped that he had allowed his imagination and anxiety too much play, but here was a down-to-earth superintendent, who probably hadn't much imagination, saying almost exactly the same as he had thought. All the same, he could see no escape from it. There must be a prosecution. He said so to the superintendent.

"Very good, Sir Gerald. We'll go and see the lady. I suggest we don't give her any warning. Usually I find early in the morning, say nine o'clock, is a good time to find these ladies in. If that isn't too early for you, Sir Gerald."

"No, that will be all right."

"I'll call for you then, Sir Gerald, at 8.45 a.m."

"Thank you. That will be very helpful."

The superintendent got up.

"Well," he said, "let's hope things won't be as bad as we fear, but I'm not very hopeful."

He started to go.

"Of course, there wasn't anything else, Sir Gerald?"

The judge paused for a moment.

"She kissed me on the forehead, if you must know."

"But there was no other kissing?"

"*There was not,*" said the judge decisively and rather loudly.

"I'm so sorry to have embarrassed you, Sir Gerald."

"You have not embarrassed me in the least," said the judge. "Good morning. I'll see you tomorrow," and he let out the superintendent as quickly as he could.

CHAPTER TWENTY-FOUR

UNDER CAUTION

THE next day, after a most troubled night, the judge set off with the superintendent, who was in plain clothes, for the house where Lesley had rooms. She was in and opened the front door herself. The judge was ready for the worst fears of the superintendent to be realized, and for her to throw her arms around his neck and call him by unsuitable endearing names. But, when he saw her, he felt relieved. He felt instinctively that anyone who looked like Lesley could not conceivably be a blackmailer. Her sweet face had a tremendous effect on him and he had to remind himself of the outrageous lies she had told, in order to rid himself of his immediate reaction to seeing her again. It was some time since he had last seen her and he had rather forgotten what an appealing face she had. And here he was with the crushing weight of the law beside him about to add to her misery. Then quickly he recalled the number of times she had assured him that she had seen Thompson and her appearance of honesty as she said it. You simply cannot judge by a face, he said to himself. The sweetest most appealing face in the world may conceal the mind of a completely unscrupulous adventurer.

"May we come in?" he said.

"Of course," said Lesley. "Please do."

They went into her sitting room.

"This is Superintendent Neale of Scotland Yard," said the judge.

They both waited for her reaction. It was not what they had expected. Her face lighted up and she said excitedly:

"Have you found him then? How wonderful."

The superintendent, though a little surprised at her behaviour, said nothing but grimly admired her performance. What an actress the woman is, he thought. She almost deserves to get away with it. And, by Jove! the judge was right when he said she was attractive. I know what my wife would say to me if she came into my bedroom in her nightclothes. His wife had not much imagination, but, he reflected, she would not require to draw very much on her small store of it to say what she thought of that situation.

No one answered Lesley immediately, and, when she saw how serious they looked, her face fell.

"Has something happened to William?" she asked anxiously. "Has he escaped again? I begged him not to try."

"No," said the judge, "he hasn't escaped."

Again there was silence. Then Lesley began again but rather less brightly:

"Then it is about him—Thompson, I mean?"

"Yes," said the judge unsmiling. "It is about him."

She could tell from the way he spoke that it was not good news.

"Has he gone abroad?" she asked. "Is that it?"

She's a sticker, thought the superintendent. But for brazenness she takes a lot of beating.

"Mrs Burford," said the judge slowly, "what do you say Thompson's real or former name was?"

"Cedric Mattingly Wilson," said Lesley, and started to brighten again.

"Then you have found him?" she said.

Wonderful, thought the superintendent. Like a captain going down with his ship. It's almost pathetic.

"Mrs Burford," said the judge. "A few days ago I went to see the headmaster of your husband's school."

Lesley went white. She was standing and the superintendent thought she might be going to faint. So he steadied her with his arm.

"No, it's all right," she said and sat down in a chair. "Just let me think for a moment."

The judge was so relieved at Lesley's behaviour that he could only feel sympathy for her. All his own fears vanished in a moment, and all he could see was a pathetic creature, already sufficiently unhappy, about to be made even more so. Then he realized that his fears might have been allayed too easily. She hadn't said anything for the moment. It's true that there had been none of the actions suggested by the superintendent, but she still might be thinking out a good lie to tell. After all, she was highly skilled in the art. No, it was too soon to be sure that he was safe.

They both waited for her to make the next move. It was at least a minute before she spoke.

"He's not really dead, you know," she said.

Really, said the superintendent to himself, this is carrying things a bit too far. Or she may be out of her mind. That's possible. However, the first thing to establish for certain was that there were not two Cedric Mattingly Wilsons. But it had better be under caution.

"Mrs Burford," he said, "I think I should now warn you that you needn't say anything unless you wish to do so but that anything you do say may be given in evidence if you are charged with an offence."

"What offence?" asked Lesley.

"Obtaining money by false pretences from Sir Gerald Carstairs."

"What false pretences?"

I'm losing sympathy with this client, thought the superintendent. Innocent baby looks and all.

"By falsely pretending that Cedric Mattingly Wilson was alive when in fact you knew him to be dead."

"He's alive," said Lesley.

"Really, Mrs Burford," said the superintendent. "Sir Gerald has seen his name on the Roll of Honour at the School. Are you suggesting that you were referring to a different Cedric Mattingly Wilson?"

"No, that's the one," said Lesley.

"Well, why do you keep up such a silly pretence?" said the superintendent. "It'll do you no good. I'm about to go to the War Office for confirmation of his death, but that's only a formality."

"I know," said Lesley. "They'll confirm it."

"Well," said the superintendent, "as I told you, you needn't answer any questions if you prefer not, but is it not the case that you have frequently told Sir Gerald that this man Wilson is alive and that you have obtained money on the strength of it?"

"Yes," said Lesley, "that's quite true. Are you arresting me now?"

"No," said the judge and added very gently, "but I'm afraid that must follow."

"I did ask you not to go to the school," said Lesley.

The superintendent had now got his bearings. These women had two well-known methods of defence. The one was the hell-cat, scratching, fighting, no holds barred method which he had feared. The other was the poor, helpless, innocent, didn't-really-mean-any-harm method, which this girl was putting on to a treat. Now *his* only fear was that the judge would be taken in by it and call off the prosecution, not through fear but through pity. He was glad it was that way, as the other would have been more embarrassing, but, all the same, he wasn't going to let this bird get away, if he could help it.

"Now, Mrs. Burford," he said, "I propose to write out what you have said and ask you if you will sign it. You needn't if you don't wish to do so."

"I'll sign it," she said. "Will I go to prison for long?"

"It's possible," said the judge, "only possible, mind you, that you won't go to prison at all. It's the first offence, you see."

"It isn't an offence at all," said Lesley, "but you'll never believe me. The man is alive."

"Now, look, Mrs Burford," said the superintendent, quite sincerely, "what the judge has said is quite true and with luck you won't be sent to prison. I'd like to help you but you make it very difficult for us if you keep on telling lies about this man. We all know he's dead now. Why keep up the pretence?"

"It's not a pretence," said Lesley.

"But the War Office can prove he's dead. What's the good of saying he's still alive? The War Office don't make mistakes like that. Not once in a thousand years."

"Then this is the thousandth year," said Lesley.

"Mrs Burford," said the judge, "are you feeling quite well?"

"I'm feeling sick," said Lesley, "but I'm quite well really."

"Why do you keep repeating this nonsense about the man being alive?"

"Because I've seen him. Haven't I told you? Twice I've seen him."

"But he's dead."

"He isn't."

"Can you explain then how he's officially reported dead?"

"Well, I can but I don't suppose you'll believe me."

"What is the explanation?"

"This man Thompson or Wilson came to see my husband shortly before the robbery. They were at school together, but they hadn't met each other for years."

"Why did you lie about their being at school together?"

"That's easy. I'll tell you. When the police first called on William he was a little anxious about what he'd been doing with Thompson on race-courses, but that was all. But later, when they identified the notes and the dust and he realized that no one believed his story about Thompson, he was terrified to say they were at school together. Just as later on I was. In case you went there and found he was dead. He felt it would be the final nail in *his* coffin. And we lied. I'm right about that, aren't I? William's case would have been more difficult at the trial if Thompson were proved to be dead."

"Well, of course. Then he is dead?"

"No, I tell you, he isn't, but who would have believed us? You won't believe me now. But I'd better tell you just the same. Shall I?"

"If it's the truth," said the judge. "But don't, if it isn't."

"You won't believe it, but it is the truth," said Lesley. "When Thompson first called on us, William was amazed, as he'd heard he'd been killed. 'I was,' said Thompson, 'or rather Cedric Mattingly Wilson was killed. My name's Thompson. It was too easy, really,' he said. 'I owed a lot all round and for various reasons it would have suited me well to disappear. I got my chance in the desert. Found a dead private and put my identity disc on him. Then deserted and got taken prisoner. I escaped and one way or another I managed to get home to start a new life as Thompson. I got ration cards and everything. Thompson's the name now,' he said."

"That's all very well," said the judge. "But first of all, this is a very old story and not at all easy to bring off. It has no doubt very occasionally happened but it's not so simple as you think. But, if this man did say all this, you knew I was trying to help you, why didn't you tell me?"

"*Because* you were helping me. You were my only hope. If you stopped helping me, there was nothing more I could do. And I felt sure that, if I told you the story about Thompson, you'd make enquiries at the War Office and find he was dead and disbelieve me. You don't believe me now, do you?"

The superintendent looked at the judge to see who should say, "No" first.

"I'm afraid not," said the judge. "You have unfortunately told me other lies and I'm afraid I can't accept what you say now."

"I didn't expect you to," said Lesley. "That's why I didn't tell you before. Can't you see that?"

"I hear what you say," said the judge.

"And why should I have done all I have, unless Thompson did exist? What good have I got out of it?"

"You've had fifty pounds," said the superintendent, "apart from some visits to race-courses and meals at Sir Gerald's expense."

"The fifty pounds were for the man who answered the advertisement."

"So you say," said the superintendent, "can you prove he exists?"

"I don't know," said Lesley, "but that sort of man isn't very free with his address."

"Well, then," said the superintendent, "from my point of view the answer to your question is fifty pounds and any more you might have been able to get out of Sir Gerald."

"Do you think that too?" Lesley asked the judge.

"What else can I think?" he said. "You lied to me on at least two occasions and now you expect us to believe a fantastic story which, if true, your husband could have told at his trial as you could have told me."

"But I've explained why we both didn't. I dare say it was wrong but then the odds were so much against us. I don't know what else we could have done. You've admitted that William would have been even more sure to have been convicted, and by your own behaviour now I can see I was right not to tell you, or you'd have stopped helping me at once. Not that it would have made any difference," she added. "I am really grateful for your help," she said, "but all it's done, so far as I can see, is to land me in the dock. Not that I care much, With William in prison, I might as well be. Only it's so unjust. We have been foolish and told lies, but they weren't crimes. Now he's doing ten years for something he never did and I'm about to be prosecuted for something I never did. Now if I told a lie now and said Thompson really was dead, you'd tell me it would help me not to go to prison. Well, I'm not going to, even if it does mean prison. He's alive and I shall say so. Doesn't that make you think I may be telling the truth?"

"A very good effort, Mrs Burford," said the judge. "It's a pity you don't use your obvious talents for a better purpose."

"I can hear you saying that from the Bench with a sneer," said Lesley. "Go on, prosecute me. But I shall tell the truth and the whole truth this time."

The *whole* truth, thought the superintendent. Were my first thoughts right? Has she tried the little girl stuff first and is she now going to try the other? Well, fortunately for the judge, she won't get very far with it now. She should have started off with that one if she wanted it to work. All the same she can make a lot of the bedroom scene if she wants to be nasty. Yes, of course, he thought, and she can say she didn't want to say anything about it, unless it was absolutely necessary. Yes, we mustn't be too confident.

Meanwhile the judge's thoughts were running on the same lines, and he felt that it was advisable to say:

"Yes, Mrs Burford, I should tell the whole truth if I were you. And, if there's anything you've left out that you'd like to tell the superintendent I suggest you do so now, though, of course, you needn't if you don't want to. But, if you bring out some further bombshell at a later date, you mustn't be surprised if people aren't inclined to believe you. You've a chance of saying it now, you see."

Cunning old boy, thought the superintendent, couldn't have done it better myself. If she says nothing about the bedroom now, she won't get much out of it later.

"No," said Lesley, "I can't think of anything else. Thompson planted everything on William and he's alive. And that's all there is to it."

The judge and the superintendent left Lesley a few minutes after the superintendent had put her statement into writing and she had signed it.

"Well, Sir Gerald," said the superintendent on their way to the judge's flat, "I think we can say that was pretty satisfactory."

"Yes," said the judge, "I think it was. It doesn't look as though there is any thought in her mind of attacking me. I must say, though, I find the way she sticks to her story odd."

"Oh, Sir Gerald," said the superintendent, "you wouldn't if you'd had my experience. Some of these people simply can't give in. All the facts are against them but they still brazen it out."

"And what has she to gain from it?"

"Nothing," said the superintendent, "nor have any of the people I have just mentioned, but they do it just the same. Well, I'll get on to the War Office straight away and report the whole matter to the Director. It's pretty well open and shut, I should say. That old identity-disc-from-a-dead-soldier yarn won't last her very long. But I'm sorry in a way, because it might land her in prison. Still, you can't say we didn't give her every chance."

CHAPTER TWENTY-FIVE

EXTRAORDINARY

AFTER the interview with Lesley the judge was as convinced of her guilt as he was before. Indeed, in some ways. he would have had more respect for Lesley, if she had not tried to impose upon them with the well-worn story of the man who puts his identity disc on a dead man. It was an insult to their intelligence. He was quite certain, as was the superintendent, that nothing of the kind had happened. And both of them were, of course, quite right. Cedric Mattingly Wilson had never done such a thing or thought of doing it.

But the judge was greatly relieved by Lesley's attitude and he then began to think of her with both pity and gratitude. After all, she might have done the things which he and the superintendent had visualized. She had tried none of them. It is true that she had attempted to get out of her impossible position by persisting in a stupid lie but that was far, far better than the method of defence he had feared she might use.

Having got to that stage, he began to ask why she had done any of the things she had done. Was it really to make money out of him? If so, she had made very poor use of her chances. Never throughout their association had she mentioned her own financial position, except when the question of paying the informant arose. It was true that very probably that was just a trick and there was no informant. But it was very odd that that was all she had done.

If her object was revenge, she had had every opportunity after the bedroom scene to give effect to any such motive, but she plainly had no such intention.

Eventually the only solution he could arrive at was that she was intending to get more money from him later. He could not pretend that he thought this was an entirely satisfactory solution but, of course, criminals went about their work in an odd way, sometimes making the most stupid mistakes and sometimes taking a great deal of trouble for no good purpose. Yes, that was really the answer. After all, the facts one could not get away from were first that Thompson was to her knowledge dead and secondly that she had pretended he was alive. No, he decided, she was just an odd girl who went about her business in an odd way. It was a pity she had such a sweet, appealing face, but, he supposed, hers would not be the first sweet appealing face in the dock and unquestionably she must go there.

Two days later the telephone rang and the superintendent asked if he could come to see him immediately. Something extraordinary had happened. The judge invited him to call at once.

Something extraordinary? What could it be? Had Lesley turned round and started the course they'd feared? He suddenly felt sick at the thought. After the relief of the last two days he felt he couldn't stand any more of that. But then the word "extraordinary" didn't suggest that at all. If that is what the superintendent had meant he would have used another expression. He would have said "I'm afraid something rather unfortunate has happened" or something like that. No, "extraordinary" wasn't at all the word to use. It was ridiculous of him even to have suspected that Lesley was on the offensive. "Extraordinary." Oh, no, that wasn't at all the right word. But then, of course, policemen didn't always have a perfect command of English, and, though the superintendent was reasonably well educated, he had probably risen from the ranks and had a limited vocabulary.

Could he have used the word "extraordinary" for "unfortunate", though? Surely not. He certainly hadn't misheard him. He had definitely said "something rather extraordinary has happened". How stupid he was not just to ask one question to relieve his mind of worry. He could so easily have said: "She hasn't started anything, has she?" or something of that kind. The superintendent could just as easily have allayed his fears on that subject in two words. Why didn't he? Why did he give himself this extra period of uncertainty and suspense?

Well, it wouldn't be for long. It couldn't take the superintendent more than a quarter of an hour to get to him. Of course, if the traffic were bad, it might be longer. Or, if any of the roads were closed for some procession. Thank Heaven, there was nothing on like Trooping the Colour. He looked in *The Times* to see the diary of the day's events. No, there didn't seem to be anything which need delay the superintendent. It was a dry day, too. Of course London traffic did sometimes get out of hand and he might get caught in a traffic block.

The telephone rang. He answered eagerly. If it were the superintendent, he would ask the one question which would prevent the period of waiting from being a period of worry too. Yes, it was Scotland Yard. Good.

"This is Detective-Sergeant Harper speaking, sir. The superintendent was a little delayed in leaving, sir, and he asked me to tell you that he had just left."

"Thank you," said the judge and replaced the receiver angrily. Confound it! There was nothing he could ask the sergeant, and now he had to trace the superintendent's journey all over again. How would he come? By the Embankment? Oh, this is absurd. He picked up the newspaper and read the whole of the first leading article without taking in a single word. He tried it again with much the same result, though by means of intense concentration he did manage to follow a few sentences. Where would the superintendent be now? These police-drivers were pretty good. But, of course, he couldn't be ringing the alarm bell and would have to take his place with other traffic. But surely he couldn't be long now. How long did it take to read the leading article? He could time it, and then read it over and over again. Yes, he'd read it aloud. He began:

"The Lord Chancellor's statement yesterday that there would soon be more judges and more Courts will be generally welcomed. It is a truism that justice delayed is justice denied but too many people have in recent years had this fact brought unpleasantly to their attention. It is, however, only fair to the Government to point out that the competitive claims upon the building materials and labour available in the country have until now been very great. Homes must, of course, have first priority, and undoubtedly even now there is still an acute housing shortage."

He stopped reading. Was that a car drawing up? He went to the window. Yes, it was. Good. A uniformed chauffeur jumped smartly out and went to the rear door. He opened it and an elderly lady emerged. The judge waited without much hope to see if the superintendent followed her, but he did not. He did not really believe that an elderly lady was the something extraordinary, but nothing was impossible. She might have been Thompson's mother.

He went back to the paper. He was tired of the leading article. He would try the letters. They were at any rate shorter, some of them so short that he could really read the whole letter and follow it without his thoughts reverting to the superintendent.

"Sir," he read, "Mr Scudley-Brown has missed the point of my letter. If he will read the second sentence before the first he will find that he is mistaken." Read the second sentence before the first? Then why didn't he write it first? How extraordinary. He must get the letter in question. Which date was it? The writer didn't say. Oh, well—it would all take up time. It couldn't be yesterday's. The day before, perhaps. But why didn't he alter the order of the sentences in his original letter if they made easier sense that way? Extraordinary. That word again. How long would he be? Why did he have to leave Scotland Yard so late? After all, he was a High Court judge. He shouldn't be kept waiting, except for something urgent.

The bell rang. He went with deliberate slowness to open it. It was the postman, who couldn't get the only letter through the letter box. It was a packet on Her Majesty's Service containing the latest Acts of Parliament. He put it on his desk unopened, and went to look for the issue of *The Times* with the original letter in it. It really would be rather intriguing to see the letter. It wasn't in Monday's; the previous Saturday's then? No. Friday was almost a week ago. It must be in that. No, this is Thursday's. Where on earth is Friday's? He always kept them in the right place. Could he have taken it out and left it somewhere? He couldn't remember. He must look again. And then the bell rang and it was the superintendent.

"Come in and sit down, Superintendent," he said. "Cigarette?"

"Thank you, Sir Gerald. I will, if you don't mind."

The superintendent took his time—what a time—in getting a cigarette out of the box offered to him and even longer to light it. He tried with his lighter without success. After several failures the judge offered a match.

"No, this works all right," said the superintendent. "Can't think what's happened to it today."

He tried several more times, still without success.

Again the judge offered a match.

"I hate to give in," said the superintendent. "Lighters are rather like horses. If you let them know they're master, they'll be always playing you up."

"Indeed?" said the judge. "Did you train yours yourself?"

"Yes," said the superintendent. "Had it from a foal."

"I suppose it has been fed?" said the judge.

He was amazed that he could talk with such apparent calm while the superintendent was wasting time with his beastly cigarette.

"Good gracious, Sir Gerald. You're quite right. I forgot to fill it. If I might have that match."

The judge handed him the box. The superintendent broke the first match and the second went out, but with the third he was successful and he leaned back in his chair.

"Well," said the judge, "what's happened?"

"It's extraordinary," said the superintendent.

"That's what you said before," said the judge. "What is it?"

"I've been to the War Office. Cedric Mattingly Wilson was discharged from the Army as unfit on the 18th February, 1943."

"There must be some mistake."

"That's what I thought. I had the answer by telephone first. I couldn't believe it. So I went round myself. There's only one Cedric Mattingly Wilson in Army records. He has never been wounded, let alone killed, and he was discharged with an indifferent character on the day I mentioned. As far as Army records go, he is still alive."

"But what about the school? They have him on the Roll of Honour."

"That," said the superintendent, "is the next thing we must find out."

CHAPTER TWENTY-SIX

THE HEADMASTER AGAIN

"LET's go at once," said the judge, "if you can manage it."

"I'd already arranged to do so."

"Good. What can the answer be? It's extraordinary."

"Exactly what I said to you on the telephone, Sir Gerald."

This reminded the judge of his uncomfortable twenty minutes, but his relief was sufficient to prevent him from being annoyed.

"As a matter of fact, I've telephoned the school and asked if the headmaster would see me at once. I didn't know at the time if you'd be able to come."

"Did you speak to the headmaster himself?"

"It's odd you should say that, Sir Gerald," said the superintendent. "The man I spoke to obviously wasn't the headmaster but he said he was. Very strange I thought it. At a school, I mean."

"As a matter of fact it was the headmaster," said the judge.

"No, I assure you, Sir Gerald, it couldn't have been."

"Wait till you meet him," said the judge. "You're going to have two surprises today."

Then the judge explained. He did not think it fair to let the superintendent go through what he had been through, though he had to admit to himself how very much he would have liked to watch the performance.

The headmaster saw them immediately on their arrival.

"You're not going to arrest me, I hope," he said. "Anyway I plead not guilty and reserve my defence."

"We've come on a very serious matter, Mr. Sprout," said the judge, "and we'd be most grateful for your help."

"Well," said the headmaster, "you never know when you may need the law, so I believe in keeping in with it."

"You remember," said the judge, "that I asked you about Cedric Mattingly Wilson and you showed me from his record card that he was killed in the last war and then I saw his name on the War Memorial."

"That's right," said the headmaster. "Someone left him some money and you want to find his widow?"

"No," said the judge, "nothing of the kind. What we want to know is where your school got the information about his death from."

"Well, I wasn't here at the time, but I suppose they saw it in the casualty lists."

"It was never in the casualty lists."

"What d'you mean? The man's dead, isn't he?"

"Not so far as the War Office knows. They certainly have no record of his being killed. On the contrary he was discharged from the Army in 1943."

"Crikey!" said the headmaster.

He rang the bell and Miss Pimple soon appeared.

"Pimple," said the headmaster, "have we still got the records from which they made up the casualty lists in the last war?"

"I'll see, sir," said Miss Pimple, "but it may take some time. They'll be stored away somewhere."

"Get the boys on to it, Pimple. I want those records if we've got them."

"What d'you think's happened?" he asked when Miss Pimple had gone.

"We've no idea," said the judge. "We only know that Mrs Burford says the man's alive and she's seen him. But she thought that he was recorded at the War Office as dead. She told us that this man Wilson told her and her husband that he'd slipped his identity disc on a dead soldier—you know the old story—and had been officially declared killed. Well, it's quite plain that he's not officially dead at the War Office, but he is here."

"What may have happened," said the superintendent, "is

that this chap Wilson, knowing that he'd been described as dead in the school magazine and that Burford knew that, spun the yarn about the identity disc. Naturally, he wouldn't expect anyone to check it up, as his name was on the War Memorial. And the Burfords believed it. As well they might."

"And that," said the judge, "would account for their both being terrified to let us come to the school and at the same time declaring that the man was alive. But, first of all, we want to know how he came to be described as a dead man. Was it just a lucky accident for him, or what? Mistakes like that have occasionally occurred, particularly with common names like Wilson. His other names, of course, are far from common, but what happens is that X. Y. Wilson's name appears in the casualty list and by mistake they put the wrong one in the school magazine, and, as it suits the man in question, he lets the error be perpetuated, and invents the yarn about the identity disc to stop people making enquiries or just because he thought it a good story."

"Oh, well," said the headmaster, "we can afford it. Our figures'll stand it."

"Your figures?" queried the judge.

"Yes," said the headmaster. "If this means that Burford comes out and Wilson goes in, it adds one to the list. Burford was in it anyway with his six months."

"What list?" asked the judge.

"If this had happened a few years back it'd have had me worried. Look, I'll show you."

The headmaster pulled up a blind on the wall and showed them a table.

"Most schools," he said, "keep records of all the Prime Ministers, Judges and Generals and so on they've produced. Well, I keep a record of all the scallywags as well. It isn't quite so easy to do because breaking and entering doesn't always get reported, while being made a Prime Minister does. So there are gaps in this list, but it isn't bad. Have a look."

It certainly was an imposing list.

"Personally," he said, "I think these lists should be published. Then you could make a fair choice. You may have a school where they've a wonderful record for generals, but they've quite a good one for confidence tricksters too. Well, you want to know, don't you? What d'you want your son to be? If you want him to be an undischarged bankrupt look at that one. There's the place for him."

He pointed to a school.

"It keeps up a good average, doesn't it? Been top of this list for bankrupts for years. Only beaten once in the last ten years. They must have a good economics master there. Or it may just be tradition, just like some schools are always good at one particular sport. Look at that one for bigamy. Wonder who teaches them that."

It really was an interesting table. Over fifty schools were on the list and against each of them was their record for the previous ten years for every kind of crime and for bankruptcy. The judge looked for his school.

"Looking for yours?" said the headmaster. "You'll find it. How d'you like it? Now perhaps you'd like to see the generals and the judges. Here."

He went to another blind and lifted it up.

"There you are," he said. "You're on that. One judge extra, whatever year that was. But, of course, you were before we started the system. It isn't a bad idea, is it? Look at this one. They got two knights that year. Now look at the other table. Two housebreakers. Pretty well cancels out. Don't suppose the knights were the housebreakers. Of course they might have been. You'd know better than me about that."

"No," said the judge, "most titled people who get convicted are charged with fraud or some financial swindle. Or murder, of course. There are no class distinctions there."

"Sorry Pimple's taking so long," said the headmaster, "but it must be quite a business going back to 1943. This case of yours would have had me worried a few years back. We were neck and neck with St. Willowbys. And one of their boys was charged with something. The trial took five days. It was like a test match here. If he was convicted, we were one up on them. If he was acquitted, we stayed equal. Then, just when things looked all right for us and the old judge was giving the defence hell—you know the way—if one of our boys wasn't charged with being drunk in charge of a car! We hardly did any work in the school that week I can tell you. But it was all right in the end. Our fellow got off and theirs got three years. But it was touch and go at one time. And if this case of yours had come up then, it'd have had me rattled. But it's all right now. We've gone ahead. They've had a couple of manslaughters and a bankruptcy to one fraud. They nearly had a murder too but they let the chap off. Juries getting a bit soft, don't you think?"

"They never like convicting if they can avoid it," said the judge.

"That's your trouble, isn't it?" said the headmaster.

The judge went rather red.

"Certainly not," he said, "it's not our business to try to get a conviction."

The headmaster whistled.

"Well," he said, "I've been to the Assizes, you know. Not one of our boys. Just to have a look. If the judge I saw wasn't working overtime to get the jury to convict, you can hang me too. And overtime's the right word, too. He was still at it at eight o'clock."

"I can't agree with you at all," said the judge. "It's perfectly true that judges do sit a bit late sometimes in order to get through the work and personally I think that's undesirable in a criminal case. I never sit late myself except in civil cases and when there's no jury."

"Well, I'm glad to hear it," said the headmaster. "But this man Burford you tried, why did the jury convict him if you were so keen on his getting off?"

"It was a very strong case on the face of it," said the judge uncomfortably. "It was only afterwards that I began to have doubts."

"I see," said the headmaster. "Second thoughts best, eh?"

The judge was relieved that a moment later Miss Pimple returned.

"Good news, sir," she said. "We've found the records. Here you are. Cedric Mattingly Wilson, killed in action 23rd March, 1943.

"Yes, but how did the entry come to be made? His name isn't in the casualty lists," said the judge.

"There's a letter here, sir, which I think gives the answer to that."

She handed them a letter which read as follows:

Dear Sir,

I am sure you will be sorry to hear that my brother, Cedric Mattingly Wilson, was killed in action on the 23rd March, 1943. As I have not seen his name in the School magazine I assume that you must have missed his name in the casualty lists. Please do not reply to this letter as I am staying with an aunt who sees all my letters and who was very much attached to my brother, and who has taken his death very badly. She is a little better at the moment but any mention of the matter now might set her back. I hope you will continue to send me my brother's copies of the magazine to the address you have and I enclose a further year's subscription.

Yours sincerely,
Richard Mattingly Wilson

The letter and address were typewritten.

"Is there nothing else?" asked the superintendent.

"Nothing as far as I can see," said Miss Pimple. "All the documents are here."

They looked through them but could find nothing else.

"So what it comes to is this," said the judge. "This fellow Wilson, pretending to be his brother, writes a letter to the school magazine announcing his own death. The editor or headmaster has no reason to suspect its authenticity. What reason could a person have for making a false report? I suppose some very careful people would check with the War Office but that obviously didn't happen here and you can't blame them for not making a check. The address is probably a false address, very likely non-existent. Hence the request not to reply. But he wants the magazine to be sent in the ordinary way so that he can see if he's duly been entered as killed. As soon as he's got it, he becomes Thompson and invents the story of the identity disc. Anything wrong with that, Superintendent?"

"Depends what you mean by wrong, sir," said the superintendent. "But I'd like to take this letter if I may, sir. I'll give you a receipt for it. But somehow I think we shall owe

Mrs Burford an apology. Of course, Burford's position isn't quite so clear. They might have been in it together. We shall have to go into that. But there's certainly a lot of work to be done on the case now. I'd better get straight back to the Yard."

"I think," said the judge, "I shall call on Mrs Burford."

"Well," said the headmaster, "very pleased to have been of some help. But, if you can help the school records by letting out Burford and not catching Wilson you'd be doing me a favour. No, don't look so unhappy. I don't mean it. You catch him. We haven't had a bank robber before and it'd be a pity to have to wash it out altogether."

The judge and the superintendent, having thanked the headmaster and Miss Pimple for their help, hurried back to London. Lesley was in when the judge called on her.

"Have you come to arrest me?" she asked.

"I'm by myself," he said, "and we don't do our own arresting. No, I've come to apologize."

"Apologize!"

Lesley jumped up excitedly.

"What's happened?" she said.

The judge told her.

"Then, when he told us that story of the identity disc, he was just telling lies?"

"Obviously. But he banked on your believing it, and nine people out of ten who'd seen his name in the school magazine would have done the same."

"What'll happen now?"

"Well, I can't be sure," said the judge, "but I feel pretty certain that the police will now make an all-out attempt to find Thompson. So you'll be off to race-meetings again—but this time not with me."

"You have been terribly kind," said Lesley.

"I've been a mixture," said the judge. "But you mustn't start to get too excited. First of all they may never catch the man."

"But you do believe me now about him?"

"Yes," said the judge, "I do. But, secondly, even if he is caught, we don't know what he'll say. A lot may depend on that. You see, your husband and he might have been in it together."

"But, surely," said Lesley, "if you find William was telling the truth about the existence of Thompson, you'll believe him about the rest?"

"I can't answer for the Home Secretary, but I'm bound to say it should at the very least raise a serious doubt as to the justice of your husband's conviction."

"That means they'll let him out?"

"I hope so," said the judge, "but it doesn't rest with me. And, I repeat, if Thompson is caught and implicates your husband, it must depend on what they both say."

"But they must believe William after this. It would be so unfair not to."

Two days later Lesley was being escorted all over the country to race-meetings by plain-clothes detectives. They had to go to more than six meetings before they found Mr Thompson, but they caught him in the end, and after they had taken his fingerprints and found that they were the same as those found on the scene of the robbery he proved surprisingly co-operative. He made a complete confession entirely exonerating William and admitting that he'd deliberately tried to plant his crime on someone with a previous conviction and then telephoned the police to give them the tip. He said that he hoped that, once they'd got someone convicted, their search for the remainder of the gang would not be active.

The reason for his co-operation became rather more obvious when, a few weeks after he had been in custody, he managed to escape from prison. The headmaster of his school was accordingly saved the sad task of adding one to the list of criminals. Confessions amount to nothing. You must be convicted before you go on the table. On the other hand it meant that the school had no bank robbers to its credit.

"Now, Spriggs," said the headmaster, "you'll have to get that Scholarship at Oxford to make up."

CHAPTER TWENTY-SEVEN

BACK TO WORK

WILLIAM was soon released and given a free pardon, but he was not awarded compensation. It was fairly pointed out that, if you tell lies to the police when enquiries are made of you, you have no right to complain if, in consequence, you are not only disbelieved but put in the dock and convicted.

The judge himself felt intensely relieved and he was congratulated by nearly all of his colleagues, particularly by those who had been most sceptical. Mr Justice Dalmunzie wrote him a short note.

"Well done," it said. "It seems that you could have safely left your bedroom door open."

Term began again two days after William was released and the judge had an interesting session with himself the night before he was to sit at the Old Bailey. He felt he couldn't entirely blame himself for the Burford verdict. He had been grossly unfair, but, had he been fair, it would probably have made no difference to the verdict. But it was in consequence of his unfairness that he had suffered such appalling suspense and anxiety. He considered having a small notice to put in front of him with "BE FAIR" on it, but, on the whole, he thought that would be inadvisable, as other people would see it. However, he did not really need a physical notice. It must surely now be so stamped on his mind that he could never forget it. And fortunately no harm had been done. On the contrary, probably, if he hadn't been unfair, William would have been convicted just the same and, much worse, served his sentence. It was only because of his own unfairness that the judge had taken the matter up. It was a pleasant paradox. Burford owed his release to the judge being unfair. But that was not to be used as a reason for being unfair in the future. I wonder what case I shall first have to try, he wondered. It would be a happy coincidence if Empton were in it to see the difference.

Mr Empton *was* in it, defending a man on a simple little charge of receiving cars knowing them to have been stolen. The cars had arrived at the accused's yard without number plates. The accused then proceeded to erase the engine and chassis numbers and to spray the cars a different colour. They were then handed back to the man who had brought them. He was known to the accused as Ernie. The accused did not ask Ernie where the cars came from or why they had no number plates or why Ernie wanted the numbers erased. He didn't think there was anything wrong as Ernie seemed a "genuine" person.

"Why," he was asked by prosecuting counsel, "do you think Ernie wanted the numbers erased?"

"Never arst."

"I know you never asked but why did you *think* he wanted them erased?"

"It was 'is car, weren't it? 'E could do wot 'e liked with it, couldn't 'e?"

Prosecuting counsel sat down and Mr Empton got up to re-examine.

"Whatever Ernie may or may not have had in mind, did you believe he was doing anything wrong?"

"Wot should I think he was doing anything wrong for?"

"So you didn't think," said Mr Justice Carstairs, "that the man Ernie was doing anything wrong?" And he looked at the jury with the look which Mr Empton knew so well but still could not describe.